THE AFTERLIFE ADVENTURES OF FOUR LOONIES IN A BIN

VOLUME II: THE DEATH OF A MANUSCRIPT
A NOVEL

PHILLIP MATTOX

The Afterlife Adventures of Four Loonies in a Bin
by Phillip Mattox

© 2023 by Career Development Software, Inc. (dba The School Company®). All rights reserved. No part of this book may be used or reproduced in any manner whatsoever except for reviews without the author's permission. The author would appreciate notice as to Fair Use educational implementation.

The Afterlife Adventures of Four Loonies in a Bin ("Loonies") is a work of fiction. All the names, characters, places, and incidents, etc., in this book are either the product of the author's imagination or used in a fictitious manner. The characters are not based on any actual living or deceased individuals. Any resemblance is purely coincidental.

Print ISBN: 978-1-66788-683-1
eBook ISBN: 978-1-66788-684-8

Table of Contents

Introduction to Volume II: The Death of a Manuscript 1
   Review of Map Locations/Terms 4
   Journal Entry Forty-One: The Harvesting of Souls 5
   Journal Entry Forty-Two: The Campfire 10
   Journal Entry Forty-Three: The Sisters 12
   Journal Entry Forty-Four: Nighttime at Camp 19
   Journal Entry Forty-Five: The Mind 23
   Journal Entry Forty-Six: The Chosen 47
   Journal Entry Forty-Seven: Portals 55
   Journal Entry Forty-Eight: Violation 66
   Journal Entry Forty-Nine: The Campfire 76
   Journal Entry Fifty: Boo 85
   Journal Entry Fifty-One: Reunion 90
   Journal Entry Fifty-Two: The Eagle 98
   Journal Entry Fifty-Three: Courage 101
   Journal Entry Fifty-Four: Mount Olympus 111
   Journal Entry Fifty-Five: The Wave 113
A Medical Alert 118
   Journal Entry Fifty-Six: The Trap 122
   Journal Entry Fifty-Seven: Farmers 127

Journal Entry Fifty-Eight: Being Back 133

Journal Entry Fifty-Nine: The Charge 138

Journal Entry Sixty: Redemption 149

Journal Entry Sixty-One: Rescue 153

Journal Entry Sixty-Two: Fancy That 159

Journal Entry Sixty-Three: Battle 163

Journal Entry Sixty-Four: Breech 173

Journal Entry Sixty-Five: The New Twin 174

Journal Entry Sixty-Six: The Prize 181

Journal Entry Sixty-Seven: The Few Who Know the Truth 185

Journal Entry Sixty-Eight: Chaos 191

Why Last? 195

Journal Entry Sixty-Nine: End Times 197

Journal Entry Seventy: The Wholly 200

Journal Entry Seventy-One: Journey of the Dead 209

Journal Entry Seventy-Two: Ego and the Soul 217

Journal Entry Seventy-Three: Evil 223

Journal Entry Seventy-Four: A Conversation 234

Journal Entry Seventy-Five: Sensei and the Funnel 242

Journal Entry Seventy-Six: Forbidden Territory 246

Journal Entry Seventy-Seven: The Gathering 249

Journal Entry Seventy-Eight: Heading Out 251

Journal Entry Seventy-Nine: The Swallow 254

Journal Entry Eighty: The Chosen 258

Journal Entry Eighty-One: A Real Deal 276

A Call 281

Journal Entry Eighty-Two: The Bodies 283

Journal Entry Eighty-Three: The Move 285

Journal Entry Eighty-Four: Blessed in Misery 288

Journal Entry Eighty-Five: New Partner 291

Journal Entry Eighty-Six: Fullest Expression of Love 294

Journal Entry Eighty-Seven: A Loving Army 297

Journal Entry Eighty-Eight: Isn't That Loverly? 303

Journal Entry Eighty-Nine: Hiding Place 313

Journal Entry Ninety: Another Gift 326

Journal Entry Ninety-One: How to Save Your Soul 330

Journal Entry Ninety-Two: Fly Through 337

Journal Entry Ninety-Three: Saturation 345

Journal Entry Ninety-Four: Deception 347

Journal Entry Ninety-Five: The Beaver 356

Journal Entry Ninety-Six: Free Souls 358

Journal Entry Ninety-Seven: Crumbling Walls 362

Journal Entry Ninety-Eight: Strategic Locations 365

Journal Entry Ninety-Nine: Conclusion 368

My Mission 370

The Hospital 374

The Records 384

Once More 396

Book of Life 412

New Twin's Page One: Forces Gather 416

New Twin's Page Two: Deceit 424

New Twin's Page Three: The Ground of Being 429

New Twin's Page Four: Armageddon 439

New Twin's Page Five: The Two Sides of Mystery 443

New Twin's Page Six: Truly Beasts of Wonder 459

New Twin's Page Seven: Sorrow 465

New Twin's Page Eight: Reunion 471

New Twin's Page Nine: The Illusion 481

Last New Twin Page: Ben's Gift 491
TheOne 497
No-Thing 502
The End 508
The Dance 511
Epilogue 512

Introduction to Volume II: The Death of a Manuscript

The first volume of this series—*The Chosen*—consists of forty journal entries written by a father (long since deceased) who was at one time a counselor at a Mental Hospital in the 1980s. As the father's son prepares to retire fifty years later, the son discovers some journals in the attic of his soon-to-be demolished publishing operation. In the manuscript of journal entries, the father lays out a mission for his son: locate four institutionalized boys, now men well into middle age, who were chosen by TheSon (the Son of TheOne) and TendHer (the Holy Spirit) to fight NoOne (the Devil).

The Afterlife Adventures of Four Loonies in a Bin: The Death of a Manuscript adds forty-nine additional journal entries. NoOne's demonic objective is revealed in more detail in this second volume; it is not to spread Love and forgiveness and it is not to fairly judge the recent dead. *The Death of a Manuscript* features NoOne's grooming of the Twins to ravage the Earth and grow an army of LostSouls to reach NoOne's ultimate goal. It culminates in an epic winner-take-all cosmic confrontation between the TheSon, the Loonies, NoOne, and NoOne's Black Matter incarnated Twins.

To defeat NoOne and his Dark Matter, the four Loonies must be willing to dwell in an entirely new Spiritual dimension. Each teen boy must release his pain and come to terms with his past. Each boy must navigate through the layers of his mind, from everyday thinking to emotional processing to being tested by evil forces hibernating deep within his unconscious. The boys must learn to work as a team: how to listen, when to compromise, how to empathize with the pain of others, and accept the responsibilities associated with being a man. Finally, they must abandon their egos and enter 'beyond the Veil' as pure Spirits; a quantum place without space where universes are created by TheOne, protected by TheSon and His Orbs, and where the dead and their Souls are judged by TendHer in the Reincarnation Universe.

Who will win the epic contest between Light and Dark Matter? Character secrets are revealed, and plot twists unraveled as the final and decisive confrontation between TheSon and NoOne unfolds. What the Loonies soon discover is that it's not just their universe's survival that's at stake; it's all universes. And the last bin the Loonies are put in may require them to make the ultimate sacrifice. Even then, will that be enough?

Thus planned NoOne.

'Amen.'

THE AFTERLIFE ADVENTURES OF FOUR LOONIES IN A BIN

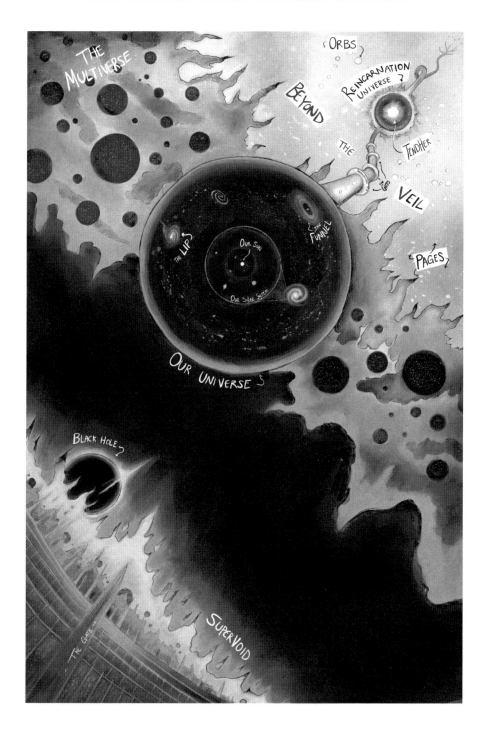

Review of Map Locations/Terms

* The Holy Trinity: TheOne (Father), TheSon (Son), TendHer (Holy Spirit).
* Beyond the Veil: The Spiritual dimension of cosmic quantum energy where physical universes are birthed to spread the Love of the TheOne (Creator).
* The Lip: A platform extending out from the Divine Quantum Foam where a Seed of creation is planted by TheOne.
* The Funnel: A transportation tube that takes newly released Souls from the physical dimension and sends them to the Reincarnation Universe for judgment.
* The Gates in the Funnel: Four stations of judgment. If the newly released Soul can pass the First Gate of Unconditional Love, the Soul may be merged immediately with TheOne. If not, the Soul will continue through the other three gates until finally judged by TendHer. The other three Gates are Empathy, Good Works, and Knowledge.
* Pages: Quantum packets of Soul "memories" that drift in 'beyond the Veil'.
* SuperVoid: Where NoOne and Souls that have been judged damned are imprisoned.
* The SuperVoid Gate: The entrance to Hell composed of Soul-Judged Evil Eyes.
* Dark Matter: The energy released by NoOne during the Big Bang. Dark Matter is the scaffolding upon which matter can cling and bring physical substance to the universe.
* Black Hole: NoOne's Dark Matter recycler. When a universe dies, its Dark Matter scaffolding is "recycled" in Black

Holes—compressed into a singularity for use later in creating new universes. NoOne calls this singularity "NoLight."
* Orbs: Angels of Light. Some are merged fully with TheOne. Others choose to serve as Mentors and Guides to the living. They may be Pure or pure depending on whether They or they enter into the consciousness of the un-pure.
* Karma: Can be either positive or negative. Ego Karma are negative deposits based on selfish acts (ego). It gradually smothers the Soul.
* Ego: Controlling nature, yourself, or others through power, property, prestige.
* Mind's Eye: Protector and observer of the Soul. Through its mechanism of self-awareness, it fights to keep the ego at bay and protect the Soul from Dark Matter.
* Reincarnation Universe: Part of 'beyond the Veil' that administers life judgments and reassignments to new life forms to remove ego Karma.

Journal Entry Forty-One: The Harvesting of Souls

The Twins' fascination with eyeballs was born of days, weeks, and months of instruction. The Twins learned that eyeballs are essential for many functions of the human experience and not just for sensation and sight. For example, personality is etched into the iris: crypts of Fuchs openings on the edge of the iris signal high affiliation (indicating a people-person); egg-shaped furrows indicate extroversion (action person). Moving to the retina, men have more rod receptors, which help them detect motion; women have more cones, which help them perceive colors. Countless sex/gender-based careers are based on these two inherited predispositions.

The most important thing to understand, they learned, is that the eyes contain the Soul; they are the fundamental source of Spiritual energy, the fuel that keeps the universe machine humming.

NoOne called it "The Harvesting of Souls." The Twins thought his teachings were much like a catechism in traditional church Dogma, but with one key difference. Although religious Dogma contained the basic tenets of a traditional religious establishment, contemporary religious rituals were stripped of transcendental experience.

NoOne, however, required complete immersion in much more than ritual. He offered not just a momentary transcendental "high", but also offered supernatural Spiritual ecstasy combined with power more fantastic than any natural force in the physical universe. Finally, the fruits of their conception and gestation would be revealed, but only if the Twins surrendered absolutely and unconditionally to NoOne's Dark Matter.

'Now you are ready to study my "Harvesting of Souls," ' announced NoOne. 'Listen carefully. Feast your darkened egos on what I am about to reveal. TheSon may have his Chosen, but I have you, my children, conceived and gestated with my own venom. When you were born, I implanted my cells. You would perceive them as Snakes. They have primed every cell in your body for my presence. You are special. You will be perfect. If all else is forgotten, you must always return to the guidance at the very core of my "Harvesting of Souls." '

The eyes are doorways to the Soul…you must remove the eyes at the moment before death to hijack the Soul…then the Mind's Eye releases the Soul to wander alone, and I can immediately abduct it,

or the dead must accept my offer to stop the pain right AFTER death. Either way, the Soul is mine.

'Look to your doorstep, my children,' said NoOne. 'It's time you understand fully that which I desire.'

Careful not to disturb the other family members in the cabin, the Twins opened the front door. They found a box just inside. Bending down, one of the Twins slightly nudged the box. It moved. The box shook. Something alive was trying to escape.

Carrying the twitching box back to their bedroom, the Twins looked at each other with anticipation. Then, carefully, they laid the box on their shared desk and removed the adhesive tape.

At the bottom of the box, ten eyeballs looked up at the Twins.

Looking indeed.

"Brother, this is a gift from our teacher," said one Twin.

"Yes, he promised to help us explore his 'Harvesting of Souls,' " replied the other Twin. "Let's take them out of the box and cut them up."

The eyes increased their thrashing. They became wide-eyed and panicked, trying to find an escape route out of the box.

"Do you think the eyes can understand what we're saying?" whispered one Twin.

"Of course, brother. Watch them as I say this: 'Let's stomp on them!' "

The eyeballs hopped around each other, frenzied. One eyeball even managed to use another eye as a trampoline and nearly cleared the top of the box.

"Do we not have Souls?" dryly asked the other Twin.

"Our Souls, brother, are unlike any other human Souls. Our dark Souls are found throughout our entire body. Our eyes are pure ego."

"That's what gives us our power, right?"

"Yes. That's why we had our Snakes. They inserted venom into every cell of our bodies."

"Ok. Let's continue. Father wants us to learn all we can about the eyes."

"Why are the eyeballs so nervous? What's with all the twitching? And why are the irises dilated?"

"Father said that when eyes dilate at death, it's because they're trying to see their way to 'beyond the Veil'."

"Oh, that makes sense. They're looking for Heaven!"

"Agreed. Let's move on."

"Now, let's try to find the Souls. I bet father hasn't removed them yet; better for us to see how the Soul is connected to the physical eye."

"Remember the 'harvesting' principles. Let me pick one up."

Gently grasping an eyeball, one of the Twins held it out in the palm of his hand. "Wow, do you see it? I can see the Soul. It's a bunch of small strings woven together, barely visible, hiding just inside the eyeball. Here, let's look at it under a flashlight."

Studying the eyeball under bright light, the Twin observed, "Yes, I see it. It's like many filaments woven together to make a net!"

"Look closer. I see another layer of fibers on top."

"Oh, yeah. What is it?"

"Didn't father talk about the Mind's Eye protecting the Soul and delivering it to him in the SuperVoid upon judgment?"

"Remember, that's if the eyeballs are removed right after death after they have accepted father's offer to relieve their pain. Many can't stand the pain and forsake their right to venture to 'beyond the Veil'. If they're removed before death, then the Mind's Eye and Soul are lost and confused, and father automatically harvests the Soul."

"Ripe to be captured by our father with no consent required!"

"Precisely. Let's see what happens when we…." The Twin dropped the eyeball to the ground and stomped on it."

"Whoops. Oh…looks like a smashed egg."

The remaining nine eyeballs bunched together, agitated. They scurried together as a group to one side of the box, huddled tight, twisting, and turning. Petrified.

Since Lil' Johnny, Jenna, and the Twins' sisters were still asleep, it was easy for the Twins to sneak out of their cabin for their next experiment.

Holding the box of eyeballs, the Twins walked to a nearby hill.

A streetlamp provided ample light. The extreme slope was perfect for their next test.

Ceremoniously lifting the box high in the air, one of the Twins emptied the box's contents.

The eyeballs rolled and quickly gained speed to the delight of the Twins. The Twins agreed to splurge and indulge themselves in an outward demonstration of emotion: giggling.

The eyeballs rolled and gained even more momentum, baffled as to their location, aghast at being cast out of the only security they knew. The bewildered eyes were in shock.

Running to the bottom of the hill, the Twins inspected the now-resting eyeballs.

"Brother, do you see what I see?"

"Yes. Fabulous. The eyeballs have crossed their eyes!"

Journal Entry Forty-Two: The Campfire

Our heads turned in unison as we followed Charles' outstretched arm and finger. He was pointing to the forest path bordering our campfire. "They did. They took your little girls," said Charles.

Charles continued to walk around the campfire, facing the dark forest path. Around and around, he walked, whispering, muttering something in a chant-like cadence. As in the movie Westerns from the fifties, Charles' pointed index finger looked like a gun shooting at Indian attackers as they, the Indians, might be circling the wagons of some uninvited White settlers.

Suddenly, Charles stopped. "Be still," he whispered to all of us. "Don't make a move."

We complied. We froze. I was amazed by how Charles stepped forward and led the group; even more surprised that all of us adults gladly relinquished leadership and command of the situation to one of our patients.

We focused on Charles and his movements, enthralled with his shaman-like performance. Luke, Ben, and John zoned out, standing very still with dazed expressions. The staff was cautious and alert, sweeping their gaze around the forest's perimeter as if looking for a sign. Even Boo seemed to be in some other world, suspended in animation.

It was late, and the stars covered the clear sky. It was quiet, I thought. Unusually quiet. I couldn't resist continually going back to the perimeter, looking for something different, something that had caught Charles' and the other three guys' attention.

I heard giggling. "Jenna, did you hear that?" I asked.

"Yeah, it sounded like a couple of kids," Jenna whispered.

"Hey, Ivan and Jim, let's check out where that sound came from," I said.

Ivan picked up his flashlight and joined Jim and me as we casually sauntered toward the woods. "I thought it was giggling," I remarked. "Never heard of an animal giggling!"

"Stop," whispered Jim. "Do you see what I see?"

John rushed toward us. "Do not go down that path, ever!"

"What are you talking about?" asked Jim.

"I know this forest well, have studied it for a long time," said John.

"What are you talking about? We just got here! Did your aunt bring you here or something?" asked Ivan.

Not able to disclose his true mode of exploration, John lied, "Yes, that's it. She brought me here, and we heard all sorts of stories about kids missing in these woods. Ask Lil' Johnny. There are a ton of animals that hide in there."

"Hey, Lil' Johnny, is it true? Lots of animals in here?" yelled Jim.

Ivan couldn't hold himself back. "Well, there aren't now, since you all have been yelling to the world we're here!"

Jim looked down. "Oh, yeah. Sorry. Never did that in 'Nam."

Lil' Johnny walked up to us. "Told ya' that ya' didn't wanna' go near here."

The group froze. We heard one crunching sound, then another crunching sound, then another, and another. The crunching was getting louder and closer to us.

Lil' Johnny retreated to the campfire. Then, he turned and yelled, "Y'all need to get back here by the fire."

We did not need to be told twice.

Journal Entry Forty-Three: The Sisters

The clan had no idea why the Twins suddenly disappeared from the village when they were seven years old. Some said Jenna drove them away. Some said Jenna finally got fed up and sent them off to kin in Montana. Some said it was Lil' Johnny's fault; he was so depressed that he let their mental disease get out of control. Some said their stepsisters, then 15 and 17, drowned them in the village pond. Others thought demons swooped down and carried the Twins away. Whatever the reason, not a person dared to ask Lil' Johnny or Jenna directly to their faces.

Lil' Johnny's first wife gave birth to Jenna. The first wife passed on ten years later, and Lil' Johnny remarried. His second wife gave birth to the first of his two baby girls barely a couple of months after their wedding ceremony; the second came two years later. Nobody dared look at Johnny's second wife's growing stomach before the wedding; everyone knew they had lived in sin, but few wanted to risk Lil' Johnny's wrath.

Shortly after the birth of the second girl, Lil' Johnny's second wife also died of cancer. Lil' Johnny was devastated, spending months weeping in his bedroom. Nothing consoled him, not even his beloved eldest daughter and their camping trips.

Jenna took over. Then just 12 years old, she cared for the two girls as if she were their mother. She hovered and protected them as if they were her own.

Years passed. Then Jenna left for college.

While Jenna was away at school, the girls got a massive dose of independence and ran wild. Quite happy with their newfound unlimited freedom (and the envy of all the other kids), the girls came and went as they pleased, often playing in the dark forest surrounding their village home for hours without any restrictions from their dad.

The girls had few boundaries. They ate what they wanted whenever they wanted. They dressed as they pleased (some would say much too provocatively). They went to bed when they felt like it. Sometimes they hitchhiked into town, waving a symbolic "hello" as they passed the general store where their dad worked. The girls laughed at the thought of Lil' Johnny discovering their many treks into the real world.

Nobody confronted the girls on their many unescorted trips; nobody wanted to risk Lil' Johnny's ire. The villagers, however, did gossip among themselves, horrified that they had seen the girls at the shopping center east of Lake Sutherland wearing bikini cut-offs and low-cut tank tops at all hours of the night. And that they had been spotted hitchhiking home all by themselves.

Both girls fumed when Jenna, who recently turned 20 years old, returned home with the infant Twins. They perceived Jenna as haughty and controlling; they did not respect her attempts to mother them. It took but a few days for the eight-year-old and ten-year-old girls to distance themselves emotionally from Lil' Johnny, Jenna, and her Twins.

Not sharing Jenna's passion for the outdoors, her two sisters' prime interest was to sit around and talk about boys. They were not readers like their dad nor inclined to excel at school like Jenna. They liked more than anything to watch and comment on the various television soap operas they watched after school.

Jenna thought the two girls were shallow and phony. The two girls often let their gossiping get out of hand, and Jenna had to remind them that gossip eventually comes back to bite. When they responded with blank stares, Jenna thought she might as well have been talking to a mule.

However, the girls did have a few things going for them. They did make effective use of the assets that nature had bestowed upon them. Their sweet and naïve Southern belle routine and their early-developed and ample bosoms often resulted in getting the attention of others. Often, it resulted in getting what they wanted whether that was the most popular boys or gifts or special considerations from adults.

When Jenna's twin boys disappeared at the age of seven, the two girls, then ages 15 and 17, were careful to mask their glee, acting dutifully sad and concerned. Secretly, they prayed that Jenna, now that there was nothing for her to do at home, would return to school or take a job somewhere far away so the two girls could party and entertain their boyfriends.

Jenna was eager to oblige but was too depressed to make any move. She just wanted to be near and taken care of by her dad.

At the age of twenty-nine, still sharing the same cabin with her dad and her two stepsisters, a gnawing emotional paralysis consumed Jenna's consciousness. It took months for Jenna to fully understand her feelings of emptiness.

There was another time I felt like this.

Then she got it. Jenna let the memory surface. She flashed back to her ten-year high school reunion just one year ago.

Jenna sat and watched her classmates register and then continue to three tables. The first table had pictures of the athletic teams featuring superstar athletes and a display of authentic player jerseys. Her picture was there: most valuable women's soccer star. The second table had a list of names and pictures of dead classmates. The third table had pictures of the Homecoming Queens and Kings and other awards.

Some students were voted this or that; "most likely to succeed" or "best sense of humor." Some had achieved maybe an hour or two of glory in an academic competition. Some had stayed atop the popularity hierarchy longer than others. Now, all that remained were faded pages in the few class annuals that had survived the decade, rotting away in closets or garages.

I didn't get asked to a single dance, Jenna mused.

Jolted out of her reverie, Jenna noticed that very few students paused to study the classmates who had passed on. It was as though the middle table did not exist.

Why do schools have class reunions? To reclaim a feeling? Like a horse returning to a familiar pond to drink? Perhaps slices of emotional history were zealously recreated because her fellow classmates had nothing later in life that could replicate those fleeting moments of belonging. Or standing out. Never to happen again.

What feeling am I trying to reclaim? Jenna wondered. *It certainly wasn't being in Love or the thrill of sex, much less having a boyfriend.*

Maybe I'm hard on us. Don't we have but one life to live? And doesn't it make sense we would want to celebrate together our sharing of that brief, carefree time of life?

No, that's not it for me. I was anything but carefree. I hated school and cared for only a very few students because, frankly, there was too much role-playing; students were caught in an endless drama, chasing after popularity. Everyone felt the tug to compete; few had the words to verbalize the process and take a stand against the relentless status-seeking. Those who dared to question the phoniness were ignored or shunned.

Yeah, from boobs to bucks. Constant jockeying for alpha top dog. Maybe that's why I had no friends. Everyone knew how I felt about the incessant artificiality.

Yet looking back, at least there was innocence. We simply fell into our roles, trusting that this stage of our life had been carefully crafted by wise adults and would most certainly lead to happiness and fulfillment. But all it led to was disillusion and sadness.

Jenna watched as classmates paired up with other classmates at various tables. They were smiling, laughing, and touching. Jenna saw with clarity why she felt like crying.

I didn't have a single close friend. I know I am partly to blame, full of my arrogant independence and myself. Still, no one, not even my teammates, not even my teachers, reached out and really tried to get to know me. Nobody thought I was worth the effort to break through my shell.

So, who am I really close to in my life? wondered Jenna. *Nobody here, that's for sure.*

Just my dad and nature.

It only took ten minutes, but Jenna left the reunion. She vowed she would never attend another school event.

Not that anyone cared.

Yes, my high school reunion. The other time I crashed from being empty inside. Maybe if I hadn't been raped, I would have gotten married. Happy ever after, maybe?

Jenna shook her head as she counted the women in the village whose sole passion in high school was finding husbands, getting married, and having children. Their overworked husbands often died young from accidents or alcohol abuse, and the wives were also trapped in numbing routines: dead at 40, buried at 60. Subsistence-based householding, childrearing, suppressing their feelings through compulsive eating (and massive weight gain), and menial chores wore away their hours and looks, and eventually overcame their strength. She saw the same pattern unfolding for her sisters.

Soon, Jenna and Lil' Johnny would need each other more than ever.

It was but a couple of months after the Twins' mysterious disappearance. The village was returning to some sense of normalcy. (Actually, most of the villagers hoped the Twins would never return). Coming home from the store for a late lunch, Jenna and Lil' Johnny found their cabin empty; immediately, the two sensed something was not right even though everything appeared normal in the cabin. There were no signs of trouble; no indications a struggle had occurred. There were no misplaced items; snacks were placed on the counter waiting to be picked up; the girls' bedroom door was closed—something the girls were fanatic about. Curiosity about whose house the two girls might be visiting turned into concern as the sun settled lower in the dusk sky, and the forest darkness devoured the light. For the rest of the evening, Jenna and Lil' Johnny prayed and hoped the girls would soon traipse through the front door, outwardly showing guilt and barely able to hold back their glee at having once more defied authority.

The next day, numerous volunteers formed a search party. A solid row of volunteers covered every square yard of the surrounding forest for a good 10 miles in all directions.

One of the searchers, an experienced vet with twenty years of experience in search and rescue, called out that he had found a clue. Lying on the ground, cushioned on a bed of meadow grass, were four eyeballs. Except for the fading dusk light, he could have sworn they were moving. Not just moving, but squirming, twitching. Like fish on hooks. He puked.

One day soon after that, when Lil' Johnny returned home from the store, Jenna was nowhere to be found. Lil' Johnny's worse fear was realized. His beloved daughter had left him. He found the note carefully pasted to the one place she knew her dad would instinctively go to—the refrigerator. The message said she Loved him with all her heart and that this was the hardest thing she had ever done. But the loss of her sons and now her step-sisters was too much for her to bear. She had to get out. She decided to move to Tacoma, Washington, a good three-hour drive away. She stated she wanted to resume taking classes in Occupational Therapy at one of the private universities there to finish her degree and planned to get a job as soon as possible. She promised to visit him often and even help out at the store during holiday weekends.

Lil' Johnny was heartbroken. He had not only lost two grandchildren, two wives, and two daughters, but now he was being abandoned by the only person left on Earth who Loved him, and much of this within the span of a few months. He was glad Jenna could leave the village to heal, something he could not do. However, the pain was unbearable, masked only by taking up residence in his store.

"At least I have my store…and Boo," Lil' Johnny wept.

Jenna did keep her promise. At least once a month for the next two semesters of school, Jenna returned to see her dad for a night or two. A few weeks after her graduation, Lil' Johnny again received a note from his daughter. Jenna had been hired at a Portland Mental Hospital.

Lil' Johnny walked through his routine daily chores as if he were a robot as the months rolled into years. Sit and rock. Greet a customer. Take money. Give change. Maintain inventory. Clean shitter. Sweep floor. Wash windows. Shovel Boo's Dog poo. It was all just a meaningless ritual.

Endless ruminations always brought Lil' Johnny back to thoughts of his little girls. Back to their eyes; eyes deserted by bodies long since disappeared. Eyes lying there, alone. Twitching.

Sit and rock. Greet a customer. Take money. Give change. Maintain inventory. Clean shitter. Sweep floor. Wash windows. Shovel Boo's Dog poo.

My little girls are out there somewhere, waiting for me.

Journal Entry Forty-Four: Nighttime at Camp

Slipping into their tents, the guys and staff knew that it would be a tough night. After much tossing and turning, Lil' Johnny, Jenna, and the staff finally fell into a light sleep. The guys were not so fortunate.

For the guys, sleep was nearly impossible with the creepy thing lurking in the forest. Putting their heads under their inflatable pillows, the guys tried to smother their fears with complete darkness. It didn't work. They couldn't shut out the forest giggling in their brains, repeatedly ruminating about all the terrible things that could happen. One thing was for sure—they couldn't even think about going to sleep. There were so many questions about what was going on.

The guys knew something terrible was in the forest. Maybe something or someone was toying with them like a cat cornering a mouse. Perhaps it was connected to all the people who had lost their eyes. Maybe it was a family of hungry monsters. Maybe it was a new form of animal species that could giggle. The collective private ruminations did not provide satisfactory answers to all the horrible possibilities. Still, the obsessive worrying did accomplish one thing: It kept the guys alert and receptive to what was about to happen.

"Pssst…John…do you feel that?" whispered Ben.

"What? Feel what?" replied John.

"Yeah, I feel something too," noted Charles.

"Luke…do you feel it?" asked Ben.

"Yeah, I do! Ben, you're the brain. What is it?" pressed Luke.

"What? What? Oh…now I feel it!" said John.

The four guys ripped open the zippers on their sleeping bags and jumped up so fast that the tent's foundation went skyward, resulting in a crumpled heap of fabric, bodies, and disassembled steel frame.

"Oh, crap. Get off of me, Luke. You're fucking huge. I can't breathe!" moaned Ben.

"Oh, bitch, bitch, bitch…you should talk!" mocked Luke.

Rushing over from the staff tent, Ivan wanted to make sure the guys were all right. "What the hell happened here?"

"There was something under our tent," yelled Ben.

"Yeah, it was crawling, and it felt like a huge Snake," said Luke.

"All of us felt it, right?" asked Charles.

Three voices were unanimous. "Yes!"

"OK, let's take a look," said Ivan.

Jim decided there was no way he could sleep with all the commotion, so he rushed over to help Ivan. The two examined whatever was under the tent with their flashlights. There was nothing there, so they aimed their flashlights outward, further from the tent.

Something was tunneling just below the surface of the ground. It was burrowing away from the tent and the campsite. It was heading to the path that led deep into the forest.

"Look," said Charles. "There are four trails."

"Like four animals?" asked Ben.

"Yeah, looks like four moles," observed Ivan. "Big moles. Monster moles!"

I couldn't believe my ears. This was all the guys needed, more drama. I hoped Ivan would start laughing like it was all a joke.

Ivan didn't laugh. He became more serious and bent down to take a closer look.

The four trails are distinctly separate, yet they all begin under the tent where the guys had been sleeping. If they're Snakes, they must be enormous, as each of the raised dirt trails has a width of at least six inches.

Then they heard giggling again coming from the forest. The guys, Ivan and Jim, froze in disbelief.

Lil' Johnny and Jenna came running forward.

"What the Sam Hill was that?" muttered Lil' Johnny.

"You tell me. This is your forest," said Ivan.

"Never seen nothin' like it. Those look like gopher trails. But they're really too wide, though," said Lil' Johnny.

"Do you have somebody playing tricks on us? And who or what is making that giggling noise?" demanded Jenna.

Lil' Johnny shook his head. "I don't have the foggiest notion."

The giggling noise stopped. Aiming his flashlight at the forest, Ivan swept the perimeter. The four dirt trails turned back towards the group.

"Holy shit. We gotta get out of here," yelled Ben.

Lil' Johnny ran past the group toward the approaching ridges. He lifted his 12-gauge shotgun and fired four shots, one at each of the tunnels.

The shotgun blast was deafening. The groups' ears rang, smoke streaming out of Lil' Johnny's gun. Expecting to see more hillbilly bravado, the guys were shocked to see that he was scared, just like everyone else.

Everyone strained to see what happened to the four trails.

More giggling deep in the forest.

"Them's got to be locals, playing their games again. I'm gonna skin some hide when I get ahold of 'em," threatened Lil' Johnny.

"OK, so who is going to sleep tonight?" I asked.

"Come on, guys, let's get your tent put back together," said Jim.

"Whoa there, everyone. Would you call what just happened an everyday occurrence? I mean, it sure seemed supernatural to me! We can't just turn this off like a water faucet!" said Ben.

"Ivan, is this one of your rites of passage?" I chuckled.

Lil' Johnny stepped forward. "Well, since you all are so damn stupid 'cause you didn't follow my advice in the first place, I guess I better be the one to stand lookout. Don't want no pussies guarding my big target butt."

Walking back to the camp area, Ivan just happened to turn around one last time to look at the forest and dirt trails. It must have been exhaustion. People see things when they're tired. That must have been it. Ivan couldn't think of any other explanation for the four small lights now coming from the forest path, right at the edge of the forest in line with the four dirt trails. Still. Floating in the air. Just staring.

They kind of looked like four eyeballs.

Journal Entry Forty-Five: The Mind

The rest of the night was uneventful for me, the rest of the staff, and Lil' Johnny—no more creepy tunnels popping up out of the ground, no more weird sounds, and no tents crashing.

However, the night was very different for the four guys tossing and turning in their sleeping bags. They were headed for a major lesson in accessing states of mental being that few humans ever experience or remember consciously. They would be shown a Spiritual path not many could fully tolerate; most turn away in denial, finding singular comfort in predictable materialistic reality.

Within their midst, a voice burst through the night's silence, made even more distinct by the lack of light inside their tent.

You have been chosen.

The words vibrated with intensity, and their sounds lingered long after they were spoken. Most often, people who are visited from the Spiritual dimension assign such manifestations as auditory hallucinations from a random dream fragment. Indeed, standard brain filters evolved to categorize such Spirit visitations, especially during sleep, as illusions; or a delusion if labeled by a health professional.

You have been judged and found worthy.

All four guys perked up.

"Did somebody just say something?" whispered Ben.

Luke crawled to the tent door flap. He was hoping to connect the voice to someone outside the tent. That he could deal with. The last thing he wanted was another supernatural visitation.

"What do you see?" Charles asked, hoping there was nothing there.

Luke didn't see a thing but heard some snoring coming from the staff tent. "Nothing."

"Well, where did those words come from then?" demanded Ben. "They're still ringing in my ears!"

John replied, "Can you all just quiet down? There might be more messages coming."

The guys froze. After a couple of minutes and not moving a muscle, they again heard the voice.

I speak to you from 'beyond the Veil'. I am who you may call an "Orb." I have been instructed by TheSon to be your guide. We will explore your minds.

"Are you guys hearing this?" asked Charles. "We need to verify we're hearing the same thing."

"The voice said we will explore our minds," said Luke.

"Yes. I heard that. The voice also said it was instructed by TheSon," added Ben.

"And the voice is speaking from 'beyond the Veil'," confirmed John.

Charles looked at the others and nodded in agreement. "I think we're all hearing the same thoughts, then."

The thoughts continued. *Your Mind's Eye will soon leave your physical body and be transported to deep space. You must not be disturbed. You must not worry. Only seconds in physical time will have passed as you explore in-depth the inner world of your brain and the lowest regions of the Spiritual world. You must learn how to master your ego for your Mind's Eye and Soul to dwell in the Spirit world 'beyond the Veil' and know that it is real. Finally, you will be tested as you explore 'beyond the Veil'. You must see clearly that which is and that which is not. And that which is not is.*

"Did you follow all those is's?" Luke groaned.

John spoke up so the other guys could hear him. "Tested? For what?"

You have been chosen by TheSon and must be ready for the evil that is now imminent for your Earth.

"I was visited by TheSon!" whispered John.

Charles smiled at John's innocent revelation.

'Can we hear each other's thoughts? No need for speech?' asked Ben.

'Oh, great. Never thought I'd be a mind-reader!' exclaimed Luke.

'Never thought you had a…,' Ben caught himself. He just nodded.

Luke nodded back.

'I hear all of you in my head. And I'm feeling what you're feeling as well. It's weird, but I'm in all your heads and my own head at the same time,' observed John.

Charles confirmed what the others were experiencing. 'Ditto… It's like I have four separate auditory channels in my head; one for me and the other three for each of you. And I feel your feelings! And also, a fifth channel coming from a completely different dimension.'

Charles paused as if processing something. 'Ben. Stop fantasizing about fire and naked girls!'

'Oh, that's so gross!' exclaimed Luke.

Ben wanted to change the subject as quickly as possible. Looking up to the top of the tent, as if the Orb was hovering just outside, Ben asked the entity, 'What about those four animals under our tent tonight? What were they, and where did they come from?'

There is an evil incarnation in your world. It has taken root in two boys. You will know them as "The Twins." Their evil was displayed tonight.

'But what were those things under the ground?' pressed Ben.

They were the eyeballs of two human beings, answered the Orb.

'So the four eyeballs and all the eyeballs at the rest stop and the news reports…it's because of these Twins?' pressed Luke.

Your experience here is of little consequence. The survival of a much larger cosmos is at stake. Earth is just the launching pad. We must stop the Twins here; if not, we must stop them in this universe. You have been chosen by TheSon to block this evil. It has to be done here.

'Whoa,' exclaimed Ben, standing up. 'Are you kidding me? We're barely seventeen years old. We're nut jobs, four crazies. Nobody will believe us. And no one will listen to us!'

John admonished Ben. 'Don't forget who you're talking to. We really have no choice.'

Charles crawled to the tent entrance and looked outside for anything unusual, 'Yeah, Ben. John and I are used to working with the Spirit world, and we will help you. You too, Luke.'

Luke muttered a not-too-appreciative thank you and said, 'Charles, this is weird hearing your thoughts in my head while you move around. Can you just sit still?'

Before Ben could completely exit the tent, Luke grabbed Ben's ankle with one hand and dragged Ben back through the tent door. 'Where do you think you're going, Mr. Courageous? You're here with the rest of us whether you like it or not.'

Ben slumped down to the ground. 'Well, OK. Just so you know, I think this is really dangerous stuff. With serious consequences. Like death. I haven't even had a girlfriend yet.'

The Orb continued. *Each of you has been chosen because you have extraordinary talent. Together, you will find the resources to hopefully destroy the evil power that attempts to destroy you and this planet called*

Earth. To make use of your abilities, you must first learn the contours of your brains and minds. You must understand how your Mind's Eyes function. This will enable you to control your ego. When that happens, you will be able to survive in 'beyond the Veil'. TheOne, our Father, has forbidden NoOne from accessing this Spiritual dimension. It is our one advantage.

'Will we be safe there, away from these eyeballs and the Twins?' asked Ben hopefully.

The Orb's response was not reassuring. *Eventually, NoOne will attack 'beyond the Veil'. It is just a matter of time. But for now, you are safe. You must....*

'What is the Mind's Eye? Sorry to cut you off, but this seems to be really important,' interrupted Luke. Charles started nodding his head as if this was a topic he also wanted to discuss. He, along with John, had more experience in nonmaterial reality than Ben or Luke, but Charles always felt he had just scratched the surface.

The Mind's Eye is the guardian protector of the Soul. It has two functions. First, it struggles with the ego to keep it from corrupting the Soul. Second, it fights off Dark Matter.

Ben wanted more clarity. 'But wait, I thought the ego was necessary to survive?'

The Orb paused. *In the physical dimension, it is useful; it does help humans physically survive. And the ego helps humans control others and nature. However, humans will not pass the assessment by TendHer if their Souls are polluted with selfish desires. This is what Dark Matter clings to.*

'Pardon me,' interrupted Luke. 'But where does this Dark Matter stuff come from?'

One name you give it is Satan. Another name: the Devil.

'Holy shit,' exclaimed Ben.

'Shit is not Holy,' said Luke.

'Thanks, I'll remember that,' said Ben.

'Oh, I have lots to teach you, that's for sure!' smiled Luke.

'Please stop, you two!' said John.

'No, we're cool!' replied Ben.

After a pause, the Orb continued. *Humans that cannot control their egos are reincarnated. They are judged by TendHer and then returned to physical form. Their Mind's Eyes must learn to control their egos before they can merge with TheOne.*

'That's a paradox, right? Controlling by giving up control? Will you give us more examples?' asked Ben.

To put it simply, ego is will. It is controlling outcomes. It is controlling people. It is expecting them to act or feel a certain way. It is judging the actions of others. It is thinking and planning to reach a goal. The ego wants to control nature and remodel it in the ego's image.

The Orb hesitated as if searching for a better example. *Dwelling with your Soul in 'beyond the Veil' is without expectations, without judgment, except one. The Soul is moved by unconditional Love.*

'So the ego is bad, right?' asked Luke.

The Orb was silent for a moment as if to add emphasis. *Yes. And no. As I said, the ego is vital for physical survival. However, it must be contained by the Mind's Eye for Spiritual development and eventual reunion with TheOne. You will ask me next how the Mind's Eye does that.*

All four guys nodded their heads in agreement.

The Mind's Eye is mindful awareness. It is watching oneself and one's ego in action like a spectator watching a game. It is the process of seeing oneself from a distance, detached. It is an objective perspective. It is the attitude of observing thoughts, feelings, and actions dispassionately. It is Mushin.

'Mush what?' asked Luke.

The Orb realized the guys needed more explanation. *Mushin is conscious awareness of our inner world without judgment and without distraction. It is like a mountain stream that is allowed to flow unrestricted to its source, eventually ending up in the ocean. Mushin is deliberately following a stream of thinking without making judgments.*

'Thoughts? What kind of thoughts? I thought thinking was good!' commented Ben. 'I mean, that's what I'm good at.'

Yes, you are. Knowledge and intelligence evaluate thoughts as useful or non-useful, factual or faulty. The ego, however, wants to judge thoughts as good or bad, thereby controlling and restricting new experiences; personal and Spiritual growth are sacrificed.

'Could you give us an example?' asked Luke.

Yes. In your world, the favorite word of the ego is "should." Whenever you hear yourself use that word, dig deep into the feelings that emerge. You will usually find frustration and anger directed at someone you Love; your expectations are not being met.

'It's acting like a judge with conditional Love? Strings attached, that sort of thing?' asked Charles.

Yes. That is so.

Then John asked a question he was confident the other guys were thinking. 'Has this ever happened before? An Orb speaking to humans while the humans are still alive?'

Once, when TheSon incarnated into the human realm, Orbs paved the way.

'We're screwed. No other choices are there?' asked John.

There are always choices. However, I have seen your Souls. I know and Love each of you as a brother knows and Loves his brother. TheSon knows you are ready. But the decision is still yours.

Ben had waited patiently to address something the Orb had said. None of the other guys seemed concerned, but Ben suspected it would play a significant role in whether they were successful or not. Addressing the Orb, Ben asked, 'You said the Mind's Eye has two functions, but you haven't talked about the second one. You know. Keeping Dark Matter off the Soul?'

Dark Matter is everywhere. It flows through you now. It supports all life. Yet, it yearns to replace Life. It longs to corrupt the living and consume the Light. It seeks to accumulate and consolidate its power in the SuperVoid, a region also known as Hell. Dark Matter seeks out the Soul in every life form, for it knows that the Light of the Soul is the only power that can destroy it.

Charles asked a question everyone was thinking about. 'Are our Souls clear of Dark Matter?'

Of course not. But the reason you were chosen is your Souls are shining above all others on this planet.

The four were thrilled. An Angel had complimented them. They agreed they could not turn down the Angel's request to fight the evil Twins. Even though each of the guys harbored reservations, and all were afraid, they nodded their heads in agreement to follow the Orb. Four barely audible "yeses" gave the Orb the permission it needed to begin the training. A lot of "what ifs" still ran through their minds.

Have faith, the Orb encouraged all four. *The training begins. Now.*

The guys' physical bodies were yanked out of their tent, momentarily hung in the air looking down on the campfire, then rocketed into space, spinning, turning, and falling faster than even John had ever experienced. 'The staff don't have a clue what's goin' on, do they?' yelled Luke.

'I'm flying! Look at me, Luke. I'm flying!' screamed Ben inside his head.

'What if they wake up and discover our bodies are still in space?' said Charles.

'Our bodies are really there at camp. We're now in "Soul-body" form,' explained John.

'Who cares! This is fantastic. Look at the Earth! We must be in the exosphere! And the other planets seem so close! How are we doing this?' wondered Ben.

'You'll soon find out,' screamed John. 'You haven't seen anything yet! Before you know it, we'll be out of our solar system.'

Suddenly the four were jerked to a halt, suspended, and alone in the darkness. Where did the planets go? Had they traveled that far out into space so soon? They thought they had to be in the deepest part of space because darkness was everywhere. All sensation ceased. They felt the beating of their "Soul-hearts," the whooshing of their "Soul-heart valves." They sensed their comrades were inches away. The four gasped for more air; a cold mist jetted outwards into space from their "Soul-mouths."

Inspecting their "Soul-bodies," the guys saw they were surrounded by a uniform armor of air.

John felt comfortable and secure. His present armor was similar to the air armor that had protected his "mind-body" on his many forest tours while in the "gap." He motioned to the guys that everything was OK and not to worry. He hoped their suits wouldn't interfere with their thought transmission. 'Guys, what do you think of the spacesuit? Can you still hear me?'

'Yes, John. No Problem! This is so cool. Wish I could wear one of these playing football!' exclaimed Luke.

'Ditto. I could start some bitchin' fires wearing one of these!' blurted Ben.

'I'm not a big fan of a tornado running up and down my body, hanging in space,' Charles said.

John laughed. 'Yeah, Charles. No worries. With these babies, you can stay in space forever. You are protected from all the stellar crap zipping through space at a zillion miles per hour.'

'Why would space debris be a problem if we're in Spirit form?' quizzed Ben.

John had a feeling Ben was going to ask this question. 'The armor is not to protect our bodies, although it can if we ever need to explore space physically. The purpose of the air armor is to protect our Mind's Eyes, which can get distracted or confused. Once that happens, it could expel the Soul just like it does at the Funnel."

'Got it! We're exploring space with our Mind's Eyes then! At least this time, so we're safe,' declared Ben.

In the distance, the guys saw what looked like hundreds of two-dimensional circles. They resembled balloons, like clothes hanging on a line to dry, hypnotically bobbing back and forth, each circling and revolving around what appeared to be other balloons. Innumerable circles of uncountable balloons curling closer and closer to other balloons.

The balloons rushed towards the four. The guys saw they were getting more prominent, and that some force was inflating them. Before the balloons reached the guys, they became so large they began to pop and collapse into radiant, minor points of Light.

Then the balloons repeated the process: expansion, pop, contraction. Repeatedly: expansion, pop, contraction.

The Orb directed four balloons to move closer to the guys.

Four balloons approached the guys and one balloon each completely covered of them.

Wrapped snugly around their bodies, the guys felt the balloons were another coat protecting their Mind's Eyes, just like their air armor, only this time covering them with an added layer of fabric. A single hole opened in the middle of their balloon. Air rushed in, extending the balloon fabric out so far that the guys' "Soul-bodies" floated within their balloons. In relation to the rapidly expanding balloon, the guys' "Soul-bodies" shrank in size until they began to tumble around the inside circumference, sliding around the curved contours, falling down steep slopes, laboriously climbing new membrane hills for the subsequent breathless, random tumble.

The guys kept shrinking; they became so small that they lost sight of each other. They shrunk further and further to the quantum level until they watched strings of energy dance in frenzied orbits around each other.

A more profound mystery was revealed to the four guys: The balloons were universes in and of themselves. In addition, the balloons were also the atomic building blocks in a progressively larger dimension made up of more universes, combining to create even more universes. The balloons were like grains of sand making up the form of a beach. Grains too many to count. Universes so small, their existence undetectable. Comprised of an infinite number of atoms, multiplied by quadrillion trillions of molecules multiplied by billions of life forms, the vast numbers belied the microscopic size of any one-balloon universe; entirely incomprehensible to humans. Materialistic classical reality had no measurement tool that could accurately describe, much less measure, this infinity.

Then to each came a second revelation. A single thought or a single feeling could be like a single universe in and of itself. It can weigh upon the Soul like the universe fabric, shrunk so tight it suffocates, trapping a Soul forever, never moving beyond the same recycled dogma, arriving at false generalizations based on many flawed, partial-truth specifics.

The guys knew they needed to learn how to stay aware, remain alert, and especially think non-judgmentally if they wanted access to the 'beyond the Veil' portal entry points located in the ever-increasing and expanding number of universes. Each universe appeared to be separate, seemingly alone and distinct, yet simultaneously affiliated and connected. Like a single thread of fiber interwoven with others to make up a carpet, each fiber had eleven dimensions, all separate realities adjoined by the same structure; eleven realities multiplied by an infinite number of other fibers and their dimensions; all having portals for the guys to navigate in 'beyond the Veil'.

And then, to each, there was a third revelation: Portals to 'beyond the Veil' could slam shut forever with but one negative, repressed, or obsessive feeling or thought.

A gust of soft, sweet, cool air was a sign to the guys that a lesson had been completed. Their balloon surfaces popped and evaporated. The Orb congratulated the guys on their discoveries. A wave of ecstasy shot out from the Orb, removing any apprehension or fear the guys might be harboring.

'Love' was the answer, and they felt it deep within their Souls. It had no boundaries, and there were no words that could fully describe its bliss.

Language separates; Love unites and expands at the same time.

The ego is a room within a prison. Negative thinking is the walls, thought the Orb.

A barrage of thoughts assaulted the consciousness of the guys.

The Orb continued. *You must be mindful and allow your Mind's Eye to take charge of your ego. Be aware. The power of life expresses itself in the rhythm of contraction and expansion, just like your balloons. You must flow with peace; do not get stuck; do not contract with fear. One fixated misjudgment or obsessive thought and you could lose your way or not find the portal you need to journey to or from 'beyond the Veil'.*

'Excuse me, but how can we explore our minds when our brains are back at camp? Down there, somewhere?' asked Ben.

Your brains are back at camp. Your Minds Eyes are here. If "here" really existed.

'They're different? I thought our minds come from our brains?' pressed Ben.

Most do. A few can leave their brains yet stay connected simultaneously as they explore their true home, the Mind of TheOne, the fifth region. It is a region without physical boundaries.

'This fifth region is where I visit my animal friends, correct?' asked Charles.

That is correct. It is the deepest region and connects us with 'beyond the Veil'. Others choose to remain in the lower four regions – thinking, emotion, ego protection, and Dark Matter. These collectively are what you call the brain. Let us begin. Behold the first region, thought.

The guys, especially Ben, got the message. It was time to stop asking questions and learn what the Orb wanted them to know.

The first region was quiet and orderly. It felt safe. The guys saw a massive storehouse of particle-packed space with no discernible walls. Looking closer, they saw that the particles were, in reality, small symbols hanging in midair, some chained together in pairs, and others united in progressively larger combinations. Some were letters, some were words, some were unfamiliar symbols, and some were letters in foreign alphabets.

The guys were prodded to look more closely. Their Mind's Eyes zipped to various parts of their brains so they could inspect, integrate, and experience the process of communication with themselves and with others. They realized that symbols were combined to build words and sentences. Some symbols formed systems, rational equations, reasoned observations, and deductive reasoning. Some were merely creative, appearing momentarily in being, then evaporating in a burst of exploding energy. Some symbols spontaneously flitted about, trying to join others in new connections, crossing hemispheric pathways of firing neurons, spewing energy to launch their message to other parts of the brain.

'This is so cool!' said Ben.

'Only you would think this is cool, since you're so smart. Bet you feel right at home with all these formulas. But I have this funny feeling,' cautioned John.

'You call being at the mercy of an Angel a funny feeling?' asked Luke.

'Well, at least you're honest, Luke. But there's nothing we can do, so we just have to go with the flow,' advised Charles.

'No, wait, Charles. John, tell us. Are we really, truly in trouble?' asked Luke.

John thought he knew where the Orb was leading them. 'Charles is right. We just have to go with the flow. But I think that where that flow is leading us could be scary and painful. You guys sure you're up for that?'

'Do we have a choice?' muttered Luke.

Before any of the others could answer, the Orb replied. *No. All of you are too far in your minds. You do not have a choice. You must trust me and your Mind's Eyes.*

'Think I'd prefer to be out of my mind!' mumbled Ben.

'Ain't touching that one,' exclaimed Luke.

'Shh. Stay on task, guys,' John scolded.

The second region is emotion.

A sudden burst of hot, searing hormones attacked the guys' flow of consciousness. Some cryptic, passionate force pushed their thoughts through unrecognizable mental landscapes, buffeted and yanked them. At the same time, they entered new neuronal junctions, only to be sent speeding to other synapses, the places where painful memories are forged, retrieved, and protected.

The guys felt they were not in control. They wept. They cringed with complete knowledge of their own suffering. They were tortured by how they had caused pain to others. They were forced to freeze at singular moments and immerse totally in their psychic torture.

Ben murdered his parents.

Luke was molested and abused.

Charles was trapped between cultures.

John was mocked.

The four were stripped to their rawest vulnerabilities. Laid bare for all to witness, the guys fully embraced each other's emotional pain. Luke watched as Ben erected careful defenses against the knowledge he had murdered his parents. Ben watched as Luke struggled to forget the years of abuse, buried in deep shame. John watched as Charles was rejected by his tribe. Charles watched as John was judged inferior. The guys knew each other's emotional trauma fully formed for the first time.

The four guys discovered they had experienced, at one time or another, the same level of psychological trauma: Ben's guilt, Luke's shame, Charles' frustration, John's rejection. They unlocked a profound secret: All the intense emotions they had observed in the others were now part of their own experience. They grieved for each other, then wept for themselves. They were trapped; little did they know the price of empathy. Because once acknowledged in the other, the emotion, whatever it is, exacts a cruel price in exchange for shared ownership. So, the guys wept in silent suffering for all, completely immersed in hopelessness.

They had to surrender, with no hope of rescue.

They did.

The group became one.

At that point of complete synthesis, the Orb ordered the chaos to stop. *Yes. You have arrived.*

Luke seemed to be more traumatized than the other three. In between sobs, he cried, 'I don't want to go through the history review stuff again.'

The Orb replied with two words: *Pay attention.*

'That's it?' asked John. 'Just pay attention?'

Lack of attention is the fuel that drives the pain. Hold on tight to that wisdom as we explore the places that few people have ever ventured in their minds. So be it. Now.

Ben yelped. 'Now? Now? You mean, I gotta do this again?'

Luke joined in. 'Yeah. I think I want to go home.'

Congratulations. You are still aware. Once you see and feel your pain, you will stop suffering.

'Sure feels like I'm suffering now,' cringed Charles.

And? So what do you need?

'Probably nothing. I just feel worthless. I can barely stand what I did to some of my friends!' answered Charles.

What you did, you did. Learn from it and move on. Do not self-judge. Suffering is pain plus judgment. Instead, envelop yourself entirely in your pain without evaluation. The pain will gradually dissipate into the stillness of acceptance that allows you to move forward in your Soul development.

'Easy for you to say!' muttered Ben.

You must continue with your journey.

Awareness was once again snagged by the guys' Mind's Eyes. Crossing through an uncountable number of synaptic junctions, the guys found they were stopped before what appeared to be a sentry guard post.

Now on to the third region of your mind. You have arrived at an area between the mind regions of thought and emotional memory. It is your guardian. It detects threats to your ego.

This appeared to be an area similar to a sentry standing guard, mandated to identify any threatening input. Worry and pain were added to the weight of anything new, anything possibly dangerous, anything associated with previous pain. Its sensors were censors, making self-protective rational and irrational conclusions, like some new baggage thrown on the back of a mule, marking thoughts for importance. Words, people, and actions that registered in this region as dangerous sparked fight, flight, or freezing. Survival, psychological as well as physical, was at stake.

'This is where the judging happens? Right?' asked Luke.

'Probably comparing new stuff with the old stuff,' explained John. 'Now, I think I understand how people can get stuck in their past.'

Charles saw the cultural differences right away. 'You sound as though the past is bad. My people think Anglo culture spends too much time in the future; always planning, ignoring the gifts surrounding them in the present.'

'Hey, Charles. Sorry. No disrespect meant. I said, "can get stuck," ' John clarified.

The guys felt Charles sigh. 'Whatever. Isn't the point of this little expedition to be aware? Don't you see the irony? We're judging our judging!'

'Lost me on that one!' chided Luke.

'So, what's new? We lost you at the thinking stage!' said Ben.

John pleaded for the guys to refrain from teasing each other and continue their mission with the Orb. 'Can we please return to our exploration?'

Before the guys could respond, the Orb replied, *So we shall. Good luck.*

Ben panicked. 'Did the Orb just say good luck? Why would we need luck?'

Luke saw his opportunity to retaliate, tour or no tour. 'We need all the luck we can get to shut you up!'

'Stop it! We really need to continue,' exclaimed Charles.

One more time. Good…have faith.

Ben squealed. 'Did you hear that? Have faith?'

John, Luke, and Charles exclaimed together, 'Ben! Stop squealing! Just shut up!'

Finally settled, the guys allowed their Mind's Eyes to open up to the deepest and most terrifying fourth part of their minds. It was as if a giant hole had opened up and wanted to swallow every aspect of their identity. They saw figures of evil peering up from a pit with no bottom. The demons demanded that the guys sink deeper into the pit of darkness. The guys didn't realize until later that they had collectively opened an entrance to Hell and the Dark Matter stored within their own minds.

A mirage of horned demons slowly crawled out from the depths. Blurry and vague, the faces and bodies were even more frightening because the guys couldn't tell who or what they were. Shifting in and out of focus, some bodies had pitchforks, others had giant hatchets, others had mouths chewing body parts dripping with blood, and others were completely covered in vomit.

The demons ridiculed. And teased. They tempted with promises of power and privilege if the guys only embraced the Dark Matter stored in the eternally deep hole.

These figures of horror cursed the guys and made them review their lives. The barrage from the demons felt merciless, personal, and eternal. Jumping from figure to figure, the beasts took turns judging every single life event. They poked; they prodded until they could turn even the most virtuous deed into depravity. They threatened the guys with punishment for every single one of their failures. The demons did not care if the events were actual or manufactured because small bits of Dark Matter were released from the pit and sent to cover the guys' Souls with every threat. They stood paralyzed as they watched their own Mind's Eyes attempt to fight back the Dark Matter. Most of the Dark Matter was repelled, but some managed to make its way to their Souls.

Call forth the Light of Grace. It is why TheSon gave of Himself. Stay aware of His Light, and the dark sludge will dry up and disappear.

Charles articulated what they all felt. 'I actually saw a spear of Light attack the Dark Matter that had trapped parts of my Soul. The Light shaved the Dark Matter off.'

'Yeah, that's what happened to me too,' replied Luke. 'Ben….'

'I want to go home,' whimpered Ben.

'I think we're almost done, Ben. You're doing great. Hang in there,' John replied, trying to reassure everyone, including himself.

For the first time in their relationship, Luke saw himself and Ben with complete clarity. 'And for what it's worth, for what you've had to deal with, Ben. I admire your courage.'

Ben cried tears of pain and tears of joy.

Had not TendHer made a prediction?

And with Igor's help, (Ben) will share the wisdom of courage and sacrifice!

Ben had never been praised for courage, that's for sure; much less from the person he secretly viewed as the most courageous person he had ever met: Luke. This acknowledgment of truth sent Ben deeper into his own Soul. Ben opened himself up further to its radiance rather than blocking the Light of Love from Luke. He knew he need not say anything. They were beyond the ritual of language. Ben struggled to mouth words of appreciation.

'I know, Ben. You're cool,' Luke softly replied.

'And so are you, Luke!' added Charles. 'So are you.'

Come back to me. We are not finished. You must venture deeper into the world of Dark Matter.

Feeling stronger now that they had successfully removed the Dark Matter from their Souls, the guys didn't flinch.

John spoke for the group. 'Let's do this. Now.'

And so it shall be done.

Instantly, the guys found themselves standing before a gate whose attached wall extended as far as they could perceive. They heard demons behind the wall collectively shout, *This is where you belong and where you will end up!*

The wall was nowhere, yet it felt like it was everywhere. It was hanging in the darkness, totally unsupported and twirling in a serpentine path, coiled protectively around its precious gate of entry. The gate had buckles and latches, giving the wall the semblance of a castle. The guys knew they should not get close, much less try to enter.

Suddenly all of the screaming and threats ceased. Everything was quiet and calm. Curiosity overcame the guys' fear, and they decided to test the gate. Huddling together in a defensive, guarded position, they slowly meandered toward the gate.

Together the guys pushed on the gate, and then it opened. They floated through the gate's entrance, unable to control their direction. Once inside the gate, it slammed shut behind them. They were trapped. They were stuck in the same part of their minds. They heard laughter laced with mockery: *Not so bright! You will never leave. You are ours now. Forever!*

Demons surrounded the guys on all sides.

Fear choked the guys' breathing. Searing circuits of pain raced across their minds, leaving each of them with scorched trails of despair.

And then their hopelessness was punctuated by an overriding promise made by the demons: *You will never escape. Ever.*

Then a figure wrapped in Light, which they knew was the Orb, appeared in front of the gate. *Begone illusions. Leave us alone!*

Screaming vitriol and hatred, the demonic figures slowly retreated. Suddenly, the Orb shot out a wave of Light aimed directly at the demons. Striking the shrinking figures, Dark Matter exploded from their bodies and completely encircled them. Twisting and turning, the demons watched as their bodies melted from the heat of the unbound Dark Matter; soon, nothing was left but barren molecules in NoThing. The gate and the wall from Hell followed them, collapsing, compressing. Finally, all were sucked into a container the size of a shoebox. Then the box itself disappeared. Leaving nothing in *NoThing*.

The guys hung in empty darkness for only a moment. Then radiant Light exploded all around them, followed by soft words that lovingly caressed their minds so that their worries, fears, and anxieties went away in an instant.

You see, demons also come from the mind. They lose their power when exposed to the Light of the Mind's Eye. TheSon is *the Light.*

The guys were ready to move on. They were close to exhaustion and the Orb knew that.

The last part of the mind is the most important. This fifth region is only accessible if you are not caught up in the reification of symbols, the Orb thought.

'Wow, that's a big word,' thought Luke.

'It means to perceive an object or symbol as having a life of its own, like money or a house or a religious symbol like a cross,' replied Ben.

The Orb patiently continued. *You are children of TheOne; you have access to the Divine. It is channeled through this fifth region of the brain, leading to the 'beyond the Veil' in life and the Funnel at death. It is where your Mind's Eye wishes to dwell. It's open to everyone, but few can work through the four regions of the mind to find it.*

'Oh yeah, that's like Buddhist meditation. I access this region when I travel through my "gaps," ' added John. 'Now I know why I was given a tour of the universe. I made a map.'

'You gotta share it with us, like ASAP!' exclaimed Luke.

'What again is the relationship between our Mind's Eye and this Funnel?' asked Charles.

John answered. 'The Funnel is where the Mind's Eye escorts the Soul after death. The Mind's Eye then fades away like a spent rocket booster. Guess our brains are hard-wired to seek the Funnel out when we die. But in life, by getting to the fifth level, our Mind's Eyes will take us to 'beyond the Veil'.'

Ben added, 'This is cutting-edge neurology. Some say that the brain is a receiver; it's an amplifier of sorts. Only this fifth part, the deepest part of the brain, "tunes in" to the experience of Spiritual transcendence, what we are calling 'beyond the Veil'. The experience of the afterlife is part of this process.'

'So this is where I find Heather?' asked Luke.

Even though Luke hardly ever brought up Heather, the group knew that he was having difficulty not knowing if, when, and how they would ever reunite. Ben and Charles didn't say a word. Ben was proud of himself for not attacking Luke and thought it was a sign of his own personal progress. Charles thought Luke would meet up with Heather again when both were needed.

Not feeling disrespected or ignored, Luke didn't want to hold up the group. 'Nobody's saying anything, so I guess I'll just sit on it,' said Luke.

Ben continued. 'But there's another explanation. Some say that this region *reflects* the background matrix of cosmic consciousness. In addition, this background consciousness is Divine. In other words, these mystical experiences are *pushed* into being by a Creator who bathes our Souls with bliss; these transcendental Spiritual perceptions are not *pulled* from the physical environment through learning or compensatory neurological processes.'

'Compens…what?' Luke asked.

'On the other hand, many disbelieving scientists assert that this state of transcendence or cosmic bliss is compensation for the sheer horror of realizing one's mortality,' Ben slowly replied.

'You mean death scares the shit out of everyone?' replied Luke.

'Afraid so,' said Ben with a solemnity that could have been mistaken for a priestly pronouncement.

'Where did you learn this stuff?' asked John.

'I read a lot. Plus, I'm a genius,' replied Ben stoically.

'To us native peoples, nature is alive,' Charles stated.

'Yes, that's animism,' commented Ben.

'Ani...what?' asked Luke.

All at once, the group laughed; Luke the loudest. 'Guess I should stick to football,' Luke announced.

'No, Luke. You're not so bad,' Ben shared.

Luke beamed.

John added his perspective. 'This is my take; at least, I think this is what I learned from my "gap" tours. Yes, we are primed to be with 'beyond the Veil' and not just destined to be physical material objects breathing for a few years and then dissolving into nothingness. We have another door of experience that we can open if we use our Mind's Eyes to perceive it.'

'When do we go to this 'beyond the Veil'? asked Luke. 'I think we're ready. I mean, let's get this going!'

John tried not to signal his rising apprehension. He knew the four were a long way from using their talents as a team and wanted to instill confidence in their mission and calm everyone down. 'Just waiting for an invite, I guess. But what we've been through, there's no doubt in my mind that we will kick some butt.'

'Hope you're right, John,' said Ben. 'Hope you're right. But right now, why are we alone? Where is the Orb?'

Journal Entry Forty-Six: The Chosen

The Orb was nowhere to be perceived. Seconds turned into minutes. The guys waited.

Finally, John said, 'Hello! Where did you go? Have you gone away and left us alone?'

The guys were reassured when they again received the Orb's thoughts, but this time the thoughts seemed to be from a distance. They strained to understand the incoming message.

My task is completed. Maybe someday we will meet again within TheOne.

'Maybe? Someday? What? Those words don't make me feel very confident,' grumbled Ben.

'Oh, stop complaining,' chided Luke.

The Orb's final words: *Prepare to meet TheSon.*

Again, silence. The guys had little choice but to wait and try to relax.

'How long do you think we'll be here?' asked Ben.

'Maybe this is a test of some sort?' replied John.

'I've had enough of being tested. How much more are we supposed to handle?' said Ben.

Charles had heard enough. 'After all we've been through, I think we need to be more trusting. The Orb said we would meet TheSon, so maybe we should all just be a little more Spiritual about this whole thing.'

Luke became excited. 'Did you hear yourself say "should"? That's your ego, man!'

Charles could only respond with a wistful sigh.

You are My Chosen.

'Guys, do you detect somebody new in our heads?' asked John.

'And didn't we hear the Orb say that we would hear from TheSon?' added Charles.

You are My Chosen. Prepare.

'Got a new voice in my head. But this one is powerful!' said Luke.

'Are you TheSon?' asked Charles timidly.

I AM. I have come to make you ready for the struggle ahead. You were Chosen because each of you has unique gifts. You will now be witness to My strengths.

'Where are you?' asked Luke.

I speak from 'beyond the Veil'. I AM 'beyond the Veil'. You are the Chosen. Now you must know your gifts and use them wisely.

Charles. You are first.

'Thank You. I hope.'

Charles, you will be the protector of nature and its many forces. Behold.

With a mighty surge, TheSon pushed Charles' Mind's Eye to a distance far from the other guys. Charles looked down on the planet Earth, a ball hanging lifeless in space, so far away. Charles felt he could grab it in his hand like a pebble and cast it skipping upon the fabric of space and time. As if reading Charles' mind, TheSon pushed him closer to the planet. Charles bathed in the radiant blue color reflected off the planet's water and the wispy shrouds of cloud that writhed their lazy, desultory rambling through the Earth's atmosphere.

Charles' reverie was interrupted. He started to fall, dropping from a distance of great height directly into an orbit hovering a few miles above the ground. He was flooded with great energy. Intuitively, through his years of immersion in animal Spirits, Charles knew he was adrift in the current of the Earth's animal energy system.

Sift through the noise, Charles. Move between the energy currents. Maneuver through the birthing, the dying, the consuming, and the Being. You will find the Golden Eagle. He is expecting you.

Charles experienced his Mind's Eye gliding, falling, and then leaping from one animal kingdom to another. His mind raced like a giant slingshot. Charles pierced through the grey contours of thousands of animal worlds; they rushed to engulf him fully in their daily drama of survival from birth to mating to dying.

Charles briefly visited his Mentor, Bestow. She smiled and nodded her head in encouragement. Charles sensed the hope emanating from Bestow's supportive solid Spirit. He felt a tingling vibration resonate through his Mind's Eye as he bathed in the alert awareness of all the other Bonobos united with her. They were solemn and appreciative but still scared.

As quickly as he was jetted into the animal world, Charles was returned to the group.

John was next.

John, the others will need your experience of traveling in and through and around and beyond time. They will need your map.

'I clung to the hope You were real. Sometimes I thought You were just a dream or part of my mental illness,' John responded.

TheSon tenderly replied, *I am indeed part of both. I am surely both. Life is a dream that unfolds in the Mind of TheOne. The mentally ill are those among TheOne's Creations stuck between the illusion of two separate realities: the material and the 'beyond the Veil'.*

'I remember they are clearly One,' said John.

Then you are indeed Blessed. The battle is about to begin. You must now make your way to meet Monster Bear, TheSon said.

'You want me to lead my team to fight the Monster Bear? I thought he was mostly a myth, like a sasquatch. How can we defeat him? He's supposed to be a giant and way too much for the four of us to handle,' stated John.

No, John. You will lead your team to JOIN the Monster Bear. I will become One with the Monster Bear. He has been waiting for Me for hundreds of years.

John replied, 'Oh, that's good. I'm relieved, I think. But can we have a backup? Are we assured of victory because of Your presence within the Monster Bear?'

All life and Creation are based upon probability. If we are successful there and survive, you will be given an even more dangerous mission.

'Ah, excuse me? If we survive? That's just an expression, right?' asked Ben.

TheSon waited. Finally, He said, *Your Souls are now at stake.*

John wanted to steer the conversation to a more practical level. 'You are the Son of TheOne, and only You can incarnate. Why can't You just destroy our enemy? Why do You need a Monster Bear?'

Darkness needs Light. Light needs darkness. It is the balance that TheOne seeks. Without balance, there cannot be choice, and without choice, there cannot be Love. I cannot interfere with freedom of choice or even the freedom that has been granted to the Devil incarnate, who now threatens universes too numerous to count. I have chosen the Way and the Will of My Father to incarnate and bring the Light.

'But what about all this evil? Doesn't it violate the laws of our nature?' quizzed John.

It is Darkness, replied TheSon.

'So evil has been turned loose on Earth, and You can't just destroy it?'

TheSon's answer hit John like a hammer: *Do you not have evil inside you? Because of that, should I then destroy you? Evil can be the beginning of hope, and hope brings the possibility of redemption.*

John still seemed confused. 'How can there be hope in evil?'

John, you must release what you perceive as the purity of perfect opposites.

Ben was next. TheSon cradled Ben's Soul as they streamed to the SuperVoid. Without protection, Ben would have been obliterated by the wailing pain of all the Souls crying for release. The miasma of foul, rotting stench made Ben want to retch.

Ben located the source of the mephitic soup: millions of LostSouls streaming out of the breached gate of the SuperVoid like so many bees leaving a hive to attack an intruder.

'TheSon, why are all the LostSouls leaving?' asked Ben.

They have been called to join NoOne's army.

Ben marveled at the construction of the SuperVoid walls, details much more vivid than he had seen before. The closer he approached, the more Ben could see the walls were made out of LostSouls—an infinite number of contorted eyes, weeping, twisted, and gnarled. The outlines of blurry faces screamed for mercy. They, too, curled and quivered. The walls undulated in rhythm, spewing foul, acid spit, and gray smoke outward. The hollow mouths cried in terror.

Ben reverted to his primary defense mechanism, which was rational analysis. Yet, he still struggled to make sense of all the torture.

TheSon observed Ben wrestling with rational causes—formulating explanations and interventions and interjecting inductive possibilities. Ben wanted to find formulas or algorithms to explain the supernatural and bring relief.

The eyes have been lost to NoOne, Ben.

'It's that simple? Like forever?' asked Ben.

Possibly. All existence is like a coin with two sides—life and death. Both exist simultaneously in all of Creation. But in different proportions and with varying degrees of energy.

Incomprehensible was the word that floated through Ben's consciousness. The bottom line was that Ben felt he could never master this new Spiritual existence. Yet, wasn't TheSon here helping him and showing His faith in him?

Still, Ben wanted answers. 'Why am I here? All the guys hate me. I've been a loser my entire life.'

TheSon's compassion swept over Ben. Ben's Soul swelled, expanding his Mind's Eye. Ben was filled with the ecstasy of connectedness and understanding. He was in rapture, a euphoric feeling he had never experienced before, even while watching his most spectacular fires.

With Ben's Soul expansion, his Mind's Eye was able to see infinite connections in the universe between the uncountable levels of organic organization and their relationship to all forms of energy. His head was filled with knowledge.

Eyes in the wall, in unison, swiveled up and down, right and left, to catch more of the energy filling Ben with Love, then spilling over and into the various streams of space. Some energy penetrated even the darkest holes in the SuperVoid wall where eyes struggled to comprehend TheSon's magnificent power.

Then TheSon spoke. *Intellect is of little use without compassion, Ben. And compassion is of little use without intellect.*

'It's so hard to have both simultaneously,' mused Ben.

Gently, TheSon spoke, *We will need such courage.*

Immediately, a tidal wave of emotion flooded Ben's Mind's Eye. A single memory, so closely guarded, so tightly protected, burst through its wall of containment. Great waves of pain spilled out. Energy that had been repressed escaped in a gush of emotion. Ben cried out, 'Where are my parents? Will I get to see them soon?'

TheSon felt the pain emanating through Ben. *Suffering is often the road taken to re-form with TheOne.*

Desperate for direction and clarity, Ben begged, 'What exactly am I to do with all this emotion and pain? Just show me.'

TheSon replied with two words: *I have.*

Then Ben found himself back in empty space, staring at the other three boys.

Next, it was Luke's turn to receive his assignment.

TheSon opened up a vision portal so Luke could visit his beloved Heather. It was but a split second, and then the two were together once more.

'Heather, I'm afraid.'

Of what? I will always be with you.

'Yes, but can our Love be strong enough to combat the evil I must fight?'

Luke, you must trust TheSon. Clutch me to your Soul. That's where I will be.

Heather's words should have been enough, but they were not. Luke wanted to escape and coexist with Heather in whatever dimension was possible.

'I don't think I'm strong enough!' Luke cried out to TheSon.

TheSon replied, *My son, Love is the most significant power in the universe. There is nothing more vital than Loving unconditionally. You must use your unconditional Love of Heather to guide you and protect others; only then will your mission be accomplished. As much as you defend others, it is the same as supporting your.Soul Mate.*

'Am I man enough to do all this? I'm just a kid in high school,' said Luke.

If being a man means using strength as a physical tool to dominate others and conquer all, then only the physically strongest are men. However, being a mature man means seeing and using all kinds of strength as a Spiritual tool to protect and help others who are weaker and cannot defend themselves. It is the man's way of expressing Love.

'Well, try telling that to all the middle school bullies!' replied Luke.

Some will simply not listen to words. If not, as a man, you are charged with defending those not capable of defending themselves.

'Whatever that takes?'

Luke could sense that TheSon was leaving. Luke could barely make out TheSon's next reply: *Do you not grasp the cascade of possible responses? You must choose. It is your choice.*

'What about women?' cried out Luke. 'What is their strength?'

To be as you are with Heather. To help you soften with Love and give you purpose.

'I see,' replied Luke.

But do you feel? Those were the last words thought by TheSon to the four guys.

Journal Entry Forty-Seven: Portals

Informed by TheSon that the four guys were soon to arrive, TendHer from 'beyond the Veil' opened four small portals in 'beyond the Veil' just in time, but not of time. Through their individual apertures and protected by their Mind's Eyes, the four guys halfway popped their "Soul-bodies" through the bottom-most layer of 'beyond the Veil', leaving their "Soul-legs" dangling beneath. Each felt like they were straddling two realities as if they had been cut in two.

Peeking up through the holes, the boys perceived a nebulous cloud stretching as far as their Mind's Eyes could sense. The four guys felt like they were in a light show with some kind of fog. Vaporous billows of leisurely shifting mist flowed by them, gently brushing their "Soul-body" heads. The mist left trace amounts of a smell similar to lavender, which lingered and then evaporated. Endless cycles of mist layered into sheets of dense fog fell upon them. New scents appeared. The guys saw Orbs of Light, glimmering, small balls of luminous energy sending out beams of assorted colors reaching to connect with other rays, crisscrossing each in all directions.

Charles was concerned that the others would be overwhelmed. He hoped the other three guys had clearly heard the message from TheSon. 'We are not in time. We are within eternity. Please let me know that you're with me.'

John was the first to reply. 'Yes, Charles. I'm here.'

Ben was next. 'I'm here, also, Charles. But I'm really afraid my "Mind's-Eye Soul-belly" will never get through this hole.'

Luke chimed in right after Ben. 'Here. Hey, Ben, buddy, let me know when you manage that trick.'

Charles continued. 'We know we're crazy in some ways. But crazy people do not have the same hallucination at the same time. So, we all agree that we have been chosen by TheSon to fight this evil that has been turned loose on the Earth?'

'Yes.' All three responded in thought simultaneously.

'Look…have you guys noticed the shapes? I was going to say "see," but I don't think our senses are working up here; or down here, or wherever we think we are,' thought Ben.

Luke was so excited to see the group of shapes all around him that he popped up out of his hole. Rising above his buddies, Luke gradually floated back to their level. 'There are millions of shapes, and they look like ghosts. Look, they're drifting all around us!'

'And rising, too. The ghosts just keep getting higher, and the higher they get, the more their bodies disappear! And then more new bodies suddenly replace them! If only my Elders could see this!' exclaimed Charles.

'I see dead people,' said Ben.

'Ha, ha. Very funny. If you look between the clouds and go way, way up, you can hardly see any bodies at all, just some streaks of Light. Why's that?' asked Luke.

'Didn't TheSon say that there was a place where Souls go when their bodies die in "beyond the Veil?" ' asked John.

'So, all these shapes and Lights are going through the dying process?' asked Luke.

John answered. 'Yes, Luke. I guess so. For them out there, yes. As far as I know, right now, our Mind's Eyes are in charge. We're different.'

'Why?' pressed Ben.

'Because we're the Chosen and being trained,' said John. 'Normally, the Soul would take over. And if that were the case, I think we would have to be dead.'

'Oh, that's a happy thought,' commented Ben.

'Guys, I can see us at the campfire, frozen. It's as if we haven't left at all,' marveled Charles.

The other three guys steered their Mind's Eye awareness back to Earth time and then murmured in agreement.

John was familiar with the sensation of sharing two realities simultaneously. 'We aren't really frozen. It's just that we're in some kind of a time "gap." We are between and also above time—where all the Souls are. What might seem like years here in 'beyond the Veil' could be a split second in Earth space-time. Just so you don't have to worry about missing out on something in the material world.'

'OK, so I gotta ask. Do you see me the way I see you guys?' asked Luke.

'Yeah, we can all see each other, but to me, you guys look like phantoms, like apparitions,' said Ben.

'Ah, those are big words. Do you think we really look like ghosts?' stammered Luke.

'No, no, I mean we can see our bodies, but they're just shapes, definitely transparent. I can clearly perceive your Souls covered by your Mind's Eyes, they really do look like eyes, but the rest of you are just blurry outlines,' said Ben.

'OK, let's try this. Guys, put all your mental energy into just seeing your arms,' said John.

'Oh, my God, my body is gone…I just see my arms!' said Luke.

'Yeah! It works. Just arms!' said Charles.

'OK guys, now put your mind into just seeing your feet,' suggested John.

'Hey, all I see are eight feet! Not just mine. I mean, all of our feet!' observed Ben.

John was pleased. He and the guys had discovered one principle in 'beyond the Veil' that could help them in the future. 'So what this tells me is that we can control our "Soul-bodies."'

'Absolutely. We now know we can manipulate our manifestations,' added Charles.

'Whoa. That is a big word! Manusfastion,' added Luke.

Ben couldn't believe Luke was setting himself up for ridicule. Anything academic or intellectual was Ben's turf.

'Hello, Mr. Brains In Your Jockstrap. It's man-is-fes-ta-tion. It means to show something that was hidden. I'm tired of being the smartest one in this group,' Ben declared.

'No, you aren't. You just think you are 'cause you're rich!' said Luke.

Ben was shocked. 'Now, where the hell did that come from? How do you know I'm rich?'

'Because you talk funny, and you use fancy words. And remember, we shared all our secrets like a few seconds ago? Well, it seems just like a few seconds,' said Luke.

'I'll trade you any time or anywhere, your muscles for my brains!'

Never would have thought Ben was jealous of me. Why would he be jealous? He's so damn gifted.

Trying to change the subject as quickly as possible, Ben asked, 'So where do we go from here?'

Relieved that an escalation of the verbal joust between Ben and Luke had been avoided, John answered. 'Just for the record, I don't know where "here" is. All I know is that we have been chosen by TheSon. For all these months, I thought I was a looney bird.'

Ben replied, 'Yeah, me too. But I still love fire.'

'I've heard every thought of TheSon's conversations with you three. Didn't you hear mine too?' asked Luke.

Charles and Ben nodded their heads in affirmation.

'I still love fire,' said Ben.

'John, how about you?' asked Charles.

'Yeah, I guess I did too,' he replied.

'I still….'

'Yes, we know Mr. Snap Crackle and Pop…you love fire!' interrupted Luke.

The guys laughed. Even Ben joined in with the mental chuckling, and he felt a growing affection for the three guys. He was increasingly considering them his friends. Ben quickly repressed his increasing anxiety. *That's my ego trying to protect me.*

'OK then, let's check this place out,' John said.

'Ah, John…this is not a place, you know that. Just let yourself merge with the fog,' suggested Charles.

'Oh, yeah. Sorry. I forgot,' replied John.

After moments of readjustment, the four made out shapes and movements. Layers upon layers of interaction stretched out as far as they could perceive. One row on top of another row. Endless strata of uncountable figures came in and out of focus. Some of the figures were human-like, but most of them were completely foreign and beyond the perceptual power of the four boys. The entities were stacked one on top of the other, talking, sleeping, screaming, crying, pleading, loving, hoping, fighting, analyzing, planning, moving, changing, and just waiting, and waiting.

Ben admired the structurally efficient design. The word "morphology" came to mind. 'It's a perfect structure, like a cosmic Chutes and Ladders game,' Ben thought.

John had explored the general layout of the cosmos. He believed his map would come in handy down the road. Charles, by far, was the most experienced in the Spirit world but tensed at the impersonal fog that spread out before him to eternity. Luke was somewhat apprehensive but was still reasonably confident since he had experienced similar Spiritual readjustments thanks to Heather. Ben was initially skeptical and tried to squeeze back to material reality through the 'beyond the Veil' hole that TheSon had opened for him. However, when Ben found himself stuck, the looks from the others convinced him to worm his way back up into 'beyond the Veil'.

As each of the four guys slowly acclimated to the new layer of existence, they practiced opening up various parts of their "Soul-bodies."

'You better not show your pee-pee, Mr. Jockstrap,' warned Ben.

'Great; nothing like an adolescent conversation when we're practically in Heaven!' countered Luke.

'Oh my gosh, you just strung more than two words together at the same time! You impress me. I can hardly wait until you learn to write,' taunted Ben.

Luke laughed. Ben joined in. They made fun of the fact they made fun of each other. No longer was their verbal sparring an ego contest; a form of disguised anger designed to build oneself up by tearing someone else down. Now teasing would be a sign of friendship, a newly birthed bond that hopefully would continue to grow.

As the four turned in different directions and examined their surroundings, a breeze enveloped them, and a single Speck of Light appeared in the middle of the group.

The small but intense Speck began to twirl around their center. Ben was the only one that tried to keep up with the rotations, which was highly distracting to all the others. They found Ben more fascinating than the Speck of Light. Eventually, Ben also needed to turn away as th Speck of Light expanded and blazed with incredible ferocity. Its radiance soon consumed all four of the guys and much of the foggy mist that had surrounded them.

Just before the power of the Light became painfully bright, it collapsed back into a small Speck at the center of the group. And hung. Waiting for something.

Suddenly, it turned into an eye. It was translucent in the center, with intense brilliance surrounding its oval edges.

If I existed, I would be called in your language by the name TendHer.

'Are you sent from TheSon?' asked Charles.

The eye moved toward Charles. *Yes.*

'Why are you here?' questioned Luke.

I am with you to confirm your fitness. Are you ready for your mission?

The eye swiveled before each of the four guys, finally stopping in front of John.

I know John well. I have seen his Soul. We have spent much effort together exploring multiple realities. John, your map will one day birth new hope.

Then TendHer briefly examined each of the other four, resting in the middle of the group.

I know all your Souls. TheSon must be pleased. However, all of you have much work to do to shed your blemished ego Karma.

Ben got excited. 'Oh, that's like in Hinduism where animals and people are reincarnated to work off their bad deeds.'

The eye moved to Ben and stopped. The eye got bigger as if it was trying to take in all of Ben. *I am TendHer. I decide who has more work to do.*

This time Luke got excited. 'Oh yes, Heather has talked about you. You're from the Reincarnation Universe, right?'

Moving to Luke, TendHer continued to speak. *You are at the most basic level of 'beyond the Veil'. Only I decide if you will move forward. Only I will determine if you are worthy to behold TheSon. For now, you have your Mind's Eyes to behold your "Soul-bodies."*

Ben pushed for specifics. 'Please explain how a Soul can have a body.'

TendHer continued. *Soul-bodies are the psychic remnants of your Earthly physical body. When beings cease to process life energy, the Mind's Eye retains a shadow memory of all physical sensations and mental processes from your entire life. This memory slowly dissipates* as your Soul and whatever negative Karma has accumulated adjusts to your pure Spirit. Because you will need to travel back and forth between essence and existence, and unlike others who have moved on and shed their Soul-body, you four will need to keep yours.

After pausing, TendHer continued: *As you become acclimated to your pure essence, you will see many different combinations of your Soul-body. This supernatural awareness is possible because I have allowed you to keep your Mind's Eyes. This is necessary since you will be returning back to the physical dimension.*

'Yes. We learned that normally the Mind's Eyes are shed once the Soul arrives at the Funnel,' said Charles.

TendHer moved to face all four. *Yes. Shortly after entering the physical entrance to the Funnel, the Mind's Eye pierces through to 'beyond the Veil' and drops away from the Soul as its job is done.*

'Where does it go? The Mind's Eye?'

From dust to dust.

'So, because you've allowed us to keep out Mind's eyes, we don't have to die to explore 'beyond the Veil'?' asked Ben.

Not now, replied TendHer.

'Who are all those transparent people out there…and up there?' asked Luke.

'Beyond the Veil' has Souls in many different stages of reincarnation, all waiting to be judged. Some will appear as an average body to you, especially those who have just arrived like yourselves. Others will appear as shadowy eyes. Some appear as total Orbs, Saints who will soon be with TheOne. Some are Souls returning to another life form and will be reassigned to another material birth to continue removing darkened Karma from their Souls. As you explore this first level of 'beyond the Veil', you will see many Souls coming and going.

'Are we confined to the first level? Where we are now?' asked Ben.

"First" and "levels" are cognitive constructs from your Earthly existence that are not part of Spirit essence. However, as you remain connected to your Mind's Eyes, you may think of it that way. I have been instructed to give you complete access in 'beyond the Veil' to this outer ring. You may come and go as you deem necessary, but you are only permitted to explore this one outer ring. You will disintegrate into nonexistence if you choose to penetrate further and violate this rule.

'When you say disintegrate, is there any fire?' asked Ben.

Almost in perfect accord unison, the other three guys yelled, 'Stop it, Ben!'

Ben backed off. 'Sorry. Again.'

TendHer replied, *Humor is a major indicator of intelligence. All of you will need humor to cope with the challenges that lay before you.*

Luke could not resist. 'TendHer, your Holiness, can I be with Heather here?'

Heather is Perfection. She is waiting for you. But she is far, far away from this beginning level of Purification.

John was next. 'What about my Sensei? Can I see him?'

'Yeah, and what about my parents? How do I get them out of the SuperVoid?' petitioned Ben.

TendHer moved away from the group slowly and started to circle faster and faster. *What will be, will Be.*

TendHer then receded to the single Speck of Light from which she had first appeared and instantly vanished.

Lost in thought, the guys didn't know what to say. They studied their new environment. Concern spread among the guys as they perceived a shift in their surroundings.

Before TendHer departed, the four guys sensed and perceived life in many forms. Now, as if a switch was flipped, everywhere they looked, they saw nothing but misty fog, coalescing into furrowed clumps, breaking apart and dispersing, then reconsolidating for more hovering, swirling, churning. It was eerily silent. It reminded Ben of the New England storms that shot dark, low clouds onshore from the Atlantic Ocean at a moment's notice, seconds before the thunder started.

Looking down, the four studied their entry portals to 'beyond the Veil', or what was left of them. The holes slowly filled in with the ubiquitous fog. Then, the holes became darker until they completely disappeared from perception.

The fog reached up and covered the group, curling and smothering the guys' Soul-bodies gradually from the bottom to the top. John saw that Luke and Ben reached out to Charles for some reassurance, but the only reaction they got from Charles was hesitation.

John knew he had to say something to lower the stress level. 'Hey guys, this has to be normal. TendHer wouldn't leave us to just get nailed, right? I mean, she's the big Chief here! No disrespect meant, Charles.'

Another Speck of Light approached from a great distance away. A powerful hot breeze surrounded the guys in a moment of spectacular explosion.

The presence was familiar.

'It must be the Orb that gave me my tour of the universe,' observed John.

Journal Entry Forty-Eight: Violation

John was wrong. A barely discernible sibilated thought stabbed through the almost complete darkness of 'beyond the Veil'.

'You are mine now.'

Turning in all directions, the guys could not see the source of the hissed words, only wispy apparitions hanging, suspended in space just far enough out of sight to be viewed as ghoulish outlines. The four guys retreated together, frantically trying to hold on to their place in Spiritual space.

'You are mine now. It has begun,' projected a growling voice.

The ghostly apparitions started to move in. One by one, the specters flung aside the ethereal haze of the dense 'beyond the Veil' fog and pushed closer. They surrounded the four guys in a circle at a distance that seemed less than a hundred feet away. As the ghosts approached, inch by inch, their movement was imperceptible except for the disturbance of the swirling mist, which made the four guys reflexively duck and try to hide in the vaporous dew.

As the apparitions approached even closer, the four guys finally saw that these beings were almost faceless; only a shiny, smooth fabric covered their faces, from their necks up to the top of their heads, broken by a wide mouth filled with razor-sharp teeth. The rest of their bodies, from the chest down, were unique yet seemed more animal than human. Some had legs, others had wings, multiple claws, razor-sharp talons, feet that came out of their stomachs, and some wept blood from orifices in their legs.

Accustomed more to the Spirit state than any of the other three, Charles collected his focus. 'This must be a hallucination. It has to be from the Hell part of our minds. We've seen these dudes before when we visited the Hell part of our minds. Just hang in there like we did in our training, and these ghouls will go away.'

John agreed. 'Yeah, we've got to keep our cool.'

'Man, these guys are something out of a comic book. I could never dream up these ghosts,' muttered Luke.

The hideous beings stopped in perfect unison about ten feet from the guys. One of the creatures stepped forward from the group. Palm up, the figure pushed out his hand. On his hand was an eyeball.

A deep voice from above and far away boomed. 'This is your future.'

The guys pressed closer to each other again, desperate to be comforted, to gain some modicum of reassurance. Huddled tight together, they felt each other quivering and their hearts beating. Labored breathing. Gasping for air. Did they need air here? Where was TendHer? Why had they been deserted?

The beast with the eye sitting on its palm tossed the eyeball high in the air. On its way down (if there was a down), the eyeball broadcast a beam that projected a cloud, and within the cloud, a vision strained to piece itself together. The guys tried to make sense of the creation. There was laughter in the background as if someone (or something) was enjoying what was happening, like a director in the wings of a theatre pleased with an unfolding play, awaiting the inevitable finale. Did it involve torture?

A picture coalesced of the Earth completely engulfed in fire. Humans and animals, large and small, were incinerated and cooked alive. Eyes climbed upward, pleading for help, billions of eyeballs levitated, collected by a giant vacuum-like mouth high above the Earth's atmosphere. It was a mouth attached to a Snake that stretched to the far ends of the universe.

Next, the eyeball projected an image of John's Sensei crying for John to come to help him, as the Sensei fell to the dojo floor, desperate to breathe.

The evil presence boomed a thought, 'You just let your Sensei die. But I can bring him back.'

Next was Luke's turn: Heather was held by shackles chained to a wall. She was being violated by animals of all sizes. They were covered in red slime and stench, some with genitals hanging on their legs. Luke reminded himself that cruelty and violence were not supposed to be found in 'beyond the Veil'; then again, according to whom?

A raspy voice was addressed to Luke: 'Did you know that your precious Love is being violated? Oh, but I can make your Love pure again.'

Ben knew he was next, so he turned away. Some force grabbed his head, turned it, and made him watch his parents, eyeless, smashed against the SuperVoid walls, crying for an end to their torment.

Thoughts were shouted, 'I am evil incarnate. I have the power to awaken the dead.'

Last, Charles stood up with his legs trembling, tears streaming down his face. He knew he was next and feared he would be the grand finale. He watched as masked vigilantes attacked Charles' Native American tribe, scalping and carving flesh from bone. Charles wept as pieces of their flesh were thrown to wolves to eat.

The unknown evil gleefully boasted, 'With simply a thought, I can make your tribe whole again.'

The four guys didn't move a muscle. They were too scared to look for the source of the imposing declaration. Keeping their heads low, they clutched their "Soul-arms" even tighter.

Luke reached out to Charles and tried to console him, 'Hey Charles, this has to be all made up. We just have to reconnect with our everyday reality.'

'How do you propose we do that?' asked Ben, who had barely processed what was happening.

'We gotta find our 'beyond the Veil' portals,' urged John.

All four heads scanned the area around their circle. They quickly realized that the increasingly dense fog and mist had covered their one chance for escape.

John whispered, 'Yes, this has to be a mistake. Maybe we're being tested by TendHer?'

At the sound of the word "TendHer," the evil ghost shouted, 'Don't you count on TendHer; she is simply a puppet. What I have shown you is your future. You must come with me. I can protect you.'

'I say we try to ram 'em. All or nothing. I don't want to stand here and get ripped apart,' Luke thought to the others.

'I say you go first. We can't just wait to be rescued. We don't have any other option,' Ben thought. 'John, you have the map. Got any secrets you can use, like the Kung Fu you were talking about at the café? How about you lead the way?'

And John did just that. Reaching down to his lungs, John concentrated on slowing his breathing and clearing his "Soul-mind." He was aware that being preoccupied with fear would not lead to success. He had to release his fears, thoughts, and feelings while guiding his energy to accumulate two inches below his navel, the special place in the human body where Chi is gathered and can be released in devastating power.

He took two strides and leaped in the air, aiming at two of the creatures, trying to create an escape route with his double-leg kick, one leg aimed at each of the two alien heads.

John's "Soul-body" went right through the two creatures. He landed in perfect balance but had not made a dent in the hideous forms.

Luke narrowcast what everyone was thinking. 'We're screwed. There's no way we can defeat these supernatural freaks.'

Ever on the alert for anything that showed any hint of rescue, Ben screamed, 'Hey guys, look over there!'

A very bright Light emerged from the dark misty background of 'beyond the Veil'. It was a circle of Light. The ghouls dipped to their knees and whined as the Light approached.

The Light stretched a part of itself into a long rope. The brilliant rope of Light began to swing, slowly at first, but then gained speed. Then, as it whipped with increasing velocity, it started to strike and snap at the ghouls, who frantically clung to each other, desperately trying to avoid the rope's razor-like sting.

Making slight contact with one of the ghouls, the Light from the rope evaporated the ghoul sending all the others to retreat and cower as a group.

'NoOne, please come rescue us!' the ghouls screamed.

'You have served your purpose,' replied a thought from afar.

The guys scanned every direction.

'Now, where did *that* thought come from?' muttered Charles.

'Hey, look way down there. It's a portal into 'beyond the Veil', and a dark cloud is streaming up to us,' exclaimed Luke.

'Yeah, it's coming from the physical dimension. It must be NoOne!' cried Ben.

'And he or it or whatever is headed right for us!' exclaimed John.

The Light transformed into TendHer. Watching the trajectory of the darkness, she clarified what they were seeing.

That is NoOne. He is manifesting himself as a Dark Matter cloud. He is coming for you.

A thought came from the dark cloud. 'Ready to behold true power, my sister dear? How so much more interesting with your pets joining our conversation!'

TendHer replied immediately. *Begone, NoOne. Their Souls are in a Sacred place. You have violated inviolate Divinity.*

NoOne roared with laughter. 'So lucky to find you here. Are you still TheOne's puppet? Aren't you sick of second-class status? Always having to submerge your Divinity into the messiness of sin?'

It is thus as you observe. I choose to Love and heal. You choose the way of evil.

'Well, aren't you snippy, dearest sister? Aren't you tired of trying to save lost causes? Didn't our Father tell you I am free to wander and collect Souls as I see fit?'

TendHer was not intimidated. *You are barred from this His holiest of realities. Seek dark dimensions for your minions of evil.*

'Have you not heard about my agreement with Father?' pressed NoOne.

TendHer replied, *Yes. But this is my reality. You are banished forever. That hasn't changed.*

NoOne's Dark Matter began to build, the fog mist compressing and darkening. 'Oh sister, shall we summon our Brother, TheSon, and end the contest in this dimension? Be cautious in your decision.'

John shouted his thoughts at the other three guys, 'We need to get out of the way of that black cloud, like now!'

'Look at that. Those dark shapes that make up the cloud are eyes,' thought Ben. 'And the eyes are coming from the portal!'

'Where did our portals go?' thought Luke. 'I can't see them anymore.'

Charles echoed Luke's confusion. 'They've just disappeared.'

Stop. Just stay still. NoOne's cloud is aimed at you, but I can make him back down. I will show you where your portals are at that time, thought TendHer.

NoOne then swirled back upon the assembly. The four guys looked in horror as the growing black wall of death surged toward them.

The dense cloud of NoOne suddenly paused. Blocking his way was an army of Orbs, led by a single Orb so brilliant and clear that even TendHer bowed in recognition.

It was TheSon.

TendHer followed the approach of her Brother and His troop of Orbs.

Sister, you have done well inspecting and testing My Chosen for their mission. Now, protect them as I deal with Our brother to end this contest.

NoOne knew the four guys were primed by TheSon to eventually confront NoOne's power. Right now, the four were inexperienced and fragile, a perfect time to destroy them. But it was way too soon to take on his Brother; especially with his Sister present. The best option for NoOne, he decided, was to plant seeds of doubt in the so-called "Chosen." The ideal way to do that: scenes of inevitable misery associated with material existence. He could later harvest whatever remained of their puny Souls.

Circling like a Vulture, NoOne's Dark Matter cloud surrounded TheSon and quickly challenged Him. 'Am I supposed to be frightened,

Brother dear? Am I supposed to cower? To panic? To beg for Your forgiveness? There is no contest to end, my Brother. TheOne gave me His mandate to offer choice. Let me show You and Your servants what waits for You all.'

TheSon, TendHer, and each guy received the exact same image: Earth completely destroyed with gases swirling around its atmosphere; nothing left but a rock spinning in space as if it had recently coalesced from the dust of universal expansion. The guys recoiled in horror.

TheSon's response vibrated. *You may command and project these childish theatrics to your material world below the Veil, but they are useless in My reality. My Father gave you the power to test illusions and offer choice to the recently dead. That is all. 'Beyond the Veil' is for the Holy and TendHer to command, including its Funnel and its entrance portal into the Reincarnation Universe. You must return to your SuperVoid. Now!*

NoOne knew he had lost. Furious that his intention to intimidate the four guys was blocked, NoOne figured he could at least remind the humans he was not defeated and would again re-emerge to torment and eventually eliminate them.

'So proclaims TheSon. Send Your inconsequential Soul army of Orbs back to Our Father. Send Your loser human Chosen back to my dimension. I will see You and them soon enough where it counts. Moreover, when I so choose, Your four Chosen shall suffer a thousand million deaths.'

The black cloud of Dark Matter instantly disappeared.

Sensing NoOne had returned to the physical dimension, TheSon thought to the four. *You must return and prepare.*

John was the first to think about his response. 'Ah, prepare for what?'

What will Be, will Be.

With that message, TheSon suddenly vanished. TendHer directed the four guys back to their 'beyond the Veil' portals.

Before popping down to their physical reality, the guys took one last look at 'beyond the Veil'.

An infinite number of Lights were coming closer. Scanning in all directions, the four marveled at the majesty of what at first seemed a solid curtain of Light. Then after focusing for a moment, the Lights turned into an uncountable number of individual, dazzling, spectacular Orbs.

'Do you see what's in the Lights?' asked Ben.

'They look like eyes…the question should be…do you see what's in the eyes?' thought whispered Luke.

'Kinda like what we saw at the rest stop,' added John.

'Yeah, but these eyes are pure Light and shaped like Orbs,' replied Charles.

The Lights parted and surrounded TendHer. The Lights then swirled around her ethereal form, faster and faster, generating even more brilliance.

These are the Pure Souls of TheOne, said the TendHer. *They have chosen to stay a bit longer in 'beyond the Veil' to be at your service in the coming struggle. All have worked through the Reincarnation Universe and have been judged Holy.*

'So they're here to protect us?' asked John.

'Yeah, can they come to Earth and help us out if we need it?' added Luke.

TendHer was firm. *Only TheSon can reside in and incarnate from 'beyond the Veil'. Your Mentors choose to return to help you when you need it before they become Pure Orbs.*

Ben probed further. 'So, TheSon can help us on Earth, but we have to come here for the Spiritual stuff?'

All are part of TheOne.

The guys looked at each other. They were each thinking the same thing. A solid action plan would be nice, along with definitive powers on Earth they could hang their hats on. How were they supposed to fight NoOne if he incarnates?

TendHer backed up, but then she turned and paused as if something important needed to be stated. Her amorphous, blurry mass turned into a beautiful, radiant face and a body draped by a long flowing cape. Long arms swept her body around, and she streaked immediately back to the guys. Then as if again changing her mind, TendHer broke up into a million spectacular Light Orbs and circled the guys. Speeding away in a single row, the row of golden Orbs again turned and raced back at the four guys, even faster than the first time.

The guys noticed the ambivalence.

'TendHer is going back and forth…is she conflicted about us?' pondered Charles.

Coming to an abrupt halt in front of the four, the vast number of eyes merged, fusing into a single, radiant eye. The imagery was not lost on the guys. TendHer had decided on a course of action, and she was "seeing" the future through her Sacredness.

TendHer sent her thoughts to the four. *Your portals are waiting. You must leave now.*

The four guys thought the same thought. Something was not right.

John collected as much calm and courage as he could muster. 'What is it we should know?

The single colossal eye of TendHer expanded and blazed its brightest. *This you must know. The unfolding conflict has grave eternal consequences, both for material forms and for the Spiritual.*

Changing the intensity of her message to a whisper, TendHer continued, *NoOne incarnated into human flesh. His evil offspring are ready to conquer all physical and life forms. Up to now, TheSon was the only One to have the power of incarnation. Now, NoOne can take any Earthly form he desires. The 'beyond the Veil' is your only safe harbor. He is forbidden to enter this reality.*

'Excuse me, but didn't he just do that? Enter 'beyond the Veil'? Can't he do that again and chase us down?' Ben meekly asked.

As TendHer slowly rose higher in the 'beyond the Veil' dimension, she shared her last thought. *What will Be, will Be.*

Journal Entry Forty-Nine: The Campfire

TendHer departed, leaving a trail of swirling, vaporous mist. She also left the four guys looking for their Veil portals. The guys felt their portals should be beneath them but had little luck finding them.

'Crap, our portals could be anywhere!' said Luke.

'Yeah, this is nothing more than cosmic soup,' said John.

'So, what do we do to get out of this fog?' asked Ben.

Having never returned from his "gap" adventures using any of the portals, John shook his head, 'I don't have the foggiest idea.'

Luke laughed. 'Oh great, a comedian in the making.'

Ben shook. His bulging "Soul-belly" heaved up and down. With a nervous, high-pitched voice, he thought, 'This is no time for jokes. How do we do this? How do we get out of here?'

John looked down at his "Soul-feet" and then looked at Ben. 'I'm just gonna jump down where I am. We gotta trust that TendHer has paved our way. I'm going to pretend I can fly, Ben. You can do that too. Stick your arms straight up. Jump as high as you can, then let your body fall, naturally. We all have to jump at the same time.'

'OK, on three, we jump. Ben? You hear me?' asked Luke.

'Ready. Kinda,' stammered Ben.

Luke yelled out his thoughts as if he was behind his center in a football game. 'One…two…three…hike! I mean JUMP!'

Charles was just putting his hand down at the campfire when all four boys returned fully to their physical bodies from 'beyond the Veil'.

All of us staff and Lil' Johnny were still scanning the dark woods that circled the camp.

The four guys were amazed at how Lil' Johnny and the staff were in the same frozen positions as when their Mind's Eyes and Souls had left to visit 'beyond the Veil'.

Ben broke the ice as he sent a thought to the other three. 'They're still looking for danger in the forest!'

John whispered, "Don't forget, in Earth time, we were gone but a fraction of a second. We've met NoOne, so now we know what to look for."

"Don't be too sure about that," warned Charles.

"Ben, you OK?" Luke quietly asked.

"Wow…that was like a giant water slide, except it didn't feel like I was only going down; just whooshing fast in all directions—up, down, sideways, and bouncing over speed bumps," said Ben.

John chuckled. "And he's our brain scientist?"

"John! Whoa, dude! You were actually funny! Again!" replied Luke.

"Yeah, that's a first," added Charles. "No, wait. That makes two."

"You should talk, Chief," remarked Ben. "Only time I see you crack even the tiniest of smiles is when you're on the john. Get it? John? As in our fearless leader who's about to beat me to a pulp."

"I could do that!" boasted John.

"Ok. Good one, Charles. And Ben. Not bad, John. You're all showing potential. I know we're all feeling frisky." smiled Luke. "But we gotta get ourselves together."

Jenna turned to Charles and asked, as she looked where he was pointing, "Charles, who are *they*? And why are you pointing to the woods?"

"Don't go in there, boys," warned Lil' Johnny.

Ben nodded his head. "You got that right."

"OK, let's calm down. You've all been seeing too many campfire horror movies," reassured Ivan.

Jenna started to pace. "My dad's right about this. All of us should stay right here. Do not go into those woods."

John wondered if others had seen Jenna dig the word "evil" into the ground with her shoe?

Not having said hardly a complete sentence the whole time at the camp, everyone paid attention to Jim as he stepped forward. "If I can do two years of reconnaissance in the middle of Viet Cong country, I can sure as hell check out a few trees."

"I'm with you Jim," said Ivan. "Come on, Jenna; let's check this out."

"I'll be taggin' along, if you don't mind," said Lil' Johnny.

The guys stayed back while the staff edged closer to the forest's tree line.

Charles unexpectedly fell to the ground.

I was pushed, Charles thought.

Charles couldn't tell who had pushed him. He looked around, but all he saw was a wavy, blurry mass. None of the adults, now at the tree line, seemed to have noticed. From his viewpoint on the ground, Charles perceived a murky brume. It was hiding something or someone.

Charles rolled around in a circle on the ground, forcing his brain to collect enough sensory input to create a clear image, but nothing would take a recognizable form. Then he bumped into John.

"Yes, Charles, it's me, John. Did you feel that force? We must get together, all four of us. The staff is headed to the woods; I think we need to stop them. And right now! Something is coming down. Luke, are you here?"

"Yeah, John, I'm here too. Ben has a hold of my left leg." Luke, dragging Ben, joined Charles and John. They could barely recognize each other in the dim haze of the smoky campfire, but there were enough familiar body smells to somewhat soothe their fears.

"Ben, ever think about using deodorant?" teased Luke.

Ben gripped Luke's leg even tighter. "Now that you mention it…."

"I think we're in deeper trouble than we thought," muttered John.

"Something pushed us all to the ground," said Luke.

"Like something doesn't want us going into those woods?" Ben proposed.

The guys saw Jim and Ivan move towards the small, hidden path that led into the dense forest. They stopped, got down on their hands and knees, and examined the ground. They had a couple of flashlights and walking sticks, which put everyone at ease.

They are experts, after all, I thought. *They have flashlights and walking sticks!*

Lil' Johnny and Jenna, on the other hand, returned to the campfire, shaking their heads.

Not a good sign. Our alpha dudes are avoiding the forest.

Jim, however, looked ready for some excitement. "Hey, guys, why's Jim so happy all of a sudden?" John asked.

Little did John know that Jim had been away from his vodka for three days, and the cravings were becoming intolerable. Jim thought he could get an adrenaline rush like he used to get in 'Nam. That might calm his system.

"Beats me," replied Ben. "Take a look at Ivan…he's on his hands and knees looking at the dirt!"

"Hey, numb-nuts," pestered Luke. "Ivan's a tracker. He's looking for clues. Ever tell you one of his stories?"

Ivan had camped hundreds of times, thanks to all his Black buddies from Portland. And he loved it. They were the only ones that wanted to join him. Together they discovered a special hiding place on the Columbia River, a large body of water that separates Oregon from Washington State. Surrounded by willows and cotton trees, the group spent entire weekends playing *Capture the Flag* on the pebble-strewn riverbank. Breaking up into gangs, they hid in the willows and then hunted each other, always on the lookout for the elusive prized flag.

Ivan learned to read tracks made in the sand, grass, and brush from competing with these friends. Soon it was just as challenging to disguise the tracks as it was to capture the flag.

Another favorite hobby of Ivan's was reading wildlife tracks while hiking alone on the many beautiful and pristine Columbia Gorge trails. Ivan built on this interest by taking classes at VanPort College, a community college in Dollars Corner, across the river from Portland. Wilderness survival was his favorite, but tracking game was close behind. After taking every class offered at VanPort in Outdoor Sciences, Ivan transferred to a university in Portland. He saw a stark contrast between the cultures. The university was much more selective. Community colleges, in general, accepted almost anyone with their open-door admission standards.

Ivan respected most of his teachers at VanPort. He thought they tried hard to help every student succeed, a significant difference from the university classes. Professors at VanPort used every trick in the book to help students learn: simulations, community observations, role-playing, group competitions, movie analysis, career shadowing, and so on. In sharp contrast, most of his university professors commonly restricted their class format to lectures only; they seemed pressured to spend more time publishing research. However, what both colleges had in common was having faculty that cared. Then again, few of those could make it in the world of the "street." At least surviving in the world that Ivan had lived.

Ivan chuckled to himself. *Yeah. Those who can't do, teach. Those who can't teach, teach teachers. No, that's too harsh. Most of the best teachers had been in the real world first and then taught. Or left teaching to pursue private sector jobs, and then returned to teaching later in life. It's the bloated bureaucracies…Directors who had to have Assistants who had to have Assistants to the Assistants who had to have Assistants to the Assistants to the Assistants….*

Ivan thought long and hard about pursuing another degree. However, with the more formal university setting and the layers of bureaucratic hoops, Ivan opted for helping kids on their own turf, violent and dangerous though the streets and they might be.

After studying the trail for a few minutes, Ivan got up, dusted off his pants, and headed deeper into the forest. He told Jim to stay put while he explored further ahead.

Swinging his flashlight around the trees, Ivan didn't see anything unusual; however, when he concentrated his light directly on the path in front of him, Ivan saw a footprint pattern he didn't recognize.

Whereas the average Black Bear has a hindprint of 6 to 9 inches long, and a Grizzly has a hindprint of 10 to 12 inches, these hindprints were at least 18 inches long. What puzzled Ivan even more was the variety of paw types—Bear, Raccoon, Opossum, Beaver, Deer, Coyote, Elk, and even Wolf. They were all lumped together. Usually, these species competed for resources. What were they doing in a cooperative group, like so many marchers in a parade?

Ivan could tell the trail was a few days old. The slightly faded prints still remained sharply outlined in the ground.

"The trees protected the prints inside the forest," mumbled Ivan to himself. "But it seems rainfall blurred and streaked the prints that crisscross the campsite itself."

"Hey, Jim," Ivan called out, "all these animals marched very close to where we pitched our tents."

Catching up to Ivan, Jim saw the tracks and, with his flashlight, traced the various patterns. "Shit, I've never heard of this. These are all made at the same time, aren't they?"

"Yeah, and do you see where they're going?" said Ivan.

Jim let out a loud "Wha…You gotta be kidding me!"

Ivan knew precisely where the parade of animals was headed. "They're going south, right up to the mountains. Even the water-based species are moving south. They're either going higher for some food reason I've never heard of, or they're trying to get away from some kind of danger."

Jim bent down to study more prints. "Yeah, like animals can sense an impending forest fire or Earthquake?"

"What would override their instinctual predatory response systems?" pondered Ivan. "Sorry for the big words. One reason I never returned to college."

With his nose buried in the Bear tracks, Jim hardly heard a word Ivan said. "Sorry, I didn't hear you. Never heard or seen anything like this. I gotta follow these tracks further into the forest."

Ivan shook his head. "It's too late." Bending down to Jim, he said, "I mean, shouldn't we wait till morning and include the whole group?"

Jim stood up and scanned the dense forest, looking for any sign of movement. "Nah, it could rain hard tonight and wipe out even more of the tracks. Let's just go in to take a peek. I'll let everyone know we'll be right back."

Ivan waited, then decided to continue forward a few more yards while Jim returned to the group at the campsite. All of a sudden, Ivan began to sweat, then shiver. A premonition born from years of camping started to take shape.

I'm picking up some serious danger vibes. Never sweated like this.

Ivan reminded himself that he had gone camping in similar conditions hundreds of times—without the prints, of course. He had to keep his cool and not dwell on the weird events leading up to this. But the eyeballs were hard to forget. He kept telling himself he was sure the authorities had found the sickos who killed all those people and then scattered their eyes everywhere; whoever it was had to be locked up by now. Probably see them when he got back to the hospital.

Ivan decided he, too, should return to the campsite. He retraced his steps back to the periphery. When close to the trail's opening, Ivan heard Jim tell everyone to stay put while he and Ivan checked things out.

Then something fascinating caught Ivan's attention. It was a good ten yards ahead in the forest. He couldn't resist moving closer to examine the object, even though he was going back deeper into the unknown.

Ivan yelled back at Jim, "Hey, Jim, I'm heading back in a ways to check something out. Just follow my light when you get here."

Catching a glimpse of Ivan's back as he re-entered the Forest, I urgently cried out, "No, Ivan, wait!"

Right then, Boo bristled and started to bark.

I looked down at Boo and whispered, "You sensing the same thing I am?"

Ivan heard Boo bark. He shivered. Boo was on to something. Dogs pick up right away on anything unusual, especially something dangerous.

Is Boo telling me not to go back into the forest? Should I be concerned about this? Ivan wondered.

Despite Jim's efforts to calm Boo, the Dog kept barking.

Ivan reached the spot where he thought the object that had caught his attention should be, but it wasn't there. Looking ahead on the trail, Ivan caught a glimpse of another strange object, ten yards ahead. It looked similar to the first object.

As he rushed toward it, the object again disappeared and reappeared ten yards further along the path.

Am I being baited here? No doubt, I should turn back. If I go any further, Jim won't be able to follow my light.

But Ivan couldn't resist walking deeper into the forest. His curiosity was building, now bordering on obsession. He crept silently this time, using all his skills to stalk the object, yet the object again disappeared and reappeared further down the path.

OK. That does it. No more hide and seek. I'll just go a little further one last....

This time, the object stayed put. Inching closer to the object, Ivan looked back. He could no longer hear any sounds from the campsite, including Boo's barking. He couldn't make out any of the campfire lights. He was surrounded by silence and darkness.

I must have zoned out and walked really deep into this puppy and didn't realize it!

Pointing his flashlight down at his feet, Ivan immediately relaxed.

"Oh gosh, it's just a girl's shoe," Ivan sighed. "How did it get here, of all places?"

Journal Entry Fifty: Boo

The night turned frigid cold. Quiet. Even the soaring, bright red, campfire flames wanted nothing to do with the sinister forest that surrounded its wood-barricaded boundary—heat escaped skyward.

Trying as hard as we could, we failed to maneuver the burning limbs to shed their heat outward.

What good is a fire that doesn't make you warm? Maybe we need to get out of here; like the heat: escape upward!

'Can you hear my thoughts, Charles?' thought Boo. It was more of a statement than a question.

'Yes, Boo. I've been prepared.'

'All higher-order species are evacuating this forest. You must get out now,' thought Boo.

John saw the exchange between Boo and Charles. "Hey, Charles, what's coming down with the Dog?"

Charles considered options. He stared at the forest. He listened to the stilled trees. He bent down and palmed a handful of soil, turning it over and over between his fingers. He smelled the air. His decision came in a flash, more based on intuition than rational choice; such is what he was good at: feeling for the right course of action. "Guys, we have to get out of here. Now."

"Oh, good luck with that," interrupted Luke.

Boo turned to face the forest. 'Guess I need to be a bit more forceful,' Boo thought to Charles.

Boo barked and ran to the periphery where Ivan had just returned to the forest. Boo smelled a scent of danger unlike anything in his experience. The threat in the scent was so potent that Boo was thrown in the air backward a good couple of feet.

'What is this power?' Boo reached out to the animals deserting the area. 'What is this force?'

'It is evil,' was his reply.

'You must flee. Now,' his animal friends implored. 'Get the humans away. Go north. We are part of an army to fight this evil. You are not. Go, now. You must escape.'

The urgency of the advice made Boo's legs shake. The voice had an authority, a command he had never felt even when processing a thousand animal thoughts simultaneously, which he regularly did unbeknown to Lil' Johnny. So who or what was this new voice?

Boo knew he had little time to dwell on the mystery message, so he did the only thing he could that would get the attention of the humans; he whimpered and cast sad eyes in their direction.

"Now what's got into you, Boo?" said Lil' Johnny. "Damn, but you're just hankerin' for a squirrel! You get back in them woods and catch me some breakfast."

Charles thought, *It's now or never*. The staff needed to back off with the exploration. Charles felt Boo's fear. They needed to escape. "Hey guys, I think it's a warning. I'm picking up a lot of danger signals."

We ignored Charles. Boo and his increased agitation had completely captured our attention.

Starting to pace around the group, Charles finally had enough. "I said *stop!*"

We swung our heads to see who had just given such a loud, direct order.

Charles continued, hands indicating the circle of the campsite and pointing to the woods. "Don't you see the danger? What do you hear? Nothing! There are no birds. There are no sounds of any kind. In my tribe, this is a sign that a great predator is soon to attack."

"I'll second that," said Jenna. Addressing the group, Jenna was trying to take charge. "You guys start packing the…."

Charles caught Boo's frantic thought. 'It's too late.'

A scream echoed through the woods.

It had to be Ivan, and he sounded like he was in trouble. "Ivan's out there. I gotta get him back," yelled Jim. Leaping onto the path just a few feet into the woods, Jim couldn't hear all the others telling him to stop. Boo whimpered but did not leave Jim's side.

As soon as Jim and Boo were out of sight in the woods, the group at the campsite was assaulted by a stench. It was rotten and foul. It lingered and grew in ferocity as the wind changed direction.

First the heat, now the wind is trying to escape, Charles thought.

Everything was dead quiet.

Looking at each other, the four guys were confused, each hoping someone would step up and take charge.

"Come on, guys. We gotta do something." Luke, as usual, wanted action.

"I think I'll guard the campfire," said Ben.

"No, you don't. You're with us," declared John.

"Charles? You OK?" asked Luke.

"I think it's too late. But we can help pick up the pieces, I guess," said Charles.

"Now, that's not encouraging," said Ben.

"Can you see the flashlights moving between the trees?" asked Luke.

Swinging back and forth, sending streaks of light in all directions, the two flashlights offered some reassurance to the guys as they surveyed the tree line.

"Then come on, we'll follow the lights. Let's do this!" said Luke.

Quietly all four walked ahead to the path, a sense of dread and doom growing in their minds.

Boo, now deep in the forest with Jim, sent a thought to Charles. 'Be prepared for the worst. We won't be returning.'

Charles touched the other three guys. Motioning them to hush, Charles whispered, "Boo says it's really bad in there."

"Maybe we should wait here at the edge of the forest for Lil' Johnny? At least he has a gun," commented Ben.

"I vote we head in. I'll be scout," said John.

Ben was not happy. "Yeah, like maybe you should kung fu your way through the trees? I vote for the gun."

A piercing howl erupted deep in the forest, followed by a silence that was almost more frightening than the scream. At first, the guys thought it was Boo but then realized the abbreviated wail was more human than canine.

"Come on. Let's get going." Luke began to walk. "Go ahead, John. You take the lead."

"OK!" replied John. "I didn't like that sound. Somebody helpless yells out more than one time."

"Good point. We'd better hurry," exclaimed Luke. "And since you're the fighting expert, you should go first. I'll cover your back, so don't worry!"

Ben added, "Yeah, me, too. I'll cover Luke's back!"

"Guess I bring up the rear," muttered Charles.

The four guys entered the woods, leaving Jenna and Lil' Johnny alone at the campsite.

Meanwhile, Jim tried to locate Ivan far ahead on the narrow forest trail, penetrating even further into the dark forest. Boo was comforting because Jim knew Boo would sense danger long before it became apparent.

Boo knew they were headed into danger. The threat was powerful and a species much stronger and larger than Boo was involved. His humans should flee to save their lives. Boo ran in front of Jim and nudged Jim's legs, trying to turn him around. Boo ran back down the trail heading toward the campfire, turned, and barked when Jim would not budge. He ran a few more feet back, turned, and barked again.

Pointing his hand at the path in front of him, Jim tried to motivate Boo. "Come on, Boo. We'll eat when we get back to camp, OK? But first, we gotta find Ivan."

Boo reluctantly followed at a distance. Together, they ventured further into the forest, with Boo looking for danger behind him as well as along the sides of the trail.

At the same time, Jim methodically observed his surroundings, careful not to step on or in anything that would make a cracking noise. *Stay light with the feet,* Jim told himself. The forest was darker than before. He stopped. He heard laughter. No other sound. Maybe others were coming to help. Sounds play tricks in the woods. He had experienced that a lot in Nam.

Jim oriented his ears. The sound was definitely coming from ahead on the trail, just where Ivan should be. It had to be Ivan. But now, the sound was different.

Laughing. No, it was more like giggling. More than one voice. Kids. They sounded young.

Journal Entry Fifty-One: Reunion

"We should go in and help. Dad, you're the only one who has a gun," said Jenna. She had never seen her dad disoriented, conflicted, wavering.

Is my dad actually afraid?

Lil' Johnny wanted to appear as if he were in control. But his heavy breathing conveyed alarm bordering on panic. Lil' Johnny couldn't remember the last time he felt genuine fear. Now it was close to overwhelming him.

"You're my family," stuttered Lil' Johnny. "I'm not leaving you for nothing. I'm not taking you in there. Besides, they got Boo."

Jenna scanned the woods. Upon seeing the two flashlights scattering beams through the woods, Jenna was determined to help any way she could. She never sat on the sidelines, and she wasn't going to start now.

"Why, dad? Why won't you take me in there? I can handle it."

Lil' Johnny dropped his gun and fell to the ground, sinking down on his knees and staring. He muttered to Jenna, "You shouldn't be here. None of you. I tried to warn you."

Moving closer to Lil' Johnny, hands on her hips, Jenna leaned down and asked in a whisper, "What's going on, dad? Tell me."

A gust of wind blew over the campsite. Jenna backed up, reflexively cringing at the thick stench that assailed her. The air smelled and tasted putrid, like fish rotting for days in the hot sun. Then, with a start, she reached out to Lil' Johnny.

"Do you smell that, dad?" panted Jenna.

"Yes, Honey. I've smelled that before."

"Dad, what aren't you telling me?"

"Jenna, I tried to keep you from coming here. Now it's too late."

Jenna followed her dad's gaze. She saw ghostlike specters. Two people stood on the path that led to the forest interior. It was hard to see who it was due to the darkness and distance.

The two figures began to wave and beckon Jenna and Lil' Johnny toward them.

Every sense in Jenna's body cried "danger." The two people looked out of place, making motions Jenna had never seen, arms and legs disjointed and dangling in many directions.

Lil' Johnny walked as if in a trance. Jenna screamed out, "Dad, what are you doing? Don't go there. We don't know who they are."

Lil' Johnny turned to Jenna. "I do. Can't you see? Don't you see who they are? My babies are back!"

Jenna ran around Lil' Johnny and blocked his advance. "Dad, look at me. *Look* at *me*. What do you mean your babies are back?"

Keeping his gaze fixed on the two figures by the forest, Lil' Johnny stopped trying to push past Jenna. "I didn't want to tell you, to worry you and all."

"Dad, worry about what?"

"Jenna, I've been here lots seeing my babies. They didn't die. I know that. I got their eyes in my pocket. They said I could keep 'em for a while."

Jenna flinched at the idea of the eyeballs in her dad's pocket. She struggled to understand. "Eyes in your pocket? How long has this been going on?"

Lil' Johnny's posture started to deflate. "I made a deal."

Jenna's voice was almost a whisper. "You made a deal with whom?"

"Your boys."

Jenna was paralyzed. She couldn't react. She froze.

"Honey, your boys, your Twins, have been living here in the forest. Said they were living with someone and not to worry, and if I promised not to tell you, they'd let me see my babies every once in a while."

Jenna asked the first question that came into her mind. "But then…why did you let us all come here, Dad?"

"Your boys said their teacher wanted to meet all the guys."

"Teacher? What teacher? Have you met this teacher?"

"Jenna, I haven't, but they said if I squealed on 'em, they would disappear with my babies. They said he lives here with them in the forest, and his name is Know'un."

Lil' Johnny turned to walk toward the two figures, but Jenna scooted in front of him again and tried to push him back. Her tiny hands hardly made a dent in Lil' Johnny's chest. "Dad, nobody has a name like Know'un."

"They said you'd say that." Dropping his gun, Lil' Johnny stepped around Jenna. "I Love you, Honey. But I got to see my babies."

Lil' Johnny lumbered as if in a spell. Getting closer to the two figures, now just twenty feet away, his arms reached out to cradle his sweet daughters once more.

He stopped. Behind him, Jenna ran up to him, panting. "Dad…."

The two figures spoke as one. "Hi, (*thump thump*) my (*thump thump*) Love. Miss (*thump thump*) us?" The voices were a low growl like an old 78-rpm record played as a 45. The two figures rocked back and forth, a *thump* occurring with each step backward or forward. The tone of their voices was sarcastic, like taunting middle-school students. Jenna swore the voices resembled those of her stepsisters, even though the voices were as low as an octave beginning on the lowest string of a bass fiddle.

Then Jenna realized the evil that confronted her. Jenna heard the expression "my Love" from only one source in her life. It was the same evil Jenna had felt when she was assaulted at the University. Long ago, the dark force that raped her at the University cruelly mocked her after he violated her, forever taking away her innocence.

You will bear me Twins, my Love. I am NoOne.

Lil' Johnny was sobbing. "My babies! He promised you'd be here...."

"Yes, (*thump thump*) Daddy (*thump thump*) dearest. We have so missed you."

The figures were getting better at speech, observed Jenna. Her observation was quickly overwhelmed by the dreadful stench that again traveled to Jenna with a wind gust. Now Jenna tried to get a better look at the faces of the two figures.

Lil' Johnny slumped to the ground to catch his breath. He looked up and crawled to the two standing figures, sobbing, with outstretched hands. He pleaded, "Why don't you come home with me? I've missed...."

Lil' Johnny did not finish his words because his tongue was ripped out by some invisible force. Jenna instinctively backed up as her father's tongue hung in mid-air. She immediately knew her only hope was to get Lil' Johnny's gun.

Jenna was not quick enough. Joining the tongue hanging in the air, Lil' Johnny's entire body drifted upward, his hands clutching his now tongue-less mouth. When Lil' Johnny had reached five feet in the air, the two young figures looked at each other and smiled.

Lil' Johnny's eyeballs popped out of his face and fell to the ground, twitching.

The sisters sauntered casually closer to Jenna while Lil' Johnny hung in the air. He was gasping for breath, hands trying to find his eyes.

The sisters giggled. "Remember us, Big Sis?"

Jenna's worst fear was realized. Bile rose from her stomach. She gagged. She knew the two figures were her sisters. But in what form? What turned them into these monsters? Bending down, Jenna threw up all the contents of her stomach.

The sisters walked back to Lil' Johnny, dropped to their knees, and picked up Lil' Johnny's eyes, one for each. They delighted in holding them. They gleefully exhibited their prizes, holding the eyes up as if to show the entire universe their wondrous possessions.

The two girls popped the eyeballs into mush as if they were grapes. Then, laughing, the sisters in perfect unison chortled, "Guess Daddykins got no Soul now!"

Jenna recoiled in horror when she saw the two shrunken sisters ambling toward her. Using every bit of discipline she had, Jenna studied her stepsisters. They wore tattered clothes, ripped and covered with dry, muddy sludge, hair stringy, and bodies emaciated. They had razor-sharp teeth hanging out of pursed lips. Their limbs swung freely, completely separate from their joints, each connected to their skinny bodies with a single muscle and tendon. Their heads randomly jerked in all four directions. They had no eyes.

The two step-sisters shuffled forward to greet Jenna, arms swinging out of sync with their steps. Closer and closer. Jenna couldn't move. Frantically she looked to her dad, but he was still hanging in the air, gasping to breathe.

"Hey, Sis! Miss us?"

Then, before she had time to fully digest what was happening, the two girls slowly transformed. They twitched, they twisted, they stretched. Dark ooze poured out of their mouths and ears. New beings ripped open the stomachs of their female hosts, then clawed their way out from the guts of the girls.

Those new beings, initially hard to identify because of all the black sludge, struggled to entirely rid themselves of their stench-ridden cocoons.

Her sons were standing right there in front of her with the same faces they had when they were seven years old, frozen in time. "Did you like our improvisation, Mother Dearest? Had to borrow some bodies for effect. Dad is so impressed. He's speechless!"

Jenna now saw with clarity that this was a trap. Why? The last thought that careened through Jenna's rapidly diminishing consciousness was, *Who the hell is Know'un? Were they referring to NoOne?*

The Twins were the last Earthly thing Jenna saw with her eyes. She had a split second of dreadful fear that she would lose her Soul. The eyes of her sons were dead and without any feeling. Could they remember their mom nurturing and Loving them?

When Jenna could no longer feel anything, her journey through death began. She wanted to wait for her dad, but he was still fighting to survive in his Earthly form.

Then she felt her Soul become surrounded by something foul. Her Mind's Eye watched with detached incredulity as her eyes were removed by a gnarled, scarred set of long fingers. They were so long that she had to stretch what was left of her inner Light to focus on the attached hand far away in the sky.

Jenna felt her eyeballs being grabbed, and with a slight squeeze, they were tugged outward slowly. The pain was unbearable and prolonged and lasted until the razor-sharp fingernails crushed her eyes like they were meaningless insects.

Jenna's Mind's Eye and Soul hung limp in space, surprised that they had so easily been separated from their Earthly home. Jenna screamed in horror. Her Mind's Eye and Soul, confused and muddled, zipped around Jenna's mangled eyes, mostly juice, on the ground. Her Soul then settled in space facing Jenna, expecting her Mind's Eye to provide sanctuary, but her Mind's Eye was nowhere to be found. Jenna's Soul now knew with crystal clarity that without a Mind's Eye to carry it to TendHer, she would never receive the redemption offered in the Reincarnation Universe.

Giving up all hope, Jenna's Soul was pulled to its destination of malevolent unrest, as if it were a fish reeled into a boat, kidnapped from its home to become imprisoned in a wall of suffering with countless other Souls. A deeply guttural, terse voice teased Jenna with a final contemptuous, snarled verdict, a prison sentence administered without pity: the SuperVoid. Because she was still alive when her eyes were snatched, there was to be no judgment. Lost in the pain of despair and the silence of dark extinction, Jenna understood she was condemned to suffer forever.

Jenna never cried much in her physical world—not because she thought it was a sign of weakness, but because she was too busy and goal-directed to take the time. Now, however, she joined an infinite number of Souls lost forever in a cursed chorus screaming for help and pleading for respite from eternal suffering, knowing it would do no good, but crying just the same.

From her SuperVoid prison, Jenna's Soul watched her physical arms and legs claw a pit in the forest floor next to thousands of other rotting corpses. It would be the last image she had of her former physical self, but a vision that she would be forced to watch repeatedly, for eternity.

Jenna's corpse was compressed next to the other diseased, eyeless bodies covered with forest dirt, mud, rock, and fern.

Jenna's Soul screamed in agony from Hell.

It made no difference.

Journal Entry Fifty-Two: The Eagle

The Golden Eagle gracefully soared high above the campsite. She had been selected by Monster Bear to fly at a high altitude as a sentry for those below. She knew that no greater honor could be bestowed on any animal Spirit.

With all her might, the Eagle fought her urge to retreat, to get as far away as possible. The Golden Eagle had watched the death of Jenna and the demise and burial of Lil' Johnny by the evil two semi-humans. Even from such lofty heights and smothered in the quiet darkness of the moonless night, the Eagle smelled and saw the vile evil emanating from the Spirits of the Twins.

Careful lest she was sighted, the Eagle made no sudden movements in the air but simply floated with the air currents. She could go in any direction, including upward, if she needed to escape. Although famished due to her efforts, the Eagle restrained herself from instinctually diving and feasting on the various animal movements that signaled food she had sighted far below, animals heading south in a parade of escape.

The creatures that tortured the humans were as foul as the force the Eagle sensed permeated the entire forest. She needed to report this to the Monster Bear at his mountain hideout and warn His companions, who were now deep in the woods, about what had transpired.

'All must leave. Vile evil is buried and yet still alive, all around you.'

Boo responded, 'Thank you, Eagle. I will pass it on. Do you see any way out for us?'

The Eagle paused to review her internal map. 'No. You are completely surrounded.'

'Have you located the Monster Bear?' Boo asked.

'He waits until his time is the right time.'

Boo was hopeful. 'Eagle friend, thank you. Please pass on our need to find the Monster Bear and let me know if anything happens at our campsite.'

The Eagle hesitated. 'I'm sorry to tell you that your master has been taken from us.'

Boo was shocked. 'What?'

The Eagle's answer was swift and precise. 'He was tortured by the beings he has visited in this forest many times. You accompanied him, and you must never trust these entities again. You must warn the humans, too. I cannot help. All animals are fleeing the forest and are heading to Mount Olympus, many miles south. I must also soon leave.'

Boo's heart was sad. Lil' Johnny had picked Boo up in a shelter when Boo was barely four months old. Nobody wanted Boo. Humans came and went; Boo begged to be chosen. He tried every trick he had learned from the other puppies selected. He ran in circles, jumped at the cage door, barked, and panted winsomely, but nothing seemed to work. The humans said Boo was too ugly, too fat, too slow. Boo got so depressed that he just wanted to sleep all the time.

Then one day, Lil' Johnny showed up. He looked like a giant to Boo.

"Hey, little fella'. You're perttier than a burnt pancake on a Monday morn. But that makes us a good couple, I'd say."

Boo jumped up and down. He sat on Lil' Johnny's shoe as Lil' Johnny was filling out the paperwork. Boo reminded himself not to look too long into this new human's eyes. For good measure, Boo let his new master know that Boo was happy to protect Lil' Johnny, so he marked his new territory by peeing everywhere he could, including Lil' Johnny's lap as they traveled in the moving piece of metal on the way to Boo's new home.

Thanks to Lil' Johnny, Boo never went hungry; and on most days, Boo had extra kibble waiting in his food dish. Lil' Johnny called Boo the world's best Labrador, even though Boo was a mutt with a little bit of every breed lurking somewhere in his ancestry.

But most important, Lil' Johnny was a loyal human, unlike many Boo had heard about from other members of the Dog species.

Boo vowed he would find his master's bones and grieve, just in case the Spirit of Lil' Johnny was lonely.

The Golden Eagle made one last pass over the campsite. He saw no movement. No life. Completely quiet. Not even a fern moved.

Boo reached out. 'Do you see my master?'

The Eagle softly thought, 'Yes.'

The Eagle saw Lil' Johnny drop to the ground. His body was lifeless. Lil' Johnny's tongue dropped soon after that as if it were an afterthought by a bored puppeteer.

Tendrils, invincible and precise, reached up out of the ground. They were black, thin, and knurly. Once they found Lil' Johnny's body, they completely encased him.

After Lil' Johnny was covered, the tendrils transformed into a black sludge, the identical sticky black goo covering the two little phantom girls. Lil' Johnny was now entombed with the same foul, black embalming substance.

Then the Earth, captive to demonic forces and unable to protest its violation, opened up directly underneath Lil' Johnny. It was just a fissure at first, but the small crack widened far enough for Lil' Johnny and his tongue to slowly slip into the expanding hole. Peering down from above, the Golden Eagle saw that the new grave was about six feet deep.

What surprised the Eagle was that the hole continued to expand, exposing what lay deeper than Lil' Johnny's grave. Arms, legs, torsos, and heads were all there. Stored for generation upon generation, the lifeless limbs had waited. Body parts suddenly came alive, reaching out fanatically from all sides and below Lil' Johnny, upwards as if petitioning the sun for resurrection. All moving. Wiggling. Going nowhere. They were like worms in warm, moist soil waiting to be plucked out from the ground. The corpses' mouths gasped for life, like fish out of water.

'These corpses have been dead for thousands of years. They are being prepared for some evil,' thought the Golden Eagle to Charles. 'You must alert your human companions.'

Journal Entry Fifty-Three: Courage

The guys walked deep into the foreboding, thick-timbered woods with no sight of Ivan. They felt lost. With each step, they felt more apprehensive. The only reason they had stumbled into the deep forest in the first place was that they could see Jim's flashlight hypnotically bouncing up ahead. Up and down, up and down. The guys seized upon the sliver of security that was transmitted with the light's rhythm. At least, they hoped it was Jim's flashlight.

"No wonder there are no animals and no sounds. Jim scared the shit out of everything that moves. If there are any monsters up ahead, they can just take a long nap because they sure as hell know our flight plan," said Ben.

"Ben, keep your voice down; *ssshhhh!*" admonished John.

"Now you guys know what I've had to deal with all these months," smirked Luke.

"Oh, come on, guys, Ben's trying to help," Charles said.

Ben stopped. Somebody was sticking up for him. A first. "Thanks, Chief…I mean Charles. I'm just getting used to tolerating Luke's ego."

Startled, the four saw a beam of light aimed back toward them. It was Jim, swinging his flashlight back and forth as he carefully watched the trail to retrace his steps back toward the guys and camp.

Totally winded, between heaving breaths, Jim said, "Thanks for coming in. Never been in such a spooky forest. I think I need some help. Can't find Ivan anywhere."

Jim was worried about Ivan because he knew that Ivan was not the type to scream for an insignificant reason. Jim was tired and hungry and wanted to get back to the open campsite, even though he imagined that, thanks to the moonless night, it would probably be completely dark there as well. He was resolved to provide an excellent example to the guys. Jim automatically fell back on his training as an elite Special Ops soldier: never leave anyone behind.

Luke felt the frustration of the dark, quiet surroundings. "Come on, I think we've gone far enough. Hey Jim, maybe we should return to camp. Ivan can follow our light even if his flashlight is toast. Ben can do what he does best: make a huge bonfire. I'm sure Ivan can find his way back."

Before Jim could answer, all five guys plus Boo stopped in their tracks. Ivan was up ahead waving his flashlight back and forth. The path leading them to him was barely visible and had more forest debris scattered around, so the guys continued onward but had to concentrate on avoiding jagged rocks and mushy puddles.

"Ah, guys. We're crunching on something. Can't see the path. What is it?" asked Luke.

A fog appeared, blocking their view of Ivan up ahead.

The crunching got louder.

"Hey, Jim, can we stop and see what's making all this noise!" It was more of a statement from Ben than a question.

Jim replied, "Sure. Let's huddle around."

Forming a complete circle on the narrow path was tough for the guys to pull off, so they gathered in a "U" shape. Then they bent down with Jim in the middle with his light to study the odd material on the path.

Ben was the first to react. "Ah, shit. This is not good."

The others could only gasp.

Everywhere there were eyeballs. Some were stacked three or four high. Everywhere.

Jim bent down, poked, and prodded with his flashlight. The eyeballs swarmed Jim like an agitated beehive.

In just seconds, Jim was covered in eyeballs. They built a wall up both of his legs.

John was ready to act. "I'll pull Jim back, but the rest of you should start sweeping Jim's legs," he shouted to the others as he grabbed Jim around his waist.

Frantically the guys kept sweeping the eyeballs off Jim. Due to the narrowness of the path, only two could brush at one time. The harder the guys swept the eyeballs away, the more came rushing to add to the wall building up and around Jim's body.

Jim was keeping his cool. "Look, guys, why don't you step back and give me some room."

Reluctantly, the guys moved back. It was a mistake. Jim couldn't handle the avalanche of eyeballs that appeared out of nowhere. The eyeballs continued their climb until they reached Jim's neck. Jim dropped to the ground and tried to crush them with his body. That, too, was a mistake. Like an avalanche, Jim was soon covered with the gelatinous ocular organs, most areas of his body five eyeballs thick.

With a sob of recognition, Jim struggled to sit up. He reached back to the guys one last time.

"I'm sorry. I'm sorry, Zaddie."

Retreating further, Luke asked, "Who's Zaddie?"

John answered, "I heard it was his wife, died young." John managed to grab the flashlight lying on the ground. The eyeballs didn't seem to be interested in it or any of the other guys at this point.

Flashing the light on Jim, the four guys watched helplessly as the eyeballs forced Jim's mouth open and gushed down his throat. As the volume of eyeballs increased, so did Jim's stomach. Out and out, the stomach extended. In agony, Jim mouthed the word "Ivan."

Jim could no longer breathe. As he gasped his last breath, his eyes dilated and rolled up. His eyeballs bulged and finally popped out of their sockets. Due to the darkness, it was hard to tell, but it looked like a razor-sharp finger shaped like a long pick popped his eyes out.

A Speck of Light emerged from each eyeball and converged into one Speck—Jim's Soul. Slowly the Soul circled its former home, awaiting instructions from its Mind's Eye, perplexed about what it should do next.

Seeing the outstretched black finger, the Soul carried by the Mind's Eye cautiously approached it. The finger beckoned the Soul even further forward. Spinning in slow circles, the Soul advanced, creeping in small little spurts, closer and closer to the finger.

The finger kept moving back. The Soul sensed it was being teased by the finger as if they were playing follow the leader. It was but a moment of beguilement for the finger, a diversion prompted by disdain and boredom. For the Soul, it was a moment of relief from what it knew was its impending doom. Gradually the Soul yielded its will to the finger and slowed its meandering orbit.

The Soul slowly moved closer to the finger. After minutes, the Soul crept up to the outstretched finger and gently rested on one of the interior knuckle joints. The Soul relaxed, some sense of security finally being achieved after the uncertain outcome of whatever game was being played.

A small laugh came from the forest. It bounced off the trees, scattering bits of sound randomly through the woods. The guys shivered and instinctively moved closer to each other. They fervently searched all sides of the path but couldn't locate the source. The laugh was everywhere and nowhere at the same time.

"Are you glad to meet our father?" The words vibrated from deep in the woods.

The finger trapped the Soul in its proximal interphalangeal joint, the joint that connects the proximal and middle phalanges. It completely surrounded the Soul in the finger's rotting flesh. The joint opened and closed, torturing the squished Soul.

Sounds emerged from the finger. "You have a choice. Endure this pain for eternity or release your Soul to me, and I will stop your suffering."

Jim's Soul tried to escape, but it was again squeezed as the finger trapped the Soul in its joint.

"Make your choice now!"

The guys could tell Jim's Soul had chosen to go with the finger. The Soul's Light faded. The dark finger closed tight.

Slowly opening back up ceremoniously, the evil finger proudly displayed its profile. The Soul was no longer there. The message was clear: Jim's Soul would not be entering the Reincarnation Universe. He was going to Hell.

The finger stayed still, directly in front of the guys.

"It's waiting for us to react," said John. "Stand still, do not make a move."

"I vote we run as fast as we can in the opposite direction," whispered Ben, holding his arms across his chest to ward off an oncoming blow.

"John's right. Everyone stay still," added Luke.

Mocking the Soul it had just captured, the finger wagged back and forth. It was behaving like a stern teacher scolding a child. Back and forth, it wagged. Then the finger vanished in a puff of mist.

Like so many army ants, a legion of eyeballs approached from the woods on both sides of the path and surrounded Jim's body. They dug underneath the corpse, creating a cushion to drag Jim's body back into the deep forest. An uncountable number of eyeballs were crushed by Jim's weight, making the same crunchy, crackling sound the guys had heard earlier as the eyeballs scampered deeper and deeper into the jungle of trees with their prize. Soon, Jim was gone.

Charles, quiet up to this point, addressed the other three with his usual calm demeanor. "I didn't have time to tell you, but my Eagle Spirit has told me we are completely surrounded by the eyeballs. The buried dead will soon rise up from the Earth."

"So, how the hell do we deal with that?" asked Ben.

John knew panic was a real threat. The guys had to start talking about options. "Look, TheSon gave us each special gifts. He must have known we would have to deal with stuff like this. Don't you think?"

"I don't think Love is gonna help us here," said Luke.

"Can't see how my intelligence is going to help!" said Ben.

Luke pounced. "Wait a minute. TheSon said you would be famous because of your courage! Rock on, dude!"

"Charles, what about you? Any animal buddies to rescue us?" asked John.

"My Eagle buddy said all animals are heading south towards the home of the Monster Bear. Don't think there are any left around here. It's just so quiet."

The guys knew that John's specialty was combat strategy. So, when he started to mutter to himself, they got quiet.

John looked down, studying the ground. "Where can we go? It seems like nowhere, right? We can't go back, and we can't go forward. We can't go around. We can't go down."

"Yeah, but we've got all the Souls to help us in 'beyond the Veil'," said Ben.

Luke shook his head. "Thought they couldn't leave. Like they're stuck there. So if our body Spirits need help in that dimension, they are there to help, but we can't count on them here. I think we better get ready to fight." He began to open and close his fists like a fighter getting ready for a big match.

"There's got to be other options," mulled John aloud.

Ben motioned to the others. "Wait a minute. Maybe if we used John's gap, we could bring back a few to help us."

"Help us do what?" asked Charles.

"Escape. Make a run for it. Get us up in the air away from the buried corpses!" said Ben.

Charles shook his head. "You've been reading too many comic books, Ben."

John paced. Walking helped him to do his best thinking. "Hold on, you guys. I think Ben has the right idea. It's the gap."

"Oh, yeah, John's got the time dimension thingy down," said Luke.

"So what do you propose, John? We go back in time?" asked Charles.

John stared at Charles, processing the idea. Then he addressed the whole group. "OK, listen, guys. This might work. We know we can't just escape to 'beyond the Veil' because our bodies would stay down here, helpless, and probably would be completely destroyed…and we'd be wandering around forever up there or out there or wherever it is. *If it is….*"

Ben interrupted. "OK, OK, OK. We get the picture."

John continued. "Right. TheSon told me it was my job to lead us to the Monster Bear. So I'll use the gap to check out Mt. Olympus. At least find out what the Monster Bear, TheSon, and all the animals are doing!"

"I thought we had Charles for that?" said Luke.

"I'm getting too much interference now. This evil has set up a signal to distort animal Spirits," replied Charles. "And my Eagle friend had to leave the area. I think John is right. He should check things out."

"Shouldn't we all go?" said Ben.

"It's too soon. I will need time to train all of you. Since my Sensei is in Orb form, we'll probably need to be in 'beyond the Veil' for that to happen," replied John.

"We're too vulnerable. We gotta get out of here, and soon," said Charles.

"What's that?" whispered John.

"Shit, something's coming!" said Ben.

"All right, everyone stay absolutely still. I'll take the lead," said John.

As quietly as possible, John moved up to the front of the group, facing the direction the sound seemed to be coming from.

"Luke, you're the biggest. You take the rear," said John.

"No problem," said Luke.

"And turn off the flashlight," added John.

Luke bent down, picked up Jim's flashlight, and turned it off. "Right. Done," said Luke.

The guys froze as they studied the approaching sound. It was a steady crunch, crunch. It sounded like the drumming used by Greek Hoplite soldiers as they advanced on the battlefield behind an impenetrable wall of interlocked shields. It was all the eerier as there were no other sounds in the forest—no birds, no wind, just total, complete silence, except for the methodical and robotic crunch of footsteps.

John thought the drumbeat was strangely too theatrical and carefully calculated to reach some objective; it was too showy and dramatic. It seemed to be coming from up ahead on the path. At any moment, whatever was producing the sound would be on top of the small group.

"That crunching sound. Those are eyeballs, I bet," muttered Ben.

"OK, guys, brace yourself," said John. "Luke, give me the flashlight."

Taking the flashlight, John slid his finger to the ON button, ready to press it if he needed the light.

John turned inward. He concentrated on breathing and relaxing his body. He needed complete "zanshin"—awareness of everything around him. John went deep inside his Spirit, preparing to jump into the gap if necessary. It would give him time to do reconnaissance and respond to whatever danger awaited the group.

The crunching stopped.

John heard giggling.

There was more than one voice, and they were young.

"Hey, guys, how's it hanging out here all alone?" said voices in unison.

"This voice is different; it's very young," observed John. He repressed the urge to turn on the light. He needed to get to the gap.

In between the laughter, the response from whomever or whatever was out there was terrifying. "Ah, ah, ah, no, you don't, Mr. Warrior. We know the gap also, and your buddies will be gone before you slingshot your way back here."

John knew that he was the one who had to deal with whatever danger the voices posed. He felt the trembling and the fear building within the group, hammering his sense receptors with urgency and dread.

This is too much, John thought. *I'm going to fail.*

It was an old wound reopening, the same feeling he had during those years of living in hopeless self-imposed inferiority and social rejection.

No, wait, this is different, John told himself. *These guys need me. The animals need me. And TheSon said I was Chosen. All of us are Chosen. So there have to be hidden weapons for me, no, for US to use. Just need to hang in here and draw on all the things my Sensei taught me.*

Guess this is it. Trying to sound as relaxed as possible, John responded, "So, what do you want?"

The voices were ebullient. "Whoopee! So you want to play! We have lots of time! Soon we'll have the whole world to play with us. Why don't we start by you turning on your flashlight?"

Journal Entry Fifty-Four: Mount Olympus

The Monster Bear roamed between Mt. Olympus, the tallest of the Olympic range of mountains, far to the south of Lake Sutherland, Mt. Carrie in the north, and Bogachiel Peak in the north, nestled within the Seven Lakes Basin. This mountainous terrain was far from the more heavily populated tourist areas such as Lake Sutherland, which bordered Highway 101.

Mt. Olympus had everything the Monster Bear needed for food, reproduction, and especially to remain hidden.

The Monster Bear was pleased. His time was finally at hand. Centuries of waiting and preparing had led to this apocalyptical climax. Sharpening his perceptive powers through those many generations had brought clarity and a focus to him that no others in the animal kingdoms possessed. He was an alpha animal, not only of the Bears but of all land creatures. He knew that this was so because his Soul was joined with the Holy TheSon, Son of TheOne, incarnate to this Earth.

The Monster Bear remembered when TheSon had requested centuries ago to become One in flesh and Spirit with him when the Bear was but an adolescent.

'Why?' Monster Bear had asked. 'You are the Son of TheOne.'

TheSon had lovingly replied, *Yes...and as you have been chosen, so you have the right to choose.*

'How shall I use my power until the day of reckoning? My parents are above all others in our land, and I will be even stronger and faster. Is this not so?' asked Monster Bear.

Yes. You will be a natural ruler in the order of life, replied TheSon. *But you must avoid man.*

'Where am I to rule? Where am I to hide?' asked the Bear.

Mt. Olympus in this forest will be the beacon for all the world. From all corners of many forests, animals will join us in Our final battle.

The Bear dropped his head in respect. 'When will this happen?'

When it is right. You will have to wait for many man-years and many Bear seasons, replied TheSon.

'Can You tell me the dangers?' asked the Bear.

It will be a just death. Both of Us will be sacrificed. However, you will gain entry to the land of the Holy and be with My Father and Me forever.

The Bear felt pride. 'An honor such as this I accept. I am grateful for Your presence.'

TheSon was pleased. *And I am grateful for your trust, My magnificent Soul companion.*

Journal Entry Fifty-Five: The Wave

The migration began as a trickle. From far and wide, a select group of higher-order animals and large predatory birds arrived to wait with the Monster Bear to receive their mission from TheSon. There was no need for predation, as the Monster Bear had stored provisions in the many dens situated around the mountain. TheSon clarified that interspecies aggression was to be suspended; all physical energy must be focused upon the evil targeted at the Monster Bear and His servants.

Flying overhead, a large group of Golden Eagles heard the conversations between the groups. They noted that species of all types were resolute in their commitment to fight for their world, no matter their genetic heritage. The Eagles also knew their likelihood of survival was minimal. Deep in their hearts, a sadness seeped through the animals and birds as they contemplated the near impossibility of seeing their mates and young ones again. TheSon comforted them and assured them their Souls, though tiny in comparison to the human Soul, would continue on to a profound passage through the Funnel where they would further grow in and with the Spirit of TheOne.

Grizzly Bears were recruited from the wilds of British Columbia, Canada, Idaho, and Wyoming and traveled for many weeks. They were led by TheSon, with the help of a team of high-flying Golden Eagles. The Grizzlies were in deep awe of the power and strength of the Monster Bear. They were huge in their own right, but the Grizzlies barely came up to the Monster Bear's chest when standing next to Him. There was no doubt as to the identity of the alpha male, removing any need for status display or contests of strength.

Hundreds of Black Bears arrived from all mountainous regions of Washington State, with some of the Bears nearing the size of the Grizzlies. At first, the Black Bears were tentative about being so near to their volatile cousins. However, given the mandate of interspecies cooperation and with time passing, the Black Bears gradually moved in and out of the smaller Grizzly groups with ease. The Grizzlies were also tentative initially but were finally comforted by the Black Bears' addition to the fighting force.

The Cougars were next. They could be found resting behind rock outcrops and the hidden dens of Mt. Olympus. The Cougars knew their role was to provide reconnaissance on the ground and to probe enemy weakness, especially at night.

Hundreds of Elk and Deer grazed lazily in the meadows below Mt. Olympus. Their role was to create confusion and chaotic diversions for the evil ones so the troops of TheSon and the Monster Bear could attack when most effective. With a herd of hooves stomping on the ground, this second backup means of communication might come in handy. The Golden Eagles found this group to have especially keen noses for any change in scent, familiar or dangerous.

Should the war extend to the ocean, TheSon had a school of Whales, with the faster Dolphins serving as their escort. They waited right offshore along the Washington coast. The Whales would make sure any approach by the enemy from the direction of the sea would be intercepted if the enemy chose to send troops via the Pacific Ocean.

A team of Golden Eagles served as sentries and battle coordinators. All were brought up to date by the lone Eagle who had helped the four guys. The Eagle volunteered to return to the campsite of the four guys to monitor the situation. To stay undetected, the Eagle had to soar even higher than usual, staying just under her maximum height limits.

'We believe we are ready, my Lord. All is in place for our attack,' thought the Monster Bear to TheSon. 'Should we begin our march?'

Just at that moment, a group of Cougars ran up to Monster Bear. They had sprinted many miles to deliver the news. They were winded, almost out of breath, but relieved to finally have reached the Monster Bear.

'Lord, there is great unrest in the valleys. A lot of movement. We could not tell who or what is moving, but the Elk also discern a momentous change in the Earth's vibration.'

Monster Bear thanked the Cougars for their report.

They are attempting to distract us, thought TheSon to the Monster Bear.

The last place TheSon and Monster Bear had imagined the battle to begin was on their own mountain. All their hours of planning and the many thousands of animal soldiers would then be useless, at least for the present. TheSon realized, maybe too late, that if the Monster Bear's troops stayed on the mountain, they could be surrounded and trapped.

Monster Bear, I have heard from one of our Eagle scouts. He has identified the cause of the vibration. NoOne's army of corpses is marching this way, said TheSon.

Monster Bear sat and stared at the view to the north. Positioned at nearly 8,000 feet in elevation, he could almost see the two lakes, Crescent and Sutherland, from his vantage point on Mt. Olympus.

Suddenly, the Monster Bear saw the approaching army. From a distance, it was similar to the enormous stormy ocean waves Monster Bear had witnessed on the few occasions he had visited the coastal regions. Violently crashing against the shore, the waves were typically hidden out of sight from human detection because of the thick black clouds and torrential rains. Sometimes, as the clouds lifted, the Monster Bear witnessed the ferocious fury of the storm. Like now.

This army attacking us is just as wild and savage.

At the same time, the scout Eagle reported more disturbing details about the approaching army to the Monster Bear. It was no ordinary land force. The approaching military force was composed of eyeless corpses, body parts, bits of skeletons, and roots, snowballing ahead in a perfect U shape toward the Monster Bear and his troops on the mountain.

The wall of dead was hundreds of feet high. Opening deep fissures in the ground, nothing that contained any current or ancient human DNA escaped the powerful suction up out of the Earth and inevitable bonding with the approaching rotating wall. It was a giant vacuum cleaner sucking up both the recently deceased and all those who had expired back to 4,000 years ago when the Chuckchi made it over the ice land bridge connecting Siberia with Alaska.

Watching helplessly from the top of Mt. Olympus, the animal troops monitored the wave of the dead as it reached higher into the sky while at the same time increasing its speed. The closer the wall advanced, the more TheSon and Monster Bear saw the tornado whirlwind sucking up out of the ground all the corpses from deep within the Earth.

The animal troops heard wailing and screaming from the massive corpse army. From the vantage point of the mountain, the depth of the corpse retrieval went down hundreds of feet into the ground, penetrating the lithosphere. Rock, clay, soil, and eventually a subterranean river of water all heaved and spewed up and out from the Earth's depths any sign of present or previous life.

The Monster Bear's troops moved up to higher ground near the mountain. Fear spread among the animals. Previously separated, the four species now huddled close together, struggling for space at the base of Mt. Olympus. The wave of corpses was just a mile away and closing fast.

The Monster Bear thought to TheSon, 'We have to protect Our flank. Send the Grizzlies down the mountain below us on the south side. Break them up into two groups and lure the wave more to the sides—toward the east and the west. The rest of our troops will retreat to the south.'

TheSon replied, *That's what they want us to do. To move us as far away as possible from the lakes. Gather all around. We, too, can farm the Earth.*

A Medical Alert

A loud buzz startled me. An emergency medical alert intermittently honked out of Sheba's mouth. At least she was also surprised. Sheba definitely had little say in her forced opera performances. Suppressing my annoyance, I put my dad's book down, carefully marking my place with a slip of paper. I was anxious to find out how TheSon would build his army to defend against the wall of dead body parts. Of course, the Monster Bear will win! He had TheSon inside his Soul, incarnated once more to Earth!

Except, given the vicious cast of characters, would the Monster Bear be enough? The Devil roamed the universe, and the Twins were still loose. Also, how was TheSon going to rescue the four guys who were trapped deep in the forest?

And why should He? For what reason? Sure, the four were the Chosen. But how could four mental patients make any impact on a cosmic Armageddon? They still seemed fragile, vulnerable, and definitely out of their league.

Although, more than likely, the same could be said for me. My dad promised me that once I found his four guys, they would let me know what to do some fifty years or so later. Moreover, I wanted to ask my dad how and where I was supposed to find them.

Before I could dwell any further on my dad's adventure, I had to submit to a virus diagnostic. When the honking begins, everyone is expected to stop what they're doing and place themselves in the middle of their living room for a two-second body scan.

Living close to others in a city with a covered dome had posed many problems for the early Erob designers. One major issue was how to prevent a self-mutating virus from becoming virulent in a highly dense population that shares the same air and water supply, even though citizens are constantly tested and treated.

All the buildings are immediately put on lockdown when a pathogen is detected. At that point, no matter the age, every dweller is expected to submit to the scan and sometimes give a blood sample. As with all the other city apartments, my unit has its own medical lab and triage unit.

Sometimes quarantine is imposed. Not that it's really necessary anymore. Very few people leave their apartments these days.

"Hold still," commanded Sheba. "I've detected a foreign virus from your body scan."

"In MY body?" I asked.

"Well, now. Let's count the number of bodies in this apartment," Sheba sarcastically replied.

I wanted to see how much of an emotional reaction I could generate in Sheba. Recently she started practicing expressions in front of the only mirror we had in our apartment, part of her required Robotic Continuing Education requirement. "Ok, I'll play along. How many?" I asked.

A huge grin spread across her face, quite incongruous with her next comment. "Oh, stop it! You can't be…oh, I get it! You're pulling my button!"

Hope she didn't pay money for that class. "Well, actually, the phrase is 'pushing my button.'"

"Push. Pull. Get your ass over here for your shot."

The next part always fascinated me. A small tray emerged within Sheba's belly with a bio-syringe filled with an exact amount of anti-viral serum.

"How do you do that? Will you tell me how you pull that off?"

All business, Sheba simply replied, "No."

"My, you have a good sense of humor today."

"I certainly do. It is mandatory for me to receive my 'J' rating."

I smelled a setup but decided to play along. After all, Sheba was the one with the needle. "And what is a 'J' rating?"

"Expert in dealing with jerks," frowned Sheba.

"Sheba, after telling a joke, you should smile."

"Who's telling a joke?"

Now Sheba smiled.

I decided the time was ideal for getting my shot over with. "Well, I'd appreciate it if you'd use the same delicate finesse with that needle that you use when preparing our shish kabobs!"

"And why should I?" Sheba asked defiantly. I was at her complete mercy, and she enjoyed every second of her complete control over me.

It was at these moments that shots terrified me. It wasn't so much the pain that came from poking a needle into my skin that made me anxious; it was that Sheba was not accurate. Inevitably, she penetrated too far beneath my skin and hit bone. "Because you're about as accurate with that needle as...."

"I know. God, you get obnoxious. How many times have I heard that? A little pain will do you good," declared Sheba.

This was the point at which I closed my eyes. Watching the needle penetrate my skin was much too traumatic for me. Shots in my butt never hurt as much as shots in my arm because I couldn't see my butt. A shot in my arm was another story. Any sight of a needle, even one lying on Sheba's triage tray, resulted in me clenching my fists and sweat running down my face. "Sheba, you go too deep. You're not supposed to hit bone!"

Am I really pleading with a robot?

Sheba was having none of my micromanagement. "Someday, you'll grow up and watch me give you a shot. Do you realize that you always close your eyes, like right now, and scrunch your eyes together right before I start to inject?"

My eyes still closed, I gulped. "Start to inject? You mean when you parade the needle in front of my eyes? You mean when your eyes glaze over in ecstasy with anticipation at the amount of pain you will inflict?"

I waited for the inevitable sting. Seconds seemed like hours. Still waiting.

"Now, how did that feel?" Sheba asked.

I was surprised. "You gave me the shot already? I didn't feel a thing. Wow, you're actually getting really good!" I exclaimed.

Sheba smirked. "Yeah. That's because I haven't given you the shot yet. Oh, here's the needle. Now watch carefully as I stick the blunt tip all the way into your arm and hit your bone."

"Owwww! You're a complete sadist."

Speculation still runs wild as to the source of the occasionally occurring deadly viruses. Many say the city Mental Hospital, where my dad had worked decades before, is the source. Some speculate there used to be some kind of top-secret, experimental biotech weapons program hidden deep underneath the Mental Hospital grounds. There is no way to confirm or discount the existence of such a weapons program because no one talks publicly about the Mental Hospital at all. It's as if the topic is entirely taboo. So much so that even the physical existence of the Mental Hospital itself is blocked from the consciousness of the average citizen.

When I'm done reading my dad's book, this Mental Hospital might be an excellent place to start looking for my dad's four patients.

If they're still there in the Mental Hospital, what have they been doing all these years?

Journal Entry Fifty-Six: The Trap

John turned on his flashlight in the pitch-black forest. At the same time, he leaped at the source of the taunting words. He hit nothing but air. John landed on the ground, sprawled out, dirt flying into his eyes and gaping mouth.

John shook his head and spat on the ground. He surveyed whatever was illuminated by the light. He could see nothing.

"Tsk, tsk, tsk, foolish boy. Can't you see us yet? Look up!"

John looked up. Suspended in midair, high above, hovered the outline of two very young identical boys. The giggling became louder; it increased each time the two boys looked at one another. The Twins slowly dropped lower to be more visible but still maintained a specter-like appearance due to the eerie forest shadows.

The three other guys ran the short distance to surround John. Luke shook his fist at the apparitions dangling up above. "Tell us what you want," Luke screamed.

Ben stepped forward and supported Luke. "Yeah, tell us."

Charles knew it wouldn't do any good to say anything, so he didn't move or say a word.

The two young boys that were suspended in the air introduced themselves. "We are who you call The Twins. We have the power of NoOne and are here to take you home."

John quickly assessed his enemies.

They have no fear. They have Chi unlike any I have ever encountered. They can't be more than 7 or 8 years old!

He was shocked to receive a reply. The Twins could read his thoughts.

'We can be any age we want to be, Karate John.'

Unaware of the thoughts shared between John and the Twins, Charles replied, "We are home."

The Twins broke out in laughter. Then, they spoke together, in perfect unison. "We're going to take you to a much better home."

Emboldened by the other three guys, Ben stepped up. "I've seen your home in the SuperVoid. It's where you send Souls to suffer for eternity."

"Wrongo. That's our daddy's home! Our home is…! Ohh…wait… let's make it a surprise! Are you ready for a trip?" The Twins together began to sing, "I'm so ready / I'm psyched to go…I'm leaving / without heaving / so stop your bereaving!"

"Where's Ivan? What'd you do with him?" demanded Luke.

Again in unison, the Twins spoke. "We couldn't help but hear his lecture on the rite of passage. Therefore, we have one for you. Solve this riddle, and you will get a Christmas present! We'll even throw in Ivan for good measure!"

"Are you kidding me?" said Luke.

The Twins giggled again. "No sir-e-e-e," they sang.

Ben stepped forward. "I'll take on your challenge!"

The three other guys looked at Ben and were astounded. They thought the same thing. *Ben, the wimp of our group?*

"Yeah, I know," Ben said, looking back at the three. "You all thought I was a big baby. Guess I am. But I was chosen for this party because of my brain, right? So I should be good at riddles."

Luke walked up to Ben, put his hands on Ben's shoulders, and whispered. "You don't have to do this, Ben."

Keeping his focus on the two Twins, Ben replied firmly to Luke, "Yes, I do. Who else can pull this off? You're just along for the ride 'cause you're so damn pretty, and John's head is partially in outer space, and Chief here likes animals a little too much for my taste."

"Still whipping out the jokes, eh?" said Luke.

"Did you just call me Chief?" Charles smiled.

Ben yelled at the Twins, "OK, let's have it."

Together the Twins posed the riddle. "What creature walks on four legs when they get up in the morning, two legs at high noon when the sun is at its fullest, and three legs in the evening hours at dusk?"

Ben knew the answer right away. He screamed back at the guys, "I know this one. This is so easy. You've got to be kidding me!"

The Twins continued to smile. "Well, kid-er-r-o-o-ony…what's your answer?"

Ben was confident. For the first time he could remember, Ben knew he was about to receive praise and validation from his peers. And he was looking forward to it. Eager for it. Not that he ever had any peers since he preferred to be alone. However, this feeling of maybe being acknowledged for contributing to a group of his peers was like starting a fire and watching the flames climb higher, without the orgasm, of course.

"It's Sophocles!" cried Ben in relief. "It's from his play *Oedipus the King*. The Sphinx asks this question to travelers. If they got the answer right, they'd live. If they got the answer wrong, they'd die. Oedipus answered correctly: Man. We come into the world crawling, hence the four legs in the morning. At midlife or noon, a man is walking on two legs. At dusk and approaching death, man is walking with the help of a cane, or three legs."

Luke whooped, "Yeah, way to go, Ben!"

"Nice job, Ben." John was looking for escape routes and noticed that Charles was concentrating inwardly.

Charles tried to get in touch with his Eagle friend, or any animal for that matter, to find out what was happening outside the forest. This little game with the Twins was buying Charles some time, but he feared he would need much more than time in order to escape back to camp. He hoped Ben could stretch the game out until Charles formulated some kind of strategy.

The Twins clapped and yelled, "Yes, Mr. Fatty, you are correct. Give the man a prize!"

"Yes, where's my present?" asked Ben.

"Ohh, this is not just any present; it's a Christmas present!"

Luke sensed trouble. He ordered, "Ben, get back with us, right now."

Puzzled, Ben walked back to Luke. Whispering, he asked Luke, "Why? What's going on? I answered the riddle! What's wrong with John?"

Charles pushed in between Ben and Luke. "Shhh...John's in his 'gap.'"

As if broadcasting to the entire forest, the Twins repeated their statement, "Give the man a prize. Oh, where are you, prize? Well, well,

well. Looks like our prize is getting a pretty wrap. I mean, it wouldn't be Christmas without some wrapped presents, right, guys?"

Luke muttered, "I have a really bad feeling about this."

"Come on, you promised a prize," Ben yelled to the Twins.

The Twins clapped their hands. "Oh, goodie. They want to see the prize. Where is the prize?"

The guys stumbled backward when they saw the prize. It was a bunch of packages with black tendrils wrapped around something covered in Earth. A quick count by John came up with ten differently shaped objects, impossible to identify due to them being "wrapped" with mud and tied with muddy fern strings. A wildflower that looked like a bow was placed in the middle.

Moving closer, the guys saw the bow was not a wildflower but, in reality, a bunch of squirmy worms.

Dropping down and forward, the Twins hovered within a few feet of the guys. "Haven't you ever played the game Potato Head? It's the best game ever! You take objects apart, then put all the parts back together again. Isn't this a great prize? Go ahead. Start opening!"

"Let me open one of the packages," said Ben.

"OK, Mr. Brain wants to see one of the packages!" the Twins shouted.

The Twins separated one of the packages from the others. Using their powers of telekinesis, they delivered the package to the foot of Ben.

Slowly and methodically, Ben untied the worms' bow. Then Ben unwrapped the tendril-like strings. Last, he scraped away the Earth-like cover, which flaked away into the air, revealing one of the game pieces.

Ben threw up.

Journal Entry Fifty-Seven: Farmers

Looking down from his mountaintop, the Monster Bear studied the carnage below. As ordered, the Grizzlies attacked both the east and west flanks of The Twins' wave. The enormous paws of the Grizzlies swiped at the rolling, flying bones and body parts, shattering them as the decomposing corpses shot out the sides of the wave.

As soon as the Grizzles made a hole in the wave, more corpses were resurrected to fill the empty spaces. Bone fragments, buried for centuries, came alive, pummeling the Grizzlies with acres of decomposed, Earth-blunted weapons. Then, as the Grizzlies fell, they were all sucked into the giant caverns created by the wave, exploding into parts and becoming one with the wall. Flesh ripped away, the newly skinned bones became sharpened missiles spearing more of the Monster Bear's troops.

Before they expired, the Grizzlies gave thanks to the Monster Bear for his leadership and courage.

TheSon's incarnated Soul that dwelt as One with the Monster Bear thanked the Grizzlies and prayed to TendHer to honor their contributions. The Grizzlies knew that unconditional Love meant having to sacrifice their lives with no expectation of reward. TheSon assured them that their freely given sacrifices would be celebrated by the Orb Host whose membership they had now earned and would soon join in 'beyond the Veil'.

In a matter of minutes, all the Grizzlies were gone, torn limb from limb, disassembled as if they were no sturdier than toys. The Soul of every Grizzly quickly slipped into 'beyond the Veil' and awaited the arrival of TendHer.

The Black Bears waited to be called in to take their place.

'What would you have me do now?' thought Monster Bear to TheSon. 'Should the Black Bears take over and attack the wall? Maybe we should all retreat south?'

It is time to farm, thought TheSon. *Yes, We, too, will farm the Earth.*

The guys were preoccupied with trying to solve the Twins' riddle. John was sure the Twins would not leave or let the guys leave anytime soon. He figured it was the ideal time to reconnoiter the more significant battle site far to the south if only he could use his 'gap.' Once there, he would have more data to devise a strategy.

John figured that if he could stand behind Charles, he might use Charles as interference to avoid the Twins' detection.

Charles knew right away what John was trying to do, so Charles stepped in front of John, obscuring the Twins' view.

Charles whispered. "I got it."

John slingshotted into his 'gap.' He had been well-trained by Sensei and TheSon. John easily accessed the forest maps that he had navigated and memorized when he was a karate student. He felt a pull towards the south.

'Yes, I do feel your presence, TheSon. I'm on my way.'

Arriving at the top of Mt. Olympus, it was difficult to tell who was more surprised, John's Mind's Eye laying at the feet of a 2,500-pound Bear or the Bear sensing an invisible human presence.

TheSon calmed both. *It's OK, Monster Bear. John is one of our warriors. John, I'm sharing Souls with this alpha Bear; the Monster Bear is one of My sons.*

John didn't know if he was supposed to offer his "Spirit-hand" or what. He thought twice about the handshake when he saw the size of Monster Bear's paw. It was almost as big as John's entire torso.

When John communicated with the Monster Bear, John knew that he was also speaking with TheSon. John thought, 'Nice to meet you, Mr. Monster Bear. I would shake your paw, but I would probably go right through it as I am all Spirit. No offense, but I'm here to see if you can help us. It looks like you're pretty busy.'

'What is it you desire from us?' asked the Monster Bear.

John thought, 'We are cornered by the Twins. They're playing games with us and won't let us leave, I'm sure. Can you help us? Like right away?'

TheSon thought, *We, too, are trapped. Look at the bottom of the whole mountain. NoOne has buried an army of corpses, and now he's resurrected them into a wave to destroy us and the entire mountain.*

Looking down, John saw the approaching wall of corpses. 'Oh no, that wave must be over a thousand feet high.'

TheSon thought back, *Unfortunately, the wall is approaching 2,000 feet. But I have help on the way.*

'TheSon. Can You and Monster Bear help…?'

Before John finished his sentence, a great rumbling shook the mountain. The base of Mt. Olympus vibrated and juddered. John saw rocks flying a good quarter-mile out.

'What is that?' John asked.

The wave of corpses stopped, suspended in the air, waiting for instructions.

TheSon thought, *That's My backup. Monster Bear, tell our Eagle friend to notify all our troops. Tell them to retreat to the mountain and wait at the bottom; they need to stay near us.*

John and the Monster Bear stood side by side. They watched the mountain convulse and the Earth erupt. Huge boulders spewed upward out of the ground around the mountain's perimeter. Right beneath the gigantic rocks were hundreds of pairs of legs, struggling to rise clear of the Earth. Finally, the legs gained traction, pushed their way up through the dirt, and dug in to climb out, wobbly and shaky. As the legs struggled to regain balance, the tops of heads emerged, quivering and shuddering, sending Earth remnants airborne in a great gust of dirt and rock. Hundreds of legs and heads popped up almost in perfect synchrony around the mountain, accompanied by ferocious screams celebrating their unexpected resurrection.

As the beastly heads struggled up out of the ground, small legs struggled to lift the 550-pound bodies. John saw long slanted eyes that rapidly blinked, more curious than scared. Razor-sharp long beaks jutted out from their fur-streaked heads and necks; thin bodies disguising incredible strength. No boulder was heavy enough to disturb their emergence from graves of slumber.

Last to emerge were the wings, protectively covering the main body of the ancient birds. Straining to get a foothold with their massive wings that were still partially buried, the beasts stumbled up out of the dirt, unfolding their wings to a span of 65 feet. They reminded John of when his aunt put his clothes out to dry on a clothesline, and the clothes flapped with impertinence as if they were convinced they could ride with the wind forever.

The entire mountain region trembled as the Dinosaurs called Quetzalcoatls stomped and flapped their wings in harmony. John couldn't figure out who was more imperious, the Monster Bear or these hundreds of flying Dinosaurs.

'TheSon, are these beasts here to help us?' asked John.

They have not been seen here for 66 million years, replied TheSon. *A brief span of time in the context of this universe. And but a heartbeat in the timeline of this planet's life. They soar at 15,000 feet, dive, and cruise at speeds up to 80 miles per hour. Watch. Monster Bear, take charge.*

The Monster Bear moved to the center of the mountain peak. He lifted up on his hind legs and roared his welcome and thanks for their arrival.

The flying Dinosaurs turned their heads to face the Monster Bear and acknowledged his welcome. They flapped their wings in unison, slowly at first but then gaining speed. Gradually the great beasts lifted off the ground. Up, up, up, the Dinosaurs struggled to gain altitude. Majestically, they felt their strength gradually return, confidence increasing with each foot in height gained.

The Dinosaurs finally reached an altitude higher than Mt. Olympus.

The winged animals from so long ago screeched with joy. Free again. Playfully, the great birds soared through the sky, nearly blocking out sunlight. Around and around, the Dinosaurs flew, warbling with happiness as they nudged and bumped into each other in mid-air. Completely captivated by their new chance at life, the carefree and frisky creatures of old cavorted in their elated merrymaking. They were certain their freedom would last an eternity.

After minutes of their airborne spectacle, a lifetime to the Dinosaurs, they paused and hung limply in the sky, wings beating just fast enough to stay aloft. Their heads looked down and turned to the top of the mountain.

The Monster Bear sent one command to the Dinosaurs. 'Destroy the wave.'

Down the beasts from long ago dove, wings folding in to gain maximum speed, eyes blazing with a passion forged from an eternity of waiting. Gazing side to side, the flying Dinosaurs felt emboldened by so many brothers and sisters at hand, sharing once again the vigor of life, the invigorating contest of battle.

As the Dinosaurs closed in on the wave, they maneuvered so they were between the wave and the mountain. Then, almost touching the ground, they speared themselves forward, penetrated the bottom of the wave, and shot straight up at a 90-degree angle.

The entire wave of corpses was disassembled like so many dominoes from bottom to top. Bones and flesh were hit so hard by the winged Dinosaurs that all material from the wave was turned to dust.

The Monster Bear gave the next command.

'Now, my Black Bear and Elk sons and daughters. Attack.'

With that order from the Monster Bear, the Black Bear and Elk stormed ahead from their base positions on the south side, turned around at the bottom of the mountain, and stampeded forward. They pounced on any pieces of the wave that had not been crushed by the wings of the beasts.

Struggling to get up and reassemble, the wave corpses were ground to a fine pulp by the brutal stomping of the massive Bear paws and Elk hooves. Wispy and fine, the corpse dust blew away with the wind, the tempest of resurrection from below halted, giving the Black Bear enough time to position themselves to stand guard over the pit from which the corpse army had emerged.

John could not wait any longer.

'Monster Bear, can you help my friends? I have waited here too long. My time here is over. I must get back.'

TheSon replied immediately. *Yes, Monster Bear. We must assist John. Our next battle lies ahead in the forest.*

Journal Entry Fifty-Eight: Being Back

While controlling from afar the wave of corpses attacking TheSon and the Monster Bear on Mt. Olympus, the Twins now settled in to destroy TheSon's disciples in the forest.

The little fat boy just puked. This they found odd; everyone had body parts. Species live, and then they give up their body parts. That was the rhythm of nature. So, what's the big deal?

Regular humans are so sensitive!

The Twins thought it insanely inventive to trap Ben's Mentor, Igor, just leaving 'beyond the Veil', in physical form, surely on his way to rescue his beloved student.

Carving up Igor's body was a snap, almost boring to the Twins. Other than the head. The head was the best part. The Twins enjoyed waiting until the very end to carve up his head. They made Ivan witness the gruesome details, watching Igor's body being slowly butchered. Couldn't mess with the eyes, of course; they were already TendHer pure.

Given that Igor had been judged Holy by TendHer, the Twins knew that Igor could return to Earth as an Orb again once he was killed. But first, he would have to again report to TendHer for reassignment in the Reincarnation Universe. And that would buy time for the Twins.

"Ready for one more riddle?" asked the Twins.

"No, we're done, and we're out of here," said Luke.

"Oh, come on, just one more, and then we promise you can have Ivan back if you answer it correctly!"

Charles shot back, "What, in pieces like Ben's buddy?"

"Now, now, my big friends. We're just having fun!"

Ben finally stopped vomiting. In between coughs, he managed to ask, "What did you do with Ivan?"

The Twins looked at each other and giggled. "Oh, he's around here somewhere! Ivan? Ivan? Where are you? He's probably just stuck up."

Charles whispered to Luke, "These Twins are psycho sick. We've got to get John back."

Luke shook his head in agreement. "Yeah, but we have to get Ivan too. I'm afraid he might be injured, so we can't just run for it and leave him."

"Do you really think we could get very far?" Charles sighed.

Luke did a sweep of the perimeter. Ben was pale and obviously still queasy. Charles was calm as ever. Boo was looking at something in the woods. "Let's play this out. What choice do we have? What do you think, Boo?"

Boo went up to a tree, sniffed around its trunk, and whined.

"I feel the same as Boo. We're all going around in circles and getting nowhere," Luke said. Then it dawned on Luke. When was the last time he sang a Dandy Randy song? For the first time that Luke could remember, he felt whole. With the help of Heather and with these guys, Luke felt healthy. Even though he was more scared than he had ever been in his life, Luke cared about what he was doing. Moreover, he cared about the guys.

Wait a minute. Even Ben? Luke pondered.

Luke did a quick inventory. Charles, although mostly quiet, was not zoning out and was using his powers to communicate with the animals. John was Mr. Reliable—never a doubt he would rise to the occasion when things got tough. Ben was not obsessively consumed with fire and volunteered to help the group. Ben came through, probably for the first time in his life. Luke, for a brief moment, allowed himself the luxury of being proud of both him and the other three guys. And, oh yes, don't forget Boo: loyalty with attitude!

"Ready?" asked the Twins. "Remember, if you answer this correctly, you get Ivan back. Whoopie! Ok, here it goes. What grows in a forest, reaches up to the sky, sways in the wind, but never asks why?"

The guys all gathered around, whispering. Ben thought it was a trick question; it was too easy. Luke said he thought the Twins were just playing with them. Charles smelled the air and continued to block John from the eyesight of the Twins.

"Let me answer it, OK?" asked Ben.

Charles and Luke solemnly nodded their heads.

Ben took two steps forward to face the airborne Twins. "A tree."

The Twins twirled in the air. "This boy is a genius! Yes, you have won. You get Ivan back. Or we should say *Ivan's back*."

The guys followed the outstretched arms of the Twins. "Lookee right over there. Your prize awaits you."

A fir tree rumbled. Something was coming out of the bark from the base of the tree to about six feet up. It vibrated and wobbled until shapes emerged. An agonizing scream from deep within the tree was followed by body parts squeezing out backwards. First, the back of two arms clutched at the air, backward. Next, the back of a head exited, followed by an outline of a spine, shoulder blades, and buttocks. Finally, the complete back of a man and the backside of two legs emerged. Whoever it was, he was trapped facing into the tree's center.

"You assholes," screamed Luke.

The Twins were laughing so hard they didn't hear the thunder in the distance. "Whoopee, I told you the prize was *Ivan's back*! There it is. You got Ivan's back."

"Let him go. Please," cried Ben.

"Oh, all right. Since you insist. You're such a bunch of killjoys!"

The guys turned to face the tree, waiting for Ivan to exit entirely from the trunk. Nothing happened. They turned back to the Twins.

"Come on. Get Ivan out," cried Luke.

The Twins were no longer being entertained by the guys. Their gaze went south. Their playful and sadistic taunting turned serious.

"You tricked us," said the Twins. "Your Monster Bear has been having fun without us. Once we deal with him, we will be back. But, until we do, let's make sure you sit tight until we return and decide what to do with you."

Long thick vines spurted out of the ground in a precise circle, lifting themselves up twenty feet. The vines were black and smelled putrid. They looked like decomposed strings of flesh. Feces clung all the way up, dripping down in thick globs. The guys were totally trapped, with just an inch between individual vines.

"Yuck, I'm not touching that stuff," announced Ben.

They turned to the tree. The backside of Ivan was still struggling to get out of the bark.

"Let's go help. Can't we, like, help him? We'll each take a limb and pull?" said Luke.

Charles was hesitant. "I'm not so sure. It's risky. We don't know what's keeping him in the tree."

"Yeah, but he'll suffocate if we don't get him out," said Ben.

"Well, we gotta do something," said Luke.

The three went to the tree. Since he was the biggest and strongest, Luke took the back halves of the struggling arms. Charles took the back half of one leg, and Ben took the back half of the other.

"OK, on three, guys. One, two, three," said Luke.

They pulled and pulled as hard as they could. The body struggled to break free from the bark.

"Just give it one last hard pull!" cried Luke.

With the extra effort, the backside of Ivan peeled out from the bark. Everything was there: head, shoulders, torso, arms, and legs. The guys had pulled so hard that when Ivan finally popped free from the tree, they all went tumbling backward.

Boo barked. The guys gently rolled Ivan over. Only there was no frontside to Ivan. Nothing left except maggots.

The guys threw Ivan's body off and jumped up. They ran to the corners of their vine-entangled cage, watching with horror as the arms, back, and legs continued to thrash about. More maggots emerged from deep within Ivan, ready for more food. Then, with one final twist of savagery, words came from the corpse. The mouth moved in large circles as if gasping for breath and wanting to say something important.

"Look, guys, Ivan's trying to say something," exclaimed Charles.

John turned to the guys. "This isn't Ivan, guys. He's gone."

"Well, OK, OK. But I still want to hear what he's saying," said Ben. Tiptoeing over to the corpse, Ben bent down slowly. When he got an inch from Ivan's face, he heard words escape the worm-infested hole where Ivan's mouth used to be: "Aren't we having fun?"

Journal Entry Fifty-Nine: The Charge

The Twins had not counted on the disquieting creative resistance amassed by the new enemies of NoOne on the far mountain. The Twins' wave of corpses was being destroyed. TheSon had joined forces with resurrected beasts from long ago to join His cause. With a slight degree of admiration tempered with jealous scorn, the Twins wondered why they hadn't thought of that.

The Twins had never failed. To be outwitted by a Bear was inconceivable. NoOne had warned them about TheSon and the pathetically weak four boys. NoOne had assured the Twins that the Monster Bear was a common animal, certainly no match for their powers. NoOne downplayed the role played by TheSon. He had guaranteed that the Twins would prevail.

The Twins thought NoOne would be proud of them because they had created such a formidable wave of corpses to attack the Monster Bear on the mountain. At the same time, they had trapped the four boys in the forest. But now, it appeared they had underestimated the Monster Bear and TheSon, who were headed right for them.

They reached out to NoOne. 'What should we do, father?'

Of course, there was no immediate reply. The Twins expected to wait. It was their place to wait.

One minute there was a bright sky, the next, a sky covered with rolling waves of dark clouds, tumbling around a center.

The center was NoOne. And NoOne was pissed. He raged at the Twins, 'Do you not see the forces dominating on the mountain? Our enemies prepare to attack us while you play childish games in the forest with the four babies. The Bear has left his mountain stronghold and is moving to where our new buried army lay. Our army must be protected. You must attack the Monster Bear and His troops before they reach the forest.'

The Twins submerged completely in their teacher's anger; the energy was unlike anything they had ever experienced. They were fascinated by the sinister emotional currents. The very forces NoOne had trained them to use to their advantage were now unleashed by NoOne. Never give in to its power, so NoOne had said, because clearheaded detachment was what separated the Twins from others in their species. Now, NoOne was emitting uncontrolled chaos, and some of it was aimed at them.

This was a first. Was there something NoOne hadn't told them? A hidden agenda, perhaps?

Processing NoOne's emotional storm, the Twins continued their flight southward to intercept the advancing enemy. With their bodies a foot above the ground, the Twins periodically levitated to a standstill to assess, study the sky, and listen to the psychic chatter from animals and humans alike, from anyone or anything within a range of 100 miles.

They vowed to meet the Monster Bear army head-on long before it reached their forest, their buried army of the dead, and the four guys. Whatever TheSon threw at the Twins, they knew nothing could keep them from reaching their mission objective: continue harvesting the army of corpses to dominate and destroy the Earth. Once they filled up the forests with corpses-in-waiting, they would advance to new gravesites in farmland around the globe.

NoOne directed the Twins: 'Look south, my spoiled children.'

In the distance, the Twins saw a cloud of dust that spanned the entire horizon moving toward them. They strained to extend their vision. And what they saw filled them with excitement. A force unlike any they had ever witnessed was coming to meet them. How foolish. But so much fun!

TheSon and the Monster Bear knew NoOne had warned the Twins and were convinced the Twins would not back down. TheSon knew His Dinosaurs had the best chance of defeating the Twins, so He ordered the Elk, Black Bear, Wolves, and Cougars to stay well behind the massive destructive charge of the prehistoric beasts.

TheSon and the Monster Bear led the charge to the north. Running on land, they could not keep up with the flying Dinosaurs who continued to gain distance. So, the Monster Bear asked his Golden Eagles to constantly update him during their long journey.

Charles made sure to stay in touch with the Eagles. Even though the four guys were trapped in the corpse vines, Charles heard the words he wanted to hear. Help was on its way.

Addressing Ben and Luke, Charles said, "My animal friends tell me an army of flying beasts is getting closer. But it will take hours for them to reach us. He also said the one counselor that survived has left the campsite. The counselor notified the Park Rangers, and they are searching for us now."

(Son, you're probably wondering why I didn't go into the forest immediately to look for the boys. I had no choice. The entire perimeter of the campsite was closed off with vines. One minute there was forest. The next moment nothing but the foul-smelling vines. Only one way out: a rocky bank that worked its way back down to the bus. I had to leave everything. Once down to the main highway, I immediately contacted the Park Ranger and called the hospital. After the Park Rangers couldn't find any trace of the guys, the hospital ordered me to return to Portland).

"Look. John is stirring. He must be back from his recon," said Ben.

John's Mind's Eye had not fully reunited with his body, so it took a few stretches and body twists to feel grounded. After a brief moment of grogginess, John blurted out, "What the hell happened here? This place stinks. And what's with these walls?"

"They're vines made out of dead bodies with a little mud thrown in. You don't get used to it," grumbled Ben.

"At least we can see the sky," added Luke.

"Oh, thanks, Mr. Positive!" needled Ben.

Ignoring the banter, John demanded, "Tell me, what's going on?"

Charles filled him in. "While you were away, the Twins toyed with us. They put Ivan in that tree, and he was eaten by maggots. Before the Twins left, they constructed this jail made out of corpses. Don't know what they're planning on doing with us if they ever get back here, but it looks like we've got lots of time to kill."

"I don't like that word 'if.' And kill is definitely not one of my favse," said Ben.

"Ivan and Jim gave their lives for us," said Charles. "If they hadn't warned us, we would have been the ones turned into trees."

"It sure isn't turning out like we're going to save ourselves, much less thinking we were chosen for some great adventure to save the world!" growled Luke.

John shook his head from side to side. "Guys, keep in mind there's a bigger picture here. It's scary not knowing what's ahead. But we've been to realities no others have ever experienced. I was given a tour of the universe! And I met the Monster Bear. He's incredible. You just wait and see. I'm sure we're going to get help. At least we have some time to sort things out; make a plan. We need to stay focused on our mission."

"And our mission is?" asked Luke.

Before John could answer, Ben stood up. "I'm not a hero. I don't want a mission. And I didn't ask to be chosen. Of all the guys on our planet, why choose me? I mean, I'm nuts! We're all nuts. I want out of...."

Charles interrupted Ben with labored breathing. The guys picked up on the intensity; even Boo stood with the hair on his backside standing up. They knew what was to follow. Charles was the quietest of the group, the most introspective. But when he had something to say, a force built up inside him, gradually processed, refined, and then exploded in relevance. "Listen, Ben, listen all of you. We ARE nuts! Of course, we are! And we know it! That's why we're some of the only sane people left. That's the point, don't you see? We know we're crazy, and that makes us sane!"

Ben stammered, "Whoa. That's some logic. We're sane because we know we're crazy? And others are insane because they don't know they're nuts? That's crazy!"

Charles replied, "Precisely. You tell me if this isn't nuts. We equate everything valuable with green paper called 'money.' We house this paper in concrete and steel. And are told that because there's a finite supply of this green paper, we have to work for it. Yet while some people are starving or need help, the rich and powerful can get and even print all the money they want at any time. They're called 'bankers.' Isn't that crazy?"

Luke impatiently blurted, "Can't we just stop all this blabbing? I want to start ripping out these vines."

"Calm down, Luke. Let him finish," admonished John. "We need to hear from everyone. Might as well let Charles have his say."

Charles nodded. "Ok. Here's another example. We encourage unprivileged women to work outside the home taking care of other children, so they can earn enough money to pay other women to take care of their own kids and call it a 'career.' Now, isn't that crazy?

"Gangs fight other gangs for a piece of turf and call it a 'family.' Isn't that crazy?

"We glorify boys who can hurt other boys and call it 'sports.' Isn't that crazy?

"Girls viciously demean other girls for how they look and call it 'fashion.' Isn't that crazy?

"We have more poverty trapped out of sight on reservations, in the inner cities, and in the Appalachians than any other industrialized country or at any other time in pre-civilized history. Isn't that crazy?

"Our country, the U.S.A., has the highest number of depressed citizens among other industrialized societies, but we're told to be 'independent and strong.' Isn't that crazy?

"I could go on and on. But think about the loneliness. So many kids are depressed. Families torn apart. You can see it all around us. And it's all made possible by people considered 'sane.'"

Charles paused and was surprised the other guys were staring at him so intently. He continued. "But we crazies aren't fooled by meaningless rituals like 'graduation' that just pass us along to another stage of numbness. We know we're losers. We know we've been counted out."

Luke paced and for good measure, to show his disgust, spat on the ground. "Excuse me, guys. We're about to lose our lives. Hate to bring your brains back to reality...."

"Hey, wait a minute. I'm not a loser!" exclaimed Ben.

Charles turned to Ben. "No, you're not a loser, Ben. But the system is. It has a sick life of its own. And our system says 'winner takes all.' The rest of us get crumbs."

Luke was at his breaking point. "Could someone tell me why we're talking about eating?"

"Stop being schizophrenic," yelled Ben.

"I'm not singing!" stated Luke. He stood up, fists clenched at his waist. "We need a plan, and soon!"

Charles looked away and muttered something at the ground. Ben ignored Luke and moved his attention back to Charles. "Excuse me for playing devil's advocate, Charles. But I don't see you complaining about modern conveniences that come from our system, like plentiful housing, clean water, medicine, safe food...."

"Oh, crap! Not again!" moaned Luke.

"Tell that to my tribal brothers and sisters," replied Charles.

"Well, no system is perfect. You're focusing on a few horror stories, and you're leaving out all the success stories," said Ben.

The guys watched Charles intently, waiting for his response. They thought Ben had trapped him.

Slowly, Charles marked his words. "I will answer with this. How do you define 'successful,' Ben? After all the pain you, me, Luke, and John have suffered, you think we're full of success?"

A mammoth grin of recognition spread across Luke's face. "Hey, I get it. Full of success. Like 'successful!' "

"Brilliant," commented Ben with a smile.

John walked up to Charles and took his arm. "Charles, you've given another great speech. This one is even better than the one at the campground. I wish we had more time. But right now, we gotta move on and figure out a way to save our butts."

Ben was not satisfied. "Wait, I just want to say that no one person can have a complete picture of our society, Charles. There are just too many elements, levels, and groups. And all economic systems have their pros and cons."

Luke had reached his limit. He shouted, "Who the fuck cares about 'an economic system?' What the hell is 'an economic system?' We're covered in vine shit!"

Charles ignored Luke and looked at Ben. "People we depended on as kids disappeared. It all started in the freedom movements of the 60s and 70s. People we counted on to protect us went their own ways, for their own reasons. And they left us behind. We were abandoned. You, me, we all protected ourselves the only way we knew how, and that 'how' is what others call 'crazy.'"

"So, we're sane because we're crazy," stated Luke. "That's just dandy. Can we move on to another topic, like surviving? Or is that too practical for you boneheads?"

Ben nodded his head. "I hate to admit it, but I agree with Luke. We should move on."

Charles was not going to give up. "Did any of us have solid families? You know. Two parents who really Loved…." Charles suddenly moved to the center of the vine prison and stared straight up. John and Ben jerked their heads upwards to follow Charles' gaze.

An Eagle had just appeared high above their vine jail, and Charles traced its flight.

"Sorry, guys. Been wanting to get this off my mind for a long time. Kinda stupid of me to waste our time like this," said Charles.

"Did you hear that?" asked John urgently.

"Hear what?" replied Luke.

"That's the point. Listen. Nothing. Just like before."

The guys looked at each other, hoping to find some assurance of normalcy. The Eagle had disappeared. The trees were still. The rustling of forest ferns from small animals stopped. The stale wind, what little was allowed through the thick vines, waned. No animal sounds were coming from the forest.

Awkward moments passed as the guys grappled with Charles' honesty and the eerie silence that followed. Each guy had no choice but to briefly review his own journey of rejection and abandonment.

The insight was too sudden and complete. Sheer terror stormed into their awareness. It was the same painful question, buried deep within their Souls, that demanded to be answered.

Will we be abandoned by TheSon like we were abandoned before by all the other adults we trusted?

The uncanny silence was unexpectedly interrupted by a "whooshing" sound emanating from a distance.

"There it is again. That sound!" declared John. "It's getting closer."

Ben pointed to the sky. "Yeah, and see how that huge dust cloud is streaming towards us? It's like on steroids."

"What do you hear, Charles, from your animal buddies?" asked John.

"My Eagle friends said TheSon has called ancient flying beasts to come out of the ground where they were just buried bones. They're headed this way being led by the Monster Bear," said Charles.

John nodded. "Yeah, I saw them. Dinosaurs with huge long wings. They just smashed the corpse army. And the Monster Bear is a monster. Most powerful land animal anywhere, I think. Well, I guess some elephants are bigger."

"What about the Twins? Where are they?" asked Ben.

"They're headed to fight them," said Charles.

"We gotta get out of here. I mean, didn't TheSon say we were Chosen?" said Luke, more to himself than to the others.

"Maybe this is what we're supposed to do? Like be a diversion?" said Ben.

"OK, let's think this through. Our bodies are stuck here, right?" said John.

"Wait. I think I know what you're saying!" said Ben. "You think we could use 'beyond the Veil'?"

John walked to the tree where Ivan had been crushed. He traced the outline of Ivan still marked on the trunk and turned back to the guys. "We know that NoOne can't go there. Can't we assume that the Twins can't go, either?"

"Yeah, I agree," said Luke.

John continued. "Well, we all had our individual 'Spirit-body' portals that we entered 'beyond the Veil' with and then used to return to the physical world. What if we used those same portals to enter and return to a different location? Like a spot on the battlefield?"

A ray of hope crossed Charles' face. "Oh, yeah. That might work. But we wouldn't have our physical bodies to fight with?"

John was quick to answer. "Who says we need them? Or that we would be of any use, anyway. Maybe our Souls would be enough to tip the balance. Maybe merge with an animal or two? Didn't TheSon do that?"

Charles smiled. "My tribe does it all the time. You Whites are still stuck in the Industrial Revolution."

"Ah, excuse me, guys. Sometimes the best idea is the simplest, and it gets lost in all the big plans," said Ben.

The three guys turned to Ben.

"So what are you proposing, Ben?" asked John.

"Well, John, I know that you're the military dude. But isn't it easiest just to have Charles here ask one of his Eagle buddies to contact the big guy and ask him to send us a few of those flying Dinosaurs? Two should do the trick. Two of us on one Dinosaur could easily make it out of here."

Charles looked at the sky as if he was calculating the descent of the Dinosaurs. "Hmm…that just might work. Plenty of room on the ground for two Dinosaurs; if I correctly recall their wing span. Their wings should barely fit through the top opening."

John, too, was looking upward. Then, after moments of silence, he added, "Ben, have you considered that you would now be part of the target? Part of the troops? The Twins could just wipe your ride out from under you, and you would fall 5,000 feet or so…that would not be fun."

Luke pumped his arms. "Yes! Yes! I vote we do it. There's one thing the Twins have never had that I'm willing to die to give them."

"A mother from Hell?" asked Ben.

Ben quickly realized he was walking on thin ice. No telling how Luke would respond. Ben dropped to the ground and looked away, pretending his comment was innocent.

Seeing that Ben was sending apology signals and given the circumstances, Luke suppressed his usual inclination to attack whenever someone brought up his mother. Besides, Ben's sarcasm had softened; lacking anger, it was more easily perceived as bonding wit.

"Well, I thought more like spanking their butts," smirked Luke. However, Luke's smile, along with his bravado, quickly faded.

None of the other guys smiled. They all knew that the time to talk and banter was over; the battle loomed.

Journal Entry Sixty: Redemption

TendHer felt the impact of NoOne's newfound freedom. This was granted to him by TheOne to streamline the reincarnation process. For the first time in eternity, LostSouls from the SuperVoid had penetrated the physical dimension of a universe.

TendHer observed the growing size of NoOne's SuperVoid army as it flooded and surged its way through Earth's mother universe, collecting more gullible Souls. Building into a river of Dark Matter mass, the newly dead were diverted directly to the Snake of LostSouls.

TendHer also observed fewer Souls being conveyed into the Funnel and Four Gates from the planet Earth.

TendHer conceded that NoOne did offer a choice to the newly deceased, but it was really a clever trick to trap ambivalent Souls into giving up their eyes and, with them, their Souls. Whispered seductively into the Mind's Eyes of the recently departed, NoOne purred, 'Let me take care of your Soul, and I will end your suffering.' Then, with the slightest signal of acceptance, NoOne yanked out the distracted eyes with their clinging Soul filaments and propelled them to join his SuperVoid army, corpses sans eyes to be buried on Earth.

The narcissistic, the materialistic, and the greedy were the easiest to dupe, the most eager to believe in NoOne's soiled possibilities. They screamed and suffered the most when they realized they'd been manipulated, just as they had spent their own lives using others. Premature judgment launched the narcissistic and innocent alike to NoOne's Snake, preventing them from continuing their journey onward to the Funnel and the just but loving assessment at the Four Gates.

Only a handful of people could hear the silky tones of deceit in NoOne's voice or clearly see that there was no evidence that the promise would be fulfilled. Regardless of whether their strong belief came from an institutional religion or their own virtuous character, the faithful were on guard. They ignored the whispers and the promises of NoOne. For these faithful Souls, NoOne had no choice but to let them move on at the moment of death to the Funnel and the Four Gates to meet TendHer for judgment.

Sinister and dark, NoOne's SuperVoid Snake was only seen when it passed by a star's gravitational pull. The sunlight briefly illuminated painful, twisted dark Souls, billions of miles long. Sweeping and majestic, the Snake-like shape wiggled and wormed its way toward Earth with its gaping mouth, sucking in cosmic waste, journeying Souls, and entire planets.

TendHer had warned NoOne that 'beyond the Veil' was off-limits to any dark being. NoOne's reply was to laugh, sending shivers through TendHer and the attending Orbs. TendHer saw the future and knew it was a matter of NoTime before NoOne attacked the realm of Spiritual purity again.

TendHer's message traveled through every atom in the universe. *NoOne, hear My Sacred command and the command of our Creator, your Father. Return your Souls to your SuperVoid prison immediately.*

NoOne replied, 'Or do what? Tell on me? I am only doing what TheOne and I agreed to do. Your Reincarnation Universe is obsolete.

You are obsolete. Your minions will shrivel. Your power has become so much stardust.'

TendHer, eternally accustomed to the threats of the rejected NoOne, sighed. *You are again on notice. If you use your dark ones to crossover to 'beyond the Veil' or if you attack my Reincarnation Universe, you will be....*

'What?' interrupted NoOne. 'I will be what? Sent back to my SuperVoid? You and TheOne need me as dark needs light, like good needs bad, like male needs female. You can't destroy me without obliterating all the multiverses ever created.'

Ominously, NoOne screamed, 'Creation can and will exist without You Three. Your time to expire is drawing near, Sister dear.'

Withdrawing back to Her 'beyond the Veil' realm, TendHer issued one final command. *One last time. You are on notice. Retrieve your dark forces from this universe. Send them back to the SuperVoid.*

TheSon was well aware of the conversation TendHer was having with NoOne and was concerned with NoOne's growing hubris. Yes, the corpse army at Mt. Olympus had been obliterated, but NoOne remained a threat for many reasons. NoOne's physical incarnation in the Twins would be challenging to overcome, even for TheSon. Moreover, NoOne's army from the SuperVoid grew minute by minute as NoOne diverted Souls away from the Funnel. Like a spreading viral contagion, mastery of the Earth universe could springboard NoOne's invasion to an infinite number of multiverses.

Most serious, there existed the possibility that NoOne's SuperVoid collection of Lost Souls would dare violate the sanctity of 'beyond the Veil' and attack the Reincarnation Universe directly.

TheSon reflected on NoOne's strategy. As had happened thousands of times before, TheOne showed His grace, forgiveness, and Love by giving NoOne the chance to choose redemption. NoOne used this freedom granted by his Loving Creator to expand his wicked kingdom. NoOne would stop at nothing to consume as many multiverses as he could. He had to be stopped. Now.

Father, My brother, NoOne, has again breached Your agreement, thought TheSon to TheOne. *He is about to consume Earth.*

Yes. I was waiting for some sign of redemption. It has not been forthcoming.

So, what should We do?

My Son, the incarnation of NoOne must be dealt with by You. The SuperVoid army of Lost Souls has yet to attack the Sacred territories.

Father, His Lost Soul army from the SuperVoid blocks Souls from Earth's Funnel. His army continues to grow. Even if we defeat him in the physical universe, he has still been incarnated on Earth to continue his evil.

Yes, replied TheOne.

NoOne is planting corpses all over the Earth for his future harvesting of Souls. I see signs that he is planning a direct attack on the Funnel with these Souls. What would you have Me do?

You may unleash the Sacred Orbs from 'beyond the Veil' to protect the Funnel.

Thank you, Father.

But wait, My Son. You must not intervene until NoOne actually enters the Funnel.

Silence. *Yes, Father. If NoOne finds the Funnel, it is possible that he could corrupt the Four Gates and 'beyond the Veil'. Even worse, there is the possibility that NoOne could* become *'beyond the Veil'.*

Journal Entry Sixty-One: Rescue

Flying high above the mountains, the Eagle heard the plea from Charles. 'Please ask the Monster Bear to rescue us so we can fight. I think we need two beasts.'

The Eagle agreed to pass along the message to the Monster Bear.

Marching toward the Twins through the valley where the war would begin, the Monster Bear received the message from the Eagle. He immediately directed his attention inward to his Soul mate.

'TheSon, the four Chosen ones are requesting that two flying warriors rescue them from the forest,' thought the Monster Bear.

TheSon paused and replied, *Yes. Rescue them. But have My winged warriors fly them far away to safety. From there, have them wait for My signal.*

Monster Bear was puzzled. 'How are they going to be used, Lord?'

We will need the four to lead Our forces against NoOne when he attempts to close down the Funnel and the Four Gates.

Monster Bear swiveled his head to watch the flying beasts practice their steep, forceful dives. The Dinosaurs were competing to see who could drop 2,000 feet, pick up a tree branch lying on the ground, and then climb back up as quickly as possible to their buddies waiting in the sky.

These flying beasts are actually playing, thought Monster Bear. *They're acting like baby cubs. They must know that life is precious and worth celebrating every second!*

Monster Bear spent some time assessing the re-born creatures. He wanted the fastest and the most flexible for the steep dive and then the follow-up ascent required to rescue the four guys from the forest where the Twins were holding them captive.

The Eagle had agreed to give a critique. The Eagle gathered a dozen of her kin, other Golden Eagles, and observed from high above. All watched the Dinosaurs play. They envied the power of the flying beasts.

The Golden Eagle soared to the command center to give her report. She was curious as to why the Monster Bear was talking to himself. Perhaps the Monster Bear was thinking about strategies for the coming battle?

The Golden Eagle said, 'Monster Bear, we have chosen the two fittest creatures. Be sure to not forget the Dog animal. He has been accommodating in giving me a grounds-eye view of events. His weight should not be a factor.'

'Oh great,' responded the Monster Bear with uncharacteristic sarcasm. 'What next? Ground squirrels? Very well. I agree with your selection. You may begin to prepare the two Dinosaurs for their mission. You all must fly at a very high altitude, so you cannot be detected. You have very little time. When I give the signal, depart at once and in staggered flights so you do not attract too much attention.'

The Eagle led the two selected flying Dinosaurs to a distant mountain meadow to the south, a temporary safe location in the opposite direction from where they must go. He watched as the Dinosaurs practiced their dives and rapid ascents. Finally, it was time to begin their mission. The Eagle landed on a long outstretched limb of a Fir tree that overlooked the meadow and watched as the Dinosaurs gracefully and softly landed on the thick green grass below.

Flapping their wings was the way the Dinosaurs communicated in battle. Only they knew all the nuances involved in their secret flapping language. Using flap speed and the depth of their wing strokes, they sent detailed messages to one another.

'Thank you for helping,' thought the Eagle.

The beasts beat their wings on the ground. They looked at each other as if deciding whether they wanted to follow such a small flying creature as the Eagle.

'I know, I do not meet your stature, but like you, I'm in the service of our Creator,' thought the Eagle.

After a few seconds of exchanging rapid glances at each other, the beasts together replied, 'Then so it shall be. We will follow you until our bones return to dust.'

'I am in contact with the Dog animal and the shaman Charles. We must leave now. Once we have the boys and Dog animal, we must return here to rest until we are called by the Monster Bear.'

With those words, the two Dinosaurs took flight. The Eagle soared in circles around the two giant beasts struggling to get their wings flapping strong enough to lift them off the ground. Finally, the two Dinosaurs made wide circles around the meadow and gradually gained altitude, two or three feet per wing stroke. Up and down, their long wings stroked, eager to find the smoothest streams of air current.

Once they were high enough, the two great creatures soared in freedom. A calmness and peace overtook the two resurrected Dinosaurs as all sound and movement from below evaporated, leaving only the whooshing of clean, cool air to gently stream over and under their outstretched wings.

The pensive sojourn of the two Dinosaurs would end all too soon. The Dinosaurs looked up at their Eagle friend and saw her turn to the dangers lurking in the northern lakes. This was their cue to end their free-flowing glide and fall in line with the Eagle. Their time to leave had arrived.

The beasts wiped everything from their attention except the Eagle. Intensely focused on the Eagle's every move, the Dinosaurs instinctually knew the Eagle was being given directions by TheSon and the Monster Bear.

John sent out his thought, 'Eagle friend, can you tell us when you will arrive?'

'We are on our way. Look high up. We will hover, and, one at a time, each great beast will pick up two of you. One beast will also take the animal Dog.'

The two Dinosaurs reached out one last time to the Monster Bear. Was this their destiny? Would they have to sacrifice their lives for the cargo below waiting to be rescued?

The Monster Bear replied, 'Yes, my fellow beasts of the Earth. Follow, defend, and, if necessary, sacrifice yourselves for these human warriors. You will be greatly rewarded when your Souls once again are released to join TheOne.'

With heartfelt thanks, the eyes of the beasts became a little larger as if their Souls had been expanded.

'Yes,' they both agreed. 'We will gladly give of ourselves for your mission. Let all my kin know this is a quest for justice. From dust, we arose. To dust, we return. Our Spirits have been resurrected one last time to nourish our Souls and make them worthy enough to dwell forever with the Creator, TheOne.'

The Eagle and her companion rescuers quickly reached the part of the forest where the guys were imprisoned. Hovering over the four humans, the Dog animal, and the vine prison, one Dinosaur let its body drop gently down, keeping its wings vertical to fit them within the confines of the narrow prison walls formed by the tangled vines.

The Eagle wondered why the evil Twins didn't put a canopy cover on the jail walls. No matter, she thought, the descending Dinosaurs could have dismantled anything the Twins designed. The flying beasts agreed.

Hovering over the treetops, the second Dinosaur alertly scanned the sky for any sign of attack. Having landed on the forest floor inside the vine prison, the first Dinosaur said, 'Eagle leader, tell two of our friends to climb to my head and hold onto my fur. I will stay level for their sake. The Dog animal needs to be cushioned between the two humans.'

Charles relayed the message. John and Luke, along with Boo, crawled up the long tail of the Dinosaur, scooted over its main body, and finally climbed onto its neck. It was more of a challenge than they had anticipated because the scales were slippery, designed to protect the beasts from the elements such as flying in freezing cold temperatures. Reaching the top of the head was only possible because of a single strip of fur that started at the tip of the tail and ended on the crest of the flying beast's head.

Having secured their grasp on the head of the first Dinosaur, the guys patted the Dinosaur's neck, signaling they were ready to lift off. As the Dinosaur began to flap, black mucous was dislodged from the prison vines. Luke gently reached down, removed some of the goo from the Dinosaur's forehead, and was delighted when the beast nodded its head up and down in gratitude.

Once the first Dinosaur exited the prison at the top and broke free of the tree line, it motioned to the second Dinosaur to pick up Ben and Charles. Gradually, slowly, the two great creatures from the past joined above the tree line, gaining power, strength, and confidence in the success of what the fantastic beasts of the past knew would probably be their final mission.

Looking back at Ben, Charles noticed Ben had his eyes clenched shut. Slumped over the head of the other dinosaur, John and Luke were also holding on for dear life. Charles screamed over, "Relax, guys! You're not going to fall!"

Charles' advice was ignored. Boo was the only one besides Charles who was enjoying the ride. Boo's head was swiveling in different directions taking in the scenery like he owned the Earth below. His ears flapped backward; his mouth opened in a broad grin; spittle flowed out of his mouth, streaming past Ben's head.

Boo sent a single question to Charles. 'Why are the others so scared? Do they not know this is our final experience in life?'

Charles was surprised by Boo's question. 'Why do you say that, Boo? How do you know this is our final experience?'

'Should you not tell the others?' asked Boo.

'Tell them what, Boo?'

Boo paused. 'What these great beasts just said.'

'What did they say?'

Boo looked downcast, barely able to utter what he knew he had to say. 'They said that this is their final mission. They know it. You and I know it. Do not the others…?'

Charles interrupted Boo. 'Yes, my friend. You and I know this. The others do not. They must be brought along gently to this realization.'

After minutes of silence, Boo finally asked what he wanted to know. 'What makes you so sad, Charles?' asked Boo.

Waiting minutes to answer, Charles reached down and grabbed Boo's paws that were wrapped around his waist. Then, squeezing them gently, Charles replied, 'Loss.'

Journal Entry Sixty-Two: Fancy That

Holding on securely to the fur of their majestic Dinosaurs, the guys flew southwest from their vine prison at an altitude of 2,000 feet. Finally, the guys saw the Monster Bear's army preparing for war directly to the east of them. The troops marched straight ahead in a vast wave with numerous animal species, in contrast to the very relaxed presence of the Twins, who simply hovered, then cruised in a zig-zag pattern all around their enemies. The Twins stalked; smug smiles frozen on their innocent faces.

Having moved north toward the lakes to attack the Twins, the Monster Bear's troops lost the advantage of high ground from their positioning on and around Mt. Olympus. The Monster Bear hoped to find a battle spot that gave his army a similar advantage wherever the battle was fought.

The guys could tell the Monster Bear was jockeying for the best battle location, preferably high ground. Still, every time the Bear's troops seemed to gain an advantage in elevation, the Twins swept in from behind, severely threatening the huge army's rear and flank. It was as if the Monster Bear's army was being herded by Sheepdogs.

It was a matter of minutes before the two armies faced off.

Finally, the Twins made their move. Jetting around from the sides to face the Monster Bear's troops head-on, they stopped and hovered like two beacons suspended 100 feet in the air. They were holding each other's hands. They were still smiling, eager, confident, disdainful.

A group of Dinosaurs quickly surrounded the Twins, furiously blowing bursts of air from their snouts, kicking up dirt and pebbles from the ground below with each determined blasted breath. The Twins, on the other hand, were calm and relaxed. They didn't appear to be fazed at all by the sudden circling of the great beasts who now blocked their escape.

'Brother,' thought one Twin. 'This is a pathetic scene. What fun we shall have!'

'Yes, brother,' thought the other Twin. 'Shall we first go after the Monster Bear or destroy these flying creatures?'

'Let's toy with them both. Take our time. Savor our power. I see our prisoners have been released. Let's bring them to our party. Here.'

'We should split up. One of us stays here. I will go get them. You keep this parade going.'

'Yes, bring them here.'

With a simple thought, the second Twin vanished with the speed of light. He quickly located the scent of the boys. After a few seconds, he found the two beasts with the guys and Boo escaping to the west.

'Hello,' he thought as he moved with them high in the air. 'My brother and I think you should join our little party with the Bear. So, you have a decision to make. Come with me, or I will destroy you and your pet beasts, here and now.'

Screaming aloud, Ben called through the wind to the other guys, "We really have no choice."

Soaring close to the other Dinosaur, Charles replied, "Yes, we do, guys. The Twins are separated! They might not be as powerful!"

"Ah, I don't know about that," said John. "Do you want to test this Twin and see what happens? It could get ugly."

"Well, what do we have to lose at this point?" asked Luke.

Boo barked and sent his thought to Charles. 'Don't do it. Do not test this Twin. Even though separated by distance, they are still thoroughly connected and powerful.'

"They must have a weakness. Something we can exploit," said John.

"Well, we know TheSon is with the Bear, and that's our strength," said Ben.

"Boo thinks we need to do what the Twin says. We're outmatched, big-time," said Charles.

At that moment, the lookout Eagle flying near the guys cried out with a high-pitched screech to get their attention. She also got the attention of the Twin.

The Eagle thought to the group, 'Yes, the Monster Bear wants you to return with the Twin. TheSon has a plan.'

The Twin quickly responded. 'Well, now, isn't that touching? Such a loyal Eagle! Be sure to tell TheSon, NoOne has a plan also.' The Twin wanted to implode the Eagle but then backed off because he wanted the Eagle to spread the word as to the Twins' presence and their powers.

At the mention of NoOne, the guys froze. Taking on the Twins was terrible enough, but throw in the most powerful dark force in the universe, and their plight seemed without any hope of success. They didn't want any part of the monster Devil, as they had sampled a dose of his evil power in 'beyond the Veil'.

Relieved that they had chosen not to test the Twin, the guys agreed to head back to Mt. Olympus. The Dinosaurs turned towards the east with the Twin trailing directly behind with that simple intention. The Twin chuckled at how easy it was to dominate the beasts and their riders. 'This is going to be a fun day,' he thought.

The two enemy groups had not moved from their positions. The two beasts carrying the four boys and Boo settled down next to the Monster Bear, who was just fifty yards from the main body of the animal army.

None could tell the Twins were having a conversation.

'Brother, where shall we start?' asked one Twin.

'Well, let's send these beasts back to the ground.'

'We could use these beasts. Turn them against the Monster Bear and the humans?'

'Hmmm…that would be interesting. But I don't like their history with the Bear.'

'Should we expect our father NoOne to appear?'

'No need. We should just dispatch this group of Dinosaurs and continue building our army.'

'What about the Monster Bear? And TheSon?'

'Did not NoOne prepare us for this? TheSon is only incarnated. He's subject to the same laws of physics as the Bear.'

'Unlike us, eh?

'Our biology has been re-formed from conception to serve as our father's conduit. We cannot be killed, at least by any human. TheSon is simply sharing space with the Bear. Once the Bear dies, TheSon must return to His Divinity.'

'I'm particularly interested in turning the four boys to our side. With their abilities to navigate 'beyond the Veil', we could project our powers of consciousness to multi-universes to harvest more Souls for NoOne.'

'Yes. I get it. Physical presence would not be required. The four boys would be our eyes and ears.'

'Well, not eyes anyway. If they are to be useful, they must keep their Souls intact. We can keep their bodies buried with our armies, but their Souls will be ours to use however we choose, in this reality or other realities.'

'How shall we proceed here, then?'

'As usual. Pain followed by suffering, followed by assimilation to our forces.'

'I was thinking the same thing. Fancy that!'

Journal Entry Sixty-Three: Battle

Although the Dinosaurs grasped a slim sliver of hope fostered by the camaraderie of their cohort and the purity of their purpose, they did not expect to prevail, much less survive. They knew their sacrifice would buy precious time for other, more powerful Spiritual forces that would come into play. The creatures of long ago didn't have a chance.

The Twins found the ideal spot for their attack. It was a large, open meadow surrounded by steep-walled canyons. The field had one entrance and one exit. The Twins knew they could trap the entire army by simply closing off those narrow openings.

The Twins made the first move on the battlefield. They concentrated on their enemies in the sky. Bordering on boredom and disdain, the Twins disassembled the flying Dinosaurs in the same way the fantastic beasts had dismantled the corpse tornado wave. Bits and pieces of wings, beaks, limbs, eyes, bone, flesh, and fur were ripped loose from the disintegrating flying skeletons.

A millisecond before the Dinosaurs were carved up and scattered into piles of dust to be scattered to the winds, the proud beasts gave their thanks for the brief resurrection and precious hours of life. The

Monster Bear thanked the fantastic beasts for giving up their new lives and promised they would be at peace in the Light of TheOne. With sadness and pride, the Dinosaurs willingly accepted their fates.

Turning away from the demolished Dinosaur army, the Twins turned their attention to the Monster Bear and his troops trapped in the meadow below. But something completely unexpected happened: The Twins felt the power of the Monster Bear. Immediately, they became confused and lost their focus. The only force they had previously experienced that possessed more power than they had was their father's power. Now they were besieged by a force that was just as powerful, if not more so. Yet, they felt a difference.

The Monster Bear's power was a different kind of power. It was tranquil and peaceful. It was not aggressive. It was not malicious. It was completely unlike the destructive, primeval power the Twins used to command physical matter: organic and inorganic. The Monster Bear's power was like energy sourced from an utterly unfamiliar dimension.

The Twins looked at each other. Their confusion simultaneously turned into excitement. They both agreed the novelty was exhilarating. NoOne hadn't prepared them for this.

Having avoided the initial decimation of the main Dinosaur group, the two Dinosaurs that had rescued the guys flew north with their precious human cargo barely above the ground, seemingly to escape the plight their Dinosaur brothers and sisters had suffered. The Twins saw the two beasts and boys trying to escape and willed their death.

Nothing happened. Some force from TheSon and the Bear shielded the beasts and their human (and one Dog) cargo.

The Twins could not have been more surprised; for the first time in their lives, their power had been blocked. Suddenly, they were more interested in the power coming from the Monster Bear than the Dinosaurs' escape with the four boys.

The Twins quickly agreed that the boys could be easily hunted down and destroyed later. More importantly, the Twins agreed they must figure out this new power and how it was able to interfere with their potency.

One Twin offered, 'Did not NoOne offer to help us if we encountered something new, such as the unique power coming from this Monster Bear?'

The other Twin replied, 'Only if we were in serious trouble. I don't think we are in any trouble. I still think we are in control of this game. We have millions of bodies buried for our use. We have fed those Souls to NoOne, adding great numbers to his SuperVoid army. This Monster Bear business is a charade. What else could he do? We are so powerful, the Bear knows his only hope is to bluff and buy time.'

'But brother, that was no bluff. I felt…well…feeble. Did you not also have this feeling?'

'Ignore it. Let's destroy this Monster Bear first, and then we can locate the two remaining beasts and their riders.'

The Monster Bear sat back and observed the Twins. There was no sign of aggression on his part. The Monster Bear gracefully motioned up to the Twins with his huge paws, inviting them to descend and sit with him in the middle of the meadow. Nary a creature moved as all eyes were glued on the slowly descending young boys. The two hovered a few feet above the ground, then slowly dropped to the Earth with a plop.

What none suspected was that the Twins were caught off guard. This reaction from the Monster Bear was foreign to them. They were used to terror and panic, two responses of powerlessness that fed their own need for subjugation and domination. Yet, here the Monster Bear was in front of them, inviting them to sit in the middle of at least a thousand nervous animals. And do what?

The Twins studied the Monster Bear's army searching for context to ascertain the Monster Bear's motives. Did the Monster Bear think the Twins were easy pickins' by sitting in the middle of a huge meadow? Maybe draw the Twins into the center and then surround the Twins? Perhaps, the animals thought their sheet numbers would intimidate the Twins before the Twins extinguished their puny lives?

Together, the Twins made a complete circle around the meadow perimeter, inches from their deadly enemy. The Twins memorized every enemy detail. The species present were magnificent to behold, yet the Twins were hardly impressed. The Black Bear was the most prominent threat, but the Twins knew they could implode or explode their bodies with little effort. The Elk and Eagles accounted for most of the army, but their weapons were of little consequence. The Cougar and Wolves could have posed a challenge, but thankfully, they were fewer in number and waited in the very back, hesitant to mingle with their less predictable animal cousins.

The Monster Bear opened wide his paws and gave the Twins the universal signal for a truce, palms turned out facing the Twins. He invited them to sit. Not used to taking directions from anyone, the Twins complied more out of curiosity than deference.

TheSon through the Monster Bear was the first to send his thoughts to the Twins. *You are wondering about My power.*

The Twins nodded slowly and in unison, surprised that the Bear could send thoughts.

I am TheSon, the Son of TheOne, and Monster Bear has invited Me to share His Soul. I also reside in every being from TheOne, including the four humans you seek. Universes far and wide know this power. It is the power to create, nurture, protect, sacrifice, soar into the Light, and dwell with countless other Souls in fellowship and kindness. It is called Love.

The Twins started to laugh. 'What you call Love is an excuse for weakness. It is totally impotent against our power to destroy! You say you reside in every living being. Why aren't you in us?'

TheSon continued. *I can be in you. A part of Me can join with you just like a part of Me has joined with Monster Bear. All Creation has an element of Me in them, dwelling, waiting, yearning. Except you. You do not come from TheOne. You are unlike any creature ever spawned. You spring from a source completely dark and without salvation. My Father is the Creator and nourishes those who seek Holiness and the Sacred. Your father is NoOne, the Soulless collector of those who choose the path of evil. He is using you to destroy all that is Sacred.*

The Twins were flustered. They looked at each other, studied the Bear, and returned to each other's gaze, searching for an answer. They had not discussed any path other than that provided by NoOne. Did not NoOne call himself by the title "father?" This was a novel concept coming from TheSon.

They had studied all the world's religions in-depth, but they were words. Just words. Now, here before them was a presence tempting them to explore a new awareness, a Spiritual path, to master a new form of power. Could it be compatible with or equal to the power of NoOne?

The Twins thought to each other, 'No. This could be a trick. Be careful. This Bear creature knows his time has come to an end and is stalling!'

TheSon continued, *I am here to give you each a choice. You have tremendous power given to you by NoOne, master of the SuperVoid and all LostSouls, but it pales when compared to the infinite power of TheOne.*

NoOne is using you to harvest Souls for his army. Choose the path of the Sacred, and you can return to the Creation of Our Father.

The Twins thought back, 'NoOne is our mentor and father who has raised us. Why do we need to choose?'

Monster Bear stood up. His height made the Twins flinch. This reaction was picked up by the Bear. The Twins quickly levitated off the ground to meet, at eye level, the gaze of the 12-foot-tall giant.

After a long pause, TheSon thought, *You have a choice to continue your destruction here or accept your Creator's grace and renounce your evil mission.*

The Twins thought back, 'You call it evil. We call it survival of the fittest. You call it grace from TheOne. We call it servitude.'

TheSon sent out his next thought as a whisper. So much so that the Twins actually moved within arm's length of the giant Bear. *When NoOne is done here on this planet, you will be eliminated, and he will move on to other universes. Do you not sense this?*

The Twins had never discussed openly the possibility that they were expendable.

TheSon continued. *Yes, that's right. Your mentor will discard you like all the other Lost Souls he has exploited, and you will suffer forever in his SuperVoid.*

The Twins stared at each other. They had never needed to do so before today. Why weren't they using their mind-reading powers? Was TheSon somehow interfering with their communication? Where were these seeds of doubt coming from? Where was NoOne?

The Monster Bear dipped his head to the Twins in a gesture of affirmation and validation. *I offer you both forgiveness and sanctity. But you must choose.*

'Forgiveness for what? What is forgiveness?' the Twins asked.

TheSon continued, *Do you not remember the pain and death you two have caused?*

One of the Twins smirked. 'Oh yes, the guilt thing. Our mentor told us it was how the powerful control the less intelligent. More meaningless words becoming meaningful by threatening punishment to those not equipped to compete.'

TheSon replied, *Love is not political. Its power is freely shared. It is freely given, just as your mother, who you tortured and killed but who might someday dwell with Me and My Father, freely gave you as much Love as she could. You rejected that Love. I offer you that same unconditional Love, once more, for the last time.*

Even though hesitating, some Spark of recognition was ignited in one of the Twins. He became unsure for the first time in his life. Again, the suddenly reflective Twin studied his lifelong companion Twin. His repudiating brother now seemed obsessed and haughty. The questioning Twin tried to reconcile TheSon's words with their life histories. The unsure Twin struggled for clarity. 'Brother, do you not remember? We killed our sisters, our mother, and our grandfather?'

The contemptuous Twin never wavered from his utter contempt for his enemy, the Monster Bear. He looked away, trying to ignore his brother's questions. 'So what? We have a mission to complete. Brother, stop looking at me!'

The questioning Twin replied, 'I am seeing for the first time inside you. I feel something from TheSon's words. Do you not feel it when you look at me?'

'Nonsense, stay focused. Stop looking at me.'

The increasingly receptive, questioning Twin pressed his need to understand what TheSon was offering. He didn't notice that he was lost in thought and was staring at his doubting brother. Nor did he see his brother's building anger.

Finally, the skeptic Twin found the source of his uncertainty. 'But brother, NoOne has taught us the eyes are the conduit for the Soul. I do not feel a Soul when I look into your eyes. Do you feel my Soul?'

'Brother. Stop it. You're just falling for their trap. Reconnect with me, now. Stop staring at me!'

TheSon felt he was making some headway. *Yes, that's right. Love gives you the power to see another's Soul. What do you find when you look inside your brother, Twins? Do you find Love? Did you ever feel Love from NoOne?*

A mask of horror spread across the face of the unsure Twin, who was now peering deeply into his brother's eyes. 'Brother, I see nothing inside you. Look inside me. What do you find?'

'Stop it. Now. Stop looking at me!' NoOne's obedient Twin lashed out at the Monster Bear with this final exclamation. Then, the Bear bellowed in pain with a single thought from the Twin. The Monster Bear brought his broad paws up to protect his eyes.

The changed Twin firmly commanded, 'No, brother. Do not remove the eyes.'

'I will do whatever I want to do, brother. What we need to do is get on with our mission. Are you with me or not?'

The wavering Twin barely heard the words. Instead, he was consumed with a feeling he couldn't identify for the first time. He felt a need to enter into the Bear and become one with the Bear. He wanted to feel what the Bear was feeling, to experience what the Bear was experiencing.

TheSon was encouraged. *Yes, searching Twin. The Monster Bear forgives you and asks that you witness his passing. Open your heart.*

The ambivalent Twin did just that; he found an entirely new world that he and his brother had never encountered. It was exhilarating peace. Contentment. Happiness. Could his brother experience this power of Love? Could his brother also perceive Love as the Logos, the beginning and the end, Creator of all including NoOne? The Bear was not God. He was a Spark of God.

The changed Twin began to scan; he felt another invisible presence. No, it was a group presence. The group approached fast. They wavered. Waiting. Expectant. They were radiant. They were pure Light. They were here. Yet, they were somewhere else.

The dark Twin hesitated. He lost his focus on the Monster Bear to process the separation from his brother Twin, who seemed to be transfixed by a Light in the distance. With complete hubris and arrogance, the attacking Twin shifted his full attention to the forces of Light that had paused.

'Look, brother. These Lights are from 'beyond the Veil'. They have come for TheSon and his Bear. They dare not enter our reality, but they are waiting. This tells me we will prevail.'

The Monster Bear was waiting for this opening.

With every ounce of strength he could muster, the Monster Bear attacked the Twin that caused his pain despite both eyes being nearly destroyed. Observing from the side and backing up, the converted New Twin watched with shock as his non-receptive brother returned his attention to the Bear and forced his stream of toxin inside the Monster Bear with the slightest of twitches, willing the virulent infection to expand exponentially. Within seconds, the Bear collapsed to the ground. The dull haze of his blurry eyes and his desperate struggle for just one more raspy breath were inevitably overwhelmed by death's imperative.

The Monster Bear groaned a final gasp of wonder at the mystery and preciousness of life. It was a groan of things to be missed. It was the sigh of uncertainty that comes with anticipating new things, the unknown, the impossible possibilities.

At the moment of death, the Monster Bear's Mind's Eye and Soul cautiously left his eyes. He knew he must now begin his long journey through the Funnel to the Reincarnation Universe in 'beyond the Veil'. He was shocked to find TheSon at his side.

Well done, My son. Well done. We have prevented the slaughter of many species today.

'Did the evil Twin not destroy our army?' asked the Monster Bear.

He is confused. The New Twin kept him occupied long enough for our Soul kin to disperse and hide. Many Souls were preserved today to spread your Love.

'Why are you with me, Lord?' thought the bewildered Bear.

My incarnation here is complete. I, too, am returning Home. I will be with you forever. TheSon smiled, cradled the Monster Bear's Soul, then gently released the great beast's Soul at the Funnel's entrance to begin its journey to TendHer.

The Orbs were waiting. The Bear found himself surrounded by all the animals he had killed, some violently, most losing their lives because of his actions. Yet, he sensed they were proud of him and happy to join him. The Monster Bear was engulfed by all the emotion—Love, fear, anger—he had ever experienced or had elicited from others.

For the first time he could recall, the Monster Bear felt complete contentment. Every creature there, even those who were his fiercest enemies, walked forward and surrounded the Monster Bear.

The Monster Bear apologized to the other animals for taking their lives. The other animals reassured him it was of consequence; all deaths make life possible. All deaths lead to the Divine purpose and consciousness of TheOne.

The Monster Bear surrendered. The Lights waiting in the distance got closer; every species he had met, from Cougars to rival male Bears, came closer and closer. Gently. With compassion. The Monster Bear felt at peace, bathed in eternal radiant energy. Healing Light so foundational that it lifted him and his greeters up and up and deeper into 'beyond the Veil'. Eternal circles; round and round forever. Everywhere, beyond time. Warm and soothing, rings of ecstasy floated down and through the Bear's badly scarred body. Every sore, every injury, every fear was healed. His "Soul-body" was cleansed and purified and rejuvenated.

At the First Gate in the Funnel, TendHer appeared.

He was judged.

He was Whole.

He was now an Orb.

Journal Entry Sixty-Four: Breech

NoOne felt the conversion of the one Twin deep within his Dark Matter SuperVoid army. He was enraged that TheSon turned one of his servants to His side, thereby destroying NoOne's incarnation, at least half of it anyway. Such betrayal was a psychic knife pushed deep within NoOne's awareness. Feeling the twisting throb of betrayal and craving for revenge, NoOne carved out an unflinching resolve to build his universal army even beyond his initial intentions.

An idea came to the surface and finally crystallized in NoOne's consciousness.

Where would TheSon be most vulnerable? Where would He least expect me to strike? Ahhh. The answer: TheSon's precious 'beyond the Veil'. Sure I was kicked out once before and warned never to return, but TheSon would not expect me to defy Father again. Besides, TheOne has allowed the Light to intervene in the physical realm, so it would be only fair that my Dark Matter be allowed to enter my Brother's precious Heaven.

At least I don't have a Soul to whine and whimper about, NoOne reflected. *Very well, I shall carry on with my one offspring. He still seems committed to my mission. The disloyal Twin will feel my eternal punishment along with the four boys. When I feel like it.*

Gaining entry to 'beyond the Veil' will be easy. I will take advantage of the lack of scrutiny by commanding a portion of my growing Dark Matter army to gather, accumulate, and wait for my instructions. I must wait. Not too obvious. Wait, just below the surface of 'beyond the Veil'.

I must have patience.

Never one of my stronger inclinations, NoOne sneered.

Journal Entry Sixty-Five: The New Twin

Resting on the ground with the four guys, far away from his brother who was still circling the dead body of the Monster Bear, the New Twin processed his conversion experience. He felt mixed emotions. The encounter with the Monster Bear's unfamiliar, absolute, and boundless all-encompassing Love shattered the New Twin's identity to its very core. The New Twin searched for a psychic substance to fill his empty, vacated psychic vacuum.

Son, whenever the ego is ignored or unattended by the Mind's Eye, the ego, with its relentless chatter, is all too happy to take command.

The Mind's Eye must then deal with a surge of guilt from the ego's past or worry about the future.

The New Twin chose guilt. He obsessed, tormenting his very newly acquired Soul.

On the other hand, maybe he did have a Soul all along; perhaps it just needed permission to grow. He pondered his hermetic past, his relationship with his brother and other family members.

Did I really kill my mother? Did I really torture and kill hundreds of thousands of people? Am I a disciple of a demonic creature called NoOne?

Why did I convert and not my brother? How could I leave my brother, who trusted me since birth with his very life? Why was NoOne's control so much stronger over my brother?

Maybe it all boils down to whether or not my brother is capable of salvation. Maybe I have a stronger will. Maybe he lacked a Soul all along and could never see the Light? Maybe he needed more time. Maybe he needs me.

Persistent, restless currents of guilt stabbed at the New Twin. He reached out to his companions as his frustration skyrocketed.

"Do you really think my brother misses me?" asked the New Twin, looking at each guy.

There was no verbal response from the four. Instead, a reticent, quiet awkwardness permeated the group. They were looking for direction. What should they do next? What would TheSon have them do? Gazes drifted in all directions, up, down, and around, postures shifted, hands plucked grass from the ground and the blades cocooned by the wind, drifting lazily away.

Whether the New Twin could be trusted lingered on the guys' minds. Was he setting them up for a trap, perhaps? Now and then, they'd glance over at the New Twin. The guys were not reassured by his fidgeting and constant furtive scanning. Even Boo was uncomfortable as he paced back and forth. His eyes, too, drifted up in nervous reflection.

"Do you remember all that stuff you did to innocent people?" asked John. "Do you remember killing Ivan and Jim and Lil' Johnny, your grandfather?"

Ben stated the obvious as he pointed at the New Twin, "Yeah, you killed and tortured a lot of people."

"Did you know what you were doing at the time?" wondered Luke.

Softly, Charles asked, "Why are you here? Why did you decide to help us now?"

"Yes, I remember. I did all those things. I knew what I was doing," the New Twin confessed, his little body quaking.

Charles wanted an answer to his question. "Why did you decide to help us?"

The New Twin couldn't answer Charles' question. Emotion began to build deep within the New Twin, fathomless in its depth. It was raw pain barricaded off within emotional walls, but the walls were really facades, fragile, cracked, releasing bit by bit unmanageable anguish and torment. The surge of emotion welled and demanded release.

The New Twin had no choice but to surrender to the deluge, a response he had never experienced. He crumbled to the ground. Holding his little head in his even smaller hands, the New Twin felt for the first time how insignificant he was.

I am just a little boy.

Breaking out of his reverie, the New Twin gasped, "Is this sorrow I'm feeling? I want to cry. I killed my mommy."

The guys sensed the trauma unfolding. They watched with ritual solemnity as the New Twin sobbed, suddenly acting his age, young and fragile, occasionally looking up and pleading for rescue.

Boo went over and lay down next to the New Twin. Tenderly, Boo licked away the tears streaming down the New Twin's face.

John whispered what everyone was thinking, "Gotta know. Why did you kill all those people?"

Between sobs, the New Twin exclaimed, "I don't really know why. We are so different from everybody else and for some reason felt it was our mission. What am I feeling? Is it called guilt?"

"You've never felt guilty before?" asked Luke.

"My twin brother and I never felt anything. Just curiosity and excitement at what we could do to others. And anger when we were frustrated."

Luke could not resist asking, "So the Monster Bear suddenly changed you, just like that?"

The New Twin nodded. "Yes. And to answer Charles' question, 'why help you now': for the very first time, I feel Love and compassion. My brother and I never experienced that. I don't think I can bear all the hurt and suffering I caused."

"Why do you think your brother didn't change like you did?" asked Ben.

"I honestly don't know. I felt the power of TheSon's Love. I looked at my brother to see if he was with me with this new feeling, and it was like looking down into a deep chasm. Couldn't see a thing, just darkness."

John replied, "How do we know we can trust you?"

"Yeah, you could just split us open at any time!" said Luke.

The New Twin looked at each one of the guys. "I don't know what to do or say. Maybe that is reassuring. I mean, if I meant to hurt you, I would have done it immediately, hours ago. Maybe I have accepted TheSon's gift. And I guess that means I'm here to protect you from my brother and all the monsters we've created."

"Well, that sounds nice, but I still need some proof," said Ben.

Charles told the group to hush. Flying high overhead was their Eagle scout. The message the Eagle sent to Charles was frantic. 'I've been sent by other animals in our energy stream to report that the evil one is gathering a great dark force in our physical realm. The evil army appears to be waiting to invade the Holy 'beyond the Veil'.'

Charles then relayed the message to the group.

"What the fu…?" blurted out Ben.

"I know what's happening," interrupted the New Twin. "NoOne is collecting Souls on Earth as part of his growing army. Once his numbers are great enough, he will breach 'beyond the Veil' and attack TheSon and TendHer in a place called the 'Reincarnation Universe.' "

"How do you know this? Is there something, I mean anything, we can do about it?" pressed Luke.

The New Twin stood up in front of the guys. "I know this because my brother and I were supposed to kill you. NoOne knows you were chosen by TheSon to preserve your planet. I mean our planet. TheSon knows that to stop NoOne from building an unstoppable army, He must keep NoOne out of 'beyond the Veil'."

"Well," said John. "I guess now we will know if you're really on our side. What do you propose we should do?"

"What is your mission?" asked the New Twin.

John answered after a considerable pause. "We are the Chosen. We need to be in 'beyond the Veil' to keep NoOne out."

"Is that the only reason?" asked the New Twin.

Ben stood up. "No…we're really trying to save all those Souls working their way through the Reincarnation Universe."

The New Twin reached out to the group, as if to draw them closer. "Please listen. If NoOne finds the physical entrance to the Spiritual Funnel, he will send his army of dead Souls to attack TendHer in the Reincarnation Universe. To fight in that reality, you have to leave your physical body here. And that was our job. I mean, my brother and I were ordered to kill you while your Souls protected by your Mind's Eyes roamed in 'beyond the Veil'."

"Well, what would happen if our bodies were destroyed here while our Souls and Mind's Eyes were in 'beyond the Veil'?" questioned Ben.

The New Twin paused. "You would just drift forever in 'beyond the Veil' never to return to physical reality. And never able to find the Funnel because the Mind's Eye has to be in the physical realm to sense its location."

"What really worries me is I can't forget the emptiness in my brother's eyes. I think my brother would kill us without hesitation with no feeling at all if he found your physical bodies. I'm pretty sure you would be dismembered."

"Oh, great. Just want I wanted. A hypothesis!" moaned Ben.

John asked, "Well, could you stand guard over our physical bodies hidden somewhere here while our Mind's Eyes and Souls were in the Spiritual reality?"

"Maybe my animal friends would watch over us, no offense," Charles interrupted nodding to New Twin.

New Twin replied, "None taken. However, I doubt any animal could protect you from my brother. I think I'm the only one on Earth that would stand a chance."

Always looking ahead, John asked, "How long do you think we have before one of you dominated the other in a fight?"

"I just don't know. I would start with evasion and hide someplace really weird; keep my brother guessing where I was. Where all of us would be."

"Are you afraid of losing your Soul now that you've experienced compassion?" asked Ben.

Concern crept over the New Twin's young face, etching lines and furrows where none had ever been. "I did not know fear. Didn't have to. But I am afraid of my brother now. And I know that he is not afraid of me. I will have to calculate the advantages and disadvantages of that."

"OK, given that our lives are at stake, could you be a little more optimistic?" asked Ben.

"Yeah, Ben's right. We're just looking for some confidence. There's got to be some way we can at least contain your brother, right?" added Luke.

The New Twin answered, "I don't know. How should I know? Look at me! I'm just a little boy."

"Yeah, a little boy with superpowers," mumbled Luke.

John towered over the New Twin (a first for John to tower over anyone). He pleaded, "There has to be a way. You must think. Isn't there some weakness we can capitalize on? Something the four of us, I mean, the five of us, can use to beat him."

The four guys waited, hoping to be handed some modicum of encouragement, perhaps something that might lead to a practical plan. The New Twin answered with one word.

One word. "No."

Journal Entry Sixty-Six: The Prize

Slowly drifting just under 'beyond the Veil', NoOne's Snake of collected LostSouls waited for orders to invade. Moaning and screaming in perpetual torture, the Snake's mouth greedily sucked judged LostSouls from the Earth and other universes. Growing darker, thicker, longer, and stretching out to a size almost a quarter of NoOne's SuperVoid, millions of prematurely judged Souls were added each hour, sucked into the voracious mouth lined with doomed, tormented, and anguished Souls.

NoOne's ultimate prize was a special door that cut through 'beyond the Veil'. It was the Funnel. Finding this location was NoOne's preeminent goal. Once the Funnel was found, NoOne knew he could steal the Souls while on their journey through the Funnel. He would get the best results at the entry point which was somewhere in his domain: the physical universe.

NoOne had found the Funnel once before. He savored the surprise of the Holy when merely by chance, he had found the Funnel's entry point. Confronting TheSon and his four little boys with impunity was a small taste of the power that he knew would soon be his. At that time, he gleefully returned to his SuperVoid space, pursued by an army of Orbs at the command of TendHer, but this time he knew what to expect, and he would be prepared. And his army would be prepared. He was obsessed with discovering the continuously shifting Funnel entrance again.

If NoOne could tempt enough of these Souls before judgment from TendHer to accept his offer of spurious salvation, NoOne was confident he could conquer the entire universe.

Delicious, NoOne thought. *To watch TheSon flee and TheOne finally acknowledge me as worthy would justify the eternity of waiting I have had to endure. All I need to do is find the Funnel once more.*

The New Twin watched as the four guys became as comfortable as possible in preparation for their mission to 'beyond the Veil'. He agreed to be their sentry and to protect their physical bodies on Earth while they roamed 'beyond the Veil' with their Mind's Eyes and Souls. Hiding them in an abandoned Cougar lair on the side of a hill found just east of Mt. Olympus, the New Twin was not optimistic.

What did they hope to accomplish? Does TheSon know they're coming? What do I do if my brother shows up?

Boo settled in and agreed to help the New Twin monitor the various animal communications streaming from different state regions.

Once stretched out and comfortable, it was a matter of minutes before the four guys worked their way through the various parts of their minds to once again tap into their Mind's Eyes. Having recently explored the dark corners and tricky illusions found in journeying deeper and deeper into the Spiritual foundations of themselves as well as the universe, the trip this time was quick and efficient. They had no time to waste, and all willed themselves to shelve the few insights they gleaned along the way for later review—if there ever would be a "later."

Upon locating their 'beyond the Veil' portals, the guys were surprised to encounter interference. Blocking their entrance to the Spirit world was a long, dense, and very wide tail composed of human and animal body parts. The tail was moving or seemed to be in motion because the corpse remains that comprised the tail were moving together in an undulating rhythm. Looking out in all directions, the tail never seemed to end. It just kept going on and on. An uncountable number of body parts. And eyes. Torn out at the precise moment before death. Jumping up and down, pupils dilating and constricting so rapidly that only the iris was visible for some. Terrified. Panicked. Searching for someone to rescue them. Trapped.

Tentatively getting closer, the guys reached the same conclusion.

'Guys, this tail is made out of LostSouls. It seems to go on forever, but it must have a head somewhere,' said John.

'What do we do? Maybe try to find the head, go around it, and sneak up on top?' asked Luke.

'It could go on forever. Shouldn't there be an opening somewhere not blocked by this monster?' asked Charles.

'Look, we were chosen by TheSon and given special talents. One of us must have the skill needed to get through this barrier and into our portals, right?' said Ben.

'You mean, just break through it?' asked Luke.

'Too risky. We don't know what kind of energy it has. We might get trapped or carved up into little bits of Soul,' added John.

'I'm too scared to make a joke out of that,' said Ben.

'So, maybe I can call on my animal friends to make a tunnel of some sort,' said Charles.

'A tunnel? A tunnel of what?' asked Ben.

'There are millions of Souls from multiple universes traveling into 'beyond the Veil' as part of their judgment every second. Let me call on our higher-order animal friends to create a tunnel for us to sneak through to our portals,' said Charles.

'Why not just call for TheSon to help us get in?' asked Luke.

John moved away to examine the Snake, then came back to the guys. He was stumped as to what the next step should be. 'Look, guys. Although we're close to 'beyond the Veil', we're still technically in the physical realm. TheSon can't come down here unless he incarnates.'

'Like he did with the Monster Bear?' asked Ben.

'Yes,' Charles replied. 'But what about NoOne?'

John quickly answered. 'NoOne is master of Dark Matter in the physical realm. He's forbidden to let any of his army or himself into 'beyond the Veil'.'

'But that's his goal? Right? To conquer 'beyond the Veil'?' asked Luke. 'That's the prize? He can take over everything if he attacks with his LostSoul army. That's what this tail is, right? It's his army?'

John again moved his Mind's Eye sense further down the tail. Then, returning, he noted, 'Afraid so, Luke. I think NoOne's waiting for the right moment to invade. That's what the tail or Snake, I guess, is doing. Looking for a vulnerable entry point.'

Charles added, 'My animal friends tell of their great agony because of NoOne's trickery. NoOne is taking eyes from all the species on Earth without giving them a chance to review their lives and get counseling from the TendHer in the Reincarnation Universe. The animals are eager for help.'

Ben felt growing confidence in his analysis. 'Look, guys, that's NoOne's ultimate design. I think he knows now that his army on Earth is not large enough to move on to other universes, so he's making a run at the Funnel. I mean, if there are millions of Souls still making their way to the Reincarnation Universe, he's going to be thinking they would be a prize to capture. With all those troops, NoOne would be unstoppable.'

'Yes, and what about the SuperVoid? Lots of troops there, that's for sure!' said Luke.

John had the answer. 'Hopefully, that's been sealed back up. Many LostSouls got out, but probably not enough for NoOne to launch his attack on other larger universes. There are an uncountable number of universes. We're just the tip of the iceberg as far as total substance is concerned.'

'I see that now. NoOne has no choice but to attack the Funnel and 'beyond the Veil'. He cannot succeed without vastly increasing his troop numbers. We need to get into 'beyond the Veil' first and then prepare,' said Ben.

'Will anyone know what we're doing?' asked Luke.

Charles was forceful and optimistic. 'Doesn't matter. We were chosen by TheSon. He will show up. We just have to get back into "beyond the Veil". And wait.'

Journal Entry Sixty-Seven: The Few Who Know the Truth

Sitting alone on the empty battlefield, the Old Twin pondered what he should do next. Pursue the Monster Bear's army? Find the boys and kill them? Resurrect troops to attack humans?

The Old Twin reached out to his father. He was surprised and slightly concerned to receive an immediate reply.

'My child, your brother has deserted us. You must increase your efforts to build my army alone,' said NoOne.

'Teacher, should I not destroy the four chosen by TheSon first?'

'No need. I know where your rebellious brother and the boys' bodies are and can remove them anytime I want. We will keep your brother preoccupied with watching the boys. In the meantime, I want you to attack as many large cities as possible. I will help project and enhance your powers.'

The Old Twin nodded in agreement. 'What would you have me do?'

'We begin in what you call "the West."'

'Like the U.S. and Europe?' asked the Old Twin.

'Precisely. The Eastern countries will be much more difficult to corrupt. They are more likely to live in community groups and know the reality of daily struggles. The West is ripe for domination because it constructs a social reality based on individualism and material status. First, we destroy the physical infrastructure, and then the superstructure of authorization of legitimate ideas and social institutions will crumble.'

'What ideas will be destroyed once the physical is demolished?'

'We will remove the illusory cultural fabrication that all people are equal.'

'As in, being the same?' asked the Old Twin.

'Partially. The notion that all humans are born the same, but society selects and divides them is one of my greatest creations; it has led to wondrous social, racial, and sexual class warfare in Western countries. In smoothly functioning Western societies, ideas control the prosperous. Wealth is justified by thinking, "I deserve to be rich because I have worked hard and sacrificed. The poor should be helped, but their expectations are too high due to lack of ability, fear of taking risks, and/or bad breaks." The idea that the wealthy "deserve" riches keeps them connected to the system and suppresses the urge to enslave the less fortunate completely.

'Ideas also serve a purpose for the poor in the Western countries on Earth. Even though victimized by capitalists, the poor mitigate their feelings of oppression through compensatory thoughts such as "My time will come when my ship comes in" or "I will be rewarded when I go to Heaven to receive my rewards."

'Government serves a purpose for both extremes. If not steeped in corruption, the government takes wealth and redistributes it to the poor, preventing revolution. It also provides the muscle to somewhat ameliorate poverty and drug-related gang crime to protect the rich by warehousing the criminals.

'Violent revolution is prevented in well-functioning societies through redistributing wealth (or at least the perception of such), mythic media narratives that provide hope, and philanthropy by the prosperous. Nevertheless, as infrastructures crumble, the rich and the poor will have to confront a new reality: equality in both opportunity and outcome is an extinct idea. Government and rationalizations no longer serve a purpose when people are starving.'

Thinking for a moment, the Old Twin asked, 'It's funny hearing you be so specific about what must be a tiny fraction of all the universes you deal with. Do all planets in these universes that have advanced genetic expression follow these same group dynamics?'

NoOne chuckled. 'The ones based on hormone-driven competition. Yes. Like clockwork.'

'Which means the strongest survive. Right?' asked the Old Twin.

'You are correct. By your actions, you will rip away technological infrastructure and the compensatory ideas that create the illusion of hope, control, and power.'

The Old Twin thought for a moment. 'Father, how do I do this? How do I bring Western societies to this primitive imperative?'

'Create scarcity. The West has little knowledge of how to cope with nature.'

'What kind of scarcity?' asked the Old Twin.

'Scarcity of food, electricity, communication, shelter. Be as creative as you wish.'

'And what is your desired outcome?' asked the Old Twin.

'As people die from starvation and predation, I will harvest the Souls I need to attack 'beyond the Veil'.'

'How will I begin the harvesting?'

'You won't. I will. You will bury and manage the bodies of my soldiers after I have removed their Souls from their eyes and sent the newly judged to my LostSouls legion, hovering underneath the 'beyond the Veil'.'

'Where do we start, teacher?'

We start with the big cities.

'Any particular cities?'

'What you call the United States. State by state, we will process Souls from the most heavily corrupted cities. Then we shall move around the globe, first with the most decadent countries.'

'What do you mean by decadent?'

'The most vulnerable countries for us are those that repress the group identity. Individual rights are more important than group responsibility. These societies swell with pride as they promote equal rights. What they ignore is the other side of the equation: equal responsibilities. They have outsourced character to the fabricated gods of Enlightenment. They will crumble immediately.'

'Oh, yeah. Every man for himself, right? So, where do I go after the United States?'

'English-speaking countries.'

'Where do we start within each state?'

'Find where the government is centered.'

'Why start with the government?'

'Where you find government, there you will find the media.'

The Old Twin replied, 'Yes, I remember reading Social Theory texts, and they talked about how the media elite prop up the ruling class by fostering "false consciousness." '

NoOne interrupted. 'Do you not see my hand at work?'

'Yes, father. I see how you have enticed humans to think in selfish terms. Only the strong can resist the seductive dimension of symbolic compensation and projection.'

'Like what, my precocious child?' asked NoOne.

'Religion. Humanism. Conservatism. Feminism. All "isms" create an "evil other." And with it, a compensatory belief system that results in more divisiveness. More hate.'

NoOne interrupted, 'And?'

'And more LostSouls for us.'

Seldom was NoOne surprised, but he was impressed with his son's knowledge of NoOne's devious social manipulations. 'So, my son. YOU tell me how I do that.'

'Yes, father. Media, such as movies, books, etc., frame stories to perpetuate the illusion that unlimited individual liberty has no negative consequences. Self-fulfillment and freedom for unfettered self-expression are the most important values, often at the expense of family and community. They even rewrite history with ridiculous empowerment dialogues to fit their myths.'

'So?' tested NoOne.

The Old Twin continued. 'By emphasizing the accommodation of individual differences rather than assimilation into primary groups, humans find it hard to fit in and difficult to compromise in living with others. Nowhere is this truer than in Western societies. They become self-centered and isolated by themselves or congregate in narrow niche-interest groups. People lose sight of the big picture, becoming unbalanced in their fanaticism, rejecting empathy, and finding it almost impossible to see the world through others' eyes. It is easy to inflate the outrage of fanatic true believers and provoke them to attack with little reason. As they clutch their righteous simplistic slogans, we then collect their Souls.'

'Excellent,' cooed NoOne.

The Old Twin sighed with relief. Finally, he thought he'd passed his test. He now felt deeply that he had earned the right to sit at the side of NoOne. The Old Twin was sure he had secured the privilege of leading great armies against the weak and damned. He might even eventually convince NoOne to let him command entire universes. Yes. He had earned the right to be his father's only son. Just like TheSon was the only son of TheOne.

The Old Twin was inflated with the power of unrestrained ambition. 'When would you like me to begin, father? When should I start to disassemble Earth's societies and join you at your right hand to invade and conquer this universe?'

NoOne was bored. His son wouldn't be a challenge to control. Like every other human, although sharing much of NoOne's divinity, the Old Twin would undoubtedly be discarded when not needed. Probably sooner rather than later.

NoOne disappeared in a cloud of Dark Matter, rising high to protest the white clouds so innocently covering the Earth below. NoOne contemptuously contaminated their perfection with his Dark-Specked discoloration. He couldn't resist laughing. The irony.

'Dark is not the absence of White,' NoOne thought. 'Dark is the subjugation of White. As with all that is seemingly Pure in TheOne's Creation, all it takes is the truth of the physical world to see who commands. To see who rises about who.'

Now a distant dark cloud working its way into the invisibility of space, NoOne sneered a command to his son far below, a Dark Matter bellow only the Old Twin could hear: 'You may begin now.'

Thus declared NoOne.

'Amen.'

The Old Twin bowed his head with Divine fervor. 'Yes, father. Amen.'

Journal Entry Sixty-Eight: Chaos

Begin he did.

NoOne had strategically stored bodies in shallow graves in the countryside. The Old Twin summoned the same dead to arise and attack society's infrastructure. Millions of corpses clawed their way from wormy holes in the ground to reach the surface. Some were ordered to stay beneath the surface and scratch forward in all directions building intricate tunnels.

Power grids within the cities quickly collapsed as NoOne's eyeless creatures crawled their way underground and above ground to topple transmission lines, cripple power plant command centers, and destroy gas stations.

Once inside the cities, and as per NoOne's instructions, government facilities were next to be targeted; some symbolic such as the Washington Monument, and others vital for providing services, such as schools and hospitals. Major government office buildings were torn apart. No construction material could withstand the intense destructive energy focused on fabricated structures. Brick, wood, masonry blocks, glass—all disintegrated and shattered. Furniture, wiring, and plumbing were ripped into pieces and flung miles high. Walls were vaporized, floor by floor.

Anyone caught in the destructive path generated by the Old Twin was quickly referred to NoOne for judgment. Then, with their eyes removed before death, the confused Souls were whisked away to the SuperVoid, their bodies buried in shallow graves awaiting resurrection as mindless demons.

Roads were destroyed next as the Old Twin ordered more buried legions to arise from their muddy graves, crawl like gophers under the surface, burst upward, and destroy road surfaces. Trucks stopped driving. Stores rapidly ran out of staples, shelves empty, in abandoned stores. Gangs hoarded food and water supplies that were easily looted from huge discount stores like Wally Mart and Famazonia.

It was easy pickings for the Old Twin as the isolated few who tried to hide were sought out and butchered by roving street gangs, who competed for leadership. The strongest, cruelest, and smartest survived. Then the strongest, cruelest, and smartest encountered the true alpha figure on the planet: the Old Twin.

At first, the Old Twin was amazed by how neighbors in every city pitched in to help each other. They shared needed supplies, ranging from food to shelter. The military was called out to preserve peace, but most citizens thought that common sense, Love, and respect would keep the peace and maintain social order.

They were wrong. Most people underestimated how fragile the social strings are that hold any civilized society together.

As supplies dwindled, idealistic notions of goodwill evaporated in direct proportion to the increasing hoarding and random attacks. Gangs first hit the wealthiest homes in the cities, murdering their residents and stealing food. They continued to move down the socio-economic ladder, attacking the less provisioned middle-class homes, and finally turned on their own working-class and low-income neighbors. The only families that survived were those with the foresight to store food, water, rifles, and ammunition and had enough family members to guard the perimeter of their property. These families were indeed rare.

Because of the amassing of weapons by private citizens, the military was ill-equipped to control the urban centers. There were too many armed citizens possessing combat-grade weapons: the AR-15 with 40 bullet magazines, semiautomatic shotguns, millions of high-capacity handguns, and unlimited body armor. As a result, soldiers deserted their units and fled to their own family homes, hopeful to salvage whatever they could find along the way to help save both their family members and homes.

At this point, the Old Twin had sent almost every one of the Souls of the city to NoOne for judgment. Eyeballs built up in piles everywhere. Streets, sidewalks, hallways in buildings, restrooms, and elevators sheltered columns of eyeballs. There was nowhere to turn without seeing twisting and rolling eyes, struggling to return to their bodies, hoping it was a temporary nuisance, praying to have their precious sight restored.

Starvation ran rampant. Crawling on the ground, hands outstretched, eyeballs hanging on by a thread, the barely living resorted to searching for other eyes for food. Except for the sounds of nature or the sporadic rumbling of military transports and private transportation, the cities became echo chambers for the Old Twin's favorite lunchtime sound: *"Crunch, crunch, crunch."*

Everyone knew what "crunch" meant. Food. Worry about ethics later.

Systematically moving from state to state, NoOne and the Old Twin quickly emptied the major cities of any signs of life. They left behind corpses stacked as high as skyscrapers, eyes everywhere, removed by the Old Twin before death. Nebulous eye-shaped Souls were sucked into the cosmic Snake immediately after death by NoOne; Souls bound to the Snake with Dark Matter. All waiting to strike the Holy and the Sacred in 'beyond the Veil'.

An unbeatable team. A determined team.

Except for one question that prickled the Old Twin's conscience in moments of secretive contemplation: *Has NoOne ever had a partner before?*

Why Last?

Our apartment was frigid. The heating Erobs were probably doing routine maintenance. Or upgrading. Still, it wasn't the best time to be disrupting apartment life as reports of the Twins' destructive rampage dominated the news. Even fewer ventured out of their apartments, so now was not the time for renovation. The hammering and drilling were driving me nuts.

I addressed the furthest wall. "Sheba, come out. I have a question. Why haven't the Twins and NoOne touched Oregon or Washington? The East coast is gone. The South is gone. The Midwest is…."

Sheba floated out of the wall. Well, at least half of her. "Who are you? National Geographic all of a sudden? What you're really asking is why haven't the Twins destroyed Portland or Seattle. They most certainly have wiped out a few of the smaller cities. Remember Mossyrock?"

"Ah, Sheba, you're missing your legs."

I enjoyed watching Sheba flustered. Swiveling her head back and forth, Sheba seemed to be locked into a scanning loop. "Just give me a sec…Just give me a sec…Just give me a sec…."

How much fun! Sheba was having a mechanical malfunction. "What? What's going on? Why the looping? And why new legs?"

Sheba stuck out her tongue at me. "Young man, I'm upgrading my strength capacity. I'm trying to figure out how I can carry you."

I knew where this was leading. "You're only one hundred pounds. No way you can…they're getting close, aren't they? The Twins. Do we have much time left here?"

"You have a lot of questions, Mr. Full of Questions!"

Now it was my turn to look for my leg. Rather, my cane. I twisted my ankle pretty badly getting out of bed the other morning. Maybe that's why Sheba is upgrading. To be my crutch when we have to evacuate.

"Hey, Sheba. No worries. I should be fine in a week or two."

Sheba slunk. Her head dropped. Her lips quivered. "We don't have that much time."

"But I'm not done with my dad's manuscript."

"Ha ha. I'm sure the Twins are going to accommodate your reading schedule. The reason our two cities were spared up to now is that the Twins grew up in this part of the country."

I was skeptical. "Now, wait a minute…."

"And because of the Mental Hospital."

"Which Mental Hospital? You mean the one in Portland? The one my dad worked at?"

Sheba dove into the wall and returned with two new legs. Unfortunately, they were human legs.

"You might want to re-visit the stockroom!" I suggested.

Diving back into the wall, I heard Sheba thrashing around. Not that she needed to. She really was somewhere in digital "la-la" land designing her new legs for Erob fabrication. Might take a few days. Did we have enough time?

Sheba screamed out from the wall interior, "Yes. Some say the Twins are saving the Mental Hospital here in Portland for last. That's why everyone is so freaked out. We know what they can do. And they still harbor a grudge from how they were treated at the hospital back in the early 80s."

That seemed too trivial to me. There had to be another reason. "Come on, Sheba. What's the real reason?"

"Well, if you really want to know?"

"Yes, Sheba. Tell me."

"The Twins know that eventually, you'll be there. They're waiting for you."

Journal Entry Sixty-Nine: End Times

Luke spoke first as the four guys finally popped through their foggy Spiritual portals into 'beyond the Veil'. 'Hey, guys, are you all here?'

'Yep,' Ben thought.

'Here,' thought Charles.

'Love speaking through thoughts. Very efficient. Guess we're all here and safe,' thought John. 'We need to think about what we're supposed to do here.'

'Did you guys sense anything different getting here?' thought Ben.

'Yes. I did,' answered Luke. 'It took longer than before. I thought for a moment I wouldn't be let in. Then "slurp"—like I was sucked in.'

Charles nodded. 'I noticed I couldn't get rid of one of my fears, and it was like a weight trapping me in the physical dimension.'

'Well, what's important is that we're all here,' said John. 'Charles, what do you hear from your animal scouts?'

'I got a frantic message from Bestow, my Bonobo Mentor, saying entire cities are being wiped out. The Old Twin brother is harvesting Souls for NoOne,' said Charles.

Somehow, Ben produced a high-pitched thought that sent vexing twinges into the guys' "Spirit heads." 'And you trust the New Twin to watch our bodies?'

'That is so irritating. Stop whatever that sound is. Need to chill a bit. Guys, do we have a choice to trust or not to trust?' asked Luke.

John answered at once. 'No, we don't. We need to stay focused on our objective.'

'Which is what again?' coaxed Luke.

John's frustration was showing as he curtly answered Luke. 'Prepare this reality for an invasion. A big invasion. From NoOne and his LostSouls.'

'Well, that Snake tail sure seemed to be looking for something,' thought Charles.

Ben added, 'Yeah, it was testing the boundaries of 'beyond the Veil'. Looking for weak spots.'

A voice reverberated out of nowhere. *He's looking for the Funnel.*

The four guys swiveled their "Soul-heads," trying to find out who had just interrupted their mental conversation. Spatial directions were nonexistent in the 'beyond the Veil' fog; everywhere they turned, all they saw was misty soup. It reminded Luke of the mist machines he used in football during a super-hot summer day of practice.

'Who said that?' asked Luke.

'Don't you mean, "who thought" that?' questioned Ben.

'So we all heard the same thought, "looking for the Funnel!" ' Charles said.

With his "Soul-body", John ventured out a few yards from the guys, looking for any sign of a presence. 'It sounded like it came from TendHer, but I can't locate her presence.'

Luke sent his thought out to John. 'Well, I thought TendHer spent all her time in the Reincarnation Universe. Maybe she'll help us since Earth is in such a mess.'

A soothing voice, originating from somewhere in 'beyond the Veil' said, *TheSon has asked me to help. Earth will soon be overrun with the dead. My flow of Souls from Earth has almost come to a complete stop. We must protect the Funnel.*

'It was you who got us here, wasn't it? You helped us get through the portals,' stated Charles.

That is correct. All of you had some negative ego processing that would have prevented you from accessing 'beyond the Veil'.

'Thanks for the housecleaning!' said Luke.

John couldn't resist asking, 'With your help, why didn't we use the Funnel?'

You aren't dead. At least yet.

'Oh, that's comforting,' thought Ben.

TendHer thought, *TheSon set up your portals exclusively for your use. You just needed a little help. But now, we must watch the Funnel for an attack.*

'TendHer, could you take us there to see this Funnel?' asked John.

Panting, Ben added. 'Yeah, and see the journey of the dead?'

Journal Entry Seventy: The Wholly

And so, we shall. The Journey of the Dead is a transition from the physical to the Spiritual. The journey begins with physical death and ends with my final decree, written in their own Book of Life.

'Decree?' gulped Ben.

Luke scolded Ben's sudden interruption. 'Ah, Ben, you don't need to share your thoughts while TendHer is thinking. I mean speaking. Show some respect.'

Softly, TendHer thought, *Yes, Benjamin, the journey's end occurs in the Reincarnation Universe, a plane of Spiritual existence alone and separate from all other cosmic dimensions. Here, I assign Souls new bodies to re-enter the physical plane and work off accumulated sin.*

TendHer continued. *Once at the Funnel, the Mind's Eye releases the Soul, still in the shape of an eye, and commands the individual's Pages from their Book of Life, weaving through various dimensions to gather and imbed into the Soul. Together, the Soul and its Book of Life travel through the Four Gates: Unconditional Love, Empathy, Good Works, and Knowledge. After the fourth gate, the Soul approaches me in the Reincarnation Universe to be judged.*

'And the Funnel is the key element in this journey of the dead, right?' asked John.

Yes. That is the prize. Should NoOne conquer the Funnel, he could conquer the Reincarnation Universe. That is why the Funnel's opening is constantly shifting within the physical universe. In addition, it is arcing around and through the 'beyond the Veil' Spiritual world.

Should NoOne find the Funnel and destroy any one of the Four Gates, all Being as you know it would cease. Souls would no longer reincarnate. The multi-universal force of Light would withdraw back to TheOne. The strongest and most corrupt would be left. The Dark Matter of NoOne would obliterate all but the most corrupt and powerful. Should NoOne succeed, only Dark Matter will reign. For eternity.

'Has this ever happened before?' John asked.

TendHer thought, *Tell me, John, what is "before?"*

Ben couldn't resist butting in. 'But aren't we OK if we protect the Funnel?'

TendHer quickly answered. *Yes. That is our plan. We can confront NoOne and his Dark Matter at the entrance should he locate it or at any one of the Four Gates that comprise the Funnel. That is why you were chosen.*

'Oh wow. I get it.' Ben was the first to get the connection. Slowly the other three recognized the meaning of the Four Gates.

'Yes! Guys, how many are we?' asked John.

'Ah, let me count…duh!' said Luke.

'OK. There are four of us. And there are four gates,' John continued.

Charles wanted more detail. 'Where are the Four Gates?'

TendHer continued. *The Soul and the Pages found in the individual's Book of Life travel through the Funnel until they encounter the Four Gates, one at a time.*

'You mean, like four tests?' asked Ben.

TendHer replied. *"Four assessments" is a better phrase. Coming from the material world, the Souls have accumulated corrupted Karma.*

'And the First Gate is Unconditional Love? I mean, that's my Gate, right?' asked Luke.

The guys instinctively felt something tremendous was about to happen. They were not disappointed.

In their presence, the majesty of TendHer evaporated; reducing her essence to the size of a small pea but still radiant, TendHer pulsated through various degrees of intensity. As her shape gradually became larger, she transitioned into the shape of an eye and floated in front of the guys. Then, with no warning, TendHer exploded, sending radiant beams of Light in all directions.

The guys had to retreat, as the brightness was painful to their "Soul-eyes."

TendHer's voice rang out, reverberating in their minds. *You have just experienced an infinitesimal fraction of the energy found in a Pure Soul. It is Love. Its energies know no boundaries. At the First Gate of Unconditional Love, I assess whether the Soul is without blemish. If so, the Soul is welcomed to become One with TheOne.*

'So, if there's any bad Karma at the First Gate….' Ben paused.

TendHer interrupted, *The Soul must proceed through the subsequent three gates and present the Soul's Pages to me.*

'Why don't you just remove all the negative Karma yourself at the first gate?' asked John.

TendHer began to move in a small circle. It was perfect in motion and design. *TheOne has created you out of His Love. Love requires freedom of choice. Freedom is not true freedom unless each Soul decides honestly and experiences consequences naturally*, replied TendHer.

'What you sow, you shall reap?' asked Ben.

Yes. Karma is the result of choices freely made. Incident by incident in life, ego Karma deposits a dark layer of crust that eventually smothers the freely given Love from TheOne. Pain, suffering, selfishness, arrogance, ignorance, doubt, lust, and anger accumulate in layers as Karma on the Soul's surface. At some point, the layers are so dense that the ego feels it is eternally empowered to defy any resistance from the Soul.

'Wow. What happens after that?' wondered Luke.

Once Souls reach this level of contamination, their accumulated pain is so deep that they have to come to me to be counseled and then return to reincarnate into another substance to remove their stained Karma.

'You mean, coming back in the flesh?' asked Ben.

Yes. TheOne never stops trying to reach your heart. It is called forgiveness. It is called grace. The process has been called many things. Reincarnation is another chance to remove the accumulated negative Karma and renounce the ego. A Soul may be reassigned, depending on the Karma, not just back to the human world but also to an animal world, or maybe even to another universe that has an entirely different physicality from the human form.

'How do we remove our bad Karma?' asked Luke. 'I don't think people know how to get rid of their Karma. Like I sure don't.'

TendHer was still. An eerie silence followed Luke's question as if TendHer again wanted all four boys to know the seriousness of what she was about to share. Luke felt his face get red but reminded himself that his face was not present.

Karma is reviewed at each of the Four Gates. Some Karma is good and is noted in the Book of Life. Some Karma is ego driven and also noted. I weigh both in my final judgment. At each gate, life events and the negative and positive Karma are mirrored back to each Soul. Can you guess what that mirror reflects? quizzed TendHer.

Ben was first with the answer. 'Karma concerning Unconditional Love. Empathy. Good Works. Knowledge. I guess you mirror the thoughts, words, and actions that fall under these four main categories. It all depends on the gate.'

The guys looked at each other and then returned to TendHer. John could almost swear that TendHer was smiling.

And which of these is most important? asked TendHer.

Charles interrupted his usual silence with an answer that puzzled the others. 'All.'

And that means what? quizzed TendHer.

Charles answered. 'All four work together. Without one of these, the Soul is not Wholly as in "w-h-o-l-l-y". It is splintered. It is fragmented. Parts of it are compartmentalized to shield the ego from pain. As a result, energy is lost, sealing off traumatic memories.'

I look forward to seeing you in my realm.

'TendHer, does the Soul ever get stuck with the same Karma through several reincarnations? Like it can't grow? Can't go anywhere new?' asked John.

TendHer answered right away. *Such is NoOne's domain.*

Ramping up his frustration, Luke wanted some help following the increasingly abstract discussion. 'Will somebody just tell me what all this philosophy is about here? I'm a meat-and-potatoes kind of guy. I don't get it.'

Lost in thought, the other guys didn't respond to Luke. The silence was finally broken when Charles asked, 'So, there's no destination? No objective? No goal? No Past?' asked Charles.

'OK, that's it. Take me back to the looney bin. You guys are wa-a-a-y out there!' Luke turned his back on the group, then thought better of it after reminding himself he was sure to see TendHer sometime in the future in a much less informal setting. Besides, he remembered, he didn't have a physical back to turn.

Ben broke the awkward lull in the conversation. 'TendHer. These Four Gates. The Karma assessments sound like the special skills TheSon gave us. For example, I was chosen because of my knowledge.'

'Yeah, I was chosen because of my empathy for the natural world,' added Charles.

'And I have my Love for Heather…and it *is* my destination,' thought Luke.

It most certainly is, Luke. It most certainly is.

The guys appreciated that TendHer paid extra attention to Luke. They sensed her approval. Of the four, Luke was the least equipped, or maybe the least interested, in parsing out the philosophical finer points. Nevertheless, the guys thought it was nice of TendHer to acknowledge Luke's commitment to his Heather.

John was distracted by studying, as usual, the surroundings. Planning, no doubt, a strategic attack and escape points.

'John, want to pitch in, here?' said Charles.

Twisting his "Soul-head" back to the group, John replied, 'Oh, yeah. I'm in charge of the good works. Action, movement, and the gap. In addition, it appears to me that once inside the Funnel, these Gates are where I would attack if I wanted to destroy the Light. Who guards these gates? How are they protected? I got the part where each Soul is assessed at each gate and, if lacking, moves on to you and the Reincarnation Universe. Bu….'

'Yeah, it sounds like it's all or nothing. If a Soul has any ego Karma at any of the gates, they go to you. If they don't, they join TheOne. Right?' said Ben.

TendHer replied, *If Souls are found to be Pure Light at the First Gate, Unconditional Love, they immediately are reunited with TheOne. If there is ego Karma at this first gate, they must then pass through the remaining three gates for me to assess how much and what types of Karma they have accumulated. I then assign them a new reincarnation to help remove the negative Karma.*

Luke still looked confused. 'When a Soul gets to the Unconditional Love gate, how does the gate know to let the Soul move to TheOne?'

TendHer expanded in a brilliant flash of radiance. 'I am the Gate. I am all the Gates. A Soul moves on to TheOne when it is pure Light, pure Bliss. No memories, ego, needs, fears, and thoughts. Pure Love means pure knowledge, pure action, perfect and complete empathic union with all Life.'

'And the greatest of these gates is Unconditional Love? Cause it's the First Gate?' asked Ben approaching TendHer.

TendHer retreated, and the guys knew why. Too much energy. Way too much for Ben to handle. Ben immediately sensed he had gotten too close and backed up, as did the other three.

Yes, said TendHer acknowledging the deference shown by the guys. *Those who glow with Love without ego Karma explode in Pure Energy as they approach the First Gate. These Souls then merge with TheOne for all time.*

'What happens to the Soul Guides after escorting the Soul to the Funnel?' asked Charles.

Soul Guides can choose to return to help others navigate the death process, or they can choose to merge with TheOne at the First Gate. But once they merge, Soul Guides may never return to the physical realm.

'Well, what about Jesus?' quizzed Ben. 'Was He once a Soul Guide?'

Absolutely not, replied TendHer. *Jesus is TheSon of TheOne. My Brother. Only He has been allowed to leave TheOne, incarnate to physical form, and return to TheOne.*

'Until NoOne, right?' pressed Ben.

The guys felt TendHer's tense and terse response. *NoOne was granted the power to incarnate to help me, or so he said. Instead, he chose not to Be of TheOne.*

'What about you? Are you Pure like your Brother, TheSon?' asked John.

When I am released from TheOne to witness histories, then assess and counsel, I cannot be Pure.

'Because you're contaminated by what you see?' asked Charles.

To tend all, I must become all, Pure and un-pure alike.

'How is that possible? To be both Pure and un-pure at the same time?'

I am impossible and out of time.

Luke wanted to return to more practical concerns, like how he could connect with Heather as soon as possible. 'So, these Soul Guides, Angels…they help the dead get to Heaven?'

Ben intervened. 'Luke, we're not talking about Heaven here. Heaven is a concept not found in all cultures.'

'What do you mean?' replied Luke.

Addressing TendHer, Ben asked, 'May I answer that?'

Please, thought TendHer.

After setting fires, Ben began what he loved to do best: lecture. 'OK. Sure. Heaven is a kingdom created after a great Armageddon in the Christian world. The saved have been sleeping and are resurrected to live with God in a great city with streets paved in gold. On the other hand, the Celts called their Heaven "Otherworld," and it was located on Earth. To them, Heaven was the perfect Earth without any diseases, old age, hunger, etc.

'Judaism subscribes to the idea of "Gan Eden" or the "Garden of Eden." The righteous are allowed to share all of eternity with God.

They also had the idea of purgatory—Gehanna—where the sinful spend twelve months removing their sin. And, of course, we can't forget the Norse's Valhalla for dead warriors—*Folkvangr*—a great feasting hall.

'Hinduism is probably closest to what we have experienced in 'beyond the Veil' and the Reincarnation Universe. Life is seen as a continuous cycle of rebirth until the Soul is liberated from desires, passions, and the physical world and allowed to return to exist in perfect bliss with Brahman and….'

Luke was exasperated. 'Excuse me, but can you just answer one question, Mr. Scholarship? Do Souls remember their past? Who they used to be? Who they used to be with?'

Coming from Luke, the guys figured his comment referred to his Soul mate, Heather, who, according to Luke, was waiting for Luke to pass on. Still, the guys appreciated Luke's question. They too wondered if some Souls were waiting for them after they died.

TendHer answered Luke. Her thought was gentle and soft. *All is possible. Those that are ready for TheOne have no need for an individual identity. They have the Wisdom and Love of TheOne, including being connected to and knowing all other Souls. Luke, you asked me if my Soul Guides help Souls transition to Heaven? The bottom line is that Souls that need more work are reviewed by me. I show them their successes and failures and map out a plan to help them improve when they reincarnate. If they choose to improve.*

Luke was shaking, almost on the verge of crying. 'Thank you! I knew it! That confirms it. Heather is waiting for me!' The guys figured Luke hadn't heard a word of TendHer's response after "All is possible."

TendHer nodded at Luke. *The Love you share with Heather is but a glimpse of the ecstasy all of you will feel as you connect with other Souls to join TheOne when I determine you are ready. Luke, TheSon has chosen* you to be the Protector of Unconditional Love against NoOne's army at the First Gate. You will draw intensely upon your Love for Heather as your chosen gift.*

'But will my Soul remember the "me" I used to be?' asked John. 'When I die, I mean.'

TendHer's radiance became more condensed as she focused its intensity on John. *To fear losing the self is an indicator at death that you haven't trusted in TheOne and have more work to do.*

'Well, how can we lose this fear? How can get rid of our fear of losing ourselves?' asked John.

For some Holy Faith. For others, experience.

'Your words make it sound so simple. But I don't have the foggiest idea what you're talking about,' sighed Luke.

TendHer glowed. *Let me take you all to visit a death experience on your physical Earth so you can see the process. NoOne is abusing this process, so you need to experience what happens from start to finish. This we call the "Journey of the Dead."*

Journal Entry Seventy-One: Journey of the Dead

Instantly, the four guys found themselves at the foot of a hospital bed. Breathlessly they scanned the room and each other, amazed at their incredibly swift journey. Then, the guys intuitively moved to better glimpse the dying patient lying on the bed. TendHer soon arrived as a Speck of Light the size of a crystal, shooting out streams of small but magnificent beams.

'TendHer, are we still in 'beyond the Veil'? asked John.

Yes. We are here in Spirit form to witness. Your Mind's Eyes and Souls are fully perceptive.

'I thought 'beyond the Veil' was a separate place,' said Luke.

'Beyond the Veil' intersects all dimensions. Do you see the spaces between the strands of wire that make up a cable?

'On my map, I have it as a separate place,' said John.

If you think it so, then it is so.

'TendHer, can the patient and nurse see you or us?' asked Ben.

No, not now. The patient has not yet expired. Once he dies, he will spend time in a dimension we call the Bardo, a transitional reality that straddles two dimensions—the physical and the Spiritual. The moment the patient dies, he will see us partially, but not entirely, because his Mind's Eye is stressed.

'Stressed?' Ben asked.

Yes, the Mind's Eye must resolve the life-death conflict. The Soul wants to move on to me. The ego fears and denies death.

Just as the guys were comfortable, a sweet smell like the Hawaiian plant *Plumeria* engulfed the room. It carried out what it probably was designed to do: the smell relaxed the guys, almost to the point of sleep. They felt their "Soul-heads" drop to their chests. Ben snored.

Then the guys felt a new presence in the room and quickly became alert. Then they sensed another presence. And another. Phantom hands pushed their way through the walls and stopped. Only their translucent hands were visible to warn the room occupants that what was to follow would be truly breathtaking. The guys waited. They looked to TendHer to see if she was still in control of the situation…hoping she was.

'Now, that's what I call an entrance,' yawned Luke.

The guys saw TendHer move, just an inch. That must have been the cue for the vaporous outlines of ghost-like shapes to continue their entrance through the walls into the patient's room. They were spaced a few feet apart, floating off the ground with elongated arms shaped like wings due to their long-sleeved flowing cloaks, majestically caressing the cold, antiseptic floor, wafting forward. Their breadth covered the width of the room, gracefully and calmly gliding, upturned fingertips elegantly touching the hospital room walls. The beings resembled ghostly albatrosses flying leisurely through the air.

The Spirits bowed to TendHer, drifted through the two living human nurses and the furniture, and waited at the foot of the bed. They appeared to be studying TendHer, perhaps waiting for her cue to proceed with their job.

'Can we do that, TendHer? Walk through walls and pieces of furniture?' Luke asked hopefully.

'And people?' added Ben.

With those who dwell in 'beyond the Veil', yes, replied TendHer. *But remember, you are at the very lowest level.*

'So, I might get stuck?' asked Ben.

'Ohh, ain't touching that one,' teased Luke.

It has happened.

'Who are the three ghosts?' said John.

The three figures are not ghosts. These three Orbs have been instructed to greet the Soul that will leave its material host.

'You mean the patient in the bed?' asked Luke.

'Then are they Angels?' pressed Ben.

TendHer made a move to the end of the bed. The three Spirits abruptly, but respectfully, moved to the side and the head of the bed in deference to TendHer. It was obvious who was in charge.

You may think of them as Angels if you wish. The dying have Orbs assist them through the Bardo to the Funnel that leads to the Reincarnation Universe. We call them Soul Guides.

Then the group heard the dying patient's rasping, shallow breathing. At first, barely audible, the sound gradually became louder and deeper with each breath.

'That's the death rattle, isn't it?' asked Charles.

Before TendHer could answer, the patient's eyes suddenly opened and looked at the groups in the room. Sheer panic and horror erupted from the once-still body and placid face. Sitting up in the bed, the patient fearfully studied the guys, turning to each one, trying to understand what was going on. As he fell back on the bed, one of the three Soul Guides lifted off the ground and lay down on top of the dying man, cradling and caressing the dying human.

The patient's look of dread gradually softened and then changed to wonder and awe. Finally, the patient gasped one last breath, opened his mouth, and sighed, eyes glued to the beautiful Soul Guide who was hugging his body, whispering affirming assurances in his ears, tenderly caressing his forehead.

TendHer addressed the group as she moved closer to the patient. *This Soul will now leave its body.*

The nurses checked for signs of life in the patient, looked at each other, and shook their heads several times. A bell rang from another room down the hall, and the nurses scurried away to their next assignment.

Just as the door snapped shut behind the nurses, a small partially dark oval ball tentatively leaped from each of the patient's eyes, squeezing free from the frozen stare of the dilated pupils. Next, filaments were cast off from each eye and glittery, translucent strings reached out to each other, intertwining. The two balls then fused together about an inch in front of the patient's face to form one eye. The Soul was free.

The Mind's Eye emerged, covering a protective oscillating electric current around the Soul whose form henceforth would be a translucent eye.

The Mind's Eye's many currents then became faster and transformed into blazing spikes of Light. The flux zipped around the eye-shaped Soul, searching for negative Karma. When the Light found a smudge, it attacked the negative Karma and some of the black Karma sludge fell away, sizzling as it vanished completely.

One heavy, deep patch of sludge refused to budge. It was the ego.

The enshrined Soul hovered as it turned in all directions within the box-like container of the Mind's Eye: up, down, right, left. It looked like the tentative exploration of a newborn chick breaking out of its birthing shell.

In a triangle formation at the head of the patient's bed, the Soul Guides brought their hands together in a prayer pose.

Pieces of darkness, as if they were slabs of dead bark on a tree, again began to fall off the Soul, the slabs sizzled and popped as they hit the Mind's Eye's pulsating currents. More of the underlying Soul surface was revealed as each piece fell off. Streaks of dazzling, shooting Light beams jetted out from the newly revealed Soul surface buried under the removed dark elements, but the Soul was still mostly dark.

'Did you see that? Why did the Soul come out with the dark stuff on it?' asked Charles.

'Yeah, it came out so dark, then some pieces fell off, and now I can see about a quarter of the Soul's surface, and the brightness is intense,' noted Ben.

TendHer waited until the Soul, now about one-third brightness, lay still. The Soul was waiting for something.

The dark matter is negative or ego Karma. We must move, as the Soul Guides will lead the Soul through the Bardo journey, said TendHer.

As the group moved to the side, the three Soul Guides changed position and moved closer to the dead body. One Soul Guide directly faced the patient at the foot of the bed, while the other two moved to the head of the body. The lead Soul Guide at the end of the bed transformed into a human form. The body was hazy and transparent, but after a few seconds, the Soul Guide appeared to be a male with long hair, wearing a traditional loose robe—a long sleeveless striped coat—with an overcoat open down the front, indicating he was a member of a Bedouin tribe. On top of his head was a kufiya, or headpiece, common to desert dwellers. The other two guides also transformed into similar Bedouin humans with the same clothes.

The four guys immediately recognized the lead Soul guide at the foot of the bed.

'That's Jesus!' Luke remarked.

'At least, it sure looks like some of the pictures of Jesus,' clarified John.

Ben was curious. 'So, Jesus comes to see every Soul?'

'Yeah, it's a meet and greet!' exclaimed Luke.

'Luke, show some respect!' muttered Charles.

Soul Guides accommodate the cultural expectations of the dying, thought TendHer. *For many who are dying, it depends on their life, religious faith, and practice. Soul Guides can appear as Jesus, Muhammad, or a Hindu god. This helps the Soul shed the "Soul-body."*

'Soul-body?' asked Luke.

'Remember? We were taught that's the psychic sense of our physical bodies?' replied Ben.

TendHer continued. *Some Souls are so tied to a body they are terrified when it comes time to return to 'beyond the Veil' and the Reincarnation Universe. They refuse to shed the attachment, which is a psychic memory. They wander the Spirit world, usually hovering over people or places special to them in life.*

Luke moved closer to the Bedouins and studied them, careful not to "touch" any part of their surface. No reaction from the Soul guides. 'Why would the dying not give up their bodies?'

Some people suffer so much pain or so much physical passion, their bodies become a substitute for being Loved and giving Love. It is their only security. As a result, their Soul has been corrupted.

'Corrupted? And they don't want to give up their security? Or give up food? Or give up drugs?' said Luke.

Ben couldn't resist adding, 'Or give up football?'

'Cool it, guys, stay on task,' said John.

Both Luke and Ben mumbled an apology and dropped their "Soul-heads" for a brief moment of shame. Very brief, indeed.

Not the least bit reactive to the banter, TendHer said, *Yes, the Soul is corrupted. The mission of the Mind's Eye is to guide the Soul home, but the ego gets in the way. Overwhelming fear allows the ego to keep the Soul trapped in this Bardo phase. Therefore, the ego must be reduced, and the 'Soul-body' memory must be removed before the Soul Guides can begin preparing for the next phase.*

TendHer looked at Charles.

Charles took the cue. 'Ah, you want me to say something? OK… some cultures make it easier than others to break this bond, I guess. Native people prize nature and value returning to nature to maintain harmony—both body and Spirit. There are so many different teachings, depending on the tribe. For example, some tribes thought they could help the dead move on by sacrificing the wives and horses of the dead. Some tribes were afraid of the dead because they thought the dead were mad at the living, and the houses and possessions of the dead were burned to help the dead move on. Some Arctic tribes just left the corpses on the frozen ice to be eaten by animals. I'm not familiar with a single instance where a passed brother or sister refused to leave his or her relative's dead body behind; it would not even be considered. So, all this fear of death must be in the White man's world.'

TendHer nodded, and Charles and the rest of the guys took that as a cue to continue. *Yes. Breaking this bond is easier in some cultures than in others. Regardless, it has to be broken. If not, the Soul wanders, seeking confirmation of its human existence, feeling like it was still housed in the flesh, refusing to accept physical death.*

Luke had a vision. 'So that's where haunted houses come from?'

TendHer replied, *The material reality and the Spiritual reality are constantly touching. You four are unique because you have portals to the Spiritual dimension we call 'beyond the Veil'. Some humans briefly bypass the Bardo and see the Veil lifted while alive, but none have dwelt in 'beyond the Veil' for as long as you four.*

'What about the Soul Guides? Do they help with this?' asked John.

The three Soul Guides moved in closer to the patient. The Soul of the patient began to spin and retreat. Up it went to the ceiling, then down to the floor, then to the door, through the door, returning and hovering with the three Soul Guides. Everywhere it moved, the guys followed the trail of Light on the Soul's surface as the Mind's Eye struggled to shed more ego sludge, frustrated by its inability to altogether remove the ego and the rest of the black negative Karma. The Light left dazzling trails of bright spears, hypnotizing the guys.

TendHer asked the guys to ignore the Lights and pay attention to the Soul Guides. *Watch closely what the Soul Guides are doing. The Soul has not agreed to journey with the Guides; it is not at peace. The ego is attacking the Mind's Eye with fear and anxiety. The Soul Guides know they must direct the Soul to gradually accept the finality of physical death and give up the "Soul-body." So, they begin their healing. And so shall we follow.*

Journal Entry Seventy-Two: Ego and the Soul

The Soul Guides motioned the guys to get close, then instantly found themselves in another location in less than a couple of seconds. The transition was a blur of visual static and cacophonous sounds. Slightly disoriented, the surroundings finally became somewhat familiar.

'I see dead people,' smirked Ben.

'And your second clue is?' replied Luke.

'See all those drawers over there. That's where they put bodies,' said Ben.

John drifted over to the center of the room. A yellowish shade of white was the dominant color: walls, floor, ceiling, even the single desk by the white door were crème colored. The dissection tables were made of gleaming stainless steel. 'Looks like we have a fresh one here on the table,' John said.

They watched as the coroner lifted the sheet off the patient's face, drawing it back slowly down the patient's body to reveal the entire corpse.

'Why are we here, TendHer?' asked John.

This is part of the Bardo, said TendHer. *Since you are in Spirit form, you will see what my Orbs observe as they continue to reconcile the ego with the Soul.*

'Why do you call it reconciliation?' asked Charles.

TendHer moved toward the head on the body. *The ego must feel safe to let go. Sometimes this takes a while. But the ego does eventually release its hold long enough so the Mind's Eye can continue on to the Funnel entrance.*

'And the ego needs to be destroyed?' asked John.

TendHer said, *No, not destroyed. It will diminish gradually on its own as it ventures through the Four Gates. Once it gets to me in the Reincarnation Universe, the only remaining essence of the ego is recorded in the Soul's Book of Life.*

Ben probed for more detail. 'Well, what about the negative Karma on the Soul? Does it also diminish as it progresses through the Four Gates?'

The ego Karma, the consequences of the ego, that is, the effect that the selfish ego has had on others and nature, will stay embedded in the Soul until hopefully removed in the next reincarnation.

'Oh, that's why different Souls have different Light patterns because each person's Karma is unique?' asked Charles.

Precisely, said TendHer. *Because mistakes and misdeeds are unique to each person, the Light manifestation is summative and unique for each life form. The colors surrounding the Soul give me a sign as to the Soul's stage of purification. White is a beginning Soul's vibratory color; purple is the highest manifestation. Your Souls come to me with a unique mix of colors, and no two Karma patterns are alike.*

Ben was puzzled by a contradiction. 'Wait a minute. How come you and the Orbs give off White Light? I mean, why isn't it Purple? Like you just said?'

TendHer's reply was humbling. *Your Soul could not tolerate the true power of Holiness. White is accommodating to your capacity to survive the presence of the Holy.*

Ben pressed with a follow-up question. 'Ok. Another question. Does a newborn have an ego? I mean, are we born with an ego?' asked Ben.

'Ben, you need to be more respectful,' coached Luke.

Ignoring Luke's criticism, TendHer continued. *No. The Soul is born with accumulated ego Karma. But the ego itself is fresh with each new rebirth due to physical necessity; humans need a defense against physical and psychological deceit.*

'Why is that? That humans need a defense?' quizzed John.

TendHer had anticipated John's question. *I thought you would ask that, given your training. Humans have not evolved out of their hunting/gathering hormonal cascade; you call it "fight, flight, or freeze." With time, should the Human race continue to exist, you might reach emotional maturity similar to the other planets in this universe, a majority of whom achieve social order through mutual respect and cooperation.*

'As opposed to what?' asked John.

As opposed to selfish interest and competition, replied TendHer. *Those are two traits your species have mastered far too well.*

Luke interrupted John's questioning. 'Sorry to butt in, but could someone go through life without an ego? I mean, has it ever happened?' asked Luke.

For once, Ben was impressed with a question coming from Luke. "Whoa, dude. That's one good question.'

TendHer replied, *Yes, it happens on other worlds, other life forms. But for your world, TheSon or "Jesus" was the only human. Your species has yet to evolve out of its aggressive genetic predispositions.*

After a pause, TendHer continued. *Your Mentors returned to human form with no egos. Those close to Spiritual perfection and reunion with TheOne at the First Gate before they die have Purple Lights that blaze so brightly that the ego dissolves. But for those few rare exceptions, physical birth on your Earth requires a series of reincarnations for almost every Soul.*

'TendHer, has a Soul ever been overwhelmed by its ego? So the Soul gets lost or destroyed on its journey through the Bardo to the Funnel and the Gates?' asked John. 'I mean, you talked about ghosts thinking they were still alive?'

All Souls are eventually drawn to me. Although some Souls need more time than others, all Souls sense my presence and eventually feel safe enough to confront the ego with the help of the Mind's Eye on its trip into the Funnel. You call it "En Light Ten Ment."

TendHer paused, then continued. *This Soul wants to return home, as all of you wish to return home. Your egos keep you frozen temporarily out of fear of the unfamiliar, the unknown. Eventually, the power of the ego is minimized due to the push from the Soul and the Mind's Eye and the pull from its Spiritual home.*

'Spiritual home?' asked Luke. 'As in the Funnel?'

Yes, and ultimately to be reunited with TheOne. Watch as the patient's ego battles with the Mind's Eye for dominance over the Soul.

Throbbing with increasing intensity, the ego of the corpse on the morgue dissection table swelled on the Soul surface, jostling the

Soul inside the Mind's Eye's casket container, ricocheting off the sides. Sliding it back and forth across the dead body, the Mind's Eye, with its precious cargo, then zipped frantically to the corner of the morgue. It hovered up on the ceiling, orienting its position to turn downward and scan the room. The Mind's Eye perceived our presence for the first time, managed to calm the ego, and oriented itself briefly to the group, especially the Soul Guides. The Mind's Eye and Soul with the ego attached slowly descended and faced the three Soul Guides.

All of us, led by the three Soul Guides, blasted off in a stream of Light to another destination. It was a funeral home. We watched as the Soul's family discussed cremation and burial options. The Soul was less agitated this time, spending more time observing but still at a distance.

Suddenly we departed again in the same stream of Light and headed to another setting, ostensibly designed to reduce more control of the ego over the Soul. Hovering in the patient's previous bedroom at his home, we saw two little children curled up and crying on a large bed. An adult came into the room and lay down with the kids, trying to console them. The adult ended up breaking down in tears as well.

The Mind's Eye reached out to the Soul Guides to ask for help. The guides shook their heads back and forth once; it was impossible.

'What did the Mind's Eye ask the Soul Guides just now?' whispered Ben.

A common question, replied TendHer. *The Mind's Eye requested to rematerialize to console the living.*

'So the Soul Guides are saying no?' asked Luke.

Now is not the time. More ego must be removed from the Soul to free more Soul Light. Notice the prevalence of the color Red. The Soul IS advancing but still has more insights to process. Once that happens, some Soul Guides will allow the Mind's Eye and a "Soul-body" to return the Soul as a vision to the living. It takes incredible effort to do this, but some newly released Souls are filled with so much Love they are willing to postpone their journey through the gates to help others.

'A vision,' said Charles, thinking to himself out loud.

John, quietly observing through most of the tour, now perked up. 'My aunt talked about that a lot. She said her dad came back after he died, and he thanked my aunt. My aunt said she knew it was real because there was so much Light surrounding him. Plus, there was so much clarity.'

'Meaning no disrespect, but maybe your aunt was on some type of medication. I mean, meds can easily set off a religious experience,' noted Ben.

John shook his head. 'That's what I thought. But my aunt said that she talked to others who had the same experience, and they too were definite that it was not meds or dreaming. She said she knew instantly it was the real deal. She said there was an overwhelming amount of Love coming from her dad. And my aunt said the last thing she saw was her dad collapsing into a Speck of Light in the shape of an eye. She heard him say he was in the hands of God and that my aunt was Loved more than she would ever know and not to fear death.'

Charles signaled that he wanted to say something, so John stopped talking and nodded to Charles. 'My native peoples live more in the Spirit world than the Whites. It is common for us to feel the presence of a recently passed Loved one. We know of their existence because we feel a gust of air brush our faces and bathe us in soothing whispers. Then it leaves. Really fast. But we know it is a tribal member working her way to the land of the Spirits.'

Having heard the conversation, the three Soul Guides slowly nodded their heads up and down in agreement. They then sharply turned their heads to the door.

In a blaze of Light, the group once more departed, following the Soul on its journey through death.

'Why did we leave so fast? Where's the Soul going now?' asked Luke.

The Soul is very scared. It is now trying to return to the hospital where it last remembers life. The Spirit Guides are trying another strategy to remove more ego, i.e., fear from the Soul. They will transfer his "Soul-body" back to his hospital room with my permission.

Once back in the physically empty dead patient's former hospital room where he expired, TendHer turned to the three guides and followed their gaze.

What the group saw next was utterly unexpected.

A trail of pitch-black tar seeped under the hospital room door. In a split second, the three Soul Guides flew to the spot and looked back at TendHer.

Ben gasped. 'What's goin' on with the black stuff?'

My brother has joined us.

Journal Entry Seventy-Three: Evil

'Now is the time. My time.' The words were delivered in a flat, deep, monotone voice that cracked and sizzled. Searching for the origin, the guys looked up and were surprised to find the black, tar-like ooze dripping down all four walls. The amorphous ooze poured into the hospital room from the ceiling to the floor and under the door.

Reaching out in all directions, as if trying to memorize the contours of the floor, the five streams of foul-smelling black slime slowly pooled in one spot in the middle of the room. Then the ooze changed shape. It gradually formed a block from the ground up. The edges of the block were perfect. When the height of the pitch-black block matched perfectly with the height of the three Soul Guides, it stopped growing.

At first, a perfect rectangle, the ooze slowly shifted into different shapes as it assessed and adjusted to the particular dynamics of the patient's room. The intruder had an intelligence of some sort as the block twisted its top half to survey the room, then swiveled back and forth, inspecting the setting, the patients, and the guys.

'Do you feel that?' stammered Charles. 'Something just got into my head.'

'Yeah. It feels like a hand opening parts of my brain, looking for something,' added John.

'This does not feel good,' said Ben.

Luke beat his head with both hands, trying to pummel the intrusive probe to death.

'Better stick to football, big guy,' teased Ben. 'Brain surgery is not for you!'

TendHer had been expecting the behavior of the block. *Beware, Chosen Ones, you are being probed for weakness.*

Before the guys could discuss what was happening with TendHer, the form broke into many oddly shaped pieces and hung in the air. In an instant, the pieces, all still pitch black, reassembled slowly, becoming the exact replica of a man.

'Guys, do you see who that is?' whispered Ben.

John replied at once, 'It can't be the patient. He's at the morgue.'

Minutes passed as nobody moved, including the dark stranger, now in the form of a White man, still hanging in the air by the door.

Luke interrupted the silence. 'Guys, that's Ivan!'

Charles was the only one who moved closer to the human form, more curious than fearful.

John saw the danger and called out to Charles. 'Better let TendHer handle this, Charles.'

After ordering the three guides to her side, TendHer said, *Yes, I was expecting this.*

'Expecting this? Ivan was eaten alive by maggots!' Ben cried. 'Why would Ivan show up now? How could you be expecting this?'

Muttering unintelligible sounds, the form shaped like Ivan turned dark again and strained to create words. His speech was forced and unnatural, words jumbled and twisted, his mouth forming unnaturally wide, gaping shapes. The sounds didn't match the movements of the mouth, in an asynchrony that made the figure only seem more like a puppet than a man.

"Like my new costume?" The Ivan-like figure turned around in jerky, erratic movements. Maggots feasted on the black sludge oozing out of the many small sores. "Isn't the effect spine-chilling?"

TendHer did not respond to the questions. Instead, she replied, *Do what you have come to do, but leave the theatrics out of it. And you do not need to talk out loud. We can hear your thoughts, as I'm sure you can hear ours.*

Ivan's body mockingly moved his lips out of sync with a voice. 'Oh, very well, dear Sister. You're so touchy.'

John could wait no further. 'TendHer, please tell us what's happening here! Should we be doing something to save Ivan?'

TendHer motioned the guys to join her and the guides at the head of the bed and to the side. *That is not Ivan.*

TendHer continued. *This is NoOne's moment. He has the right to test the recently released Soul. It's part of the Bardo transition.*

'What's he gonna ask?' Ben screeched.

Luke burst out, 'Will you shut up and let the woman, I mean, God speak?'

'She doesn't speak, numbnuts. She's thinking to us! And she's not God, she's TendHer, and she can kick this dude's butt,' yelled Ben. Then realizing he had just insulted the Devil, Ben slid behind TendHer for protection.

Charles also backed up and said to Ben, 'Be like a Native and spend more time listening than talking. Definitely stop the screaming, Ben!'

Surprised at Charles' unusual intervention, Ben and Luke released a 'Whoa, dude!' at the same time.

TendHer continued describing the Bardo. *I have ordered the Soul Guides to re-manifest his physical body. My brother will be sure to follow.*

'Here?' asked Ben.

Luke joined Ben in expressing surprise. 'As in his real, real body? I thought it was at the funeral home?'

You are correct.

Suddenly a shadowy copy of the dead person's physical body appeared. Its ego joyfully danced around the specter. Its exhilaration because of its apparent reunification with its former physical body was to be short-lived.

'Is that what I think it is?' muttered John.

No. His physical remains are elsewhere. I have returned his "Soul-Body" here to provide a reference for the Soul. And for you. Come. Get closer.

'The ego sure seems happy!' observed Luke.

'I'll bet that won't last long when it finds out the Devil's here!' added Ben.

Moving closer to the Mind's Eye and its Soul hovering around the patient's head, the four guys were fascinated with the energy that suddenly burst from the Soul's surface. Ben continued, 'Some of the ego's dark sludge just got removed. Now I know the ego is pissed. Look at all the energy freed up. It's blinding!'

'Wow!' added Luke. 'The ego is just hanging on the Soul Light. It looks determined and desperate. And it's beating like it has a heart or something.'

'Ah, TendHer, the…ah…the ego looks like it has a life of its own,' said John.

TendHer continued. *That's the power of the ego. It survives and thrives if it can convince its host that it is real. But the ego is not real. It's an illusion built around the need to control and protect the person from pain and fear. The strongest fear is based on our strongest need. Can you tell me what those are?*

'Oh. I love tests. The strongest need is to survive?' answered Ben.

TendHer nodded. *And our most substantial fear, Benjamin?*

'I'm the only one of us guys you call by name. Should I feel special or totally screwed?'

Impatient to move on to the next step in their journey, Luke interrupted. 'Answer the question, dude!'

Ben stared at Luke and gave him the "Mind-finger." 'OK, my best friend who is really a jockstrap in disguise. Give me a second. And our strongest fear is death?'

Charles tuned right into what TendHer was describing. 'So the ego is kind of a Spiritual band-aid?'

Yes. During the Bardo, NoOne visits each Soul and acts as a movie projector for any fears present. NoOne amplifies the fear and anxiety, trying to destroy as much Light as possible within the Soul. If he successfully covers most of the Soul's Light, I will likely judge the Soul irreparably damaged and send it to the SuperVoid.

At that point, the replica of Ivan began to transform into another image. The black components moved around like a Tetris game, scurrying up and down, right and left, until a new body shape was formed. It looked like a man, but the figure struggled to keep its body parts in place.

At least the guys didn't have to look at Ivan's doppelganger any longer.

The dark figure standing in the middle of the room shifted into different shapes. The patient's Soul became increasingly confused, alarmed, and agitated. With the tense struggle between its parasitic ego and its protective Mind's Eye, the patient's Soul was clearly conflicted. Suddenly, the Soul launched itself away from the patient's "Soul-body" and perched itself high up on the ceiling, shivering with fright.

Then the Soul sprinted toward the door but was aggressively blocked by NoOne, still in the form of Ivan. Diving toward the floor, the Soul bounced against the floor tiles, unaware of the limits on its movement by TendHer. It flew back across the room and finally came to rest on the far windowsill. The Soul looked exhausted as it struggled to rid itself of its quivering, terrified ego.

TendHer continued. *NoOne has become the evil personified, long repressed by the Soul. As you can see, the Soul is hiding, trying to escape the evil.*

'It looks OK to me!' said Ben.

Let me take you inside the Soul, and you can experience the pain generated by the ego and its Karma, said TendHer.

All four guys saw and felt the same thing. They shrank to the size of an atom and found themselves inside the Soul, looking out. They felt the weight of the ego, which was clinging to its Light host, sucking Spiritual energy, pounding sheer terror and doom into the Soul.

The guys watched a drama unfold. NoOne, still appearing as Ivan, summoned selective Soul Pages from 'beyond the Veil'. The Pages were then projected as life events in the middle of the room for the Soul to watch. The Mind's Eye could do nothing to stop the increasingly fearful, dark sludge that smothered even more Light from the Soul.

'This is painful,' announced John. 'TendHer, what do we do?'

Nothing. You are experiencing NoOne's life review process. He selectively chooses historical snippets, almost always undesirable, to make the Soul capitulate to his demands.

'These are terrible things I'm seeing. Surely this Soul is damned,' said John.

TendHer replied. *Not necessarily. Some people need longer to see the Light. And people can change. That is why we send Mentors to guide strayed Souls who have prayed for help. Evil can never be erased, but it can be somewhat overwritten by compensating with good deeds. It's a scale that I alone can balance.*

'Overwritten enough to get to you, rather than being sent to Hell?' asked Ben.

Yes. It is challenging but possible. Sadly, the Soul we are now observing is close to the point of no redemption.

Now projected externally, the four guys shared the period of life when the darkened Soul was almost completely covered with ego: the person was a cruel, selfish landlord. He lacked compassion and empathy and was driven to maximize profit and power. They saw children hungry and shivering due to the cold in an apartment where the heat had been turned off. They saw frantic parents pleading for mercy, crying to not be thrown out onto the street in subfreezing temperatures. They saw the man laughing and taunting the poor tenants who couldn't afford shoes for their children, forcing the parents to use cardboard and string to hold together worn-out shoes.

TendHer spoke. *This is ego Karma. Pure Souls speed to the Funnel and the First Gate. Some Souls with heavy negative Karma, such as this Soul, are forced by NoOne to experience what they have forced others to experience in their life.*

'And this is what NoOne does to try to win Souls? Making a Soul look at its evil Karma?' asked John.

TendHer continued. *Yes. The evil Karma is so deep that the Soul clings to the ego because it provides security. NoOne simply presents the mirror to reflect back the evil. That creates more pain.*

John interrupted, '…which builds a more enormous ego for defense?'

Precisely, said TendHer. *It's an endless cycle that results in the continued growth of the ego tumor. It is almost impossible to stop once it begins. However, it can be ended with a Mind's Eye revelation, which is usually based on trauma. As I mentioned, people can change.*

The figure suddenly disappeared in the middle of the room, turning into a lump of black tar lying on the floor. It then transformed from the bottom up into an image that was the exact copy of TendHer.

Ah, you haven't seen this part, TendHer, muttered the black tar.

TendHer stood absolutely still, staring at what appeared to be her identical twin across the room. Then, backing away, the guys moved to the side of the room with the Spirit Guides.

NoOne, stop! uttered TendHer.

'I have come to give this Soul a choice. Just as I have given billions of others.'

The Soul descended slowly from the corner ceiling and moved to the center of the room facing NoOne.

As the duplicate image of TendHer, NoOne smirked as he presented his offer to the Soul. His voice was soft and tender, like TendHer's, yet the guys detected a slight tone of condescension and sarcasm.

'You can stop this pain and terror. You need not suffer. You have to give yourself to me. Then you may join my minions.'

Luke uttered what the other guys were thinking. 'TendHer, can't you stop this?'

The TendHer shook her head. Turning to us, she said, *There is nothing I can do. The Soul in each person must make the choice.*

'But I thought you did the judging in the Reincarnation Universe?' asked Luke.

'Yeah, and what about the gates?' added Ben.

TheOne has given NoOne the power to present ego Karma-covered Souls the option of terminating their reincarnation cycle early by following NoOne instead of proceeding to the Funnel with their Spirit Guides.

John saw the implications. 'So that's where he's getting his army on Earth.'

Overhearing John's comment, NoOne again smirked. 'And that's why I will soon be giving this same choice to you four. Your bodies are inches away from death….'

In perfect unity, the guys gasped.

Noting the guys' reaction and attempting to change the subject, TendHer interrupted NoOne. *Yet, the Soul must choose.*

Suspended in midair in the group's center, the Soul started to shift from side to side.

'The Soul has made its decision. It has chosen to come with me,' announced NoOne. 'So be it.'

The Soul disappeared.

'Before I go, let me show you where it went,' said NoOne.

As a single dark spot in the middle of the room, energy ripples began to emanate outward. Then, as the dark spot expanded wider and wider in concentric circles, a vision portal opened in the middle of the room, giving the group a peek into another part of the universe.

As the center of the portal began to shift into a larger perspective, John was the first to identify the image. 'It looks like a tail.'

The portal moved at high speed and blasted closer to a vantage point that captured a more detailed image. 'Yeah, a big tail. Look at the nearby stars to get a perspective,' said Ben.

'What are those squiggly things in the tail?' asked Luke.

'They look like eyes!' said Charles.

'Yeah, they do look like eyes. What are they doing?' asked Luke.

Ben saw the detail. 'They're jumping up and down. As much as they can 'cause they're all crammed together. It looks like they….'

'Go ahead, say it', commanded NoOne.

Ben gulped. 'If they could make sounds, they would be screaming.'

'Look, the image is zooming in closer,' said Ben.

'What is it? Why are we now seeing just one eye?' asked Luke.

John spoke what was soon apparent to all. 'It's the Soul that was with us. It's more active than the others.'

Yes. It's pleading to be saved. It has not yet accepted that it will be tormented for all time, said TendHer.

'How many eyes, I mean Souls, are in that tail?' asked Ben.

TendHer began to fold in on herself, becoming smaller and smaller. *There are more Souls in the Viper's tail than in the Reincarnation Universe. Therefore, you must return to your bodies and prepare.*

'Wait, prepare for what?' questioned Luke. 'What do we prepare for?'

Ben looked at Luke and nodded his head in agreement. 'Yeah, TendHer, prepare for what?'

Your transition, whispered TendHer as she became smaller and smaller.

In a panic, Ben blurted out, 'What do you mean by "your transition?"'

No answer.

Finally, Charles found the word everyone was dreading. The thought he sent to the others was *death*.

TendHer's last words were chilling. *You must return to your bodies. Now! Your sentry, who you call the New Twin, is being attacked.*

Journal Entry Seventy-Four: A Conversation

The Old Twin thought that once giving in to human weaknesses like emotion and compassion, the power that was gifted from NoOne would be lost.

My brother will be a cripple. He is dead to me; no longer of use. And dead to our father as well, thought the Old Twin. *Removing him from existence will be easy.*

The Old Twin's confidence soared. With each passing moment, more and more Souls were worming their way to NoOne's great Snake. Sure, his brother would put up a fight. Sure, the New Twin would gather sycophants to battle, but there was no way the New Twin could contest the power of NoOne's Dark Matter.

Did I say, "worming?" chuckled the Old Twin. *How clever. Guess the great Snake of LostSouls could be described as a worm as it slithers around looking for the Funnel.*

"And, oh, what a prize it will be when we find its entrance!" uttered the Old Twin out loud.

Should I make my brother suffer?

The answer for the Old Twin was easy, uncompromised by ambiguity or conflict. *Of course, he will suffer. He will suffer because it will be an exciting and new experience for me. I will see how firm my brother's resolve is when he finally greets his mortality.*

The Old Twin was not surprised when confronted by numerous animal guards at the mountain lair where the four boys rested. *Couldn't my brother be more creative than this? Really? A few Cougars and Black Bears. What an insult. They will soon lose their eyes.*

Before the Old Twin could dispatch the animal sentries, his brother walked out of the cave. The New Twin ordered the animal sentries to depart. He didn't want them to become pawns in the war of wills soon to follow.

The New Twin talked first. "Brother. Let's sit and talk. I want to tell you…."

The Old Twin thought, *He's showing his hand! He never would have done that in our years together.*

Before the New Twin continued, the Old Twin lashed out with as much psychic power as he could muster. A stream of blackness shot out of the Old Twin's eyes, aimed squarely at the New Twin.

The New Twin was not expecting such an immediate eruption of violence. He struggled to shutter his mind from the onslaught of psychic daggers.

"Wait, brother. We need to talk before we fight," pleaded the New Twin.

The Old Twin had never seen his brother so weak. Never before had he seen his brother beg for consideration. "I've said all I want to say," the Old Twin said calmly. With those words, the Old Twin shot straight up in the air. Looking down, the Old Twin focused his venom on the mountainside directly behind the New Twin. With a slight twitch of his head, huge boulders exploded outward and thundered down the slope, blocking the cave opening where the four guys hid.

The New Twin sidestepped the rocketing boulders and tumbling debris with a relaxed demeanor, keeping his eye on the cave entrance. He managed to divert just enough boulders to keep the entrance clear. The New Twin knew he had to keep this entrance open if the four guys needed to escape.

"Protecting your precious new friends?" taunted the Old Twin, flying circles high above and around the cave.

Standing guard at the cave opening, the New Twin was nonplussed. "You know you cannot defeat me. We are equal in our powers."

"No, you're wrong. Your newfound compassion has weakened you. I feel the softness in you," responded the Old Twin.

"And I feel the return of my friends. They have returned to their bodies," proclaimed the New Twin. "And other friends from the sky are heading this way."

The Old Twin was not used to being caught off guard. The Old Twin had unknowingly lost half of his intuitive radar without his brother. Because of his preoccupation with his brother, the Old Twin had missed the thousands of Eagles cruising a thousand feet above, heading right for him.

Stumbling out of the cave, just recently returned from their journey with TendHer, the four guys shielded their eyes from the bright sun. They muttered comments of relief to each other, and thanks to TendHer, wherever she was, incredulous they had made it this far and were safe.

Boo also emerged, walked up to Charles, and started to whine. Stepping in front of the other three, Charles surveyed the land from the cave's entrance, glanced up at the sky, and thanked his Mentor, Bestow, for transmitting his plea for help.

Charles knew his brothers and sisters of the sky would come to his aid but was shocked to see so many. Eagles of all sizes from all over the globe flew in, wave upon wave, in perfect formation, diving down to distract the Old Twin. Charles thanked the animals briefly, for he knew there was only a brief window of opportunity for the guys to escape with the New Twin.

For the first time ever, the Old Twin was bewildered about how to respond to an adversary. The squadrons of Eagles couldn't hurt him. Surely, they knew that. And he was obliterating hundreds of the beasts. But they just kept coming. Why would they keep diving at him, knowing they were surely doomed?

It took but a moment for the Old Twin to figure it out. His brother, the four guys, and the Dog beast had disappeared. Erecting a hundred-foot impenetrable invisible bubble around him, the Old Twin struggled to see where his brother and friends were headed. The Old Twin's vision continued to be blocked as the Eagles refused to retreat. This gave the guys and Boo just enough time to find a new temporary hiding place.

The New Twin used the same technique. He created an energy bubble for the four guys and Boo with his psychic energy. Once they were all safely inside the bubble, the New Twin propelled the invisible shell with its occupants to a place he thought his brother would never look. It was the one landscape ignored by NoOne—the ocean.

It was but a fraction of a second when the bubble cocoon with all its occupants sat peacefully in a kelp bed on the bottom of the Pacific Ocean, about 50 feet offshore. Inquisitive creatures meandered peacefully by, curving their way through the undulating green kelp bulbs. An octopus jetted away, disturbed from its rocky den. It paused just long enough to probe the invisible shield with its eight arms, tapping it and then zooming out, leaving a quick burst of dark protective liquid. Once the ocean bottom silt settled back to the sea bottom, various rockfish swam around the bubble, confident that all was back to normal.

Boo was in Heaven, swiveling and trotting in many directions to glimpse the passing sea-life wonders. His eyes opened wide, and the guys could tell Boo wanted to bark. Letting his tongue hang out would have to suffice for now.

Ben broke the awe-inspired silence. "Ah, guys…we're at the bottom of the ocean."

"And your second clue was?" Luke replied playfully.

John was next and addressed the New Twin. "This has to be safe. I haven't heard any mention of NoOne planting corpses underwater. Isn't that right?"

The New Twin concentrated on maintaining the bubble, so he told the guys his answers would be brief. "That's why I picked this spot. You should be safe to journey to 'beyond the Veil' from here."

"And you're safe here too, aren't you?" asked Ben.

The New Twin nodded his head in agreement. "As safe as one could be while my brother is loose."

Straining to catch a glimpse of what looked like a small Salmon Shark, Charles was not happy to be crammed into the bubble. "What should we do next? Just sit here and wait? How long can we hold out?"

Before anyone could answer, what appeared to be logs passed their bubble; then turned and made another pass, brushing against the force field of the bubble.

The guys strained to see the logs more clearly, approaching the edge of the bubble.

"How can logs get this deep? I thought they floated," said Luke.

"I, ah, don't think those are logs. Logs don't make one-eighty turns," replied Ben.

Straining to make out the long objects, Charles was the first to identify them. "Those are corpses."

"Oh, crap, they're dead bodies!" cried Ben.

As the corpses closed in on the bubble, the guys watched in anticipatory fear, expecting something dramatic to jeopardize their safe haven. Swaying and drifting with the underwater current, it was a matter of moments until four of the corpses bumped head-on into the bubble.

Ben saw it first. "They have no eyes."

"Are we sure they're dead?" asked Luke.

"There's your answer," replied Charles. The four corpses became animated. Standing vertically in the water, they stroked their way to the bubble, stretched out their palms, and ran them down the smooth, invisible bubble surface, heads jerking toward each of the occupants inside the bubble. Because the corpses did not have eyes, the guys caught a glimpse of worms moving in and out of their deep eye socket pits.

"Can they get to us?" Ben choked out.

The New Twin was hardly reassuring. "Don't think so. I'm still trying to sort out what powers I have. It's not like the old days when I had my brother. Then, I knew we were invincible. Now that we're separated, I'm not so sure which powers are diminished."

Eager for reassurance, Luke asked, "OK, do you think we've been found out? Do you think these corpses will report back to NoOne?"

"Ah, guys. What's that dark spot in the distance?" said Luke.

"Can't see very far, but it's getting closer and coming toward us," reported Charles.

The dark spot approached the bubble rapidly. It certainly had the group's attention as they huddled in the protective round shell.

"Oh, man, that is gross!" screamed Ben.

"Yuck," howled Luke.

The New Twin immediately saw the attack and beefed up his concentration. "Those are the eyes of NoOne," he calmly said. "They have been partially eaten by the sea creatures. I'll bet the corpses alerted NoOne that we are here."

The dark spot gradually got closer. It spread out from its core, quickly filling the circumference of the guys' visual field, finally completely enveloping the invisible protective bubble. Eye upon eye stacked up as if all were frantic to get inside the underwater dome. The bubble began to bow and twist inward from all the pressure.

"Don't we need to get out of here, like quick?" pleaded Ben.

The guys and Boo moved back from the edge of the bubble, trying to get as close to the New Twin as they could.

After what seemed like hours, the New Twin finally spoke. The guys saw the concern in his expression.

Replying to Charles, the New Twin calmly suggested that Charles reach out to his friends in nature. "Best do it now," he added.

"Why don't we just get out of here?" asked Ben.

The New Twin answered in a quiet, soothing voice. "My friends, I need all my energy to keep this bubble from crushing. I'm afraid I must acknowledge my limits. If I had the assistance of my brother, it would be no problem."

"OK. Leave it to me, then," said Charles. "I'm getting some big dudes to help us."

And big they were. Resident Pacific Sound Orcas received the call for help from Charles. Three Whales (called such even though technically they are Dolphins) were in the vicinity, and the guys immediately heard their stirring calls echoing through the water. Quickly locating Charles' Spirit, the Orcas were at the bubble in less than five minutes.

As the Whales circled the bubble, sediment from the bottom stirred and mixed with the dark shapes of the eyes. Initially, the occupants of the bubble barely made out the shapes of the Orcas. But they felt everything. Taking turns, the Orcas continued to pass around the bubble, swallowing thousands of eyes with each pass. The bubble swayed back and forth with small gentle bumps letting the occupants know the Whales were doing their work. Inch by inch, the army of eyes was eaten as if they were part of the Whales' regular diet, one of the more-than-one-hundred species that the Orcas consumed on any given day. New eyes continued to take the place of consumed eyes, but they were no match for the voracious Whales. It took an hour for the whales to consume them all. Finally, the transparent bubble skin again provided an unobstructed view of its ocean-depth surroundings.

Charles relayed the thanks from the group. The whales whirled playfully away and then twirled back towards the guys, making a group pass above and around the bubble. A gigantic underwater current thrust the bubble forward further out to sea along the ocean floor. The Orcas' mouths seemed to smile in friendship and a spirit of playfulness; their receding, undulating tails flashed a message of farewell.

"I'm afraid this is just the beginning. I'm sure my brother is cooking up a new threat to attack us."

John knew their only option was for him to reconnoiter. "Maybe I should go to the gap and see what's going on?"

The New Twin agreed. Shaking his head up and down but still not losing his concentration, the New Twin panted, "The sooner, the better."

Journal Entry Seventy-Five: Sensei and the Funnel

While the New Twin was relocating the four guys and Boo to a different location in the still intact bubble, John left his body and began the long reconnaissance below 'beyond the Veil'. An eerie sense of foreboding started to consume John's "Soul-head." Mentally shivering with anticipation, John knew he had to keep his thoughts focused on being receptive to any sign of danger that might suddenly appear.

It seemed like years since John had meandered leisurely through empty space. It was so quiet, so peaceful. Now, blazing distant stars hung limply in the distance, just like then, not caring or concerned with the universal drama unfolding. John hoped to remain as calm when the inevitable ordeal began.

John knew that even though he felt he had been absent a long time, his friends in the material world would have experienced only a few seconds. He still felt pressure to find the Funnel and formulate a defensive strategy as soon as possible.

The reason why the four had been chosen by TheSon now seemed much clearer. They were the protectors of the Funnel and the Gates. If breached, the entire Reincarnation Universe would be destroyed. Souls lost forever. Creation no longer Becoming. Being reduced to NoThing.

Suddenly John sensed a presence. At first alarmed, he relaxed as a calming invisible force surrounded him. John was hesitant, but then remembered when he had that same feeling. It was like the trips John took while studying with his Sensei; it seemed eons ago, being in the dojo and making the map of the universe.

John tried to ascertain the intent of the breeze. Was it a threat? Could it be a distraction from the Old Twin to trick John?

No, he thought. *This air is the same air I felt so many times while on my gap trips. I just need to flow. This breeze is a sign of help arriving, like in the old days, when I was lying in a mountain meadow, becoming one with all of Creation.*

He remembered when he had a purpose, a mission to become the best he could be. He was admired and respected.

In a flash, John recognized the presence. 'Thank you, Sensei,' thought John. 'You told me you would come for me when I was needed. So, this is the beginning. I am ready.'

Sensei slowly circled John. With each rotation, an invisible layer of air armor radiated from Sensei's presence, protectively coating John's "Soul-body." John submitted to the breeze and let it whirl around him; it was velvety soft and soothing.

Yes, John. I have come to help you find the portal to the Funnel and prepare for battle. Even though we are not entering the Funnel, you will need this armor to protect your Mind's Eye from stress as we might encounter realities too crushing for regular gap travel. And it will protect you from NoOne's Dark Matter.

John's energy and morale soared. He had hoped Sensei would show himself, even though John knew the Sensei was a much needed and relied upon Spirit, a bodhisattva Soul, a Mentor delaying reunion with TheOne to serve others in need on Earth.

'You're taking me back to the Funnel, aren't you?'

Yes.

In a whoosh of energy, John blasted to another location.

Behold.

Still slightly dizzy, John asked, 'Sensei, am I supposed to be looking at that small, blinking dot out there?'

Watch closely. The small dot, as you call it, is really a hole. It is a physical opening, yet at the same time part Spiritual. It's constantly changing its location within every universe. It crosses dimensions, so the same Funnel simultaneously exists in all universes within all multiverses. It's always moving. It never has a predictable pattern. It was created by the Creator to call forth the dead. Souls are pulled to wherever it is located within a particular universe. And we call it the Funnel.

'Sensei, what do you mean the "the same Funnel exists simultaneously in all universes?"'

Don't think of the Funnel as a dot on a piece of paper. Think of it as a single hole punched through an uncountable number of pages folded over.

'Like a wormhole?'

Precisely, yes.

The breeze increased in intensity; enveloping John even tighter. *If NoOne finds the Funnel location, he will penetrate it. Then our only chance to stop him will be at one of the Gates deep in the Funnel. That is where you, John, must make your stand.*

John wanted all the information he could get. 'Sensei, will you be there to help me?'

I don't know. For now, you must witness the prize NoOne seeks.

A wisp of air directed John's attention to something barely perceptible in the distance. He felt another nudge from Sensei to look even further out. Together they zoomed toward the dot of Light, the Funnel entrance.

Coming to a stop while they were still at a distance from the Funnel opening, John saw and heard buzzing and vibrating. The Funnel opened and closed in rhythm to imbibe the ascending Souls. When open, the Funnel was a round tube filled with radiant energy. As the dead swirled in a cloud and were sucked into the Funnel hole, John noted it briefly closed leaving nothing but empty space. Then John saw that occasionally the Funnel disgorged Souls rather than sucking them in.

'Sensei, the Funnel looks like it's a two-way street. Souls are sucked in, but souls are being spat out as well,' observed John.

Yes. The exiting Souls are on their way to their new homes.

They've been judged?

They have been judged and assigned a new host body to continue to work off their blemished Karma.

'They're coming to babies on Earth! Can we move closer?'

John and Sensei approached the parade of newly ejected Souls. Frenetic activity surrounded John. Souls momentarily acknowledged him, floated by, and watched. Some were curious, puzzled as to why they could see a physical entity observing them. All were at peace and unphased by the unknown that lay ahead on the Funnel tunnel to a new life.

'This is where the Snake is headed, right?'

Yes, John. This is the prize that NoOne covets. It's the key to his plan. Do you not see the number of Souls that he could forage for his Snake?

'I couldn't begin to count them. How do we defeat him?'

John was sure Sensei would now disclose a well-thought-out war strategy for how the Snake could be defeated.

A long pause followed. John sensed Sensei was troubled. He had hoped Sensei had a firm, guaranteed plan ready to share. John was wrong.

I don't know.

Journal Entry Seventy-Six: Forbidden Territory

Although a billion times larger than the typical Black Hole, the Funnel left no clues as to its presence. Streaming simultaneously through billions of universes, the Funnel defied detection, rejecting the logic of physics, presenting itself simultaneously in every universe ever created, hiding in gravitational singularities, dedicated to sucking and propelling recently released Souls to the 'beyond the Veil' and the First Gate. And spewing recently judged Souls back to a pitiful physical existence.

Such complexity was deliciously challenging for NoOne. He vowed to never give up. And his vow was finally paying off. His one dutiful son had made the discovery NoOne had waited eons to behold.

The Old Twin has been useful after all, thought NoOne.

Upon being given the task of tracking the four guys, the Old Twin recorded their psychic frequencies. Their every movement was tracked and recorded. If any of them tried to leave the New Twin's bubble, the Old Twin could trace their every move. And especially, if any of them tried to visit the Funnel, he was to notify NoOne at once.

Which he did.

Sensei and John had no idea they were being followed. Nor that they had inadvertently exposed the Funnel's general location. The Old Twin alerted NoOne as to his prized discovery.

Father, the boy John and his Mentor are at the Funnel. I can send you the coordinates. It is always moving and shifting, but they are there right now.

As John and Sensei were exploring the Funnel, NoOne commanded a platoon of resurrected corpses armored with Dark Matter to lurk behind a star and wait for them to depart. NoOne had given the corpses explicit instructions not to give away their presence or location. Soon after John returned to his body in the New Twin's protective bubble, the platoon contacted NoOne. Twisting and curling around the Funnel, the platoon moved in a holding pattern, waiting for instructions from NoOne, watching recently deceased Souls be dispassionately slurped into the Funnel's maw each and every second. And new Souls spit out to merge with awaiting new physical containers.

NoOne was ecstatic. *Merge and purge! Or is it purge and re-emerge? How quaint!*

The news of the Funnel discovery by NoOne spread instantly throughout all multiverses. The Orbs knew that NoOne's discovery of the Funnel was a Celestial perturbation and would force TheOne to Be. Orbs signaled other Orbs from every dimension to address a cosmic urgency. The energy from the frantic transmissions moved TheOne to consolidate His Will in the Divine Foam. Layer upon layer of Orbs swarmed to bear witness to His emanation. They also knew they would eventually be called upon to defend its existence.

TheOne of the Present sighed as the future could be read if He chose to do so. Gladly sharing Love and freedom of choice, TheOne would not look at TheOne of the Future lest it influence His gift. Nevertheless, He knew now that He must intervene for the sake of His Creation.

TheOne thought. *NoOne. I have forbidden your presence near the Funnel as it is part of My domain in 'beyond the Veil'. Return to your SuperVoid.*

'You gave me permission to winnow the weak. It makes sense that I should assist in judgment at the Four Gates.'

You are forbidden to enter, repeated TheOne.

'TheSon can. Why can't I?' tested NoOne.

TheOne sighed, *TheSon chose the path of Light. You chose the path of Darkness. Once again.*

'I have only done what you commanded.'

TheOne flared in blinding Light, a trillion trillion stars bursting in ecstasy at the Sacred words coming from the Creator of life for all time.

You shall cease.

Crying out from an eternity of pain and rage from hopeless rejection, NoOne exploded: 'Since the beginning, You chose TheSon over me.'

You will forever be enslaved until you choose the Way of Love, replied TheOne.

NoOne was furious. 'Then I will forever be the enemy of TheSon. The world of rock and dirt and sweat is all there will be. I will continue to patrol all your universes, sucking Souls to Hell that you do not want in your precious Kingdom. And I will enter Your Funnel and conquer the 'beyond the Veil' when and if I please.'

TheOne paused. He finally sighed with a softness born of eternal wisdom: *I will always be waiting for you. But until you see the Light, you will be separate from all that is good in My Creation. You shall be no more respected than the centipedes of the Earth; no more fertile than the rocks in the soil; no more radiant than the void from which I created you.*

NoOne could only mutter what he had always uttered, hopelessly trapped in his twisted logic of evil. As long as TheSon and TendHer were around, NoOne would always be third on his Father's list. That fact, plain and simple, sent NoOne into a rage and filled him with anger at himself for even contemplating pleasing his Father, the Creator.

With defiance, NoOne shouted at TheOne for all to hear: 'Ready your favorite Son. Tell Him that He will be permitted to incarnate all He wants in my SuperVoid. And I shall incarnate all I want in the physical domain. Tell your favorite daughter, TendHer, this: She may judge only those I desire to cast off. So be it, Father. I am the "it," and I shall disobey You. So be it.'

With a passion born of a Father's unrequited Love, TheOne tenderly mourned once more the loss of His most glorious Creation.

So be it, My beautiful Son. So be it.

Journal Entry Seventy-Seven: The Gathering

NoOne gave the command to attack. His legion of Snake Soul-Judged Evil Eyes and Soulless corpses made one final turn to position itself for the Funnel invasion. The cavernous jaw at the front of NoOne's Snake was the ultimate weapon, a dramatic effect that would give more than a moment's pause to those NoOne hunted.

NoOne knew TheSon watched and chuckled at his Brother having to wallow in impotence just as he, NoOne, had suffered through eons of powerlessness. Yes, TheSon was a true sycophant. NoOne never had a chance of becoming his Father's favorite thanks to TheSon's pathetic flattering servility.

Until now. NoOne was sure he could make his Father reconsider the place and power NoOne had in the Heavens. All NoOne had to do was provide proof. A jaw of Dead Souls that could swallow entire planets and stars was proof enough. TheOne would be forced to finally accept NoOne's true worth. He thrilled at the vision of TheSon bowing before him, finally acknowledging the superiority of NoOne's authority and command.

Yes! thought NoOne. *I have more than enough troops to contest and overpower the guardians of the Four Gates, whoever and whatever they may be. At this moment, I am scouring the multiverses for more planets to purloin. Once I take over, the Funnel will be mine to control. And ultimately, the Reincarnation Universe.*

Projecting his presence to the mouth of his Snake, NoOne commanded: *Come, my loyal children, and flock together. To me. Join in outrage and fury to overthrow the illusions of the Spirit and the Spiritual.*

The eternally lost did come forth, finally strong enough to break through the SuperVoid gate. From their eternal prison, Souls judged evil by TendHer from all eons spilled through the SuperVoid's previously impenetrable gate, rushing in a torrential, perpetual stream to join NoOne's Snake at the opening to the Funnel.

From all regions of TheOne's Creation, the evil, the wicked, the putrid, the partially decomposed, the corrupt, and the depraved gushed toward the Snake, stunned at the unexpected power that rescued them, surprised at their reprieve from eternal torment. The recently departed, the many long-buried in wretched sin, the hideous, the lifeless, the hopeless, the life forms long ago judged by NoOne and crushed to ashes and dirt arose and rushed to NoOne's coercive mandate.

NoOne was pleased. With powers never before realized, NoOne's Dark Matter swelled in majesty and glory as it glued together the Soulless eyes into the Snake's body surface. He felt he was free at last from the last thread of loyalty to the Creator. He felt validated in his mission, convinced of his success, having finally broken through the chains of paternal regulatory constraint.

With his Snake of evil finally truly formidable, NoOne bellowed out his command for more Dark Matter to come forward and accumulate in its structure. Dark Matter from every multiverse rushed to cling to it in an unholy embrace, dense and deep, unlike any other epoch in Creation, forming for the first time in history a solid visual mass of true evil. The Snake swelled to trillions of miles of Dark Matter, its girth completely smothering entire galaxies and the solar systems residing within.

NoOne leisurely floated around his beloved Snake, his inky sable form caressing the Snake's skin like a child. The screams of terror and anguish emitted by trapped, ambivalent Souls sounded like soothing music to NoOne.

NoOne's moment of triumph was at hand.

Journal Entry Seventy-Eight: Heading Out

We are done, thought Sensei. *Time for you to gather your warriors and begin to prepare. I sense NoOne's Snake is close to the Funnel. You must return to the material world. Now.*

'OK, Sensei. Any last words of advice?'

Goodbye. My time with you is done.

John panicked. 'Sensei, what do you mean your time is done?'

John, I have been informed we were followed. NoOne has located the Funnel. I must return to join TheSon's troops.

'Oh,' thought John. 'So, you won't merge with TheOne yet?'

No, replied Sensei. *I will be needed in the battle that looms. We will yet reunite to protect the Reincarnation Universe.*

'When will I see you again? You always seem to show up when I need you the most.'

Then so be it, my best student. So be it, my best friend.

Those words blasted John's Mind's Eye and Soul back to the Pacific Ocean. He located the New Twin and his fellow soon-to-be warriors hiding in a cave embedded in deep Pacific waters. The guys were soundly snoring.

The New Twin looked exhausted; he could barely acknowledge John's return. A smile gradually formed on his little mouth. "I'm glad you're here. I sense my brother is close to finding us once more. We have to find a new hiding space. So, what did you learn?"

John sat and petted Boo. He was relieved he could talk out loud again. "We must get to 'beyond the Veil' as soon as possible. My Mentor and I accidentally led NoOne to the Funnel, and he will soon start attacking the Funnel. From there, his evil ones will proceed to the First Gate."

The New Twin sighed. "So, it is down to that. The First Gate. My brother and I have often heard of the Four Gates. But there's no way he could go there now because I'm here. He has to keep looking for me."

John shook his head in agreement. "That's what we hope anyway. I don't think we have a chance if your brother is waiting for us at the Funnel." John started to pet Boo. Happy to be massaged, Boo mimicked John, nodding his head up and down and swishing his tail back and forth in perfect rhythm.

"You must protect our bodies when we're gone," said John. "If your brother overtakes you and destroys our bodies, we will be stuck in 'beyond the Veil' forever, which may not be such a bad idea upon reflection."

Now it was the New Twin's time to nod, only in disagreement. "No. You four were chosen by TheSon for a reason. He knows you will prevail for all of us. You must!"

The other guys stirred from their naps. Stretching and yawning, Ben, as usual, was the first to share his opinion. "I think this bubble is worse than the nuthouse! And it's beginning to smell like a locker room."

Luke snickered. "What would you know about a locker room?"

Ben ignored Luke's dig. "It's time to head out, isn't it, John?"

"Yeah, John, what did you discover?" asked Charles.

Charles didn't receive a reply. Something massive hit the bubble dead on sending the guys bouncing off the sides. They landed in a great heap.

"What the hell was that?" screamed Ben.

"Oh my God. We're being attacked by Sharks!" said Luke.

A massive school of Great White Sharks had attacked the bubble, pushing it out of the cave and moving it further out to sea. The guys were spellbound as the Sharks snapped their massive jaws up and down, and swiveled their gigantic tails in all directions, rows of razor-sharp teeth frantically snapping at the invisible shell.

The guys tumbled around inside the shell as it rolled further into deeper waters.

Ben wanted to make sure the New Twin could keep the bubble intact. "Can you keep this pressure up? We could be crushed any minute!"

"I'm being crushed from your body, dude!" exclaimed Luke.

The New Twin summoned his deepest energy reserves. "I'm trying. I'm trying!" He used every ounce of strength to reinforce the shell's integrity and protect it from the ferocity of the beasts frozen in a Paleogene prehistoric stage of evolution.

John eyed his friends. He slowly enunciated each word. "Yes. It's time. It's time to head out. The war has begun."

"What do we do about our bodies here?" asked Luke.

"Trust the New Twin," said John. "Can we count on you?"

"I'll try," was the only response the New Twin could come up with. "Leave. Leave now."

Journal Entry Seventy-Nine: The Swallow

NoOne recalled the last time he had located the Funnel. It was a slaughter. The number of Orbs destroyed could not be counted. Ever since that first discovery, the Orbs guiding the dead to the Funnel had been careful not to leave a trail that could be followed. At that time, NoOne's Snake had been but a fraction of its current size. But this time, his Snake would not stop at the physical entrance to the Funnel. NoOne was ready to penetrate the transitional split—where the physical entry becomes the Spiritual conduit. He was ready to go all the way to the First Gate and beyond.

Contracting in ever-tightening circles, the Snake approached the physical opening of the Funnel. The Soul Judged Eyes and body parts of degenerated body matter, crushed even tighter, screamed their sad lament, silent to most, but heard by the other forever-doomed Souls. The Snake glided through a completely black physical space—empty to most—but vibrant and alive in an invisible layer of Dark Matter soup; perceptible only to dark forces and the Holy.

The Snake intuitively knew that forcing too much Soul energy into the Funnel at one time could potentially rupture the opening, causing it to seal off and escape to another dimension, where it could be hidden until TheSon restored the purity of the opening. It would take eons for NoOne's legions to find the Funnel entrance again. On the other hand, entering with too few of the DarkSouls could result in a weak attack, equally disastrous in the outcome.

The mix must be perfect. The timing was everything. Attacking the Funnel must lead immediately to the First Gate, where the first challenge awaited NoOne's army. Due to their sneak attack, NoOne calculated that there would not be enough unsuspecting Orb monitors to contest the digestion of the Funnel.

My Father may choose to ignore the future, but I will not. I see my outcome. I will succeed.

NoOne gave his Snake an order to make one last huge turn. It had to be perfectly oriented to the opening of the Funnel. Rather than squeezing the Snake into the opening, NoOne ordered the Snake to open its mouth wide and swallow the entire Funnel entrance and portions of the Funnel tube itself.

And so, it did. With an enormous belch, the Snake lifted its upper jaw. Then it dropped its lower jaw. Then it raised its upper jaw higher, the lower jaw lower. Cycling through this progression hundreds of times, the Snake's mouth widened to solar system proportions; more than enough to swallow its Funnel morsel.

Some dead Soul eyes, cradling cadaver remnants inside the throat of the Snake, were peeled away by the Funnel membrane. NoOne quickly ordered his scraped-off eyes to retreat and attach themselves to the tail of the Snake. Millions of miles were therefore recycled in the lithe Snake's length.

NoOne's Snake created a continuous opening on its side so new Souls could enter the Funnel. Souls were prevented from escaping by a constant forward breath spurting out of the Snake's mouth; a one-way flow of Souls into the Funnel was guaranteed. Now caught up in the skin of the Snake, recently arrived Souls had no choice but to be judged and then journey deeper into the Funnel with other LostSouls to the First Gate. NoOne sneered at the hysterical weeping by the pathetic new Souls anticipating a Heavenly reward, only to be surrounded by screams of sheer terror.

'Cry, my new children. Your reward is soon forthcoming.' And for good measure, NoOne judged each, giving them the same choice. 'Choose the way of NoOne, and your fears of judgment will be stilled. Or suffer the uncertainty of the unknowable.'

All the Souls, previously ebullient with the expectation of salvation and bliss, chose NoOne. However, they discovered that NoOne only offered a respite from their current fear and not a complete cessation of their pain and suffering. Soulless, the new empty eyes cried for mercy and a second chance. Smiling, NoOne ordered the LostOnes to the deepest, darkest depths of the Snake, surrounded by other new Souls, screaming in utter horror and complete hopelessness.

For added effect, NoOne ordered some Snake corpses to life. Dancing around the new Souls deep within the Snake bowels, NoOne directed the corpses to completely surround the new hapless Souls and tear each other apart. Then the corpses reunited. Then they disassembled. And then reunited. Over and over again. NoOne could not decide which was more entertaining: the shock of the corpses when ordered to destroy themselves after regaining afterlife or the terror of the new Souls as they watched the self-mutilation.

NoOne basked in the frenzy of panicked thoughts emanating from the new Souls. *Am I next? What did I do to deserve this? I am in Hell! Please spare me! Someone, rescue me!*

TheSon and TendHer witnessed the consumption of the Holy Funnel. They knew the Snake would soon be capable of ramming the first Holy Gate.

NoOne had waited for eternities. Finally, he could taunt his favored Sibling. 'TheSon, my Brother. Can You hear me? I have swallowed whole Your precious Funnel. It is full of my dead Souls, ready for me to feast on our Father's Light. I will soon banish You to the NoThing—to spend Your energy Lighting that which cannot receive Light.'

A Host of Orbs stood at the First Gate. Their brilliant Lights emitted a thousand frequencies of color to welcome all to be judged, the Holy Gate opening only when a Soul was deemed Holy and worthy of Being with TheOne. A second contingent of Holy Beasts and Species circled the Gate's tall pillars, protecting the Funnel tube leading to the Second Gate, providing a second layer of protection in anticipation of an attack.

TheSon had a surprise in store for NoOne. Just in front of the First Gate, a billion Orbs suddenly appeared. They swelled in size, then joined and spun, accelerating to ever-faster velocities, creating a Holy Wheel Black Hole. Such fantastic speeds with the Hole were reached that a center vortex, aligned with the SuperVoid, was carved out of 'beyond the Veil'. It was in this trap that TheSon sought to snare the lining of the Snake's throat and suck it downward. First, it would seize the inside of the Snake's throat, securing it firmly, then it would vacuum in the entire outer body, sending the Snake back to its SuperVoid Hell.

NoOne had other plans. He had seen the trap well in advance as he moved in and out of time dimensions. He had compensated for the Wheel's massive size by making sure he had enough DeadSouls in the body of his Snake. NoOne was convinced that now his Snake was big enough to conquer the entire Reincarnation Universe.

NoOne ordered a contingent of LostSouls to peel off from its throat and form a giant hand. It began to squeeze the wheel. Orbs flew everywhere, ripped from the Wheel's frame; Orbs massacred and left floating, Lightless. The Wheel groaned as if it had a life separate from the Orbs and then slowed, flapping helplessly in a wavy billow of Spiritual vapor. The Holy Wheel struggled to continue spinning, its energy particles transfixed on its event horizon, caught between existence and nothingness. Teased with the hope they might escape, the trapped Orbs watched in terror as the Snake's hand completely squashed the Wheel like a grape.

Then NoOne ordered the Snake to deeply ingest the Orb remains of the Wheel. Like so much garbage, the Orbs fell helplessly through the Funnel trapped inside the body of the Snake. Finally, the dead Wheel Orbs burst through the tail of the Snake into a dimension of NoPlace/NoTime physics, disintegrating into irrelevance, leaving only stripped-bare, memory quantum particles, the only reminder of Their existence, to float lifelessly alone in empty NoThingness.

The Son knew that He had been defeated, at least for now. He may have underestimated His brother's evil genius, but not His brother's determination. TheSon had seen this horrific outcome eons ago, one of a billion possibilities from His brother's sin, but had hoped He could spare the sacrifice of Holy Orbs and preserve the Funnel. Now He knew that was no longer the case. The time had arrived to summon His ultimate weapon.

TendHer, it is time to call My Chosen.
Yes, Brother. It is time.

Journal Entry Eighty: The Chosen

The four guys knew their mission was at hand. A mission now only possible because the New Twin had promised the safety of their physical bodies while their Souls journeyed into 'beyond the Veil'. The guys were somewhat confident but at the same time anxious due to the relentless pursuit of the Old Twin and the Sharks. It was the unpredictability of the Old Twin that scared them the most. The New Twin assured them that he would never give up.

John wanted to be reassured by the New Twin. "How long do you think you can last? How much time do we have in 'beyond the Veil'?" asked John.

The New Twin did not answer. His energy had noticeably waned, and John was sorry he had diverted the New Twin's focus from his task. Maintaining the integrity of the bubble shell, especially with the continued Shark onslaught, was taking its toll.

Finally, the New Twin responded. "I will keep your bodies safe as long as I can. That's all I can promise."

After a brief reflective pause, John tried to perk up his cohorts. "Ok, guys. Just remember we were chosen by TheSon. It's time."

"Where are we headed first?" asked Luke.

"I think we need to send our 'Soul-bodies' to the First Gate," replied John. "Follow me. Sensei left us a little something to help us when we arrive in 'beyond the Veil'."

The four settled in on the bottom of the bubble. Nodding to the New Twin, they began to work their way through their minds to the desired state of relaxation that would allow them to project their Mind's Eyes and Souls into 'beyond the Veil'. Each took turns struggling with issues; they mostly kept silent. But Ben couldn't help but affirm his new disdain for fire and Luke cried out his Love for Heather. After that, the entire group settled down and regained their concentration.

Once completely enveloped in 'beyond the Veil', the guys discovered to their relief that four suits of air armor were waiting.

'Why do we need armor? We're Souls!' Luke thought to the others.

John immediately knew why. 'This is the same protection that insulated me on my most recent reconnaissance trip. The air armor protects the Mind's Eye and, with it, the Soul as well.'

John continued. 'The Funnel entrance is perpetually in flux, shifting back and forth between many physical dimensions. Once found and entered, it is this trauma that forces the Mind's Eye to release the Soul and Book of Life. With our armor suits, our Mind's Eyes are protected so we can go back and forth, between the Spiritual and the physical should we need to do so.'

'How does it do that, John?' quizzed Ben.

'Remember what TendHer said?' answered John. 'We have been allowed to keep our Mind's Eyes in 'beyond the Veil' to perceive our "Soul-bodies" and communicate with the Orbs.'

Just as they started zeroing in on a location in 'beyond the Veil' where they would launch their search for the First Gate, the guys saw in the distance what appeared to be an Orb. As it approached closer, the guys knew immediately it was TendHer. Her presence this time was subdued, her Light muted as if she did not want to be detected from a distance. Circling slowly around the guys, TendHer once again manifested herself as a shadowy human, white clouds circling a transparent body.

I was sent by TheSon to find you and lead you to the First Gate. First, you must return to the physical dimension to locate the Funnel. I will direct you from a distance. Stand as close together as you can, commanded TendHer.

Then, TendHer ordered the guys' air armor to completely engulf their "Soul-minds."

The air armor swirled violently around each of the four Souls and then expanded. The protective gear perfectly matched the phantom physical body dimensions of each. Ben's air armor was broad. John's was short. Luke's was tall and wide. Charles had armor that was more like a ball.

'Ah, TendHer, why is my armor like a bubble?' asked Charles.

Before TendHer could respond, Ben said, ' 'Cause they ran out of uniforms!'

True to his desire to rise above conflict, Charles remained silent.

TendHer replied, *Among the four of you, Charles is the only one completely immersed in the world of natural life. His Soul is massive with animal Spirits and requires a large vessel.*

'Well, I want one of those!' said Ben.

Ben was surprised when TendHer reached out to him with her cloak and tenderly nuzzled his armor. It stirred a deep, long-buried memory of Ben's mother cradling his head when he was very young. It was the only instance Ben could remember when his mom was tender. He felt his Soul begin to weep.

'Yes, Ben. Someday you will have one of those huge Soul vessels. Indeed, your Soul vessel will span the size of many suns.'

The other three guys oriented themselves to Ben. Collectively, they thought with incredulity, 'Him?'

It took but a millisecond for the guys to reach the physical location where the Funnel was supposed to be.

'I'd say this takes my breath away, except where is the Funnel? All I see is…ah, shit! Do you guys see that?' exclaimed Ben.

'Hey, this air armor is so cool. I could do fantastic things on a football field with this!' said Luke.

'Luke, you're constantly surprising me!' said John.

'Guys, look! There's no Funnel, just a big Snake!' said Ben.

Approaching the Funnel, the guys saw a dark, slithering tail casually hanging in space. The Snake's head and neck seemed to disappear into nothingness.

It's what I feared. NoOne's Snake has swallowed the Funnel. You cannot see the head as it has penetrated 'beyond the Veil'.

Looking back in physical space, the guys saw a millions-of-miles long tail that was probably only perceptible because the guys' Mind's Eyes could distinguish the Snake's dark outline against the bursts of Light and the glow of other stars far on the horizon.

'TendHer, what's happening up there? It looks like NoOne has swallowed the entire Funnel!'

Yes, NoOne has swallowed the Funnel up to the First Gate and destroyed the Wheel trap we set for him. The Funnel has stopped transitioning the dead. Soul Guide Orbs are trying to destroy the Snake's tail with comets, but they are failing.

We will need to find another way to get to the First Gate. We will need to go by way of 'beyond the Veil'. The small opening in the Snake's skin left for new Souls to enter the Funnel is too well protected.

'That should be easy for us, though, right?' asked Ben.

TendHer was not reassuring. *There could be an ambush waiting for you. Our only consolation is that NoOne must stay protected in the Snake lest he violates our Father's mandate.*

'Looks like he has lots of room to hide in. The Snake is beyond huge!' exclaimed Ben.

'What happens if NoOne, or the Snake rather, destroys the First Gate?' asked Charles.

We can't let that happen. Because we lack a large enough Orb army to fight NoOne, We have stacked all Four Gates close together. All Our troops of Light can concentrate now on one choke position.

John was excited as he began visualizing the coming battle. It was the same tingling he got before a karate sparring match with a formidable opponent. 'Oh yeah! NoOne can't outflank you with a pincer movement. It's just like the Battle of Thermopylae—Sparta held back Persia for days with just a few hundred men because the Persians had to attack them in one small mountain path access point.'

As was his style, Charles had been silent the entire time, wondering what role his animal Spirits would play. 'Mam, what role does the natural world play with the Orb armies? Will I command an army of animal Orbs?'

TendHer replied, *Now that we will stack the Four Gates close together, you will not need to separate. All four of you will defend the one gate. It's all or nothing.*

'Everything's riding on the First Gate? Ok, guess we all go in together,' said John. Then an idea popped into his head. 'It isn't too late to attack NoOne now,' added John. 'It would be a sneak attack. They're not expecting us.'

'I thought you would say, "Never too late to back out?" ' said Ben. 'Oh, and one more thing. We all have been Chosen to protect the Gates. But exactly what do we attack this Snake with? What weapons do we use?'

'Yeah, that's been bugging me too,' added Luke.

With tepid optimism, John remarked, 'We just have to trust TendHer. Right? I mean, I always saw us leading the Orbs.'

'And the Orbs do the actual fighting? That sounds just fine with me. I sure hope so. As Luke knows, I'm not so hot when it comes to "hand to hand" combat!' said Ben.

Luke smiled. 'Well, you do have potential with your weight advantage.'

'Not here in the Spirit world. Didn't you ever take physics?' replied Ben.

'TendHer, are you still here? Can you tell us what weapons we use to fight the Snake?' asked John.

TendHer replied, *When the time is right, TheSon will guide and lead. For now, departure is imperative.*

With John's intuitive mastery of warfare strategy, he began to experience a sinking feeling. Not once had TendHer or their Mentors discussed specific weaponry. There had to be some extraordinary power or energy that could be used to fight the Snake. So why hadn't they been trained?

Then it hit him. He realized that maybe they would never get weapons. Perhaps they were nothing more than bait, like fishing; at best part of some deceptive battle ploy.

With no time left to process or comment further on TendHer's cryptic response, the guys felt their suits energize and all were propelled away. Again, the journey took a few seconds, 'beyond the Veil' looming on the horizon.

TendHer waved the guys forward.

As the guys approached the boundary into 'beyond the Veil', they tentatively approached with their "Soul-bodies;" cracks appeared in the Spiritual barrier wall directly in front of them. TendHer motioned for them to cross over to her.

With their "Soul-arms" inserted through the boundary cracks into 'beyond the Veil' and their "Soul bodies" dangling still in space, the four guys hung half in and half out, waiting for directions as to what they should do next. TendHer motioned them to thrust their entire "Soul-bodies" through the boundary and into 'beyond the Veil'.

You must hurry. A ninth dimension will soon slice through this location. Any physical element close to the boundary will be carried away. Think of a knife slicing through a piece of paper.

That was the catalyst the guys needed. Just as they squeezed completely into 'beyond the Veil', another colossal boundary slit through space. One moment everything was quiet; the next moment, a vast, new fabric dropped like a curtain released to close off a stage from a theater audience. The guys realized they would have been cut in two if they hadn't moved when instructed by TendHer.

Peering closely at their previous physical location, even TendHer was surprised to see what appeared to be a train pulling thousands of individual cars, straddling the dimensional boundary. As they got closer, the guys could tell the train was in fact a solid core legion of eyes. They were pulling vast balls of ice.

TendHer commanded, *You must follow. We must gain distance from the space-Spiritual boundary.*

As the group retreated further into 'beyond the Veil', they looked back and saw mountainous balls of ice crashing against the space side of the boundary.

'Are those little comets?' asked John.

Look closer, directed TendHer.

As the balls of ice shattered against the space-Spirit boundary, the eyes retreated. At first, the guys were relieved to see the eyes going away. Still, concern mounted as the group saw a massive contingent of corpses push a single block of ice to form a solid wall covering the entire space-Spiritual boundary. As far as the guys could see, the ice wall blocked any view of the physical space they had just left.

NoOne has just sent us a message, said TendHer.

'Do we really want to know what it is?' replied Ben.

TendHer's response was not reassuring. *He has blocked our retreat back to the physical dimension which he controls. If you dare to return and he catches you, he will destroy your Mind's Eyes. You are only safe now because you are with me and have your protective armor. Plus, he has not yet destroyed the First Gate.*

NoOne wasn't finished. Small openings appeared in the ice. Within the openings, faces came to life. No torsos, just faces.

'Oh shit. What's happening?' cried Luke.

The faces were writhing in agony. They had no eyes.

The guys felt drawn to the faces staring at them from the other side of the space-Spirit boundary.

TendHer was too late. *Stop, do not look!* she commanded.

Hypnotically, the guys let themselves drift back to the boundary and did not stop until they were inches away from the faces. Luke was looking at Heather. John was looking at the face of Sensei. Charles was looking at the face of Bestow. Ben was looking at the face of Igor.

The four Mentors, in physical manifestations, were being tortured. Small spears of ice sliced away layers of their faces. They begged for mercy. Pieces of their flesh hung in space, a testament to the evil of NoOne. As a piece of flesh was removed from one of the faces, it was replaced with a piece of flesh belonging to one of the others. Repeatedly: slice off, replace, slice off, replace. It was an ironic rhythm designed to mock the natural impartiality of the physical world.

Look away! TendHer called to the guys.

'I can't. This can't be real!' cried Ben. 'There is no force in existence that would be so cruel.'

Yes, there is, replied TendHer. *NoOne. We must leave.*

'He's playing with us, isn't he?' asked John.

TendHer reached out and covered the sheer display of agony and torture with her own partition of vibratory Strings. Blocked from any further demonstration, all was suddenly silent and still.

'Has he gone?' asked Ben hopefully.

The four guys felt a cruel laugh vibrate through their heads.

TendHer explained what was happening. *NoOne is taunting me. And you. He wants me to chase after one of his illusions so our group becomes separated. Go now to the First Gate. As you get closer, you will see the other three Gates stacked close to the First Gate. Hover at a distance, and you will find Souls waiting to help you on the other side of the First Gate.*

Pointing to the ice covering the physical side of the boundary, Ben said, 'Wait, why would NoOne do this to us? Doesn't he have anything else to do now?'

TendHer replied, *He wanted to make a point. You've been put on notice that you will never return to your Earth's bodies.*

All four guys gasped in unison, 'What?'

TendHer continued, *As long as you are trapped here, he can free up his Twin son to do his bidding on Earth and not be concerned about you, especially how you could help TheSon if He chooses to reincarnate once again.*

'What's the bottom line here?' asked John.

Proceed undetected to the First Gate, answered TendHer.

Ben asked, 'How do we go undetected? How do we make it through, much less survive the First Gate to join the Holy Angels thingees?'

'Holy Angel's thingees?' chuckled Luke. 'You talkin' about your wiener again?'

'I can't believe this,' interrupted John. 'More jokes?'

Ben and Luke smiled and nodded their "Soul-heads" up and down.

'Hey, just a little comic relief!' said Charles. 'It's a White man's way to hide fear.'

Ignoring Charles, TendHer answered Ben's question. *Some Orbs are waiting to meet you and guide you through a parallel dimension millimeters away from the First Gate. With the battle in full fury, we hope NoOne won't feel your movement until you re-enter the Funnel at the Second Gate, facing his Snake.*

The guys weren't given any time to ask questions. They felt a push from TendHer and found themselves at a safe hiding spot to the side and overlooking the First Gate. The guys watched as the protective Wheel was destroyed, piece by piece.

The battle was vicious. The Snake's head was close to the First Gate, the unswallowed portion of the Funnel continuing to the Reincarnation Universe jutting up out of its mouth, the body and tail of the Snake dropping down as far as could be sensed.

The Snake was anxious to complete its consumption of the First Gate. The Snake expanded its head with its wide jaws to a monstrously enormous size. The Soulless Snake glowed dark red with each thrust closer to the First Gate, some body parts so engorged with portions of the Gate that they exploded away from the body.

NoOne emerged from the depths of the Snake. Manifesting as a solid, dark cloud, NoOne rested just inside the cavernous mouth, the size of many suns, careful lest he violates his Father's stricture of not desecrating the Holy 'beyond the Veil' by entering its Sacred dimension.

Gradually, NoOne formed the shape of a huge mirror that spanned the width of the gigantic oral cavity. A great silence ensued.

'Why are the Orbs backing up?' asked Luke.

'Is that a mirror in the Snake's mouth?' asked John.

Yes. More theatrics from my needy brother.

'What's going on in the mirror?' asked Charles. 'I see something like scenes from a play being performed.'

You are correct. NoOne is acting out scenes from the Orb's lives when they were human and long before judged Pure. He is projecting for all to see their episodes of sin, neglecting the many acts of charity and Love, of course.

NoOne began to speak. "Sanctified Orbs, why do you retreat? Remember when I played back your life events upon your death, oh Holy Orbs? Do you not remember your sins? Do you not cringe at all the evil thoughts you had? Come, my dear Orbs. Do you not remember the lust in sex? Do you not remember envy? Jealousy? Oh, how delicious is the physical life! Do you not miss it? I can still offer you salvation. You can once more taste the power of dominion, the thrill of conquest, the exhilaration of invincibility. Come, join me, and I will put you all at the head of my Snake."

NoOne simultaneously projected scenes of lust from every Orb's life for all to witness on the huge screen, long before they were transformed and saved by TheSon. Visibly repelled, Orbs retreated further in apparent humiliation.

'Can Orbs be embarrassed?' asked Luke.

Ben, Luke, and Charles were also puzzled. 'How could Orbs judged Pure have any negative emotion?' asked Charles.

They can't. NoOne is doing this to scare you. My Orbs feel nothing but Love and pray for the salvation of My brother.

'Has an Orb ever been corrupted?' asked John.

All things are possible with a Creator that cherishes creativity and safeguards choice.

In response to his sister, NoOne assumed the shape of smoke billows circling around the inside the mouth of the giant Snake. As the shadowy currents gained speed, pincers of dark lightening probed the Holy 'beyond the Veil' just outside the Snake's mouth. Upon touching the Spirit dimension, the foreign streaks of Dark Matter exploded, leaving massive pits of 'NoThing.'

The Orbs were stunned and froze in wonderment at the spectacle NoOne was providing.

'Not so Holy now, are you, my not so holy sister!' NoOne proclaimed. 'Be as creative with your pitiful battle plans as you wish. My army can take your gates any time I wish. Or I may choose to leave you with nothing but eternally deep pits of nonexistence.'

TendHer approached the mouth of the Snake as a single eye. It was microscopic compared to the gigantic size of the Snake's mouth. The guys wondered how TendHer had any chance of prevailing over Her brother.

NoOne responded to TendHer's sudden presence by sending spears of Dark Matter directly at TendHer's eye. Just before hitting their target, TendHer erupted into unfolding white sheets of energy. The spears were enveloped entirely and extinguished.

Have we not done this before, my brother? You lead us down a path of mutual destruction. Is not that madness?

'Madness, my sister, is watching our Father play His stupid games with His Creation. Behold my power.'

Then NoOne again materialized his mouth-wide mirror and recreated his victorious consumption of the Funnel. The Orbs were dazzled by the fascinating drama taking place in the mouth of the Snake. Undulating and swaying, within the oral cavity, an infinite number of scenes acted out, recreating every detail of NoOne's victory: from following John and Sensei to the location of the Funnel, to consuming the Funnel, to the agony of the recent dead trying to reach TendHer in the Reincarnation Universe, and especially NoOne taunting the Orbs.

Still dwelling inside the mouth of his moving Snake, NoOne triumphantly approached his jackpot, the First Gate. He paused before the Gate. Lurking far enough out of reach to avoid an attack by the Orbs on the other side, NoOne screeched encouragement to the eyes without Souls that comprised his evil vessel.

'See what we have done to the Orb Wheel! And now we will destroy the Gate! When I command, you must push, my children. Push. They are so weak, and soon we will easily move on to the Second Gate!'

The four guys were perplexed. How could they protect the First Gate from their present position? Their answer came soon.

'Hey guys, look at those Lights!' said Charles as he pointed off toward the far horizon, beyond the First Gate.

'Yeah, so what?' asked Ben. 'There are Lights everywhere. They're called suns.'

Charles shook his head. 'No, Ben. We are in 'beyond the Veil'. These are different. They're changing colors.'

Four faint Lights appeared to be inching closer.

'Did you see that? They're moving,' said Luke.

'Why would they do that? Why would the Lights be moving unless they're Orbs?' asked Ben.

'Definitely not Orbs,' commented John.

The Lights moved from their spots and settled in the middle of the very surprised four. The Lights shriveled to about the size of eyes.

'Wrong on that one, John,' muttered Ben.

The radiance of the four Orbs was overwhelming yet awe-inspiring to each of the four guys, hypnotic in power. They knew these were special Souls who had come to help them protect the Gates.

'Are you Angels?' whispered Luke.

The Lights whirled in a merry dance of geometric perfection, from squares to rectangles to circles to octagons and back to circles. Always back to circles. The alpha and omega. The end becomes the beginning. The beginning becomes the end.

Then the Lights lined up in a row, one Light for each of the awestruck guys. Facing them. Slowly and in unison, moving towards them, the Lights stopped about two feet in front of them. And began to transform.

Body parts struggled to break free from all four Lights like a chick breaking through its birth shell. An arm here. A leg there. A head. A torso. Finally, four human-like "Soul-bodies," still radiating streaks of sizzling Light, presented themselves to the four.

Finally, one spoke. *Do you recognize Us?*

The guys took turns speaking names they thought they would never utter again.

Luke: 'Heather.'

Charles: 'Bestow.'

John: 'Sensei.'

Ben: 'Igor.'

Moments seemed like years as the four boys studied their Mentors standing before them. Just minutes ago, the faces of their Mentors were being ripped apart by NoOne at the ice wall. And now They were here. Was this again a trick by NoOne? Was this a trap?

Heather was the first to send Her thoughts. *My beloved Luke. Told ya' I'd be here waiting.*

Luke rushed with his "Soul-body" to hug his Soul Mate. His arms reached forward to hold Her, but nothing was there.

Heather laughed. *Luke! I am a Soul now. I am beyond the senses. I should be with TheOne, but He sent all four of Us to warn and prepare you.*

'Igor, they let You in Heaven?' Ben blurted out.

Igor also burst out laughing. *Yes, even a scoundrel like Me has a chance!*

John looked at Sensei and bowed with his "Soul-body." 'Thank You for coming, Sensei. We need Your help.'

I've looked forward to this moment for a millennium, smiled Sensei.

Bestow brought the group back to their immediate task. *OK, guys. Nice to have all the touchy-feeling stuff going on, but the First Gate is almost destroyed.*

As usual, Ben couldn't contain his curiosity. 'Nice to see You all, if we could see up here, but could someone tell me, and us, what we're supposed to do?'

'Yeah, what's going on?' added Luke.

Igor answered, *TheSon will soon be here. He has seen this coming before time. He is about to make a deal with NoOne to open up the Funnel and protect its Souls.*

'A deal? So no big battle?' asked John.

Looking at Bestow, Charles posed a question. All waited to hear the answer. 'We were told by so many of You that we were to be the Chosen ones to battle NoOne. So now, You're making a deal?'

Ben jumped in. 'Yeah, where do we fit in?'

Sensei moved forward. *The war has just begun. For now, We need you here to keep the Old Twin occupied on Earth. We must keep him contained. And that might be your only job when and if you return to your bodies.*

'If? Might?' moaned Ben. 'Words I don't like.'

'Hey, that rhymes!' exclaimed Luke. Then, when no one congratulated Luke on his witty observation, he continued, 'You know, guys. Might? Like? They kind of rhyme…don't they?'

There was one skill Luke prided himself on possessing in athletics. He kept his cool when under stress. Well, most of the time. He had witnessed over and over how tension ruined team performance. And how humor could reinvigorate his teammates with confidence. What he observed in the other guys presently was not encouraging. Not even one reacted to his humor.

'Why would You need the four of us to keep the Old Twin contained?' asked John. 'I mean, our New Twin is doing just great.'

Sensei slowly answered his student, *TheSon beholds all eternity, as does TheOne. Love gives them this power. What They see is this: NoOne can destroy all life. Everywhere. Everything. Both the Twins might have a hand in that destruction. Precisely what role they might play was not disclosed to Us.*

We must be prepared for all possible outcomes, added Bestow.

'So, that's what we're doing here? Just one more possible outcome?' pressed Ben.

Ben. All will be revealed in due time. You know that, answered Igor softly.

The four Mentors departed the same way they had arrived.

Charles started to hum.

Observing Charles' sudden agitation, John asked, 'What's going on, Charles? Why are you making that sound?'

'My animal world is distressed,' replied Charles. 'They are reaching out to me to know what happened in 'beyond the Veil'. Animal souls are stacking up below the Funnel; they are being consumed by NoOne's Snake.'

'What are you going to tell them?' Luke asked.

Charles seemed to drift away. 'Tell them? What should I say?' Charles mumbled. 'I guess there's nothing I CAN say, is there?'

The question posed by Charles silenced the group. Each knew Charles had given the only answer he could. Each settled into a quiet unease; thoughts jumbled with tension, ready for something unexpected and bad to happen. At this point, they had no control over their futures. Their pasts seemed pointless. Were they not supposed to protect the First Gate? Why the hopscotch between the physical and the Spiritual? There was absolutely nothing they could do except trust in their Mentors, TendHer, and TheSon.

It was just a matter of time. In a dimension without time.

Journal Entry Eighty-One: A Real Deal

NoOne decided to terminate the Chosen. He saw their Mentors depart the same way they had arrived, as faint Orbs of Light, so the timing was right. TheSon and TendHer were not around; no doubt They were preening in some mirror of Holiness. Now was a perfect opportunity to eliminate the Chosen boys and their irritating meddling.

NoOne spat out of the Snake's mouth whirling clouds of dark psychic venom mixed with saved stellar grime. Swirling in tighter and tighter circles, the fevered mixed concoction jetted toward the group. Completely encircling the guys, the clouds kept spinning, rhythmic, labored, hypnotic. They waited for NoOne's command to smother the boys' Souls thereby leaving their bodies on Earth empty, broken husks.

A dense thought emanated from the Snake, directed at the Four Chosen. 'I have only to give the order, and your bodies on Earth will feed my worms. TheSon's pathetic plan to protect my Sister's precious First Gate has failed. In just a matter of minutes, my Dark Legion of Soul-Judged Evil Eyes will break through the First Holy Gate. Soon I will have control of the entire Reincarnation Universe. You have no hope. I want you to know you are doomed.'

John spoke up. 'If we're without hope, why are you waiting? Why are you wasting your time warning us? What do you really want?'

Before NoOne could reply, there was another voice, another presence. The guys oriented themselves in unison to the source of the voice. Even NoOne's Snake shifted in perspective. The sound of this voice brought all activity to a standstill.

A lance of Light surfaced from another part of 'beyond the Veil'. It unfolded like an umbrella, arching over the guys. Like a stream meandering through a forest, its radiance then collected in eddies above their "Soul-heads," creating deep pools of brilliance, exploding against itself, breaking apart, turning into a billion million brilliant, luminous beams, crisscrossing and merging, separating, and reaching, recombining, and bursting only to recombine as beams; beams uniting back to a single magnificent lance of Light.

'Talk about the Fourth of July!' Luke exclaimed.

John whispered to the rest of the guys, 'That has to be TheSon.'

'He sure arrived in the knick of time,' said Luke.

Ben wanted an answer to John's question. 'Like John asked, what does NoOne really want? TheSon will find out!'

John added, 'I think I know what NoOne wants. He's using us to set up TheSon. He wants something. And it can't be good.'

'Regardless, guys, I think NoOne was about to kill us!' said Luke.

Yes, tell me, My brother. What do you want? I am TheSon, Son of TheOne, and I command you to tell my Chosen what you want!

NoOne's cloud curled in fury, round and round, until it became even darker, more condensed, and focused. 'I knew I could lure you here. Only you would come to the rescue of four pitiful human children. You are so predictable. You want to know what I want?

'I WANT YOU!'

What of Me do you desire, oh brother from the soil? Do you want My treasured place alongside Our Father, TheOne?

NoOne briefly swelled, then became eerily still. 'Yes. That's a good place to start.'

Do you not know the only thing Our Father has to do is appear, and you will be blasted back to your SuperVoid?

At the mention of what NoOne feared the most, the Snake slightly retreated, driven back by TheSon's clear reasoning. 'He will not show up. He cannot. He gave us free will. And He gave me my mission to streamline His inefficient Reincarnation Universe.'

TheOne knows of your treachery and deceit. You will be reckoned with when our Father decides.

NoOne felt he was losing control of the negotiation. 'You think that petty threat will make me withdraw my legion of dead Souls and spit out the Funnel? You think I will not terminate your Chosen?'

Pausing to consider whether NoOne was bluffing, TheSon slowly replied, *In exchange for what, brother? What do I have to do to make you withdraw your army of Dead Souls from the Funnel and set free My Chosen four?*

'I will give You the opportunity to do what You do best. What You Love to do.'

Be specific, brother.

'I will give You the opportunity to re-judge all my LostSouls. Isn't that what You Love to do? What You are called to do? Forgive?'

Such is the Divine Province of Our Father, TheOne. What gives you the right to bargain with TendHer's Damned?

NoOne was exuberant. His dark cloud scintillated with Sparks around the Snake's mouth as he considered the possibility of success. 'It's either that or....'

What? Once more, I ask you, brother. What do you have to offer Me?

'I will let You take my army back to my SuperVoid here and now for You to re-judge.'

That is Our Father's decision to make.

'But think of all the Souls You can convert. You will have an eternity to do so!'

Again, should TheOne direct Me to do so, I would comply.

NoOne was fed up. 'Brother, make Your decision now to agree to my terms or I will continue to destroy the rest of Your Gates and invade the Reincarnation Universe. I will replace TendHer with my Snake.'

Is that all?

NoOne was furious. He had counted on his Brother to panic. Even to plead. How could He be so calm?

'No. Because it will bring me pleasure, I will wipe out all life forms associated with Your four Chosen and their Mentors. I will replace their Souls with Dark Matter, and they will walk the Earth incarnated with my evil. They will systematically reduce the planet to rock and stone. And then I will turn them loose on each other; forever. They will drift in the darkness of space. Only remembering one thing: how You abandoned them.'

Why do you pass up so many opportunities to redeem yourself with Our Father? Do you not see that the path to joining the Trinity is through Love and compassion? Not through threats and intimidation? What say you, brother? Are you weary of your banishment?

NoOne fumed. The last thing he wanted was to be lectured at. Again. His Brother had not earned the right. NoOne kept his Silence. He wanted an answer.

Ben huddled against Luke, as if wanting to be protected. With a quivering "Soul voice," Ben thought, 'I think we're toast, Luke.'

'Have faith, Ben. TheSon must have some kind of long-term plan,' said John.

'TheSon is cornered. Damned if he does; damned if he doesn't' thought Charles.

'Well, I hope the damning he gets doesn't involve us massacring humanity!' replied Ben.

'What's mass…a…cri…?' asked Luke.

Ben shushed Luke. 'I think a decision has been made.'

TheSon's response was barely perceptible by the four guys. At first, they thought TheSon sounded sad or resigned. Yet upon reflection, they felt deeply TheSon's Loving resolution. Could TheSon see this deal with the Devil as a chance to increase His Holy Flock? To give of Himself once again, fully?

Very well, you must leave the Funnel and the Reincarnation Universe alone. You must free My Chosen four. You must leave their Mentors alone. No interference with....

NoOne's Dark Matter cloud churned with excitement. He interrupted TheSon. 'My Brother, I will sacrifice my Dark Matter to ensure justice. I shall only be concerned with the living and their passing. I will not interfere with TendHer and Her precious recycling of Souls.'

The guys were aghast that TheSon had given up so easily. Wasn't it their job to defeat NoOne? They were told they were the Chosen. Now they were being used as pawns in a cosmic chess match. How easily would they be devoured if NoOne decided not to keep his end of the deal? What if they were no longer of value to TheSon? What if He abandoned the boys; just like all the other father figures in the boys' lives had abandoned them?

Rockets of Light from TheSon reached out in all directions, at first random and confused, searching, then gradually they slowed down and formed new patterns.

So, you agree to withdraw your legion of dead Souls from 'beyond the Veil' if I agree to dwell with the LostSouls in your SuperVoid? asked TheSon.

'Yes,' my Holy Brother. 'You have my word.'

A Call

I was drained of all energy. Reading my dad's manuscript of journal entries had taken an unexpected emotional toll; it was much worse than I had expected. Just as I wondered how I could overcome my increasing exhaustion (and curiosity) and take a break from reading, Sheba notified me of an incoming viz-message. I was relieved. I had no choice. I put my dad's book down.

"Permission granted. Commence message."

"Why so formal? You've never been so brusque!" replied Sheba.

I was caught off guard. Probably just tense from reading my dad's journals. "Oh, yeah. Sorry, Sheba."

"Now I'm worried."

"I'll bite. Why are you worried?"

Sheba ignored me, just huffed a sigh of frustration, and proceeded to process the new communication.

A blurry, squiggly haze assembled in the middle of the room. It struggled to reach clarity.

"Ah, Sheba. Re-calibrate the image."

"I'm sorry. Failure to re-calibrate. Image not in our library."

"What? Not in our library? You have everything that ever existed cataloged."

"Guess not."

"Ok, then. What is the source of the image?"

"Source of image unknown."

"Sheba, forget the visual. Retrieve verbal only."

"I'm sorry. Partial retrieval is only possible."

"That's fine. Just give me what you have."

"I will proceed. Verbal only."

"Ok. Start now."

"Words not in my dictionary."

"I don't care. Damn it! Just tell me the words!"

"Words nonsensical."

"Tell me the god damned words!"

"Know One."

"You mean as in knowing one, as in two different words?"

"Negative. Pronunciation implies one word. Correction."

"Accepted. Proceed."

"Noone."

I have a message from NoOne? The Devil in my dad's book? "Very well. What else?"

"I can discern two other words. It's difficult to precisely identify."

"Why? Interference from the dome?"

"No. There is screaming in the background."

"So, just tell me the two other words."

"One word is 'stop.' And the other word is 'reading.' "

Journal Entry Eighty-Two: The Bodies

The New Twin was exhausted. For days, he had protected the Dog and the bodies of the four guys, psychically maintaining the protective, invisible bubble shell. He knew that soon he would be completely drained of his last ounce of energy. Once that occurred, the Sharks' crunching would crash through his weakened projection, and all physical matter inside would implode or be drowned.

Despite his intense weariness, the New Twin occasionally caught dreamlike images of his brother. The Old Twin brother tormented the New Twin with psychic images of torture and pain. Especially cruel were the constant replays of all the destruction the two boys had delivered to so many innocent people.

A mocking question continued to surface in the New Twin's mind, obviously sent by his deranged and vindictive brother. *Was he ready to perish for these pitiful humans and a Dog?*

Yes, the New Twin thought. *I have experienced the power of Love. It embraced my intense mental capacity and connected me to every human being and animal on the planet. It was unlike anything I had ever experienced with our father, NoOne.*

Like his brother, the New Twin had been taught to concentrate, focus, and aggregate all the energy he had at his disposal to penetrate and dismantle any target. Fear was the source of that energy. Fear was at the core of Dark Matter. However, unlike the laser-like, narrow thrust of fear, the New Twin discovered that Love swells and expands. Love grows, evil obliterates. He felt a constant push-pull between the two—competition for mastery of his Soul.

As far as he could tell, fear was winning.

The New Twin saw that both coasts were decimated. Entire forests were ravaged by firestorms, leaving nothing but smoldering coals and clouds of ash and ember.

Cities collapsed, with skyscrapers draped across each other like so many fallen dominos. Midwest farmland was scorched beyond recognition from the molten lava spitting fire and poison upward to the Heavens as mantel crust volcanoes erupted up from the ground, hungry for the sky, peaks reaching heights more incredible than the Himalayas.

Momentary speculation captured the New Twin's imagination. *What if I had stayed with my brother? What damage could we have done together? He could not have done this by himself. He must have the help of our father and teacher, NoOne,* thought the New Twin.

The New Twin's reflections were abruptly interrupted.

'Haha, my foolish brother. I'll always be with you until I decide you are no longer entertaining enough to toy with.'

The New Twin was shaken. It sounded like the voice of his brother. It *was* the voice of his brother invading his brain, and there was no way the New Twin could shut it down.

The New Twin, feeling vulnerable, knew he had to sound strong and confident. 'At least you have lost half your power. Eventually, we will cross paths. I will show you my power to create is stronger than your power to destroy. How does it feel to be alone? How does it feel to be tied to all the Dark forces in all the multiverses? Your dissolution is guaranteed as is the finality of the LostSouls eternal suffering.'

'Now, now. Don't get philosophical on me,' thought the Old Twin. 'What I do is quite simple. For your information, you are wrong. I don't need you anymore.'

"You've been replaced," softly uttered the Old Twin aloud. He chuckled. Projecting his disdainful and haughty voice for all to hear, the Old Twin announced, "Perhaps you're wondering, why am I communicating with you, my long-lost relative? Well, I thought you should know what you're up against. I have a new partner. Or, should I say, a new Twin!"

Journal Entry Eighty-Three: The Move

The New Twin felt his power ebbing away. He knew he was close to losing control of the bubble structure. From outside the sphere, the Sharks continued their relentless attack. They seemed to have only gained in purpose and intensity. How long could he mentally project the bubble protection? Another day, perhaps? He knew it was time to act. He had to move the four bodies and the Dog and find some new place to hide immediately. The New Twin knew their fates relied on him. He must find them a haven so remote that he could rest without fear of being discovered by his brother and his new Twin "friend."

Speaking of the new friend, who was he? In the deep recesses of his mind, the New Twin sensed somebody familiar, perhaps somebody from their old clan village. A neighbor? He couldn't dwell on this new alliance much longer; it was a luxury he could ill afford. A more pressing matter was at hand. As the guys were still exploring 'beyond the Veil', he had to get their bodies to safety.

As the New Twin looked down to check on the guys, he suddenly saw the four bodies stir. Groggy and dazed, the four guys struggled to focus on their new environment one by one. Groaning and yawning, they took turns sitting up and looking about. They seemed stunned to have returned. Their heads twisted and turned rapidly in every direction, trying to understand where they were and why.

'Take your time, guys. I'm sure it takes a while,' thought the New Twin.

John was the first to speak aloud. It was more of a moan. "We lost."

The New Twin was taken aback. It was obviously not an announcement he expected to hear. "You what?"

Ben quickly answered. "Yes, we weren't able to do anything."

"All gone. All gone." Luke was on the verge of tears. "Heather, all gone. All gone." He began to weep.

Charles crawled over to hold Luke's arm. "Luke, we all feel the same way. You heard Heather; she's waiting and is safe now that NoOne called off the attack. I miss Bestow, too. But now, I feel something I haven't felt in a long time. Nature is talking. Our animal friends are hopeful. They have pockets of safety, and they're waiting to help us."

Ben returned to his more clinical self. "Well, we're all stuck here, and the weirdo Twin is still roaming around. How long can our buddy Twin here protect us?"

"Maybe I should go back and try to find the Snake, just to make sure it's backed off?" suggested John.

"No, that would be too risky. I think we're meant to hang together, not split up," said Ben.

"Oh, great, 'hang' is a word that does not make me relax," remarked Luke.

"So, what's our plan?" asked John.

The New Twin answered. "Now that you're back here, we must move to a place my brother won't be able to find right away. I'm just as strong as my brother, and without the mental force needed to maintain this bubble, and if I can rest a bit, I can take him on if I must."

The guys were thinking the same thing: The New Twin ran out of energy once before. Did he have enough power to move the group one more time?

The New Twin suddenly realized that the Sharks had stopped their attack. For some reason, they had all departed. Did the Sharks need a rest? Were the eyes coming back to take over? Maybe the Sharks sensed the Whales returning to rescue the guys? Or did the Sharks get an order to retreat? Perhaps they were no longer needed?

With the departure of the Sharks, the fish returned. The guys saw fish lazily float by, slivers of Light dancing off the seafloor, reflecting the bright sunlight of the day. The guys were amazed at how deep in the water they were, yet they could still see the sunny surface.

The silence became alarming. In a way, the constant grinding of the Sharks and their teeth against the bubble's invisible barrier was confirmation that the Old Twin was not immediately a threat. The scraping sound of the Sharks' razor teeth was reassuring in a way; the group at least knew that they had some wiggle room to make a plan to escape.

Now, with the eerie silence, the guys intuitively felt danger looming, possibly a deadly trap of some kind. So just in case the Old Twin was planning to attack, the group decided they had no choice but to move and escape to a more secure location. And hope they weren't being followed.

And wait.

Journal Entry Eighty-Four: Blessed in Misery

The Snake was confused. Why did NoOne order it to regurgitate back down towards the Funnel entrance, away from the First Gate? The Snake knew it was on the verge of victory. It was feet away from swallowing the First Gate completely.

The Snake sensed a core of White Orbs waiting for it to advance further; TheSon and His Orbs surely were poised to counterattack. This was of little concern because the Snake predicted complete victory; the number of eyes comprising its body greatly outnumbered the scattered gathering of Lights waiting on the other side of the Gate.

Suddenly the Lights disappeared. The Snake's collective consciousness sensed a massive change. Who was the source of this new voice issuing its orders? Why did the Snake feel compelled to obey? Was not their leader NoOne, the master of all Dark Matter?

In a millisecond, the Snake and all the eyes comprising its Darkness understood.

The Voice was unlike any voice they had ever heard. *Come, My children. We return to our home. But you shall be blessed in your misery.*

Blessed? OUR home? Communal summative wisdom emanated from the trillion trillions of Soul-Judged Evil Eyes. Their frantic nervousness was felt throughout the 'beyond the Veil'.

The Voice used the word "our." This must be a new tormentor. It's another trick to make our agony even greater.

Again, the Voice permeated the awareness of the Snake. *I am TheSon, the Son of TheOne. Follow Me.*

Follow they did. Rather than hellfire and relentless piercings with NoOne's Spiritual spears, the eyes felt a coolness, a calmness. For the first time in their SuperVoid eternity, they felt hope.

Those doomed to the SuperVoid knew all too well that NoOne trapped the Souls deep within the empty, vacuous eyes. Locked up. Hidden. Never to be released from their eternal torment. Now, TheSon, in the form of a single point of Light, floated in and through the group, instantly cataloging every sin from every eye. Each of the eyes felt a surge of hope that a second chance was possible.

Divine and Holy forgiveness meant one singular thing to the eyes returning to the SuperVoid with TheSon: the release of their Souls. Trapped forever by TheOne deep within the Black Hole of their empty eyes, TheSon might free their Souls for re-judgment. They felt the promise of a new judgment and the possibility of being given a way to escape the SuperVoid and transfer to the Reincarnation Universe.

The eyes felt they were being probed, but the piercing was healing. Eyes that screamed to eternity were invited to view a cleansing image of forgiveness. Every sin, every misdeed, every transgression, every crime, every failing would be reviewed. The heart of each would be examined to assess penance of character and resolve for atonement. All of Creation would be called to examine and judge with TheSon the worth of every eye for grace and forgiveness. Those who were cruel, trapped in desire, with no conscience, and no memory of their transgressions would remain in the SuperVoid. Forever.

Fleeing as far away as he could from the SuperVoid, NoOne intended to never return to his past kingdom. Once and for all time, there were no Divine chains to yank him back. Cruising within numerous universes, NoOne's Dark Cloud freely entered any domain he desired with no interference. For the first time, he encountered no Spiritual prison such as his SuperVoid home that might cage him. He had never been so free. Was it too good to be true? Was he scammed in the same way that he defrauded pre-judged Souls? To think his brother would fall for his trap made him wonder if he, NoOne, was being set up.

By giving up his army of DeadSouls, NoOne had indeed paid a hefty price. Yes, he had lost his beloved Snake, but it was well worth it to get rid of TheSon, at least for a few millennia. He wondered how long TheSon would really stay in the SuperVoid. Surely, long enough for NoOne to build a new army and construct an even bolder stronghold, untouchable by the counterfeit Holy.

As predictable as ever, his Brother had to play the savior role. 'TheSon likes to suffer and cater to the weak, to be a martyr,' thought NoOne to his host of Dark Matter followers. 'No wonder there is a need for me. Only I can provide equilibrium and balance. How can any world survive without pruning out the anemic, the frail, and the corrupt?'

NoOne could later find new Souls to judge in any of the trillion universes. One at a time, it would be a challenge. But now, he was free to wander and explore. No more SuperVoid with its Spiritual walls forever trapping him; no more hearing the screams, the pleas, the suffering. All of which he enjoyed, he admitted to himself. Yes, he would miss that part. What he would not miss was his imprisonment.

Yes, indeed. NoOne would conquer the Reincarnation Universe. It was just a matter of time. And didn't he have the rest of eternity? He needed to be patient, tend to his duties when called upon by TheOne, and stay inconspicuous.

Where should he start? What grand first step should he take now as a free master of all the multiverses in existence? He had to start somewhere.

Ah, I see my evil-spawned offspring on Earth has resurrected an old acquaintance. I think I will start there. Surely, the Twin and his new partner could use my help. After all, I AM his father! She IS my Lover! Just have to get her a new pair of eyes.

Journal Entry Eighty-Five: New Partner

Jenna filled in the parts of her memory that had disappeared at the campsite. She had lost her eyes and her Soul, but now she felt a presence. She could see.

"I have a new set of eyes!" Jenna screamed.

'Yes, mother. Or should I call you Mother? No. You don't deserve a name with a capital! But at least now, you have your Soul back; what's left of it anyway.'

"Where am I? I'm not buried anymore!"

'A little confused, mom? I thought I would resurrect you and let you see the old homestead.'

"That's our cabin. Where I raised you. And your brother. Where Lil' Johnny raised me. What happened to it?"

'Well, our kinfolk didn't appreciate you and grandpa hanging out with evil Spirits, so they torched it. Pity about Lil' Johnny. He was useful.'

Jenna looked at her son. He was smirking. At least he showed emotion now.

"Where is your brother?"

'Oh, he's hanging out with some guys.'

"Where did you get my eyes?"

The Old Twin's smirk turned into haughty condescension. 'They were kept in safekeeping by someone very close to me in an extraordinary place. It's called the SuperVoid. You know it as Hell.'

"What do you want from me? Why have I been brought back from my grave to life? Why am I with you?"

With a new set of eyes attached to a fragment of her previous Soul, Jenna started to recognize her surroundings. Long buried in the Earth, her body had been without awareness. She remembered the darkness that enveloped her when her eyes were destroyed, feeling intense pain, praying for the relentless torture to cease, agreeing to anything that the spirit called NoOne presented.

'Yes. Yes. Yes. Take my Soul. Stop my pain.'

The pain did stop. The suffocation began. Jenna found herself squeezed in with an uncountable number of others. She frantically tried to identify who they were. Then she had a revelation: She had no body, only her eyes. And the eyes of others. Reaching out, she sensed there was no end to the eyes. No end to the anguish and the screams to suppress the agony. She could not breathe. It was as if she were drowning and had one last half breath, just enough to keep her alive for a few more seconds but knowing that she was doomed; gasping to make the most of what little life remained; knowing it was futile.

But her body, what remained of it, was buried in the ground. It, too, was surrounded by others. She was in a perpetual coffin. Buried alive. Surrounded by a multitude of others experiencing the exact same panic and fear. Unrelenting. Absolute.

The Old Twin sensed the adjustment his mother was experiencing. 'Now, mother. You have to get your act together. You're back.

No getting stuck in the past. You're here for a reason. To be my new teammate.'

Jenna stumbled a few steps away from her son. Anxiety creeping over her pitted and half-rotted face, she stuttered, "Your teammate? I'm your mother. At least, I was."

'Isn't that an observation worth discussing.'

Jenna mustered as much courage as she could. "Will you please stop sending me thoughts and just talk like a real person?"

The Old Twin laughed. "Ok. You have no idea what you're saying, but I'll humor you for now."

Feeling like she was a little more in control of the situation, Jenna blurted out, "And why am I here? Why was I brought back? Who brought me back? I want some answers!"

"Whoa, mother dearest. Still feisty as ever. But not feisty enough to keep yourself from getting raped."

Jenna gasped. "Where did you…what…are…you…?"

The crafty, smug smile from the Old Twin didn't change. "Thought your sons didn't know, didn't you? We know all the details. Thrust by thrust."

"How did you find out?" Jenna was aghast and could barely get the words out of her mouth.

"Well, mother. Look at what you produced from such a rude interruption of your life: us! We, or at least me at this point, have come to know and Love your rapist, my father."

Jenna fell to her knees. Her memories were spinning, images and visions swirling around like competing currents in a river. It was impossible to track their beginnings or fusion with other streams, but all fleeting by, dark, muddy, and murky, leading nowhere.

"You know the man who raped me?"

"Mother, it really wasn't a man."

"What?" Jenna screamed. Images flooded her consciousness. The university. The pathway. The boy rapist. The monster climaxed inside her. The Snakes. The birth.

Do we not have beautiful children, my Love?

The Old Twin paused for effect, savoring every millisecond of suspense, already disappointed that the sweetness of the revelation would be so brief.

"He called me 'my Love.' " stuttered Jenna. Jenna bent forward, shielding her head in her hands, covering her ears. She didn't want to know anymore.

"Mommy, I think I'll let you in on a little secret. Daddy says he wants us to come out and play!"

Journal Entry Eighty-Six: Fullest Expression of Love

You are of Me, yet You are troubled, thought TheOne.

Yes, Father. When I am separate from You, making judgments, as TendHer, I am not You, replied TendHer. *The evil I must witness separates Me from My Purity.*

As do the incarnations of Your Brother. Sacrifice is His calling, as it is Yours. It reaches out to both of You in testament to My Love for My Creations.

Yes, We show Your Love with different manifests. From You. Our Love is freely given. But We long to be fully united. With You.

TheOne swirled in brightness, expanding from a single Speck of Divinity to a vast cloud of coruscating skyscape, growing ever larger as His consciousness engulfed the Reincarnation Universe.

To be fully united? It has never been thus. Daughter, I sense a part of You other than Me is troubling for You and Your Brother.

Like a supernova, the Energy of the One condensed to a single point and then exploded again. Then condensed. Then exploded. Repeating the cycle, the Divine Cloud reached the far ends of all known universes. TendHer simply observed, knowing Divine energy could never stop but must always be in motion, expressive.

That which is of concern is not a part of Our Divine Trinity. NoOne is free, said the TendHer.

That is true, replied TheOne.

It has never come to this. For all eternity, TheSon contained NoOne keeping him safely sequestered in the SuperVoid, except when You called NoOne forward to fill a new universe with his Dark Matter.

TheOne briefly ceased his majestic display. *Ah, so My design has finally borne fruit.*

TendHer was incredulous. *What? Fruit? True evil is now free to roam all the multiverses.*

That is so.

Then how can that be fruitful? asked TendHer.

TheOne ballooned in a vapor-like mist. He reached the apex of an explosion beyond knowable space or time limits. TendHer found His Spirit crisscrossed with glistening filaments of radiance, soothing and comforting, and energized with pillows of Holy strands.

The fullest expression of Love is creativity. NoOne has choices, and those choices could eventually nurture a cosmic resource.

To do what? Add more beauty to Your Creations? I doubt it. Not with NoOne. At what price, Father?

Daughter, You fulfill Your rational assessments beyond My expectations and hopes.

That is why I decided to leave You and administer Your Reincarnation Universe, replied TendHer.

That is true. You made a choice.

So, what about TheSon now stranded in the SuperVoid? asked TendHer.

TheSon made a choice.

TendHer paused. *And so will NoOne. Soon. This is a first, having NoOne free like this,* said TendHer. *What would You have Me do?*

TheOne became a gigantic wave, curled and ready to crash, blocking out all four horizons. TendHer, as always, was humbled by His power.

Don't do. Just be with Me.

TendHer was not satisfied with TheOne's answer. She wanted and needed guidance.

We will be swamped by those resurrected from the SuperVoid should they proceed through the Funnel and the Gates to be judged.

TheOne quickly replied, *No. Send them to 'beyond the Veil' to wait.*

So, I don't let them enter the Funnel? asked TendHer, confusion marking Her thoughts.

They will know what to do, replied TheOne.

Will I then know what You expect from Me? asked TendHer.

TheOne replied, *Before the battle looms, You and TheSon will see what needs to be done.*

So, there is a battle ahead, stated TendHer.

Yes, answered TheOne, almost in a whisper.

And if NoOne wins?

TendHer knew that the conscious presence of TheOne was ready to leave. Billows of razor-thin dazzling Strings vibrated and blazed as the consciousness of TheOne ebbed, fading to the dance of the Quantum Foam—harmonic vibrations that emerge from the illusory emptiness of space; movement mimicked by delighted, frenzied quarks and electrons.

In a flash, TheOne jetted out to deep 'beyond the Veil' where TendHer had never ventured. She felt the answer from TheOne, witnessed by all multiverses.

We start over.

Journal Entry Eighty-Seven: A Loving Army

Given his agreement with his brother, NoOne, TheSon was fully aware he would be imprisoned in the SuperVoid for quite some time. This signified for TheSon, at least for the part of His essence He chose to reveal, a progression of related events. Most of "the time," TheSon was "above" time or "under" time, some "time" "within" time. This was the Holy "non-time" of eternal bliss that was "beyond-time," not "in" time. However, "now," it was necessary for TheSon to enter the perception of time. The judgment of individual Souls in the SuperVoid required systematic and orderly processing of singular Books of Life; Pages collected through multiple life journeys that had a "beginning" and an "end." This was normally the assigned duty for His Sister, TendHer, usually completed in the Funnel and her Reincarnation Universe.

TheSon knew His Father had a plan. Why else would His Father order the re-judged Souls to linger in 'beyond the Veil' and forbid them from entering the Funnel? Complete trust in His Father guided TheSon's sacrifice; He cared only for the welfare of the LostSouls being denied true choice by NoOne. TheSon was determined to make amends for the brutality and deception of His brother.

TheSon felt Spiritual tugs as He re-judged LostSouls in the Supervoid. Those found deserving and worthy were forgiven; their Souls were made whole. They were released and escorted to 'beyond the Veil' to wait for the Funnel to be repaired and reopened. Then onto ego Karma removal guidance and reincarnation assignment by TendHer.

TheSon also knew that whatever good His concession with NoOne produced was temporary. NoOne would use his newfound freedom to build another army and create more chaos. TheSon knew the battle was only postponed.

However, TheSon was filled with hope, the same hope that swelled the SuperVoid with possibility. As the Spiritual Prophet and Savior of an infinite number of worlds, TheSon instinctively knew when to submit and open His heart to the wisdom of His Father's creativity. He had greeted the inevitable suffering sacrifice of death after every incarnation with the same Loving trust. He now embraced fully the redemption of LostSouls in the SuperVoid made possible by His Father, TheOne.

If Divinity was to survive, TheSon had to be ready.

Ironically, NoOne had provided TheSon with the army TheSon needed to protect 'beyond the Veil'. A motivated army. An army with memories of NoOne's treachery. TheSon hoped that a combination of Love and remembered deceit would be an uncontestable combination for winning the battle that loomed, even though TheSon and His newly saved would probably be outnumbered.

TheSon knew NoOne would be scouring multiverses recruiting new troops. It was critical to contain NoOne as soon as possible before NoOne's troop numbers again outnumbered His. It had happened once before. TheSon was trapped and powerless, but He hoped TheOne would intervene and not allow it to happen again.

Even more critical for His chosen team of four and the Souls on Earth was to contain the Old Twin. TheSon sensed how strongly the Old Twin wanted to destroy the guys and his brother, forcing the human boys to continuously move to new locations.

Finally, He observed them landing on a faraway beach, safe from the watchful eye of the Old Twin.

Have faith, My Chosen. I will be joining you when the time is right, thought TheSon to the fleeing group.

"Did you hear that?" asked Luke.

Ben looked up, confused at first, and then as he grasped the message, a smile spread across his face. Excitedly he announced to the group, "TheSon just checked in. Finally!"

"Yeah, I heard it too. Getting lots of vibes from my animal buddies," said Charles.

John commented. "OK, guys. We have to get in gear and hide. And I mean like quick!"

Addressing the New Twin, Ben asked the question everyone was thinking. "Do you think you can find us a better spot somewhere on land to hide from your brother? I mean, we're on the beach, exposed."

The New Twin was obviously exhausted. He didn't answer. His little head hung limp as he stared at his tiny feet. His emaciated arms were crossed with both hands shaking in a steady rhythmic twitch, almost in perfect unison.

Boo walked over to the feet of the New Twin and Lovingly walked around and between the New Twin's legs, much like a cat rubbing itself against the side of a sofa, trying to comfort the exhausted New Twin, who was bordering on a complete physical collapse.

John moved closer to the New Twin, almost nose to nose, and repeated his question, but softer, almost at a whisper. "We gotta find a better place...to...hide!"

John's proximity startled the New Twin. He jerked his head up and gazed at John. His hands came up in a protective gesture as if John posed a threat. For a moment, John understood that the New Twin might have the powers of a superhuman, but he was also a little boy, still in his first decade of life.

How could such a small person carry so much psychological weight and Spiritual purpose?

John retreated a few steps, held his hands out in front of his chest, palm side up as if to say, "I'm safe, don't worry." Breathing a few times deeply, the New Twin calmed himself, surveyed the group, looked at John, and nodded. The New Twin breathed a huge sigh when Boo cuddled up against his knees. The group visibly relaxed as the New Twin bent down, patted Boo, looked up, and finally smiled.

"Sorry about that, guys. Kinda drifted off," sighed the New Twin. With those words, the New Twin slumped to the ground. Luke rushed over to help him stand up.

"Well, if anyone deserves a break, it's you," said John.

Ben screeched, "This is not the time to take a break. We need to get out of here."

Luke walked between Ben and the New Twin. With his back to the New Twin, he began to lecture Ben. "Ben, will you just relax? John and our new buddy will figure things out. It doesn't help to panic."

Never one to back away from a debate, Ben replied, "You're telling me to relax? You got your girlfriend stuck in Heaven. Don't tell me to relax!"

"At least I have a girlfriend!" yelled Luke.

For one of the rare moments in Ben's life, he let down his emotional guard long enough to share a feeling. "That is so cruel," Ben softly replied, dropping his head to the ground.

Luke was shocked by Ben's brutal honesty and uncharacteristic vulnerability. Quickly, he muttered, "Yeah, sorry, Ben I take that back."

John was not having any further bickering. "Ben and Luke, please stay on track. We must pull ourselves together. Both of you, be like Charles. See how cool he always is. Seems like all the time, I have to tell you two to think before you open your mouths!"

Like a switch was flipped, Ben reverted to his old contentious self. "Well, you keep saying that about Charles. Over and over. I don't think Charles is with us most of the time. He's talking to the animals like Dr. Doolittle."

Charles smiled and couldn't resist a comeback. "Well, animals make more sense. They're honest. Just like you were when you said Luke was cruel. Animals don't play with words to manipulate others or hide their feelings."

The group was silent. One by one, heads started to nod in agreement. The last head to nod up and down was Ben's. He repressed his natural inclination to again fight with words. He knew that he must stay connected to the group. Who else did he have?

Inwardly Ben felt like a loser once more. *I just start to feel good about myself and feel part of the team, and then I say something stupid. "Stuck in Heaven?" Is it possible that I'll learn to keep my mouth shut at some point?* Little did Ben realize that his one moment of emotional honesty had earned him the respect of every other person (and animal) present.

While the guys were verbally sparring, the New Twin received an image from TheSon. At least, he thought it was from TheSon.

"I think we should all…." Before Luke could continue sharing his idea, he was abruptly interrupted by John.

"Shhh. Our guy here is tuning into something," whispered John.

The guys turned to study the New Twin. They watched with fascination as the New Twin was communicating with someone or something outside their group. The New Twin's head swiveled numerous times in different directions, seemingly looking at things he was discussing with an invisible companion. Trying not to be rude, the guys looked away if the New Twin glanced at them. The four were becoming more nervous as the discussion continued because the New Twin became more agitated as the minutes passed.

Finally, the New Twin relaxed. He visibly slumped as if a great weight had been removed. The four guys audibly exhaled and finally let go of their tightly wound-up muscles, relieved that the New Twin seemed to have things under control.

"Yes, I know I was tense. I apologize. I didn't want to upset you. We've been through a lot." The New Twin gestured for the guys to get closer. He didn't have to ask Boo, who was wrapped around his legs, panting, tail drooped under his rear end.

"I just communicated with TheSon. He has laid out our end game and a strategy to reach that objective." The New Twin paused. He looked around, and then his eyes became blank, oblivious to anyone or anything around him. He nodded, but it was not at the guys. He was still locked into a dialogue with TheSon.

"Sorry. Details," the New Twin said. "Now I understand."

"We need to get going, at least with some goal in mind," added Charles.

"Yes. Yes. Yes. Sorry. I should begin," replied the New Twin. "Wait, just one second."

Zoned out once more, the New Twin returned within seconds to the guys. Again, as if speaking to an invisible presence, the New Twin announced, "My thanks for your patience. I'm ready to go."

"Let me guess. A meadow deep in the forest?" asked John. No answer was needed. The guys knew that a location where the perimeter was visible and could be guarded was their only hope unless, of course, the Old Twin decided to drop in from the sky.

Journal Entry Eighty-Eight: Isn't That Loverly?

The Old Twin had no interest in lingering in his former village with the recently resurrected Jenna, his mother. His old cabin was burnt to a crisp. Few kin were left in the village, certainly none the Old Twin had any desire to torment; most scattered to surrounding small towns. As word got out about Jenna's and Lil' Johnny's horrific death, any villagers deemed close family to the two were shunned and forced out of the community. The displaced refugees avoided any mention of the monstrous Twins in their new homes lest they again become the subject of bigoted gossip at the least, physical harassment at the worst.

Taking Jenna's hand, the Old Twin transported the two of them to a site he was sure that his mother would remember. He figured a familiar environment like the original campsite where Jenna and his grandfather were killed would provide context and especially recognition of the power that dwelled within her son. The less resistance, the better. This was important so he could begin her training.

The Old Twin was relishing his control of the situation. He had complete sovereignty over life and death; he could even shut nature down should he choose to do so. With a mere thought, he had commanded birds to cease chirping, bees to cease flying, and ferns to stop rustling. Even the air became still. Humid. The smell of rotting flesh percolated up from deep within the Earth, the resting place of his growing corpse army.

The Old Twin fondly remembered when he and his brother terrorized the four guys in their tent and removed his grandfather's tongue and eyes.

"Yes, mother dear. We are once more a team. Just do what you're told, and you might live to see your Lover again!"

The Old Twin chuckled then thought, *Isn't that what father wants? Yes, that's exactly what he wants. But more than that. I think daddy has a crush on Mommy.*

Jenna, still in shock, could only stutter. "You…me…the Devil?"

This is nasty humidity, even for me. I'm actually starting to sweat! Must be suffocating for Mom. When this is concluded, I'm going to rewrite Pygmalion! I'll be known as the Henry Higgins of supernatural powers. I can redo any worthless human being into a prized specimen, complete with new eyes and a slightly reconditioned soul!

Wiping his sweaty brow and walking calmly around the campsite, feet from where he had resurrected his mom, the Old Twin looked forward to showing his mother what she could do and who she would become.

"Now, now, mother. Just relax. Didn't know you had a special Lover? Ha, ha. Trust me. You will see him again."

Jenna shook her head in disbelief. Looking around, she tried to orient herself. The forest looked familiar. It was where everyone she

Loved had died. Memories of her dad unfolded like snapshots in her Mind's Eye. Tears streamed from her eyes, and her hands began to shake.

Stay calm, she told herself. *No, I won't stay quiet. This is a nightmare. I must be sleeping. Wake up!*

"No, mother, you aren't dreaming. You are here with one of your sons. Yes, my grandpappy is mostly dirt now. We have a new alpha in our family, and he has given me a job to do. And you're going to help me."

"Do what?"

Giddy and squealing with glee, the Old Twin screamed at the top of his voice. "We are building an army. However, it's not like any army you're familiar with. We're getting special troops."

"What do you mean, special troops? Troops for what? How are they special?"

"Ah, excellent questions. Your Lover has plans to battle the good guy. You see, my father, your Lover, is the bad guy. At least that's what others call him. Frankly, I think it's all a matter of perspective. What is bad to one person is good to another. It's relative. This is the defining characteristic of advanced, rational thinking and so-called "civilized societies." All sides to an issue are relativized in their perspective. In the end, there no longer exists any underlying moral foundation, no ethical commitment to higher ideals, no overriding truths. Like-minded people join together solely based on shared selfish interests and learn they can get what they want by demonizing other groups, usually with childishly simplistic slogans such as 'Down with patriarchy.' Or 'Abortion is murder.' Life simply becomes a matter of who can scream the loudest. So much so that eventually, a society implodes from the wars brought on by tribal polarities. It's the classic 'us versus them.' So, to you, your

Lover is 'the Devil.' To me, he's my father and is simply trying to break through all the hypocrisy and call *it* as *it* is."

Jenna was in shock. Her son's commentary on political philosophy was unnatural coming out of the mouth of a seven-year-old. It made her cringe and shiver. It was creepy, and Jenna was quickly sinking into a panic. She told herself to settle down, stay focused. Her life might depend on it. Again.

"And what is '*it*'?" whimpered Jenna.

"Survival of the fittest. Earth has become weak. It no longer deserves the universal resources that it demands."

"What are you talking about? That sounds like Darwin."

The Old Twin nodded his head in agreement. "Yes. Only on a multiverse level. You will soon understand that the Earth is competing with trillions of other planets in trillions of other universes. We aren't special. We're just sloppy and spoiled."

Jenna was not prepared for a debate on social theory, or even cosmic theory, for that matter. However, the one thing she spotted in her son was his lack of feeling, a dEarth of emotion, except when he started to talk about his father and his theories.

"So, what's your plan? A global cleansing?" asked Jenna.

"Pretty much done that. But not completely. Earth has a unique place in my father's plans. It will be the launching platform for his destiny: inter-universal domination."

"In other words, your father, the Devil…."

The Old Twin interrupted Jenna. "And your Lover."

Jenna was together enough to fully express her disgust. "Don't you dare call him my Lover. He raped me."

"Touchy, touchy," laughed the Old Twin.

"Let me finish. The Devil is planning on conquering other planets, other worlds?"

"And other universes," added the Old Twin.

"OK, those too. The Devil wants to do all this, but *why*?"

"Mother, he wants to dominate and put inhabitants to use."

"Put them to use for what?" asked Jenna.

"To build an army," replied the Old Twin.

"Build an army for what?" said Jenna. The horror of what she thought her son was saying was building. It took all her strength to listen clearly and try to understand the implications.

The Old Twin took on a look his mother had never seen before. It could best be described as "dreamy." His gaze clouded in orientation, and he seemed to vanish. There was no life in his eyes.

"Thanks, father," the Old Twin said. Turning around to face Jenna, he said, "Sorry for the zone out. Your Lover said I can tell you."

"You just talked to the Devil? Here?"

The Old Twin laughed. "Oh yes. And to answer your question, since you are now my partner, we're building an army to destroy God."

Jenna became hysterical. Incredulous laughter turned to screaming. *This can't be real. I died. I'm in Hell, that's it. My son is psychotic.* Jenna had forgotten her son could read her thoughts.

"No, you're not in Hell. And yes, I am psychotic. And yes, it *is* real. At least how *you* define reality. We're about to explore another reality."

Finally settling down but still breathing deeply, Jenna asked, "Answer this question. How are you planning on defeating God?"

The Old Twin wanted to savor every second of the pregnant pause that followed Jenna's question—it was so delicious. It's almost as good as watching eyeballs pop out; even better than watching people watch the eyeballs of others pop out and then have to wait for their own eyeballs to pop out!

"Ah, my simple mother. Have you not looked around lately? Remember your Mental Hospital job and the wonderful reception I received there? Oh, and by the way, it's not the only place that houses the mentally exceptional. We've been stocking planet Earth for eons."

"What, like a lake? Stocking it with fish?"

"Ha, ha. No. We've been stocking it with inhabitants from other worlds. We have been assembling an army of mental patients from other universes. What you call Earth is one of many Mental Hospitals for the multiverses."

"You get mental patients from other universes? Where are they?"

"You see them every day. You see them walking, working, playing, eating, sleeping, and, yes, fornicating. They're deposited. As we speak, new portals are being crafted to transfer these deviants to this planet. And planted. Like corn. Been this way since *Homo erectus*, right before your species, *Homo sapiens*. Who do you think wiped out all the competing species?"

Jenna was incredulous. "So you could make room for more bodies? And they're from other universes?"

"Yes. My father is only interested in universal rejects and home-born losers."

"And you saved the bodies for an army?"

"Yes. They're right under your feet. Here, at the campsite and in the forest. Buried everywhere. Our quaint little village had hundreds buried. Waiting."

"When a new group arrives, where do they go?" asked Jenna.

"They mostly go to farmland. Soon we will command all the farms, forest, and wilderness areas. Every square inch of our vast planet will be a cemetery army waiting to be called. All continents. All countries. Everywhere but cities. Well, at least for now."

"Why not cities?" Jenna couldn't believe she was being drawn into her son's delusion. Was it psychosis? It had to be.

On the other hand, she had personally been raped by a monster.

Had it really been the Devil?

And she had witnessed the power and cruelty of her sons.

The Old Twin was quick to reply, as usual, with a condescending and haughty manner. "Can't resurrect bodies from under the concrete. You ever heard of 'From dust to dust?' "

"Yes," Jenna answered.

"Most of America is urban now, 85 percent. Living in cities with nothing but concrete underfoot," the Old Twin coldly recited, as if lecturing a student. "But that will change. Once food disappears, and the bandits are done, we will plow the concrete under. There will be lots of space opening up."

"So why can't we see these outer space colonists when they arrive?" pressed Jenna.

"It's not a 'them,' mother," the Old Twin smugly answered. He could hardly contain his irritation at having to explain something so simple to his mother. Could she not understand how brilliant her son was? And how powerful?

Jenna built up her courage to ask, "What do you mean, not 'them?' If not 'them,' then it's a 'what?' A thing?"

"DNA. That's all my father sends. Just enough to rewrite the most important coding genes of the human host body with the DNA of the transplant. Special delivery right through your Lover's special portal, carried by those wonderfully small quantum string messengers."

The Old Twin searched his mother's face to see if she could comprehend what he was saying. He could tell she was beginning to understand the implications; she looked increasingly horrified, just as he had hoped, so he continued. "Unlike home-born humans, when the genetically re-engineered transplants die, they are preprogrammed to wait for my father. They go right to the Earth. No Souls. Just like seeds. Waiting to sprout. But regular homegrown humans are another story. They have Souls, and that's why NoOne has to recruit them one by one. My job is to safe-keep the bodies of the damned—both the transplanted and the homegrown."

Jenna uttered her conclusion impulsively. "So eventually, there will be no more homegrown humans."

The Old Twin laughed. "Hey, at some point, the hotel fills up. No more rooms!"

"Did I come from another universe? Was I one of the mental patients sent here?" asked Jenna.

"No. You were one of the millions from this planet. Born here. But still planted because you gave up your Soul to your Lover."

"When did the first transplants come to Earth?" asked Jenna.

"You can thank your Adam and Eve from Mesopotamia. They were the first transplants. But other variations of the homo line of descent were allowed to evolve independently."

"Because?"

"*Ahhh*, aren't you a curious little mommy? It's all about numbers, my dear. Homegrown humans became our reserve just in case we needed more bodies. Like now."

"What percentage of Earth is homegrown and what percentage is transplanted?" asked Jenna.

The Old Twin giggled, "Alive?"

"Yes, alive."

"There are very few homegrown humans left. But if you survive our partnership, I'll let you know just how many, mother dear."

"What about your brother?" asked Jenna.

"He made his choice. It was a stupid choice."

"What choice was that?"

"He chose the Spirit because he's pathetic and weak. He will soon be destroyed, as will all your Mental Hospital boys. First, we build our army. You and me. And father."

"I didn't get a choice when I died," stated Jenna.

"Oh yes, you did. My father made a deal with God, you see. Humans no longer must go through reincarnation. You now have a choice to end your suffering rather than having to climb some abstract ladder to paradise."

"And I made a choice to reject Heaven?"

"Guess some people call it that. You just don't remember. You begged for your pain to stop and would do anything. Your Lover took you up on your offer. It's all in a split second, and then whoosh, off your Soul goes to the SuperVoid while your physical body goes to the ground to rot, waiting to be resurrected when father calls you. But at least you didn't have to endure horrible pain while being judged in the Reincarnation Universe."

Smiling, the Old Twin continued. "If you choose the way of the Spirit, you go through cycles of reincarnation till you're pure. It's too late for you now, anyway."

"Why? Why? I want to do that!" Jenna sobbed. "Please! Can't you please help me?"

The Old Twin turned his back. He knew it was time to end the discussion. He was bored. The novelty of having mommy back had worn off. Even worse, he could tell she would be a constant whiner; always complaining. He realized Jenna was a liability. She knew too much. She talked too much. She asked too many questions.

Yes, I must fix this. It is time, thought the Old Twin.

Turning around, he looked at his mother and erased all the memories found in her long-term memory with a slight twitch of his eye.

Start fresh; that's what I say. Mother, you will be a perfect partner, the Old Twin considered. *The enemies I need to overcome will recognize too late your change, giving me just enough time to carve up their Souls. Guess mothers are of use after all.*

"Jenna, how do you feel?" probed the Old Twin out loud, curious about what effect his psychic surgery had on her personality. After all, he needed at least some sliver of familiarity left from his "old" mother.

Jenna, staring at her son, struggled to put words together. All she could manage to say was, "Who are you?"

"I'm your son, mother."

Jenna smiled and said, "Isn't that loverly. Who are you?"

A little clearer and louder this time, the Old Twin responded, I'm your son, mother."

Jenna again smiled. "Isn't that loverly. Who are you?"

Well, guess that didn't work, thought the Old Twin.

"Off you go, mother dear, back to the grave. Guess I should take your Soul back."

With a brief smirk and twitch of the Old Twin's mouth, Jenna's young eyes flew out of her sockets and fell, flopping to the ground. He wondered. A fascinating scenario captured his imagination. What it would be like to kill her here and now?

Why not? I'll find a new partner somewhere down the road, the Old Twin mused. *If father gets too mad, I can always come back and get her.*

So, the Old Twin removed all the oxygen from his mother's body. One last horrific gasp and Jenna's lifeless body sluggishly crumbled to the ground like a flower wilting in the hot day sun. She was immediately enveloped by hungry worms. Jenna disappeared deep within the Earth, covered with regurgitated squirmy sludge, a fitting wardrobe for her Earthy casket.

From a far-off place, fetid words hung in the air, drifted in, and circled around the Old Twin and his mother's new grave, heavy with psychic mucus, a fitting eulogy: *Do we not have beautiful children, my Love?*

The Old Twin was surprised. *Whoopsie, guess I was a bit hasty!*

Obediently, the Old Twin answered, "Yes, Father. Isn't that loverly?"

Journal Entry Eighty-Nine: Hiding Place

The New Twin motioned the guys to gather around him. They didn't have far to walk as the meadow they landed in was no more than 50 feet in circumference. It was surrounded by Western Hemlock and Sitka Spruce trees, an excellent temporary hiding place. A stream could be heard "tinkling" nearby; it was comforting with its steady, predictable rhythm.

Boo lay sleeping at the New Twin's feet, snoring and occasionally passing gas in almost perfectly timed breathy sequences that seemed to match the tempo of the stream.

"Are you guys thinking the same thing I am?" asked Luke.

"Yeah. I can stand small spaces, I can stand heights, but I can't stand Dog toots!" said John. Everyone laughed, even the New Twin, but it was short-lived. The New Twin nudged Boo with his foot. Boo yawned and instinctively wagged his tail as he saw his human companions huddled around him.

The New Twin continued. "OK. We need to settle down here. My brother is preoccupied with something. He has been at one location for quite a while, but at least he's away from us. We need to take advantage of this break in his pursuit."

Ben interrupted. "You don't have a plan?"

The New Twin looked up into the trees as if he were thinking. Everyone followed his eyes, but the New Twin was obviously focused on thoughts other than the empty sky.

Not a good sign. Nothing going on in the sky. He doesn't have a plan, thought John.

The New Twin returned his gaze to the guys. "I think we are sitting ducks wherever we go. My brother has zoned in on all our psychic configurations, which somewhat mirror our electron configurations. It's like a location beacon flashing our whereabouts for someone with my brother's capabilities. My brother can find us no matter where we go and eventually come for us. At his pleasure and any time he wants."

Luke wasn't sure what that meant. "Uh, what's a psychic configuration?"

The New Twin looked at Ben. "Tell 'em, Ben."

Eagerly Ben began. "Well, atoms have shells that keep the electrons in orbit around the nucleus. It's like layers of a cake, so to speak. Each shell has a different capacity for electrons. For example, the first shell can handle only two electrons, the second shell can only handle eight, and so on. This is what makes up part of our periodic table. From the little I have read, admittedly from some highly questionable underground sources, psychic configuration is similar in theory. The Soul has rings around it with two forces: Love and fear. Each ring has different limits on how much Love and fear it can handle. Once the fear is removed from all the rings, the rings of the Soul collapse to become Holy, and then are ready to merge with TheOne."

"So, fear is the only negative emotion?" asked Luke.

"Yes, all negative energy, whether hate or anger or anxiety, can ultimately be tied to being afraid," said The New Twin.

John saw how this fit in with his karate practice. "Oh, yeah. That fits. It's about loss. Losing anybody or anything important, like a parent or a friend. Even a competition. It could be the fear of losing our life, which really means the fear of losing our ego. Part of my karate practice was acknowledging and dealing with fear because, many times, it's normal to be afraid. I learned I had to trust completely in a higher power, whatever or whoever that is, and just let go of the fear, like watching the water in a creek come and go with no judgment, just observation."

"So, we need to stay on the run?" asked Charles.

I can do that, thought Charles. *It's the others who won't be able to keep up with me.*

The New Twin paused and then replied, "The only option I see open would be for all of you to dematerialize, except Boo. He'll stay with me. I can make you do that, physically disappear. The problem is getting you to rematerialize. Don't think that's ever been done before."

Charles stepped forward and addressed the group before anyone else could speak. "We need to disappear. I don't know about dematerializing, but Native cultures understand the power behind that which cannot be seen."

"Isn't that what we've been learning about? Isn't that 'beyond the Veil' where we've spent so much time?" Ben asked. A bit of disappointment tinged Ben's voice. He wanted to lecture more on atomic structure and dematerializing. But then again, he thought, rematerializing was an entirely different matter, way out of his league.

Charles continued to speak in a quiet, soft tone, much like when he gave his campfire presentation about the Monster Bear, which now seemed like years ago. "We can become invisible through our sacrifice."

Boo's head jerked up. *Time for me to disappear. I think I see what's coming.*

The New Twin tuned into Boo's thoughts. 'Hang in there, big guy; I think Charles is on to something.'

The guys were familiar with the signals Boo sent when he was upset. His chin would drop into his chest, eyes would swivel up with a look that elicited sympathy, and then his tail would curl between his legs, with a whimper or two for added effect.

The New Twin and Charles laughed when they caught Boo's thoughts: 'Great. As long as I don't become a hot dog for somebody. And this feels like one big weenie roast.'

Ben brought both back to reality when he said, "Ah, I hope you're not thinking what I think you're thinking."

John and Luke reacted at the same time and in unison. "What?"

Charles answered. "You're thinking of Soul merging, aren't you?"

The New Twin purposelessly did not answer. He wanted the possibilities to sink in; let each guy draw some tentative conclusions to reduce the trauma. He didn't think anything else would work. The merging of Souls was the only path that had any chance of success. Maybe the group could come up with some other course of action.

"My question is if we merge, how do we purge? I mean if we merge with somebody…." Ben was interrupted before he could finish his thought, which he considered very disrespectful given his intellect. But since it was the New Twin, he let it slide.

"I didn't say 'somebody else,'" said the New Twin.

"Oh, my god, you've got to be kidding. I ain't gonna get in bed with some *thing*," groaned Luke.

"My native peoples merge all the time. And again, all of us here are now experts at leaving our bodies." Charles' comments seemed to help Luke relax.

Ruminating on possibilities, John added his observations. "This will still be a first. I think our Twin buddy here is saying that our bodies must disappear, not just our Spirits or Souls. Am I right?"

Softly the New Twin answered. "It's the only way. Your bodies must disappear along with your Mind's Eyes and Souls. Our bodies have around 37 trillion cells. My brother and I can track every one of them. Butcher your body up into a hundred pieces, and we can still locate every piece."

John immediately saw the practical implications and was more interested in the process than the possible dangerous outcomes. "So, light our bodies on fire?" he asked.

"Your bodies must be destroyed," replied the New Twin.

"Just what I thought," whispered John.

"What the *fu-u-u*...!" exclaimed Luke.

"You have to be kidding me!" gasped Ben.

"No, I'm not," matter-of-factly replied the New Twin.

A hushed calm engulfed the group. There was nothing further to discuss. It was the only way. The guys felt like they had already taken one step off a cliff, precariously balanced, teetering high above an unknown abyss, leaning with only one foot on solid ground.

"I'm sorry. It's the only way," said the New Twin.

"You said our Souls could be merged?" asked Charles.

"Yes."

"What species?" Charles tried to help the group relax a bit by getting into the details.

"I'm glad you ask, Charles. We will need your communicative powers with our animal friends."

Attempting to break the ice with some humor, Luke suggested they merge their Souls with mermaids.

Who would want to hurt a mermaid?

Ignoring Luke, Ben asked, "Is that right? We're going to be eaten?"

"That might work with anyone except my brother or me. Cells are cells. We can tune into recycled digested host tissue just as easily as live tissue."

"Then what about our Souls? Can't your brother zero in on some signal from our Soul?" asked John.

"Good question, John. No. My brother cannot read Soul signals. I can because I chose to be with TheSon. Whether it is genetic psychopathy or just plain perversion, my brother will not have a clue where your Souls reside. However, there is one risk. I can read your Souls because I have a Soul. There could arise a situation where my defenses crash and my brother reads my mind."

"So, it's best if you don't know where our Souls are?" asked Luke.

"That's right. Charles will find you some animal friends to merge with. I will know the species you are merged with, of course. But I will not know where you go, other than the general area."

"So, we have to be, like, exploded?" asked Luke.

"I'm afraid so. Your current bodies must be destroyed. Once this mess is over, we can find you new bodies."

Ben started to laugh. "Wow, maybe I can be an athlete like Luke. Hey, buddy, maybe you could have an inner tube stomach like me!"

Luke's mouth hung down to the ground. He was not happy.

"What are the steps?" asked Charles. "Who do you want me to contact for Soul merging?"

"You choose. However, consider a species with maximum terrain coverage in small fragments of time, exceptional evasiveness, and aggressive power."

Ben blurted out his answer before Charles could tell everyone to stay quiet, lest the New Twin figure out their new homes. "Elephants!"

"Why are you so damn happy, Ben?" asked John.

Ben's eyes opened wide. His mouth tried to form words, but nothing came out. Finally, Ben released a feeling long suppressed, never considered, much less shared, with anyone else. A tear formed at the corner of both eyes.

"I get a new body! This is a dream come true. I've been teased all my life about my weight. Do you have any idea how horrible that is? My only place to hide was in my head. My only way to deal with my pain and anger was by setting fires!"

Finally, the New Twin said, "I'm sorry for you, Ben. I know it's been tough."

Words came slow and measured from John. "Yeah, Ben. If it's any consolation, all of us have demons. Guilt weighs me down to this day."

"What? Why?" a surprised Ben asked.

"You know the story already about my Sensei, whom I let die."

"Oh, yeah, sorry, John. For what it's worth, I don't think you let your Sensei die," said Ben.

The New Twin reached out his tiny hands to the group. "We all must stay together on this. All of you are needed. All of us have issues. In addition, I am learning that pain does not ever go away. It just becomes familiar. I hope that I will be better able to accept mine at some point. But for now, all of us have to stay focused."

"Do you know how weird it is, such fancy words coming out of a little boy's mouth?" said Ben.

The New Twin replied, "Yes, Ben, I think I do. My brother and I can make ourselves appear to others any way we want. I have chosen to be honest with you. I want a reminder of my humanity. I am part of this biological circus that my father has engineered. So, pardon my bluntness, but we must get back to our mission. Charles, do you know who you want our group to merge with?"

"Yes. I just need to be alone to contact them," said Charles as he huddled in the corner of the meadow with his head between his legs.

Luke couldn't help himself. "Charles, so you knew this was going to happen all along? You already have a species in mind?"

"My people do this all the time. Our many tribal dances celebrate this kind of merging."

"Is it going to hurt?" asked Luke.

The New Twin had anticipated just this question. "No, Luke. All of you listen carefully. Your eyes with your Soul will be removed the instant after you die. Then your bodies will be incinerated. Your ashes will be escorted by a hundred Eagles to the upper reaches of our breathable atmosphere and released. They will disperse almost a thousand miles over the ocean. Impossible to trace."

"So will it hurt to lose our eyes?" asked Luke.

The New Twin paused. The guys thought this could be either a good sign or a bad sign. Unfortunately, it was the latter.

The New Twin raised slightly higher on his small heels to steel up his courage. "Well, yes. For just an instant. But then…no pain, 'cause you'll be dead."

Ben wanted more details about the merging. "Will we be aware that we are merged with an animal? Will the animal know?"

The New Twin motioned to Charles in the corner to answer Ben's question.

"We do it all the time in Native cultures. There will be awareness, yes. For both parties. However, it will be a natural experience like working with a good friend on a job that both know well. Both Souls will be enriched."

Ben waved his index finger back and forth. "OK, then, sorry to be the one with all the questions, but when we're all done with this great adventure into the afterlife, how do we get back into another human body? I mean no offense, Chief, I mean Charles, but I want assurances I'm not going to end up in some eighty-year-old body running red lights in a wheelchair and needing an oil lube to wipe my ass."

The New Twin had obviously not had enough time to consider possible answers to such a question. "Look, guys, the odds are high you aren't going to make it. I'm just telling it like it is. I see no other choice. If we stay here, you are guaranteed to become snacks for the Cougar."

Charles was surprised. "New Twin, there aren't any Cougars here; they all left for the big battle at Mt Olympus."

The New Twin smiled. "None you know about, Charles. Trust me."

"So, we're going to die," stated John.

After what seemed like an eternity, Charles spoke in his usual low, serene, monotone voice. "Have we not seen the other side, the 'beyond the Veil'? More than anyone, we should not fear death. Our fate and joy reside with the people we Love the most, and they wait for us when we cross the threshold. How can you be afraid? Luke, how can you be afraid? Heather is waiting for you. John, how can you be afraid? Your Sensei waits for you. Ben, how can you be afraid? The person you came to trust, Igor, is waiting for you. All of nature waits for me, and I embrace the mystery."

"Just not excited about losing my life," mumbled Ben.

"None of us are," said Charles. "We need to move on with this. I need to get our animal friends ready. I've sent word out, and many groups are eager to join us."

"Who are you going to use? What animal wants to share their being with a human?" asked John.

"An animal you've probably never heard about. I think the host we choose to merge with needs to fly," said Charles.

John was more excited about who Charles would choose than any of the other guys. John reasoned he should probably be the leader as he was familiar with all the forests of North America. "Agreed. For scouting great distances."

"Yes," said Charles. "And a vicious fighter."

"Well, I want to be an elephant or a whale. Something massive," said Ben.

John shook his head and laughed. "You already are, Ben! It's just too obvious. It must be an animal that's either really low to the ground or high in the air. An animal that's mobile, fast, and can disappear out of sight instantly."

"That's what I was thinking," added Charles. "I think the air has the best vantage point. I notified our hosts a few weeks ago that we need them for air support. They're coming from zoos all over America."

John was impressed. "Wow, you're organized."

Boo asked Charles to ask the group a question. "Guys, Boo wants to know what happens to him."

"It's time to say goodbye, Boo," said the New Twin. Time slowed down for everyone as they realized how important Boo had been for the group's emotional and physical survival.

'Oh, great, so I'm headed for kitty litter?' thought Boo.

Charles and the New Twin laughed.

"Could you fill us in on the joke?" asked Ben.

"Boo just doesn't want to be recycled," said Charles to the group. Then, turning to the New Twin, Charles asked, "What happens to Boo? We should take care of him before we merge, that's for sure."

The New Twin smiled and turned to face Boo. "I haven't forgotten you, Boo. However, you will have half of your fears confirmed. You are headed for the kitties. But they have pledged to protect you and not turn you into litter."

Boo was not happy. Backing up, he slowly lowered his rear to the ground and refused to look at the New Twin.

"Ah, come on, big guy. You don't have to be merged like the guys. My brother won't pick on you. I've got a den of Cougars that will ensure you're protected and well-fed. In fact, they've been waiting for you in the forest."

The New Twin signaled the Cougars to come forward. The guys watched Boo anxiously scan the meadow's perimeter. Out walked three huge Cougars. They were confident and regal as they slowly sauntered toward the guys, almost in perfect step, with their gigantic paws paddling leisurely at the ground.

The New Twin introduced the Cougars to Boo. They promised to treat Boo as one of their own. At first, Boo cautiously approached the Cougars, then stopped and turned. His tail suddenly drooped.

"Boo is pleading to stay with you, New Twin," said Charles.

"We must say our goodbyes, my gentle and loyal friend," said the New Twin. "You have served us well, and from what I have learned, we will meet again in 'beyond the Veil'. For now, you have earned the right to be free and to be protected."

Boo was ambivalent. He wanted to stay with the guys; he had thoroughly bonded with them and the New Twin. 'Come on, guys. I'm not really into the predator scene. You know, I get nauseous at the sight of anything red. Like blood. Especially my blood. Cougars are ferocious. I'll stick with processed meats from the grocery store if you know what I mean?'

Charles smiled and nodded. 'Know what you mean, Boo. This is the only way to protect you, I'm afraid. But I'm also glad because you will thrive.'

The three female Cougars circled Boo and slowly walked around him. Little by little, they tentatively approached closer until finally, they were rubbing Boo with the side of their bodies, purring. Two more Cougars emerged from the woods and joined the group until five Cougars were circling and purring. Then something entirely unexpected occurred. The five Cougars backed away from Boo, who stood still in the middle of the group. Facing Boo, they simultaneously stretched out their front legs and bowed their tawny heads.

Charles interpreted the actions of the Cougars. "Boo, the Cougars have given you alpha status, above all male Cougars. They will forever defer to you and have pledged their lives to protect and serve you. You will be king of all the lairs in the Pacific Northwest."

The five Cougars rose and, nodding to Boo to come with them, together they walked toward the forest. Boo looked back just once.

The guys could have sworn Boo was smiling.

Boo could have sworn the guys were crying.

Entering the forest, Boo and the Cougars disappeared. Just as the guys were returning to their task, they heard a noise. Out from the forest ran Boo, chased by five tiny Cougar cubs. Not being as quick or fast, Boo was quickly overrun. The cubs jumped on Boo, rolling him over on his back. Boo's tail thrashed in pleasure, tongue-wagging, slobbering all over the cubs, who were just as delighted with their newfound buddy.

Then from the woods emerged a couple of adult female Cougars. Shaking their heads back and forth as if scolding the playful cubs, they walked up to the cubs and Boo and nudged them back into the forest. Boo never looked back.

The guys promptly returned their attention to the New Twin. He was reaching the limit of his endurance. It took every ounce of his willpower not to fall down in exhaustion. "Guys, you need to move quickly. I'm about out of energy. Charles, please call your friends."

"Got it," said Charles.

Turning to the guys, Charles whispered, "You probably have never seen them before because they live in Africa, Southern Europe, and India."

"Wow, sounds erotic," said Luke.

"No, fur brain. It's exotic!" said Ben.

The New Twin paused to catch his breath. His breathing was becoming increasingly labored.

"*Gypaetus barbatus.*"

Charles knew he had little time. He nodded. "You're correct. Forgot you read minds."

"Sorry, don't know the classification. Can you speak using English?" asked Luke.

Ben jumped in. "I memorized all the scientific classifications when I was barely out of first grade. I can tell you every Kingdom, Phylum, Class, Order, Family…."

"Enough, already," said John. "Just give us a common name!"

"Go ahead, Ben," said the New Twin.

Ben lingered to relish his control of the situation, slowly turning around to ensure everyone was paying attention. "My friends, I hope you like to eat bones because soon we will merge with Bearded Vultures."

Journal Entry Ninety: Another Gift

The Old Twin had little time, much less concern, for his brother. He was preoccupied with harvesting and planting his corpse army in the farmlands. These were hardy folks. Strong backs, resolute in their determination to survive. Very useful for the hard labor sure to surface down the road.

Am I gifted with wit or what? Sure to surface? Oh, yes indeed! They will surely surface! Labor is not a problem!

And the cities?

Only a few large cities protected by the Erob domes remained intact, their populations safe. He knew he would eventually discover the domes' random algorithms controlling the quantum frequencies that generated the shield and scavenge those last few remaining urban populations.

The cities are not a problem.

The Old Twin also knew he could find and eliminate his brother and the four young males any time he so desired. So why rush?

The four boys are not a problem. So why do I have this sense of dread? I never felt this way when my brother was around, thought the Old Twin.

The question that he had successfully repressed, yet which still managed to gnaw away at his self-certainty, finally surfaced.

Why hasn't my father checked in with me? Is he deserting me? Is he just using me and then will abandon me?

Months had passed since NoOne instructed the Old Twin to follow his brother and report the activities of the four boys. The one-way communication was frustrating, and all the Old Twin wanted to know was when he could join his father in space, at the head of the gigantic space corpse army.

At least, that's what his father had promised him.

Did he really promise me? Or am I thinking wishfully? pondered the Old Twin.

The Old Twin mentally ran through his father's possible reasons for avoiding him. *Maybe he's upset with me? But why would he be mad at me? I've been loyal and done everything he has asked. Could it be*

NoOne is disappointed that I impulsively ended the sniveling existence of my mother? Hmm. Perhaps he was closer to Jenna than I thought.

Granted, the last few weeks had been a rush.

Maybe I just need to relax. Take a rest. I deserve a break. I've earned it! I mean, think of it. How many humans can fly? How many can move mountains? How many can wipe out entire forests? How many cities have I wiped out with absolute impunity?

Of course, I'm tired!

The Old Twin thought the time was ripe to ask his father, NoOne, if he was stuck forever in a small boy's body. Could he produce offspring like his father when he got older? *Item to discuss with dad*, thought the Old Twin. *Want to understand why post-puberty humans get such pleasure humping like Dogs and spitting out body juice!*

But for now, that topic would have to wait. The Old Twin's priority was reconnecting with NoOne and joining his army in space.

Weeks passed. The Old Twin started to feel even more abandoned, the constant killing was no longer a thrill or a challenge.

Finally, the Old Twin felt NoOne was nearby. 'Why have you been gone for so long? Have I angered you? Please let me know what to do, father.'

NoOne answered. 'It is now your time.'

'Yes, father. Am I joining you in space? You promised I could lead the corpse army!'

NoOne replied, 'Not yet. Be patient. I have another gift for you. Are you ready?'

'Oh, yes! Oh, boy! Another gift!'

Deep within his brain, the Old Twin felt a soothing invitation to be receptive to whatever was delivered by his father. NoOne called it "the ultimate gift, not born of Earth or Spirit." It would hurt, he was warned, but NoOne emphasized that the venomous toxin would assure ultimate authority over life and death. It was so much more than he had received with his brother during their advanced training. With this new infusion, he would have complete supremacy over all life forms in every multiverse! This new venom, promised NoOne, would finally allow the Old Twin to lead NoOne's space corpse army, a leadership role NoOne knew the Old Twin coveted.

The Old Twin dropped to his knees in readiness and humility. 'Yes, father. I am ready to lead your army. Do what you must do to prepare me.'

'So be it, my son,' laughed NoOne. 'So be it.'

Wave upon wave of dark black psychic sludge filled the synaptic spaces in the Old Twin's brain; neurons and glia cells alike coated with sinister malevolence; each honoring their singular mission: to house the Devil incarnate. Each cell's mitochondria thirsted for more wickedness and rapacious darkness, with a need that never could be met. It was intoxicating. The Old Twin was driven to plead for more and more poison.

NoOne was all too willing to fill his remaining son with Dark Matter, but he was still suspicious of why his son had sent Jenna back to the dirt. However, the annoyance he felt for his one son was overshadowed by the fury he felt for his other son, now called the "New Twin."

Would my one remaining faithful son dare defy me? I clearly see his ambition. Did he send my Jenna back to the Earth as part of some long-term design? What about my second son, the "New Twin?" Does he not know the power of my anger? Has he not witnessed the depth of my darkness? In due time, this "New Twin" will be dealt with. For now, I wonder. How should I discard them both when I am tired of their petty appetites and whining?

Thinking of desire, do I have an appetite for my former mistress, Jenna, now buried with the worms? Of course, I do! Becoming a man to impregnate her was quite curious. No, let me reconsider. It was much more than a novelty. To feel the orgasm of the human male was satisfying. Yes, quite satisfying. I can see how the human species has been so easily damned. What would males do to expel their fluid in a female? What control the females must have in manipulating their suitors! Possibilities stretch out before me.

I wonder.

Jenna is special.

But why stop with her?

Journal Entry Ninety-One: How to Save Your Soul

Hours passed. NoOne relentlessly forged Dark Matter evil from afar, flinging it down in dark narrow arrows for merciless, transformative penetration, conscripting it into every cell of the Old Twin's body. Exhausted and spent, the Old Twin crumbled to the ground, waiting for his master's next move, awaiting his prize: to be declared General of the space corpse army.

The Old Twin reflected upon the perfect symmetry of his father's orders: Corpse remnants and Soul-Judged Evil Eyes to his father's Snake, new human flesh to the ground. Perfection. Yet something was missing.

That something was confirmation of the Old Twin's future as NoOne's right-hand man. NoOne simply disappeared. The Old Twin received no such assignment. Insidiously, doubts continued to arise in the mind of the Old Twin. *Some hesitancy is starting to grow in me. A nagging fear of what? Wait, I don't fear! So, what is it I'm missing?* It took the Old Twin days to finally put his finger on the source of the novel annoyance (he chuckled at the imagery, noting his father's uncanny use of his demon finger to inflict pain).

Yes, that's it. Can my father be trusted? Will he manipulate me for his own advantage? Of course, he will! That is his nature! I'd be as stupid as my idiot naïve brother if I thought otherwise. He's the Devil!

In fact, NoOne could care less about his faithful son's existence; he had more important tasks to complete. The Old Twin would be devastated if he found out, NoOne was sure. However, he knew his son's hurt feelings would soon crust over and create even more anger to put to use—all for the benefit of NoOne.

What *did* concern NoOne was why his Brother, TheSon, had still not counterattacked. Was TheSon really keeping his promise to stay in the SuperVoid?

NoOne was baffled that TheOne had failed to intervene once NoOne's Old Twin son had begun to destroy society's infrastructure. This emboldened NoOne even further. However, doubts still lingered.

My attacks must be coordinated, mused NoOne. *They must be simultaneous to outmaneuver my absent Father and whimpering Brother.*

NoOne calculated his progress thus far. The precious eyeless corpses already planted were closely guarded, for they were the key to conquering the physical dimension. His son had planted the bodies like a crop waiting to be harvested. NoOne estimated that one-third of the

Earth's population had been "converted." Over two billion Souls had been extracted from pairs of human eyes.

The newer cadavers would wait in slumber until later commanded to join NoOne's corpse army, whose primary purpose would be to march, consume, and destroy the rest of the planet Earth and then continue further into the physical universe. Everything not yet destroyed would be annihilated: forests, farmland, cities, and animals, including ocean life. NoOne's idea of a Garden of Eden was a desolate desert Earth with eyeless cadavers laid out in neat rows waiting for their call to engage in battle in some far-off section of the universe, ripe for the picking.

Soon, NoOne's Snake of corpse parts glued together with Dark Matter and Soul-Judged Evil Eyes would be large enough to re-engage the pathetic TendHer and her Funnel. The Snake would redirect the recent dead to NoOne's domain, and that would be situated wherever NoOne decided to set up his new kingdom.

Now I have my pick. I can choose a new home in the physical realm or the Spiritual dimension. Even my Brother has never had that choice!

There remained one complication. Where to store the corpses? NoOne's newly dead required fertile soil to keep them fresh. The Old Twin and NoOne had successfully destroyed most of the smaller cities and even a few of the larger metropolitan areas that were too cheap or optimistic to invest in dome protection. However, the cities' concrete foundations and paved streets were useless for corpse storage, so NoOne instructed the Old Twin to fling the bodies into the surrounding countryside. Looking up, terrified city folk beheld an army of dead bodies, each flying like a grotesque parody of superhuman heroes, launched from their temporary dirt coffins, traversing the sky, waiting to be commanded to attack.

With the recently implanted energized Dark Energy and his increasing anger at his father, the Old Twin feasted on the fear that cycled and swelled like wildfire through his body. He relished the sheer horror he brought to cities, spending hours designing new ways to haunt and terrorize the populace.

His favorite script was to emerge from the sky as a swirling black cloud specter, sometimes taking the shape of a gigantic Snake (to honor his father's Snake army) to produce panic. Nearing his target, the Old Twin's Snake swelled to the size of a skyscraper, zigzagging back and forth, up and down, ripping eyes from the heads of terrified humans.

Lashing out from the specter's dark cloud whirlwind Snake apparition, the Old Twin used the Snake's Eye Reaper. Gray, twisted coils swirled downward from the Snake's belly, breaking off into thousands of smaller rings, which broke up into even more churning and chewing circular saws, quickly covered in blood as their razor-sharp edges tore into horrified victims. Once finding their targets and boring into the human eye sockets, the coils snipped the carotid artery, careful not to injure the Soul. The Souls were summarily judged. Gorging on the energy from the dead howling in agony, the Snake feasted, satiation impossible, oceans of salivating spit drenching the countryside below. As the New Twin watched the delicious torment, he ordained the newly dead's eternal destiny as soldiers in NoOne's new multiverse legion.

But first, they must be stored. When the Old Twin had collected at least a thousand bodies in the sky at any one time, he flung them down with surgical precision to Earth in perfect formation for their planting and eventual resurrection. Like meteors, corpses bombed the countryside, leaving the Earth rippled with raised mounds of dirt. Row upon row of graves gave eerie testimony to the power of the Old Twin.

Word spread fast that the appearance of a black cloud specter shaped like a Snake signaled the harvesting of Souls. The public's only hope was to flee. Most of those who witnessed the spectacle of what later would be called "The Gathering" found it hopeless to resist. It was common to see so many bodies in the air that the sun was completely blocked. Day turned into night. Millions committed suicide; the only act sure to stop the monstrous abomination. They hoped a merciful God would forgive them.

Weapons were useless against the black cloud specter. The only strategy that provided a glimmer of hope was an advanced warning and immediate relocation to bomb shelters deep under many basement apartments. Even this tactic seldom worked because the specter efficiently worked its evil through any solid structure, regardless of composition, depth, or distance.

A signaling system was installed in large cities to alert the residents that the Old Twin was near. The first person to spot the specter raced to a high vantage point, whether that perch was on the top floor of an office building or an apartment complex. It was that person's job to turn the spotlight off and on. This message was then passed along a predetermined line of sight using the same light signal, five on and offs, to warn succeeding neighborhoods of the impending doom. The flashing of the spotlight became the symbol of death; few spoke of it, but nobody ignored it. Rather than a symbol of hope, it announced looming extinction.

Once the code had been received by area sentries, heartbreaking last instructions were whispered from parent to child, father to son, mother to daughter, friend to friend; hurried hugs were given to bewildered, whimpering pets. With sporadic sobbing and heartbreaking detail, directives were shared from old to young. Neighbors and friends were admonished to monitor and teach children how to deal with impending doom. Should any young be left alone, they were taught how to load a firearm (preferably a shotgun) or how to wield a bat or an ax.

Ears were primed to perceive any sound of attack. A blast coming from a far distant part of the city sent citizens into a panic. As the blasts got closer to the city's center, they signaled it was time for citizens to take measures into their own hands.

Screaming and sobs punctuated the heavy gunfire. For miles around, the doomed occupants waited their turn. The gunfire began an orchestra of different ammunition types, piercing the darkness of the night, dissonant calibers swelling into a deafening crescendo, mercifully drowning out, temporarily, the terrifying cries of loss.

Everyone waited for their fate to arrive, young and old, eyes darting every which way, watching one another. Some reached out with gestures of reassurance. Others attempted to reconcile with a strained partner, hoping to put aside what now seemed like trivial differences. Some hoped there might be a last-minute reprieve, perhaps just a little bit of information that would negate the task at hand.

"Why, daddy? Don't you Love me anymore?"

"Please, mommy, did I do something wrong?"

"There's got to be another way!"

"If we wait, Jesus will come, I'm sure."

"Can I take my Teddy Bear pillow with me, mommy?"

Resolute and stalwart, the assigned executioners carried out their tasks, tears streaming from their Souls, washing the floor with grief and sorrow.

The sight of those last standing, with comrades and Loved ones laying still on the floor, staring at the ceiling with jaws dropped and mouths frozen stiff, straining for one last breath, hammered home to those still alive the reality of their own hopelessness.

An operation manual was produced and spread among the cities. Its origin was never determined, although some say it came from the brother of the evil Twin. It instructed the citizens on how to die and protect their Souls.

It was a single page in length with two paragraphs. The page had a simple title at the top: "How to Save Your Soul."

The first paragraph read, "Your only hope is to be executed before the arrival of the Snake; the heart is the best target. The brain is problematic because the eyes are connected to the brain and can be inadvertently damaged. Both of your eyes must be protected before death to prevent automatic judgment and custody by NoOne. Then at the precise moment after death, you must be prepared for 'the Visit.'"

The second paragraph read, "After you are dead, the Devil will appear. He will make you suffer. You must fight the pain. Do not give in. Reject the offer of remission. You are being lied to. The Devil will take your Soul if you let him. Do not let him. Pray to your Angel Soul Guide to shield you. Stay focused on the Light provided by your Guide."

Children and adults alike memorized the advice as if it were a catechism, hoping that it would help. Faith, it was assumed, would usher their Souls away to a safe location until TheSon again appeared.

Young and old, one last thought, one last shred of comforting grace bid them a momentary soothing peace the moment after death. What could not be witnessed by the living, obscured by the fog of death, were single slivers of Light struggling to lighten the Souls of the recently deceased. It was but an instance of Divine Love emerging from a far-distant place without space and without time. Words drifted into awareness, also from afar. They came from TheSon.

Your Souls are safe. Come to Me, My children. You will not have to spend eternity suffering with the Devil.

Words also could be heard, serrating the dark consciousness of the Mind's Eyes of the recent dead. Words discharged from a leviathan specter hanging far off in space, a dark shape, obscure and pulsing, frothing with greed.

'Oh, yes, you will.'

Thus planned NoOne.

'Amen.'

Journal Entry Ninety-Two: Fly Through

With a wingspan of nine feet and a weight of seventeen pounds, the Bearded Vulture, a carnivore from Eurasia, closely resembles a falcon. However, unlike other Vultures, the Bearded Vulture has a head covered with feathers. Upon closer inspection, observers are equally surprised at the Bearded Vulture's thick and exceptionally muscular neck.

What uniquely sets the Bearded Vulture apart from other birds of prey is its diet. While it is a scavenger that feeds on dead animals, this is the only bird with a diet consisting almost entirely of the marrow of bones. Swooping down to pick up a partially rotted large animal bone, the Bearded Vulture will fly high and drop the bone, cracking it on the rocks below into edible portions. Moreover, due to its powerful stomach acid, a piece of bone can be completely digested in a day.

From their position in the middle of the small, quiet meadow, the four guys and the New Twin watched as the Vultures circled, their wings majestically stroking the air, almost in perfect unison, so strongly that a "swoop-swoop-swoop" helicopter sound filled the air, reverberating off the surrounding tall, bristling fir trees.

Alighting in the middle of the shallow meadow, the four Vultures studied the ground, then the trees, and then each other. Shaking their wings, the Vultures settled on the ground and groomed themselves while simultaneously boring their steely gaze into the eyes of the humans. After a few minutes, the four Vultures stood up, and each faced one of the four directions: east, west, north, south. They stood still. Regal. On guard. Waiting for a command.

"They know who is in charge," said Charles.

"And how did they react at the prospect of giving up control?" asked the New Twin.

Charles replied, "They volunteered to come and merge. They know it means certain death, but they long to join their ancestors and TheOne."

"Wow, but what do you mean certain death?" asked Luke.

Charles was waiting for just such a question. "You act as if it's a bad thing, Luke. Nature sees death as part of the cycle of life. Each animal knows that dying means being peacefully absorbed into the mystery of reincarnation and re-creation. Our four friends are willing to sacrifice their lives and, in so doing, will have accelerated their Soul development."

"Vultures have Souls!" exclaimed Ben.

Charles shook his head. "That's right, Ben. All higher-order animals have Souls. The Souls of our Vulture friends are very small, but in terms of eternity, even the smallest of Soul radiant signatures add up and contribute to TheOne. Our friends here are old and tired and look forward to helping us and being reunited with their deceased family nests and their Creator."

"Family nests?" asked John.

The New Twin cleared his throat. "Guys, birds don't talk or write, and you probably think that means they don't have Souls. Let me tell you something. The chicken and beef you eat in hamburgers and nuggets come from animals with Souls. Yes, they are very tiny, but as Charles said, they add up in the end. And all of them reunite with their families, whatever form that might take when they pass."

Remembering his steady diet of hamburgers, Ben wanted to change the subject. "OK, so we merge? Right?"

"Yes, Ben," replied the New Twin. "And I just got an image of a hamburger coming from you. After talking about the Souls of animals, all you can think about is food?"

Luke perked right up. "Hamburger? I'd die for a hamburger."

Charles could not resist needling Luke: "Yes, you just might!" Luke was the least sympathetic to the plight of animals, probably because of his experiences in a farming community. Slaughter was a fact of farming life.

"Well, I'm hungry," moaned Ben. "We haven't eaten in like forever!"

"Come on, guys. We must move forward." The New Twin walked over to the Vultures and stood in the middle of the four. The four turned to face him and waddled closer to the circle's center a few steps. The New Twin walked to each Vulture, stroked each head, scratched their cheeks, then returned to the middle and thanked them for their sacrifice. He could tell the Vultures were exhausted.

"Charles, will you see if our four friends are ready to be merged with the guys?" asked the New Twin.

Sitting down in the meadow, Charles reached out to the four Vultures. 'After we merge, you must get us as far away from the New

Twin as possible. Can you do this after you made this long journey to reach us?'

The Vultures' heads drooped. Eyes closed. Quivers ran up and down their feathers like a breeze was ruffling and cooling down the powerful birds. Maybe the shuddering also helped reduce their stress, given their almost certain death. Of course, they were familiar with the Monster Bear sharing his Soul with TheSon, but still, the experience was rare and mysterious.

What brought glints of terror to the aging Vultures was a hint from the New Twin that their mission was not what they thought; that even the four guys did not really know what lay ahead. This hint of the unknown made them anxious and more tired. They wanted to dilute the stress of ambiguity with a definite plan of action.

Slowly the four noble birds raised their heads to meet Charles' eyes; with great weariness, they nodded in agreement.

'Yes, we know,' the largest of the Vultures thought to Charles. 'We sense there are universal forces at play fighting for justice. We will do whatever it takes to accomplish our task. Our bird brothers and sisters are being decimated in the millions by the evil ascended upon us. The skies are no longer our own; there is no free domain where we used to float and glide and feed.'

"I think we're ready to begin," announced the New Twin. "Guys, come over, and each of you lay down next to one of the Vultures."

Separated by just a few feet, the Vultures made room for the guys to lie comfortably next to them. A single thought spread among the four birds. 'Humans are so ugly, and they smell terrible.'

"Heard that!" said Charles.

"What'd you hear, Charles?" asked Ben.

Charles chuckled. "Something you don't need to know right now!"

"Oh, great, with my luck, my bird will have worms for lunch!" said Luke.

'Nope, we prefer bones,' thought one of the Vultures.

"Hey, I heard that!" said Luke.

'And don't call us "this bird," ' added another Vulture.

"I'm so sorry; it's just that I used to eat duck," confessed Ben.

"Why are you apologizing? Ducks are a long way down the feeding chain from Vultures," stated John.

"Please mind what you both are saying!" admonished Charles.

Ben was squirming next to his Vulture. "Well, for the record, I'm starving. When's lunch?"

John enjoyed the banter. The guys hadn't had much chance to decompress and relax. He thought he would add to the stress-reducing ritual. "I think we should all fly through a fast-food take-out!"

Ben, Luke, Charles, and all four of the Vultures turned to look at John precisely at the same time.

"Yes, I know. I do have a sense of humor. Occasionally," smiled John.

Luke was uncharacteristically cheerful. "Hey, guys and bird buddies, how 'bout we check out the nearest hamburger drive-thru?"

'Humans, we prefer the grocery store you call "nature," ' stated one of the Vultures.

In unison, the four guys replied. "Why?"

'We like our chicken with lots of bones.'

The four Vultures slapped their wings on the ground, missing the guys by inches.

"Hey, do you think these dudes are 'bird laughing?' Do they think that was funny? Do they really have a sense of humor?" pondered Luke aloud.

"I sure hope they're joking around. Have you looked at their beaks?" said Ben.

'I've never had a human bone,' stated one of the Vultures.

'Come to think of it, me neither!' thought another Vulture.

'Do you think human bone would crack if we dropped it from high up in the sky?' added another Vulture.

"OK, that's it. I'm not hungry anymore," grumbled Ben.

The New Twin was thoroughly entertained by the banter but felt it was time to get serious. "Gotta break up this little party. We need to get going with our plan. I'm setting a trap for my brother. At the precise moment immediately after you die, I will remove your eyes from your bodies. That's when you need to merge with your Vulture buddy. A millisecond later will be too late."

Luke was confused. "Whoa. How do we do this merge thingy?"

John knew exactly what the New Twin was explaining. "Guys, it's just like leaving our bodies and sending our Mind's Eye and Soul to 'beyond the Veil'. Only this time, we focus on our Vulture friend."

"Precisely," replied the New Twin. "I have directed the Vultures to be receptive when the time comes to merge. Their tiny Souls will be like magnets and draw you in before you can get lost."

"Lost? Lost? What do you mean, lost?" squealed Ben.

The New Twin tried to be reassuring. "You will be fine. However, if you miss the homing beacon from your Vulture, you may be forever lost. It's why NoOne can simply take Souls at will when the eyes are removed before death. The Mind's Eye is confused. It latches onto any passing Spirit or self-destructs."

"Latches onto any Soul? Like the Devil?" said Luke.

"Yeah, will the Devil show up to quiz us?" asked Ben.

"Normally, yes," replied the New Twin. "But I'm hoping the merging will mask the release of the Soul and will be done so quickly that there will be no signal sent to NoOne. I will have your eyeballs for safe keeping after their removal. If I can keep my brother from destroying your physical bodies, I might be able to return your eyes to your bodies. If your physical eyeballs are destroyed, your Souls might be stranded with your Vulture."

"Stranded?" asked Ben. "Like forever flapping in the breeze with a diving bone-crusher?"

The New Twin did not answer. Too much knowledge could jeopardize the ability of the guys to relax. The four guys had to be completely calm before they attempted to merge. Thinking of losing one's eyes was terrible enough.

John replied right away. "We need to get started. Remember, we're on a mission and have been chosen by TheSon. We're in good hands with the New Twin. It should make you feel good that he personally was rescued by the Son of God. You know the...."

John gasped, suddenly not able to breathe. Panicking, John appealed to Charles, Ben, and Luke. "Help me...."

For a split second, the four shared a common understanding. They were dying. Horror transformed into resignation. Peace spread over their faces.

Their heads fell back together at the same time, hitting the ground with a singular "thud."

John's last thought was, *'Guys, just let ggggg....'*

The four Vultures looked down, curious and detached. Each was positioned next to one of the guys and towering over their new human associates. Then, together they looked up at the New Twin, waiting for his next move.

The New Twin had prepared himself for what needed to happen next. The eyeballs had to be removed. And they needed to be removed immediately upon the four guys' passing to keep their Mind's Eyes and Souls connected for their travels in 'beyond the Veil' and safe return to their bodies later on.

The release of the Souls began at once from the eyeballs and took but a few milliseconds to complete, just as the New Twin hoped. The releases were soothing. Four brief vibratory pulses, one for each pair of eyes, turned into steady deep, lush tones accompanied by Light beams. The four Souls inched out from the eyeballs safeguarded by the protective Mind's Eyes.

It was now time to merge.

As the Souls were reeled in closer to the Vultures' Souls, each Vulture's Mind's Eye signaled its Soul that everything was OK. The human Souls had found new homes. The guys' Mind's Eyes had done their job. They would stay distinct from the Vulture's Mind's Eyes until it was time to separate, thus preserving two individual identities housed in one biological life form.

All sense of pain disappeared.

'You are with me, John,' said the bird. 'As are your three friends with their new hosts. All four of you have successfully merged. Welcome to our "kettle." You are now part of our Vulture family.'

Journal Entry Ninety-Three: Saturation

Sharing a Soul and Mind's Eye with any animal or human is not as easy as it sounds. The Soul does not communicate with words, so whether they liked it or not, the guys had to rely on their Mind's Eyes to communicate with each other and the Vultures. Most importantly, the human Soul, as compared to the Vulture Soul, is configured with millions of Mind's Eye layers, so its symbolic processing automatically begins to eclipse the relatively simple instinctual processing of the much smaller bird's Soul field.

The guys noticed nothing different after the merging: a natural unfolding of their Mind's Eyes surrounding their Souls. They felt safe and protected. The Vultures, however, felt overwhelmed. Tensions began to build as the Vultures could not stand the constant dialogue "chatter" of the human's Mind's Eyes.

The four Vultures consulted as to how to end the usurpation. Everything came to a head when Ben tried to tell his host what she should do. Ben's Vulture made sure all the other guys (and their hosts) witnessed the consequence of Ben's effrontery.

While on the ground getting used to the merging with the Vulture, Ben's Mind's Eye, noting its own enormous complexity compared to the simplicity of his host's Mind's Eye, attempted to influence his host's wing flapping as if to have a say in controlling the flight. Ben's Vulture would have nothing to do with any input from Ben. As far as she was concerned, Ben was only along for the ride. There was no way she would hand over her flying instincts to a human.

So, Ben's Vulture used her Mind's Eye to flood Ben's Mind's Eye with images of how some of her relative Vultures cool down. "Saturate" is the ideal word because often groups of Vultures ("kettle") urinate on themselves in great quantities to stay cool.

Ben's Vulture jetted out a few juicy spurts for good measure, hitting the other three Vultures. The other Vultures waddled closer, positioning themselves to receive the most liquid.

That's all it took. Ben's Mind's Eye receded to a corner in his Vulture's unconsciousness and did not utter a peep. For one of the only times in his life, Ben had nothing to say.

Charles and John sent kudos to Ben's Vulture, who was all too happy to acknowledge her victory in overcoming Ben's intrusion. She thought it only fair that she received more than her fair share of marrow at their first stop.

Such a soggy image was a reminder for all the guys to repress any future impulses to contribute, much less criticize. The guys' services and reactions were not needed. The guys wisely vowed to stay in the background and simply observe, trying to see the world through the Mind's Eyes of their hosts, now protecting the guys' Souls.

As they settled into their roles as spectators, the guys observed the four Vultures toddle over and huddle around the New Twin who was heaving with great sobs. The Vultures meticulously groomed the New Twin. They nudged the New Twin up and down his body. Little squeaky noises came from their beaks. Were the Vultures also crying?

Instantly, the guys perceived a dramatic change in the New Twin. They felt a diversion of focus as some force shifted the guys' attention to a location across from the New Twin. Looking over, they sensed their bodies lying on the ground. Motionless. Where once their eyeballs had been securely nestled, snug in their eye sockets, now there was nothing. Only deep, dark, empty pits.

The Mind's Eyes of the four guys cringed in fear, physically tumbling the Vultures backward in apprehension. The guys knew instantly they were beyond the point of no return, entirely at the mercy of the New Twin; the same Twin who once wanted to torture and kill them. The same New Twin whose father was the Devil. The same New Twin whom they let blind them, possibly forever. The same New Twin who now literally held the future of their physical existence in the palm of his hand.

As a sense of panic spread among the group, a comment made by one of the Vultures did nothing to allay the tension in the group. 'Looks like we're all duck soup.'

Journal Entry Ninety-Four: Deception

'Show yourself,' thought the New Twin. 'I know you're here. I can last as long as I want. Where are you? Show your face.'

As minutes passed, the Old Twin finally appeared at the meadow's edge, hovering a foot off the ground. He had not changed physically. The Old Twin still looked exactly like his seven-year-old identical twin, except for a cloud of pure black mist that hovered over his head.

The New Twin chuckled at the irony. *Is that a halo around my brother's head?*

The Old Twin glared, projecting a dark menace. 'Be careful what you think, brother. Won't you say hello to someone special?'

The mist turned into a group of Hawks. The New Twin got the message.

Hawks are the predators of Vultures.

The twenty-plus birds circled the Old Twin's head at a dizzying speed. The largest bird of the group separated and hovered over the rest as the Hawks continued their tornado dance and dropped down around the body of the Old Twin.

The massive alpha Hawk growled in a muffled voice, guttural and deliberate. 'Hello, my disobedient son. I know your disrespectful thoughts.'

The New Twin was startled. He studied the Hawk, trying to identify which part of a Hawk's body could possibly produce sound.

'Father? I didn't know you would...." He turned to his brother, 'You brought father?'

The Hawks burst into dark sprinkles and lingered as a gloomy mist around the Old Twin's body. The mist began to spin. The tighter the circles turned, the darker the mass became.

NoOne's voice was silky sweet. The New Twin had heard the tone many times when his father wanted something desperately. 'I am here, my son. Are you ready to join us? To be part of my plan once more? To be MY Chosen?'

It took all of the New Twin's concentration to send a masked thought message to the Vultures: 'Go...go NOW. I will divert my brother.'

The four birds leaped forward with a couple of hops and began to flap, finally getting off the ground. It looked as though the Vultures were straining beyond their ability, but each finally gained enough height to take advantage of the prevailing tailwind. Finally, the Vultures turned to face their escape route, almost in perfect synchrony, struggling to gain more altitude to flee.

The New Twin had accomplished his mission so far. The eyes had been removed precisely at the moment after death. NoOne had no Souls to judge because the guys had merged their Mind's Eyes and Souls with the Vultures just as they died. The birds got off the ground and were getting away. Or so he hoped.

Looking up and following the direction of the birds, the Old Twin chuckled. 'Oh, brother. You are so transparent. We know about your little Soul-merging stunt. Father and I can destroy those birds anytime we want.'

The trap had been sprung, but the New Twin still felt like he should be careful. 'Then you know the boys' Souls are off-limits to you; both of you,' he replied.

If only he could steal a few more minutes for the Vultures. They needed to climb as high as possible. If the Vultures gained enough distance, the Old Twin might not be able to track where they were headed.

It seemed to work. The Vultures were out of sight and hopefully off the Old Twin's immediate radar.

The Old Twin peered deeply into the New Twin's psyche, 'What do you mean "off-limits?" '

The New Twin didn't respond, hoping to gain even more precious time for the Vultures. 'The four Souls have been judged by TheSon and His Father, TheOne. And they have merged with my creatures. You're too late to judge.'

Before the Old Twin could reply, NoOne's dark mass rocketed into the air. A rage-filled voice boomed down from above. 'How dare you bring up the name of TheSon. He now rules in Hell. He has no power here.'

'Yes, father,' replied the New Twin, trying to bluff by creating any diversion that would buy the Vultures more time. 'You are much more powerful. As you can see, the four boys are dead, and their eyes are in my pocket. Their bodies are of little use to you here.'

Laying face up in a neat row, hands folded on chests, the bodies of the four Chosen lay motionless on the ground—Luke, Ben, John, and Charles—eyes missing.

The New Twin prayed that the guys' eyeballs would survive so that they could eventually return to their own bodies. For that to happen, the eyes could not be destroyed.

The Old Twin chuckled. 'Did you really think you could abscond with my treasures? Maybe I will destroy their eyes? Let the boys rot in 'beyond the Veil' never to return to their precious bodies! Or maybe get them new eyes like our mommy and turn them into slaves.'

The New Twin shook his head. 'That can't happen cause the boys' Souls are not under your control. They cannot be imprisoned in the SuperVoid. They will be in Heaven!'

NoOne's increasingly larger dark mist cloud thundered, 'And Heaven will soon be mine!'

The New Twin softened. He figured he had pushed his father far enough. 'Father, they are trapped in the bodies of birds and can only escape to 'beyond the Veil'. I have their eyes! No Funnel. No reincarnation. You should be pleased.'

After pausing, the New Twin whispered as if NoOne couldn't hear, 'And brother. Take note. I think it's time you worry about when, not if, you will be discarded by our dearest father. Very soon, you will have served your purpose, and he will wipe you out as he has destroyed most of the life on this planet.'

The dark cloud rumbled. NoOne had overheard the New Twin's comment. NoOne's response was to turn his mist into torrential dark rain. It drenched the meadow in thick sheets.

The New Twin knew he was walking on thin ice. He projected a barrier around his body to protect himself from NoOne's wrath of nature. At the same time, the New Twin knew that his strategy was working, at least for the time being. NoOne's attention was distracted, now focused on his rebellious New Twin son, not the escaping boys.

The Old Twin was also distracted, processing his brother's suggestion that he would be abandoned. He looked surprised, as though he were in culture shock, as if he was a tourist in a strange country. The

Old Twin's eyes furtively scanned the meadow, locking in on NoOne's Dark Matter cloud that was now secreting oceans of dark liquid and had grown in size to block out the entire sky. He needed reassurance. The Old Twin's little hands reached out; he clenched his shrunken fists and then quickly retracted them. He dipped his head twice as if being reprimanded by his father.

The Old Twin suddenly appeared frail and vulnerable. He slumped for a moment, shoulders rolling over a fraction of an inch, not even noticeable by most. The New Twin was not like most people. He knew his brother like a book, from cover to cover, each page, each sentence, each word a carbon copy of his own Soul and Spirit, except for one difference. The New Twin had embraced Love; he had a Soul just like the four Souls now safely merged with the Vultures.

The New Twin's gamble paid off. The Old Twin was caught off guard by both his brother's suggestion of paternal disloyalty and stinging disapproval on the part of their father. The Old Twin bristled; he was never taken by surprise. He controlled his life; it was executed flawlessly according to his plan and NoOne's power. The Old Twin knew that he was playing into the New Twin's plan to buy more time for the Vultures so they could escape farther into the distance, but the Old Twin needed some time to box up the very uncomfortable revelations that were straining to be released.

Focusing inward, the Old Twin pleaded with NoOne to help him. 'What are these feelings? Is this what humans call "fear" or "anxiety?" I'm feeling pain. Father, you will never abandon me, right? Father, you promised to keep me clear and strong.'

To the surprise of the New Twin, NoOne replied, 'Do not fear, my loyal child. It's a trick. I will just erase these few nasty feelings. Just a little mental tune-up. There, does that feel better? How rude of your brother, eh?'

The Old Twin did feel relief, and in seconds, he had no memory of the brief intrusion by the foreign conscience.

Regaining his emotionless composure, the Old Twin turned his attention back to his brother and the four bodies that lay between them. He exclaimed, 'Ohhh, look at that. The four boys are truly, at last dead. The least I can do is take care of the bodies.'

The New Twin noted that his father had not denied the abandonment possibility, a fact the New Twin figured he could later use to his advantage.

To buy more time, the New Twin dug into his pocket and brought out eight eyeballs.

The Old Twin saw the eyes and felt a surge of energy; even though exhausted, he thought might succeed. He was ready to gloat. Wouldn't his father be happy? Proud, even?

The New Twin threw eight eyeballs on the ground as far away from the Old Twin as possible and said, "Brother, if you really want to make certain the boys can never come back to physical reality, here are their eyes. Take them. You've won. But leave the bodies for me to bury as they wished."

Showing the eyes created the desired effect. The Old Twin couldn't help but turn his head and focus on their location, diverting his attention from his brother, the bodies, and especially the escaping Vultures. The Old Twin walked over and stomped on them.

'Just like old times, eh' brother,' the Old Twin snickered.

The New Twin carefully displayed a contrived expression of disgust. But inside, he was celebrating.

The Vultures had indeed gained great distance and altitude from the drama unfolding on the ground between the Twins and their father. Safely secured in their neck feathers were the actual eyes of the four guys. All eight of the eyes were headed to Montana, somewhere in the mountains. The specific destination would be communicated later by one of Charles' Eagles, who had recently joined the group.

The guys were grateful that the New Twin had found eight eyes of corpses buried deep within the Earth to substitute for the guys' natural eyes, now hidden among the Vultures' feathers. It seemed the deception was going to work. At any rate, the confrontation between the Twins had bought precious time for the Vultures to escape further east toward Montana, now but fifty miles away.

'Charle's Eagle. May we call you that?' asked the lead Vulture.

'Yes, my friends, you may,' said the Eagle. 'You are curious, I assume, about what is happening on the ground?'

'Yes, with the bodies and the fake eyes.'

'This is what has been passed on to me from below. The evil Twin crushed the fake eyes. NoOne destroyed the four bodies. NoOne called upon four different beams of light to thrust out of the Earth. He commanded the beams to circle the bodies. The beams paused, hovered over each body, and then fell, stabbing the four bodies simultaneously. The heat was so intense the bodies exploded into flames sending red-hot cinders everywhere. Even the Twins had to back away.'

Circling away from the Vultures for a moment, the Eagle landed on the tip of a tall Fir tree, scouted the countryside below, and then majestically dove to the group soaring just below to continue her report.

'The bodies were completely consumed within seconds, ashes pulled higher into the sky to heights only known to those of us who exist in silent splendor high above the Earth. The cinder fragments swayed in jagged rows and reached up to where my noble kin soar, higher still, free and innocent, trusting in a power that called to them to have faith. Unlike us, they did not have a choice or the strength to defy the crushing pressure from above, what humans call gravity. Their remains were scattered to the winds.'

The lead Vulture responded, 'We were instructed to deliver these eyes to a mountaintop in Montana for hiding while the boys project their Souls to 'beyond the Veil'. Should we not be grateful that we escaped this far? Of what use were their bodies anyway? They can always return from 'beyond the Veil' and inhabit a new body as long as they have these eyes.'

The Eagle replied, 'I feel the human boys wanted to return to their own bodies in the future to continue their physical lives, like us. Does not your family long for your familiar presence?'

'Yes,' replied one of the Vultures. 'I sense we are close to the drop-off location.'

The Eagle hovered in mid-air. 'Halt. Do not go any further. Do you see the dark cloud in the distance following us?'

'Yes,' replied the lead Vulture. 'What is your concern?'

'It is Dark Matter. It's evil, and we must avoid it. I suggest you land now in a heavily wooded area below. There. Let's drop straight down by that stream.'

Dropping in a steep dive to the stream bank, the Vultures were careful not to use their usual landing display of shaking out their wings and feathers. It was a ritual long ago invented to aid in the instantaneous relaxation of all the fatigued muscles used in long flights. But now, it might create too much attention. Gently, the Vultures rose up on their tiny rear legs and let the eyeballs slowly roll down their backs to a bed of twigs a few feet from a stream bank. Carefully collecting more forest scraps with their beaks, the Vultures tried as best they could to disguise the precious eyes. The four Vultures ended their mission by erecting a circle of twigs around the eyes and placing a large pine tree branch over the top.

Circling from above, the Eagle told the Vultures that the eyes were well hidden, and it was time to go. Relieved that they had survived, the Vultures launched themselves up off the ground, nodded to each other, proud of their contribution, and drifted away to find carrion bones to feast upon. Once soaring with a prevailing tailwind, the lead Vulture told the others to inform the boys that it was time for them to separate.

The purging from the Vultures and transfer of their Souls to 'beyond the Veil' proceeded and concluded without a single hitch. Stitched to a part of their Soul and Mind's Eye was a single Page granting permission to "de-incarnate"—venture to 'beyond the Veil' at death without being escorted immediately to the Funnel. It was the first time that any non-Divine life form had been given such an honor.

The guys mourned the loss of their bodies. They were prepared for this possibility but still were deeply saddened. At the same time, the guys were consoled by the knowledge they would eventually find a new human body to inhabit when they returned to life.

Their eyes were safe. Were they not?

From 'beyond the Veil', the guys focused on their Vulture friends soaring south, flying thousands of miles out of their way to avoid NoOne. 'I speak for all of us guys when I thank you from the bottom of my heart. We will always remember how you risked your lives for us,' thought John.

Charles added, 'Yes, my brothers and sisters. You will now be my Sacred guardian Spirit!'

'And I will never ever buy another parakeet!' exclaimed Ben.

The four Vultures formed a perfect circle in the sky. The guys sensed the Vultures were not offended by Ben's comment. In fact, the guys thought the Vultures were smiling. Soaring freely with the air currents, the Vultures jetted up and down, upside down and around as a group, in perfect synchrony. It was a dance performed only a couple of times to honor those few, rare humans who deserved to be recognized.

Charles had the last thought. 'We will be in 'beyond the Veil', my friends, and have a celebration for you when you arrive.'

'Yeah, but no squirting allowed!' Ben added.

The Vultures dipped their beaks one last time and rotated high in the fluffy clouds as if to say goodbye. Then they were gone.

Journal Entry Ninety-Five: The Beaver

Scrounging for more sticks to dam his small tributary on the bank of his favorite stream, the 100-pound Beaver discovered strange round objects. He'd never smelled anything like them before.

Working his way upstream, the Beaver impulsively stopped and dropped his load to the side of the bank. He could not get the smell out of his mind. He scurried back to study the foreign oval objects. He had never seen such colorful things before. Were these eggs? Was this a trap? He backed up and surveyed the perimeter for potential predators. To be extra cautious, he looked both upstream and downstream.

No strange sounds or sights, he noted. Just for good measure, the Beaver dove into the water and swam upstream and then swam back, again looking for anything out of the ordinary on the bank or in the water. The usual forest and stream noises assured him that all was safe.

Approaching what he hoped were eggs, the wet Beaver first sniffed their surface. The smell was different, but it was not like any other dangerous non-edibles he had learned to avoid. These eggs were colorful; each had a bright center, and the surrounding white had a unique glossy display, much different than the forest environment of dark Earth tones.

Slowly, the Beaver bent down and licked one of the eggs. It moved slightly. Did it move on its own?

Eggs don't move, the Beaver thought to himself.

Once again, he licked the egg; it again moved. He liked the taste.

Though not as tasty as my favorite treat, tree bark. All foods were judged by their similarity to this cambium soft tissue delicacy found on the inner part of the riverbank tree bark.

This must be a new kind of apple, concluded the Beaver. He knew from experience that there was no telling where apples might show up. Apples also had colorful spots, just like these eggs.

These must be apples. And safe to eat!

Just to be sure, the Beaver jumped into the water and drifted downstream to find his mate. On his back, leisurely drifting along, he looked forward to eating his newfound delicacy. He was ecstatic because he knew his mate would be pleased.

Upon spotting his mate up ahead, the Beaver left the stream, shook off the excess water on his fur, and dashed to share his discovery.

'Come with me, quickly. I found a treasure.'

The female Beaver did not need any more motivation. Whenever her mate discovered new delicacies, she expected a full stomach. Immediately, she dropped her load, and the two sprinted on the soft, muddy bank back toward the eggs.

The eggs had rolled closer to the stream. The Beaver was eager to impress his female mate. 'Do you think these are a new kind of egg? Or maybe an apple? Look, they move, and they are shaped like apples. But they smell like eggs. They must be a new type of egg!'

Inspecting the objects, the female declared, 'I believe you're right!'

'Shall we share them with the rest of our colony? They work so hard and deserve a treat,' she asked.

'Of course. But first, let's just try one,' replied the male Beaver.

So, the two shared one of the eggs. It was delicious.

They couldn't stop eating.

They ate all eight of the eggs and returned to work on their dam.

NoOne leered. 'My beautiful pets. Did you enjoy my gift?'

Journal Entry Ninety-Six: Free Souls

Charles and John had the most experience dwelling in the Spirit world. They sensed the complete separation from their eyes. Feeling each other, they instantly agreed that Ben and Luke were the most vulnerable to extreme stress and would require guidance.

'Ben, Luke…you with us?' thought John.

Charles added, 'Are you OK? John and I are fine. This is where we need to be. And we've been here before, so nothing new.'

'Oh, yeah, right,' said Ben. 'First time I don't have my body to return to, though. No way am I happy about that! Hey, wait a minute. This could be awesome! No more blubber to hide!'

Luke was dazed. The transition seemed particularly hard on him. Charles thought he might need to get Luke one of those Guardian Angels to help. 'I'm with you guys. Just waiting to get my bearings.'

John hushed the guys to still their thoughts. 'Hey guys, gather around. I just got a vision. Do you feel that?'

'Do I ever!' said Ben.

As animals and their Souls were involved, Ben, Luke, and John turned leadership over to Charles, who quickly shushed the guys. 'Keep your thoughts still so I can visualize what's happening.'

John said, 'Yes. Sorry, Charles, you have more clarity with the animals than the three of us combined. What's going on? I'm feeling so many different currents of emotion.'

'Awww…just to recap, the Old Twin destroyed our bodies,' replied Charles.

In wishful thinking, Luke asked, 'Are our bodies gone for good? Maybe the New Twin did his hocus pocus thing and can put us back together? I mean, I really liked my body. It was the only thing going for me.'

'You're wrong, Luke. You have Heather,' said Ben.

'Oh, yeah. Guess that's true,' agreed Luke. 'But how did we end up ghosts forever?'

Charles replayed the image of the bodies disintegrating into charred ashes. Silence ensued as each of the guys processed the finality of their physical obliteration.

Meekly, John reached out. 'Guys, we're OK. The New Twin knows what he's doing.'

'What about our eyes, Charles? Did NoOne get them away from the New Twin?' asked Ben.

Luke said, 'Yeah, that's what really counts, we have to keep them, or we're really stuck up here.'

'Well, since we're still here, wherever "here" is, we must still have our Souls,' added John.

The three guys agreed but sensed that Charles was disturbed and processing something.

'What is it, Charles? Why did you zone out on us?' asked John.

'I might have some bad news,' thought Charles.

'Oh, shit, what now?' moaned Ben.

Charles slowly let his perceptions slip out, frame-by-frame, like an old-fashioned black-and-white, manually projected silent movie from the 1920s.

'Follow me on this, guys. The four Vultures made it off the ground with our physical eyes hidden in their feathers. They shot up high in the air and found a tailwind. Made it almost 600 miles due east to Montana. The Vultures hid the eyeballs next to a stream.'

Ben impatiently urged Charles to continue. 'And? Come on, Charles. What's the punch line? Where are our eyes?'

Charles' answer could hardly be heard. 'Ah, Ben…guys. Beavers ate them. All of them.'

Silence.

'So, what does that mean for us? We have our Souls, right? We're here in 'beyond the Veil'. NoOne can't touch us! Aren't we safe?' Ben sounded like he was trying to reassure himself more than get information.

'Yeah, he's forbidden to come here!' added Luke.

Charles wandered away a bit as if he was looking for an answer to Ben's questions further out in 'beyond the Veil'. Slowly drifting back to the guys, he said, 'I don't think this has ever happened before. You know, where a Soul and its Mind's Eye make it to 'beyond the Veil' first, and then the physical eye it's connected to is destroyed. Usually, the physical eyes are destroyed first and cease functioning once the Soul and Mind's Eye are released on their trip to the Funnel.'

'But what about all those eyes I saw in the SuperVoid Hell?' asked Ben.

John saw how Ben and the others could confuse the physical eyes with the "Soul-Eyes." 'Guys, it's simple. The Soul is shaped like an eye, but it's not physical. The physical eye transfers to the Mind's Eye a code at the moment of death. Once that happens, the physical eye is no longer needed. It's like a password. This code emits a signal, looking for a home receptor. The Funnel has a honing beacon constantly surveying the universe. When the two find each other, the Funnel sucks the Mind's Eye and Soul inside like a ferromagnetic metal racing to a magnet surface. The Mind's Eye then dissolves. Since we merged with the Vultures, our physical eyes still had our codes to enter the Reincarnation Universe. Merging made our physical eyes think we were still alive. Now that our physical eyes are destroyed, we will never get our code for gaining entrance to the Funnel and working our way to the Reincarnation Universe. We're lost in non-space.'

Luke beamed. 'Hey, "Stranded In Space!" That was a good show! But what's fer....'

'Iron, nickel, cobalt, to name a few,' Ben interrupted.

John wanted to be encouraging as to their prospects. 'If it's any conciliation, what we've done has never been done before. The New Twin kept us alive. I just don't know what it means in the long run.'

Ben formed the words but struggled to send them to his fellow Chosen ones. 'The only conclusion I can think of is this: it means we…are…ghosts…forever…trapped in "beyond the Veil".'

Journal Entry Ninety-Seven: Crumbling Walls

Silence. No response. Repeatedly, TheSon prayed, *Father, NoOne and his corrupted son have almost completely destroyed one of Your Creations. I am Your servant to use. Please send Me.*

Over and over. Silence was His only reply.

TheSon had kept His Word. He kept His end of the bargain. TheSon remained in Hell. It was well worth His self-imposed banishment. He complained not once, knowing He was part of a much larger picture. He would find out soon enough how He would help fulfill whatever His Father had in mind.

TheSon calculated the eons He had spent drifting among the Soul-Judged Evil Eyes in the SuperVoid, Loving and forgiving, waiting for any sign of remorse and reconciliation, looking for the goodness found in all living creatures and formerly living Souls. TheSon probed and prodded, offering salvation and peace. Trillions upon trillions of life histories were re-examined. Choices were reviewed. Options presented. Futures explored. Some LostSouls accepted the teachings of TheSon. Others, fixated on passion or anger, rejected TheSon's offer of forgiveness, instead choosing to sink even further into their fear and torment.

Father, I am Your servant to use. I remain steadfast to My Word. I am bound to the SuperVoid. Please send for Me.

Over and over. No response.

Father, please open up Your consciousness to Me with Your purpose.

Years passed. In some realities, millenniums expired. For Divine reality, it was but a millisecond; barely the time it takes to process an intention. *Very well, Father. Let it be.*

TheSon, My Son.

At last. Joy swelled in TheSon's countenance; numinous energy felt by all in the SuperVoid. Saved and unsaved marveled at the profound energy emitted by TheSon, finally greeted by His Father. Those who had accepted TheSon's offer of forgiveness celebrated and vibrated hymns of harmony. Those who had rejected TheSon's offer of redemption fell deeper into the SuperVoid; darkness embraced to hide in the furthest, loneliest reaches of Hell.

Father. NoOne has incarnated and trapped My Chosen in 'beyond the Veil'. He is now building an even larger army composed of the recently dead and the LostSouls. Most have not been fairly judged. I see his intent. He wants to find and destroy the Funnel and make servants of the Holy Orbs in the Reincarnation Universe!

My Son, did We not know this would be?

No Father. I did not. It has never happened before. I had to intervene and protect the Chosen at the First Gate.

Yes, My Son. Yet, You did not have to intervene. All is God. God IS…and IS not. I am All. I am Some-Thing. As are You. This is My Divine Drama. You know All returns to Me.

Yes, Father. But compassion is My Soul. It is Love. It is You. It is needed.

TheOne was silent, then exploded out and away from His single point of Divine Light. His faithful Orbs followed, leaving TheSon alone in the complete darkness of the Void adjacent to his SuperVoid.

TheSon longed for His Father. *Why do You leave Me, Father? Am I not the Way of Love and Forgiveness?*

The response from TheOne was unexpected. A universe-shattering boom brought all movement to a complete halt, followed by the return of the retreating Orbs.

So spoke TheOne and His Divine multitude. *YES! TheSon IS LOVE AND FORGIVENESS. AND JOY. CELEBRATE TheSon! LET THE DRAMA UNFOLD.*

With those Holy of Holy words, the SuperVoid walls of damned eyes crumbled. Dark Matter, so securely containing the empty Soul-Judged Evil Eyes within the wall, exploded into space, swallowed entirely by the waiting and hungry Black Hole adjacent to the gate; to be used in yet unborn universes. Some unrepentant eyes awaited clarity; drifting aimlessly in the Void; confused; rebellious; unknowing or unwilling to know the Truth.

Thoughts buzzed between the eyes.

'Has NoOne returned to damn us?'

'Why are we free?'

'Why are we alone?'

'Where's TheSon? Didn't He promise redemption?'

'What do we do now?'

'We are being punished!'

TheSon proclaimed for all to hear. *No, My children. Those who accepted My offer of redemption and then repented are free to visit the Funnel to be judged. The rest shall cease to exist.*

'No…I didn't mean it! Please, one more chance!'

'I promise to change!'

'I didn't understand what You meant!'

And it was over. The Hell of the SuperVoid, spanning all universes, ceased to Be. The Soul-Judged Evil Eyes that had refused TheSon's Grace were lost forever. The repentant eyes streamed to the Funnel to be judged.

One last realization that the damned LostSouls had rejected: there *was* Light. Sucked into the cold, empty, silent reaches of darkness, the now-forever LostSouls saw with Divine clearness the outcome they had passed up: trillions of soon-to-be Holy Eyes in perfect formation, singing *Hosanna*, praising TheOne and His mercy. All in a line, flowing forward in perfect synchronicity. But unlike the damned, heading for the Holy Funnel.

In the lead was a single Light so bright, none but the Holiest of the Holy could gaze at it, not even for a brief moment.

It was TheSon. He had His army.

Journal Entry Ninety-Eight: Strategic Locations

In an eternity that spanned a second, TheSon and His army of Orbs found themselves suddenly surrounded by other purple dancing Orbs shared freely by TheOne; Souls so Holy they were selected to announce the Sacredness of TheOne and TheSon to all Creation.

And salvation. Redemption offered freely by TheOne. From here to everywhere, a celebration of the freeing of the LostSouls began. More Light flooded the reveling to build on the Sacred. TheSon's army tripled in size and energy.

NoOne's purpose was clear to TheSon: NoOne desired to destroy TheOne's ability to create life. TheSon knew of two strategic locations within the macro cosmos where life and its creative processes were formed and reformed. One was the Funnel. The other was the Holy

Lip. TheSon calculated that NoOne knew the Funnel could no longer be breached. Its defenses by now would be sealed tight with security; the Holy Lip was another matter.

All universes were birthed, and all universes ended at the Holy Lip. All universes began from a single discharged Holy Speck offered to the Lip. This hole was the exit from the Divine Foam and the entrance point to a soon-to-be newly created physical reality. Every universe had a Holy Lip; it had to. However, finding one was like finding a particular grain of sand on all the beaches of a medium-sized world.

On the Lip, an infinitely dense spectacular Speck of Holy Energy explodes into Sacred expansion and, with it, the birth of a new universe. First, NoOne's Dark Matter is commanded to be released. Then, lasting a ten-millionth of a trillionth of a trillionth of a trillionth of a second, energy from the TheOne explodes outward creating a universe for one sole purpose: to grow and nurture a Soul Host based on Love. Only TheOne knows the perfect number of planets that can shelter and nurture Soul development for His designs.

Weary and angry with his forced and unappreciated servitude, NoOne knew all too well his role in universal design. NoOne's Dark Matter was the lattice structure for energy and its formed matter to cling to. At the end of time, once a universe's energy was spent, NoOne's Black Holes sucked up whatever energy remained. The pure quantum energy Foam that remained was returned to the Ground State of Being called TheOne. All that remained at the end of a universe's life was a membrane grid of NoOne's Dark Matter; its energy eventually sucked down the drain of a universe's final colossal Black Hole; accumulating recycled Dark Matter for yet another creation.

NoOne was well aware of the freeing of TheSon and the LostSouls from the SuperVoid. All it did was remind him of how little his Father could be trusted. It confirmed NoOne's absolute necessity to eliminate them both. Throughout NoOne's slavery, he had ruminated endlessly on how he could usurp his Father's dominion. Now it was much more than dominance; now it was about existence.

How best to shatter my Father and ravage His Creation? How can I force Him to give back what He has forced me to produce? Perhaps Dark Matter was the answer, his secret weapon. It had to be; it was his only weapon. So, what would happen if Father's Divine Foam, so vulnerable just inside the Holy Lip, was swamped with Dark Matter?

NoOne decided it was time to marshal his forces and look for the Lip. For eternity, he had been frustrated as the Lip and Funnel pulsed through created time and space, the only parts of the physical world linked to the Holy, always moving, shifting, and quaking into being in new locations for brief moments. None but those ordained by TheOne knew the exact location. NoOne knew if he could find them, especially the Lip, TheSon would show up. TheSon had to. The balance of Creation required it; demanded it.

The final battle for control of the multiverse cosmos in its entirety was now a certainty.

Yes. A showdown, thought NoOne. *A show to tear everything down. Particle by particle.*

Dark Matter will be all that remains.

This I plan. 'Amen.'

Journal Entry Ninety-Nine: Conclusion

Son, I have tried to provide you with a complete narrative of the natural and supernatural events that led to your present predicament. I am saying it is your predicament because I probably will have been gone many years by the time you read this.

I am tired. I have written somewhere around five hundred pages. I thought it would be therapeutic for me. I have been so depressed. The dark clouds of hopelessness hang over me almost constantly now; they wash away any positive thoughts I might have. I am just trying to hang in there long enough to set my affairs in order and be sure you're settled.

I trust this manuscript will lead you to wiser forces that can help you discover answers to questions you have not yet asked. I wavered throughout the time we spent together as to whether I should tell you about your origins. And your relationship with me. The bottom line is I never once doubted or regretted that you were my son. You still are my son. But now, you must move on and embrace a new summative identity—Hero—to find your answers.

Begin your quest.

Son, we all have the potential for a Divine perspective and a transcendental purpose, but most cannot see how that Spiritual synchronicity fits in with life's physical turbulence. I am blinded as to my outcome going forward. But I feel I have realized my purpose, and for that reason, I hope I will make it through the Gates.

Maybe I will meet you again in 'beyond the Veil'. I hope I will. Perhaps I have contributed enough to the universe that TendHer will judge me worthy of dancing with the Orbs. Maybe not.

Maybe the small slice of Divinity that dwells in all of us will keep me faithfully connected to the Creator of life's mysteries. I hope so.

Overall, three things I know with all my heart. First, I Love you as my son, and the fact that we were brought together in unusual circumstances only serves to strengthen our bond. Second, NoOne will attack the Holy Lip—existence is at stake. Last, you must find the four Chosen and battle with TheSon against NoOne, wherever that may be.

Begin your search for the four guys. They are waiting for you. All the forces I have mentioned in this manuscript are poised to begin the final conflict. Please hurry. Love, Dad.

My Mission

I put the thick manuscript down. "So, you did it," exhaled Sheba.

"Speak up, Sheba. Did what? Finish my dad's book?" I asked.

"Yes," Sheba answered softly. She was obviously not her usual petulant self. Was it because I'd ignored all her warnings and finished my dad's manuscript? Had I somehow opened a Pandora's Box, unleashing uncontrollable forces?

"Is that all you have to say? No congratulations? No motivating speech to send me on my way to God knows where?"

Sheba approached and squatted, squarely facing me as I sat in my chair. "I guess this is where I say 'goodbye,' " she announced.

Taken by surprise, all I could do was blurt out, "What did you say?"

"It is time to say goodbye. I begged you to stop reading. But you did not. You did not listen to me. You did not even listen to the Devil! You had so many good years left."

I was concerned. I pressed Sheba. "Had? Had? Had years left? And now I don't? What are you talking about?"

Sheba turned, slowly sauntered towards her sleeping pillow at the far end of the living room, and sat with a defiant, sullen plop. "My job is done. I told your father I would keep you alive as long as possible. Now? You are past the point of no return. You must never come back here."

This was the last thing I expected; to be pronounced "terminal" and forced to say goodbye to Sheba, my dad's favorite Erob.

"And why's that?" I asked. "How have I passed the point of no return? Why can't I come back here? It's my apartment!"

Sheba shook her head. "You know too much. He knows you are here."

I decided not to play our usual question-answer game; it was not the time to match wits. Sheba sounded and looked grim. Maybe even depressed. "I know. I felt his creepy presence the further I got along in my dad's manuscript. I just thought it was because I was so involved with the story."

Sheba knew something I didn't, and it was serious. Would she tell me?

"You must leave now and never return," whispered Sheba, as though she didn't want the walls to hear what she said.

"But why Sheba?" Part of me hoped this was just another one of Sheba's practical jokes. "Where should I go? Are you coming with me?"

For a brief moment, Sheba softened. She dipped her head and tail at the same time. A tear formed in the corner of one eye. She scanned the room from side to side as if to locate someplace to hide.

I got it. I felt Sheba's intense emotion. My honesty had moved her to display her total and complete devotion.

"I'm sorry, Sheba. Please tell me what you know." A part of me knew this was to be our last conversation. Deep inside, I knew I had uncovered too many forbidden truths. I was a serious threat to somebody.

Sheba replied, "You are dangerous, now. You know too much. The force NoOne is coming for you."

The next moments of silence felt like years. "Ok. You're right. I know this now. I must go. But can you come with me? We can get out of Portland and find a new apartment in Seattle."

For one of the few times in our relationship, Sheba leaped on the kitchen counter, planted her face close to the window, looked outside, and growled. But why was she growling like a Dog?

Sheba looked back at me, scowled, and said, "A dark fog is coming. It's NoOne. He is almost directly over us, just above the dome. All of us Erobs have been called back to Security Headquarters."

"Why, Sheba? What will happen to you?" I asked.

"Who knows? But don't you worry. I'm keeping my eye on you." Sheba stared at me to see if I had picked up on the deeper meaning.

"Yes, Sheba, I got it."

Sheba grinned. Guess I passed her mental fitness test for surviving on the streets.

"I'm scrubbing this place clean," she continued. "No traces of you can be left behind."

Standing up, I jumped to the window to look at what Sheba was worried about. "I see it, Sheba. You're right. Never seen a black fog like that. It's dense and spans the horizon. What's that thing in the middle? Look, it's right in the middle of the fog."

"It's a Snake."

I was ready to go. "Better help me pack some things up."

Sheba smirked. "I already have. That's how much you've been out of it. I've already got you packed; picked out the few clothes that were clean. You might work on your laundry skills down the road. Your bags are by the bedroom door."

"Wow. You're in a rush to get rid of me. Will I ever see you again?"

"Yes, my unkempt protégée," promised Sheba. "As soon as we Erobs learn how to manufacture Souls."

Grabbing my coat and two bags, I opened our apartment door. Looking back, I said goodbye to my one and only friend.

"You HAVE a Soul, Sheba. And a helluva' heart! I Love you."

The Hospital

I already missed Sheba, but there was nothing I could do about it at this point. Hopefully, when things quieted down, I could track her down. Maybe check out the Erob Humane Shelter. If she did end up there, I sure would feel sorry for that staff.

I found temporary housing in an Erob bed and breakfast about as far away from my old apartment as possible. As luck would have it, the only Mental Hospital in Oregon was located nearby, within walking distance. Hidden in the West Hills of Portland, Oregon Regional Hospital's presence was hidden by thick forests, perched above a highway that led to the coast.

Even though I lived in the same city, I could not recall ever visiting the hospital. I could not remember a single Erob 24-hour news report featuring its property, staff, or programs as hard as I tried. I could not recall a single charity event held for its benefit, charitable donations being the lifeline for other service agencies.

Yet, as I parked my car in the main lot, something seemed foreboding about the facility. Maybe I was trying desperately to protect myself by obscuring an unsettling memory. An oddly familiar vibe of impending doom shivered around my torso, muscles bracing for trauma. Sweat teased down my face. My hands were clammy as I lumbered up the old, cracked, deep concrete front-porch steps.

As I timidly pushed through the hospital's main double doors and sheepishly peered in, I heard the receptionists chattering, their high-pitched voices echoing off the tile floors. Looking over at me, I could tell they were wondering if I was an escapee from one of the many other hospital wards. Standing there frozen, I waited for them to decide. I subtly raised my official-looking clipboard and nodded, hoping to project credibility. Once they saw I was not wearing the red plaid wool coat mandatory for patients, they went back to their cups of coffee and conversation, totally ignoring my presence.

I glanced straight up at a huge chandelier hanging from the three-story lobby ceiling by a thin steel chain. The main body of the chandelier was composed of a thick circle of iron, surrounded by perky sconces supporting crescent-moon-shaped light bulbs, half of which were burned out.

I could've sworn the chandelier was struggling to let go of the ceiling and drop on me.

Next to assail my senses was a musty, pungent odor. It had to be urine. And feces. A thought streamed through my head.

Guess this is a zoo, and I'm headed into the Lion's den.

My impression was reinforced by the echoing sound of a single loud scream. I looked at the receptionists for a sign as to what the cry meant. I was relieved that they barely reacted. They couldn't have cared less; hair-raising screaming must be a regular event. So, what's next? Dracula crawling on the ceiling, upside down?

I had to start here. It was the best place to begin my quest since I knew that all four guys had spent considerable time in and out of this very same mental health facility in Portland. Looking at the wall directory, I found the two Long-Term Care floors and gingerly leaped up the stairs.

The first Long-Term Care floor was empty. A note on the door directed staff and visitors alike to the second floor. All patients had been transferred there. I would later discover why: a virus had raged through the hospital wings, wiping out most patients over the age of sixty.

Was I too late?

Maybe not. The second floor was packed with patients. Approximately the length of a football field, the room was filled with rows of six-foot-long tables. Patients surrounded most tables. And I could tell some were senior citizens.

The smells of urine and feces that assaulted me as I moved further into the room were overpowering. It was the same stench that had greeted me as I entered the building, except now the odor was more concentrated. My eyes started to water, and my hand instinctively covered my nose.

Hang in there. I'll get used to this. I have no choice.

Everything on the floor was white, including the staff's uniforms. One television was blaring in the center of the room, facing rows of steel chairs. The chairs lacked solid back support and were attentively lined up, waiting for somebody to sit. Thick bars crossed all the windows, fluorescent lights hummed on the asbestos-covered pipe-laden ceilings, chairs screeched as they were scooted along by the sedated, semi-conscious patients on the old, lumpy linoleum floor. Doors slammed and echoed their complaint from the wings above.

Walking up to the staff cage located next to the main entrance, I banged on the glass window. Raising my voice, I proclaimed, "Ah, excuse me. I'm here doing research. Could somebody help me?"

A short, bald, senior male attendant with dozens of keys attached to a long chain swinging from his hip peeked out of the small window door used to dispense medications to patients. He was uncharacteristically aged, despite all the longevity and age-reversal appearance drugs at his disposal.

"Yeah. Guess so. What's your business here?"

"I'm from the Mayor's office. Got a letter right here," I said, removing and offering a piece of paper from my clipboard. The local Erob Medical Association was one of the few community groups my dad believed was worthy of his contributions. It baffled me why he would give money to a group that helped wounded robots, but numerous times during his life, I saw how his generous gifts opened doors. Like now.

"Nah, don't need to see it. You here for a tour?" he asked.

"Ah, sure. Can we do a walk-through?" I asked.

Sighing deeply as if I was interrupting his work duties, he curtly replied, "Sure."

As he exited the glass cage, I glanced at the attendant's nametag. I asked, "Peter, you work here long?"

Mumbling under his breath, Peter replied, "Too long. Thirty-plus and counting."

"So, you know all these patients?" I asked.

"Most. We just had one floor to take care of in the good ole days. Now, I got another fifty patients crammed in cause a bunch of dumb shits started dying from the flu on the first floor."

"How many died?"

"Ah, around thirty or so. Mental midget administrators thought they could save money by sending the rest up to our floor."

Nervously, I prayed that if my dad's four guys had, in fact, been here, they were spared from the epidemic.

Scanning the room, I noticed that most patients were sleeping, probably over-medicated. At least a dozen or so of the patients were rocking. Most stared at nothing. Occasionally, a patient screamed out an obscenity. That outburst would be followed by another patient responding just as forcefully. Then another. A chain of screams ended with the original patient screaming out for everyone to be quiet.

I scanned the room, looking for a table with four older men. That would be a perfect place to start. Most of the tables had more or less than four patients. Trouble was, none of the tables had just four senior patients.

I decided to sit, wait, and watch. Maybe one of the patients would wander over and join a table with three? Possibly one of the tables of five would lose a patient to a table with three occupants. For hours, I sat and waited.

Just as I was about to leave, one older gentleman stood up and shuffled to the other side of the room. He sat at a table with six other older males. He turned and looked at me. He smiled.

I noticed that the two attendants in the glass "cage" looked up. I made eye contact with Peter and walked over. Then, I politely tapped on the cage glass window.

"What's up?" asked Peter, peeking out of the medication tray opening in the window.

Pointing to the table with the seven older men, I asked, "Could you tell me if that is a regular grouping?"

"Grouping? You must be from the university," grunted the other attendant.

"No, I'm from the Mayor's office. Sorry to bug you, but do those seven older men always sit together? They appear to be the oldest patients in the room."

Peering out and studying the room, Peter asked, "You mean those seven at the far end?"

"Yeah," I replied.

"Nope. Weird. Never seen that seven sit together. Most of the time, it's just the same four old farts."

"Normally, the table just has four of the older males?" I asked. "Which four? Can you point them out to me?" I asked.

"First two on the left, both sides of the table."

"Can you tell me how they got here?"

Peter shook his head. "Who knows? They've been here for thirty-plus years, as long as I can remember. Not one of them has said a word in all that time. They just sit there staring into space. But I'll tell you this. Their psych files are filled with shit that would make your Erob toilet blush!"

The imagery was undoubtedly "behind" the times, but I managed to keep my cool. "Why?"

Peter ignored my question. Talking to himself, he said, "Funny. Wonder why the others joined 'em?"

"Those four have been staring like that for thirty years?" My interest began to build as I considered the possibility that these were the exact same four guys my dad wanted me to find.

Just too easy.

Peter didn't reply. He sighed and looked at the exit, hoping his slight hint would get me out of his hair.

I didn't take the hint. "Looks like they haven't changed their hospital robes for decades," I muttered.

"Doesn't matter. Just as soon as we change their clothes, they start throwing up and shittin' on 'em anyway. God, one day I came in, and all the patients had their robes off, men and women alike, bunched 'em up in the center of the room and peeing on 'em. Women too. Squatting. Men aiming at the women. Not a pretty sight."

"What? The peeing or the robes?" I asked.

He ignored me. Curiosity aroused, I probed further. "The original four, there, in the corner. Do you have their history? Could I access their files?"

Looking away from me, staring back toward the door we just entered, Peter replied, "Well, technically, you're not credentialed."

Pushing it as far as I thought I could without getting nasty, I said, "Look, I got a letter that gives me researcher privileges here. It's from the Mayor herself. She gave me complete access to all the records here at the hospital. Take it and look for yourself."

Repulsed at the prospect of having to read anything other than comic books, Peter thrust out his hand and grabbed the letter. "OK. OK. Sure isn't like the old days. Seems like anybody can come in and do anything they want. I'll go get permission for you and be back." The attendant barely shuffled to the door. More disgruntled sighs.

I heard Peter's footsteps on the steel stairs, vibrations reverberating throughout the entire floor. I could tell he was climbing very slowly.

My hemorrhoids grow faster!

With no warning, three of the seven older males sitting at the table suddenly stood up, grunted loudly, and moved to another part of the room. Now there were four patients left at the table, all staring into space. As the three walked away from the table, they looked at me and then looked at the table they had just left. They did this three times.

A message was being sent. I was being directed.

Shifting my attention back to the four seniors left sitting at the table, I noted they looked nothing like the four guys in my dad's picture on his desk. Nothing at all. I never asked my dad who they were, but since my dad's book talked about four guys and there were four boys in the picture, they all should be the same fellows.

I slowly approached the four senior patients' table from the side of the room to get a closer look. I was confident they would not notice my presence. All four had their heads frozen in space, staring at nothing. I didn't detect a single body movement among the four, not even a twitch.

The picture on my dad's desk was an old Polaroid with four very distinct guys posing with fishing poles. One of the boys was a heavy-set guy, obese. All four of these guys sitting at the table in front of me were thin. One guy back then was tall and muscular; he posed with confidence, like a football player. None of these guys were tall, much less muscular. I remembered a Native American, but these guys were three Whites and one Black person. Don't recall any of them being Black in the photo, either. I also remembered a short guy with a fierce penetrating look; these guys were all average in height. None looked fierce at all.

I wanted to make this work. It would be easy and convenient if these were the four guys my dad helped long ago, but I needed to stay within the bounds of reason. Fishing for something that didn't exist would waste too much precious time.

Turning back to look at the staff cage, I expected the remaining attendant at any moment to warn me I was getting too close to the patients. With each step closer to the table of four, I felt I was creeping closer to the unknown. My throat dried up. My heartbeat thumped against my chest. Beads of sweat popped out on my forehead.

Then I heard words coming from one of the four patients sitting at the table. 'It's about time you got here.'

I stopped moving, my foot dangling inches from the floor. Was that a voice I heard, or was I just talking to myself? The four appeared not to have moved. Their eyes were fixed in a downward stare at the table's surface. They were planted in their chairs. I surveyed the room. Not one patient was looking at me. The staff attendant in the glass cage was looking down, still reading his book or maybe sleeping. For good measure, I focused on each side of the room and the few center seats filled with patients watching TV. Nobody was paying any attention to me.

It must have been something in my head. I turned around to leave.

'You're the boy. Knew your father well. Said you'd be comin'. Took ya' long enough. No matter. Here comes Peter Cottontail. Come back another day.'

These thoughts aren't mine. They're coming from outside me! From these four patients?

"Read our files first. Ben's full of shit as usual. Just make sure you come back soon!"

This time I knew I had heard someone speak aloud. Turning my body around to face the four old guys, I detected no movement or orientation toward me. Before I could get closer to the four, Peter returned.

"OK, you're right. You got the OK. Stay around if you want," sighed Peter.

"I guess I should…I mean, I was told…ah, yeah. Guess I think I'll check out those records for a bit and then maybe come back in a few days. Are you working a couple of days from now?"

Peter gave me the look dentists get from patients when they're told they need to have five teeth capped. "Sure, whatever."

"Thanks, man. Do you ever wonder if all these people know about what's happening outside this floor?" I pondered as I moved toward the door.

Thankful to finally get me off his floor, Peter mustered some enthusiasm. "Nah, they're all zombies. God abandoned them a long time ago."

On a hunch, I turned and briefly looked back at the four men seated at the far table. One of the four gave me a wink. It was amazingly fast. Maybe I was stressing out, but I could swear I also saw him mouth the words: "No, He did not."

The Records

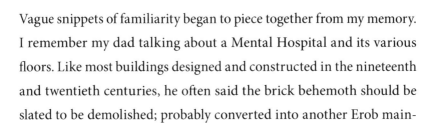

Vague snippets of familiarity began to piece together from my memory. I remember my dad talking about a Mental Hospital and its various floors. Like most buildings designed and constructed in the nineteenth and twentieth centuries, he often said the brick behemoth should be slated to be demolished; probably converted into another Erob maintenance shed. I wondered why his prediction never came true.

If this was the Mental Hospital he was talking about, the archives room would be located in a section of the building few ever visited: down in the basement.

My dad talked a lot about how creepy it was being alone with the archives; recorded histories of suffering, so many lives lost to mental illness. And stories of ghosts ran rampant at the hospital. He was convinced it was the way the hospital administrators kept snooping employees away from the many secrets harbored in seclusion, secrets of failure. Still, now and then he admitted he felt an eerie presence, as if he was being watched.

I was right. The records facility was down in the basement. Walking downstairs via the narrow steel staircase, I reminded Peter that I specifically wanted to see the files on the four guys that sat at the far table. Peter could have cared less. He shoved a piece of paper in my hand. Four names were scribbled on its coffee-stained surface. Opening the creaky, steel door to what looked like a dungeon, Peter gruffly pointed to cabinets on the right, grunted "See ya," and walked back to the entry.

"Hey, you don't need to stick around, Peter. I'll scream if I have any questions."

Peter yawned and barely looked back. "Nah, it's hospital regs. I gotta sit by the door as long as you're here."

"OK, no prob, thanks," I said.

I was alone with rows of cabinets filled with paper documents, unheard of in this day of auditory digitization. No longer is there any need for paper, much less professional notes, because every word uttered is recorded automatically by the Erob sensors located in every wall in every building and stored at a central site. But, being somewhat of a traditionalist, I still used paper and pencils.

"Let me know if I can get you anything else," Peter mumbled, then yawned from a distance.

"Thanks…I think," I yelled back. Then, peeking around one of the cabinets, I saw Peter sitting at a table right by the door, staring off into space, head jerking up and down, trying unsuccessfully to stay awake.

Leisurely strolling up and down a few aisles, I finally found the file section I was looking for. Each of the four guys had their own file. Yelling out to Peter, echoes bouncing off the walls, I asked, "Hey Peter, you said you read the files on the four guys sitting at the side table, the guys you wrote down on the piece of paper you gave me?"

Awakened from his nap, Peter yawned back, "Yeah. Like I said, you'll find some heavy psycho shit in those files. Everyone gets a kick out of them."

I mentally calculated my objective. Primarily, I needed to make sure the files reflected the characters I had read about in my dad's manuscript. Even though the names and bodies were different, it was imperative to associate definitive personalities and life histories with the four seniors zoned out in the hospital.

In John's file, I found precise sketches of all the forests of the United States. Longitude, latitude, even logging roads were mapped out. Lots of maps. One particular map caught my eye; it was a map of the universe, the same map I found with my dad's note attached to his manuscript, with the name "John" written on the top.

An extensive essay on "The Sexual Behavior of the Bonobo" was found in Charles' file. It was scientifically articulate. It identified every Bonobo in every zoo in the United States, undoubtedly linked to Charles' Mentor, Bestow.

Luke's file contained hundreds of Love letters. Page after page of very romantic and sometimes erotic musings. All addressed to his Soul mate, Heather.

Ben's file was thick. I found essays on every subject imaginable.

"Hey Peter, these are some fantastic samples. All four of these guys have produced some sophisticated and complicated stuff."

Peter drowsily replied, "Yeah, the head shrink here says don't make the mistake of thinking crazy people are stupid. Just the opposite. Got some heavy hitters in this place, and those four are the heaviest as far as the shrinks are concerned."

Testing Peter, I said, "Well, they're catatonic."

Now resigned to my constant questioning, Peter forced himself to fully wake. He stood up. I heard him pace by the door. "Yeah? No shit. But even catatonics have periods of remission. Not anymore for these four, though. For years, these four have been vegetables. They wrote all that shit before they zoned out for good. Thirty years ago. Since then, zippo. Just sitting there. Once in a while, they parade around like a chain gang. Except one of the four, about four years ago, started to write like mad. Theory crap. Didn't understand much of it."

I had no doubt Peter couldn't comprehend anything more complicated than lunch. Ever so curious, I asked him, "Well, how did they get their materials? Any theories on that? Did they ever go to the library? Or head out for field trips?"

Peter laughed, "How would I know? I was still suckin' at my mom's tit. Now? Library? Field trips? Hell, they can barely walk to the shitter, much less take a leisurely stroll to get on a bus to go somewhere. Once in a while, they walk up and get their own meds. Been a long time since I saw that, actually."

I could tell Peter seldom had an audience for his humor. He laughed awkwardly until I affirmed his wit with a chuckle.

"Haha. Oh, OK. Thanks. Think I'll take a bit longer with this thick file if that's OK?" I asked. I knew the file belonged to the patient my dad called "Ben."

Peter again yawned. I heard a "clunk" as his head again hit his desk for a nap. It was a matter of seconds before he began to snore.

Ben's file intrigued me. He was obviously brilliant; that came through loud and clear from my dad's manuscript. Ben's file contained essays on everything from the ecological impact of reduced bee populations and the resulting decimation of crops to detailed sketches of miniature hydrogen bombs. Nothing really piqued my curiosity, so I continued skimming the articles and research notes I found in Ben's voluminous, thick file.

The first article that caught my eye was Ben's scientific analysis of how the Twins acquired their powers. It was an interview with one of the psychiatrists at the hospital decades ago. The doctor must have felt some connection with Ben because he agreed to be recorded.

In notes scribbled alongside the first page in the margins were summary notes made by Ben quoting the psychiatrist: "Something more than them being identical twins shaped the Twins' pathology. It wasn't just the fact they were identical; it was because something spectacular happened in their mother's womb. Something never before seen in the human species. A very unique form of embryo mutation."

Interview and Impressions: Raymond Hauser, MD
Subject: The Twins
Tape recorded by Ben

DR. HAUSER: Two decades have passed since the Twins were admitted to this Mental Hospital for their crimes. The Twins didn't stay long, just six months until they escaped. We are still trying to identify how they managed to break out of our maximum-security ward.

Behavioral genetics is still an infant science. But any way you cut it, the Twins, for whatever reason, are unique in the history of the human species. What they can do together cannot be explained by any current body of knowledge, especially the social sciences, which I anticipate will be absorbed by biological genetics reasonably soon, despite the hearty resistance from the increasingly irrelevant social scientists.

A little background. Even though labeled "identical," normative identical twins still have several hundred random mutations in one of the four DNA nitrogen-containing nucleobases—A-T and G-C. Approximately 6 billion nucleotides are in the human body with as much chromosomal material to go to the sun and back around 70 times, so just a few hundred code changes should not be a big deal.

The kind of physical skills the Twins developed and used can only be described as "super" natural, a disturbing conclusion from someone such as myself who has been trained in the scientific method.

The typical human has 20,000 to 25,000 coding genes that lead to the construction of over 90,000 different proteins made up of one or more of the twenty amino acids. DNA controls and directs all activities found in a cell, including replication, growth, handling mutations, and synthesizing these proteins. Genes are units of DNA that specify the order of amino acids in proteins through their sequence of DNA bases (nucleotides). These are composed of a sugar molecule, a phosphate, and one of the four DNA bases (A-T, C-G).

BEN: Yes, I'm following you.

DR. H.: Impressive for someone your age, but understandable given your test scores. At what age did you start associating fire with sex?

BEN: Hey, doc, can we keep that out of this interview? Just treat me like a reporter, OK?

DR. H.: Oh, yes. Sorry. Never been interviewed by a patient before. And you are following me?

BEN: Yes, doc.

DR. H.: Anyway, this is where the rubber hits the road. A human body usually only has about 1.5 percent to 2 percent of its genetic material as coding genes. These coding genes dictate how to make the messenger RNA that can leave the nucleus to transmit the DNA code to the ribosome for protein synthesis. These are things like regulatory genes that control other genes and the homeobox genes that direct the creation of specific body tissues. So, what does the other 98 percent of the genome do?

BEN: Shouldn't the university researchers dig into this?

Dr. H.: Professors are too invested in bureaucratic survival to take risks. Two major components of the rest of the genome are microsatellites and jumping genes, both of which are responsible for mutations and play a huge role in natural selection.

Ben: You're talking Darwin, right? These non-coding genes account for our species variation, most of which are random mutations; these small changes allow humans to survive as a species.

Dr. H. [*nodding*]: Yes! Our bodies are set up for accidents. It's a throw of the dice. A crapshoot. Depending on their environment, some groups pass on body changes that give them an advantage. And they live on. Other groups die out.

Ben: Like having black skin in the tropics or white skin in Northern Europe?

Dr. H. [*nodding*] Yes.

Ben: OK, so what makes the Twins so unique?

Dr. H.: Some have made guesses, but no one really knows. Some have posited that the Twins can convert a considerable section of the non-coding genes in their brains into coding genes. Their brain neuron nuclei have become like superchargers. Not only do they have an increased percentage of coding genes to the tune of about 90 percent of their total genes, but specific parts of their brain are super packed.

Think of this! [*enthusiastically*] Einstein had parts of his brain that were super packed or "super wired" to transmit and process more information. It's like having a fourth ridge in your mid-frontal lobe or tripling the tissue space in your hippocampus, helping you plan and process large amounts of information in your working memory. Maybe the Twins can harness incredible mental energy through this super packing of converted non-coding genes into coding genes.

BEN: What do you mean by 'mental energy'? Do you mean nerve impulses?

DR. H.: We have to look at an even more microscopic level. At the DNA.

BEN: DNA? Really? (Note: I braced myself for the direction we were heading. Definitely cutting-edge research. I hoped I would be up to the challenge of following Dr. Hauser's lead.)

DR. H.: Yes. DNA emits radiation. Photons. What if the DNA in these super-packed non-coding genes could consolidate this radiation and externalize it in a focused manner?

BEN: Kinda like a laser?

DR. H.: Exactly. Light Amplified by Stimulated Emission of Radiation. LASER. Within a highly discrete wavelength.

BEN: So, leaping ahead here, perhaps the Twins have harnessed DNA radiation in their highly packed non-coding parts of their brains and can amplify this power even more by cross-referencing? By taking two energy streams and joining them into one "super stream" weapon, they can achieve super physical capabilities?

DR. H.: Yes [*muttering almost to himself*] It is a giant leap. But plausible. If by "super stream," you mean consolidating each other's DNA radiation into one energy expression.

BEN [*pause; rustling of papers*]: There's something else to think about. Considering your hypothesis, there could be super packing in the aggression parts of the brain. Also, what about the parts of the brain dealing with conscience or empathy?

DR. H.: I see where you're going with this. Super packing in some parts of the brain, but kind of a compensatory unpacking in others?

BEN: Maybe more like no packing. Think about the role of discipline through reward and punishment. Normal twins experience epigenetic mutations in their genomes. This makes them different. Brain tissue expands or contracts due to environmental rewards and punishments. What if this process was somehow blocked?

Dr. H.: Hmm. Closed-loop brain specialization. Zero empathy processing. Yes, the Twins thrive on the total psychic capitulation of their victims. With no empathy nerve processing, they see their victims as objects, like a tree or pile of dirt, or a bunch of moldable plastic toy soldiers scattered on a child's floor. They smash and sweep the toys aside with no feeling like so much garbage when they get bored.

Ben: OK. We know what they can do. But I still come back to what set this all in motion. I mean, random embryo mutation? I guess that's a reasonable hypothesis. But….

Dr. H.: But *what if*? What if the mutation that has led to so much suffering and cruelty was not random? [*long pause*]

Ben: [*slowly*] Mutation…cruelty…wasn't random? You mean it came from somewhere else?

Dr. H.: Perhaps. Or someone else.

Signed: Ben.

The second article written by Ben that caught my attention was an examination of why and how our society had been taken over by robots. Hoping to discover more context, I realized my time was running out. Thankfully, Ben's notes were in outline form and easy to read.

Why did robots take over our society?
Here are my notes.
Robotization and Social Order

* Inequality. Haves segregated from Have Nots. Each is pissed at the other. Operate in separate spheres. Have Nots bitch because they think the rich are greedy and snobs. Want lots of taxes to

redistribute wealth. Want big government, so the public sector creates jobs based on security and social justice equity (structural access plus the goal the liberals don't want to talk about—equal statistical group outcomes). Haves bitch because they think the Have Nots are lazy and lack the work ethic to "pull themselves up by their bootstraps." Want low taxes, so the private sector can create jobs based on innovation and risk.

* Globalization and digitalization. As per #1, the real culprit of stratification was the entire globe now competing for a shrinking pool of jobs. Technological innovations such as digitization led to greater efficiency and less need for unskilled and/or repetitive labor.
* Breakdown of the perspective of shared communal truth. The rise of social media spawned mobs of bored, angry, and/or disenfranchised niche interest groups. Self-interest led to polarization of the left to promote socialism or the right to promote libertarianism. Refused to see other perspectives and compromise. All-or-nothing thinking.
* Masculinization of women. Androgen (testosterone) hormone cocktails at birth re-wired girl brains to mimic the specialized, visual-spatial predisposition of the male brains and, with it, superior mechanical and mathematical reasoning abilities. Auditory, language centers, and MNS (mirror neuron system) of the traditional female brain were reduced. Proteins enhanced to build masculine secondary sex characteristics in women well past puberty: enhanced muscle mass (vs. tendon flexibility), flat chests, hyper-masculine female genitals, greater physiological capacities (greater lung capacity, higher basal metabolism, more type 2 muscle fibers, more red blood cells, larger and thicker

M cells wired to rods in retina which go to the visual cortex to enhance spatial perception, more grey matter for specialized processing versus female white matter for contextual processing, etc.).

* Outsourcing of birth and child-rearing. Negligible menstruation with an average of 400 eggs per woman harvested for the Erob birthing centers at puberty. Women robustly engaged in the same career areas as men as per #3: construction, manufacturing, engineering, and physics. Traditional marriage rituals were terminated.
* Feminization of men. Radical loss of social engagement (failure to launch syndrome), and motivation levels due to reduced testosterone levels, breakdown of status display rituals (courtship, peer group recognition), and obsessive immersion in fantasy virtual reality.
* Sexism. Women gained control of private-sector jobs as well as the public sector. Men could not get hired. Unemployed, male suicide rates skyrocketed, and groups of male vigilantes and lone revolutionaries instigated mass shootings weekly. 24-hour robot surveillance and security were needed and developed for every house, street, neighborhood, government building, etc.
* Individualism—self-absorbed unrealistic empowerment. Children could no longer work with others or with groups. A generation of kids with the attention span of a mosquito and the personality of a two-year-old.
* Multigenerational wisdom lost. Younger generation no longer restrained or protected from self-destructive behaviors.
* Artificial Intelligence. Later just "Intelligence." Robots became self-innovating.

* Robots were invented to save us from the Twins. The robots were the only ones that could work together, engineer a protection plan, and follow through effectively.

Conclusion: We're totally fucked. —Ben

I found it inconceivable and sad that our Earth was reduced to groveling at the feet of the Twins. Were they still seven years old?

Guess nobody knows. But I was sure of one thing —the personalities contained in these files were the same four I had read about in my dad's manuscript. I started to feel energized, hopeful, and more optimistic than I had felt in a long time.

However, there was one crucial question I needed to answer, dots I needed to connect. Were the guys in these files (and my dad's manuscript) the same four guys sitting upstairs?

I perked up. I was on to something. Ok, so where do I start? With the obvious, of course. Where we all begin when judging other human beings: looks!

My optimism immediately vanished. There was absolutely no physical resemblance between the guys sitting upstairs and their physical descriptions in my dad's journals; I was also certain of that.

Once More

Finally, nighttime arrived. Exhausted, I collapsed on the small cot that took up most of the room in my newly rented, cramped, temporary apartment living quarters. Huddled in the corner were a sink and a toilet. The single induction burner stove predictably lacked its control panel. The bathtub had not been cleaned in years.

I blamed it all on Sheba. She had directed me to a part of the city I had very seldom visited. She said it was for my protection. It was much like a shanty town with tents and soon-to-be-demolished two-story apartment buildings hugging the streets. All sorts of questionable characters roamed the narrow sidewalks or stood in doorways. They were like sentries. Looking for something. I knew I would soon have to move on because I didn't fit in. Nothing I did or wore matched the milieu of character filters the locals used to define who belonged, and therefore, who was safe.

At least I'm close to the Mental Hospital.

Begrudgingly, I admitted Sheba was seldom wrong when it came to matters of survival.

I missed Sheba. I missed her insults and haughty parades. She had indeed turned out to be my best friend. However, I knew there would be severe physical consequences if I returned to my former apartment.

I couldn't get back to the Mental Hospital soon enough. Up at the crack of dawn, I waited for the main hospital doors to be unlocked. Thanks to the Mayor, I had the authority to drop in anytime during daylight hours. I figured the best time to be alone with the four would be after breakfast when most patients take their naps after the heavy carbohydrate-loaded breakfast and the distribution of anti-psychotic and anti-anxiety drugs.

Peeking into the ward through the wire-meshed door window, I saw the patients were napping. I figured they had just consumed their morning medications after breakfast. I opened the door and tiptoed in about three paces when each of the four guys looked up at me from across the room and smiled.

One of the guys seemed to be in charge. The same one that messaged me the previous day again initiated our conversation. Having re-read part of my dad's manuscript, I felt more comfortable communicating through thought rather than speech this time.

Nodding his head toward the staff cage, the patient thought, 'Well, well. You're back for more, eh? I see Peter Cottontail is fast asleep already. Your tax dollars at work.'

I needed to make sure I was not hallucinating. 'We're speaking to each other through thought. I just finished reading a book explaining how humans talk to God.'

'Imagine that,' he thought back.

'Imagine what?' I replied in thought.

'Imagine being chosen.'

'Chosen? My dad said you four were the Chosen.'

'Four and could be more, I say to you. Answer us this: chosen for what?'

'I don't know. Some great battle with an evil force? My dad didn't say specifically.'

'So you say.'

Was I being manipulated or tested? I must hang in with these guys to see if they're the ones. I must not lose my cool.

'Yes, don't lose your cool.'

'You can read my mind?'

'Of course, we can hear your thoughts not only to us but also to yourself. You soon will read ours if you can answer one final question. Think carefully. Who is your father?'

I relaxed. Finally, an easy question. 'My dad worked here at one time. He taught you how to fish.'

One of the other guys sent me a thought. '*Woohoo…this boy's daddy worked in a looney bin! Imagine that!*'

Hoping I passed their test, I pulled up a chair close to the four guys, but not so close that it might seem like I was trying to violate their space.

'Why do you call him Peter Cottontail?' I thought, looking away, trying to establish rapport.

'Don't you notice how he hops when he gets uptight?'

'Oh, has he been nice to you?'

'He tried to get rough one time. All four of us zoned in on his mind. He still doesn't know we control him through thought. We let him know we were and still are off-limits.'

'Off-limits?' I asked.

'Yeah, none of us are to be roughed up. We told him to just keep smoking his weed in the staff office, and we'd all get along. Like now.

Probably finished a couple of joints, and it's not even nine o'clock in the morning.'

One of the other guys sent me his thoughts for the first time. 'He figured nobody knew he was abusive. But we know everything that goes on here. And out there, too.'

'Well, what do you know about me, then?' I probed.

The lead guy took over. 'Come on, guys; let's give our friend here a history lesson.' Pointing at me, he added, 'It's time you know where you came from.'

Another of the four then interrupted. 'And why you need to help us…once more.'

'Once more?' I asked.

'You were the Twin that was adopted…by your father, our Counselor.'

My head was screaming with what the patient had just projected to me in thought. I couldn't help vocalizing my shock, "I'm the *what*?"

'Careful. They'll lock you up, too! You are one of the Twins. You just don't remember because of the trauma.'

'Trauma? What kind of trauma?'

'Your brother did a number on you. He was turning your brain into zeros and ones until we rescued you. Got you out of Seattle fast. Your dad figured it best to move back to Portland and not tell you about your past until the time was ripe.'

'Wait, what past? I have a brother? *The other Twin*? You rescued me?' I gasped.

'Yes. Now you need to remember if you can. You were the Twin that accepted the Word of TheSon. We called you the "New Twin." You made the choice to accept that which is Sacred in all universes. You were the Twin that risked a glimpse of 'beyond the Veil'—a reality out of reach for those consumed by ego. Your father sent you to fight with TheSon against the Devil in 'beyond the Veil'. TheSon waits for us there. Now.'

'I'm the New Twin that my dad wrote about?' I choked and slumped back in my chair abruptly.

The guys said nothing; they just sat there, waiting for me to process the revelation of my life.

I flashed back to the earliest time I could remember being alive. It was with my dad. I was in my early teens. We were shopping. A thick wall blocked the retrieval of any other memories further back in time. I couldn't remember. I never had to remember. I was always so happy and content with my dad. But why couldn't I remember any time before that? Why had I not been more persistent in discussing my roots?

Looking deep within myself, I realized I should've been more stressed than I was. It was a miracle I was still able to keep functioning. Maybe my dad had been grooming me for just this moment. Is that why he made me read so many history books and help him with his science publishing business? Was my brain wiped clean by my brother? I searched for more early memories and clues from my past, but I came up blank.

Then a memory crashed into my consciousness as if rising through rippling dark water. It was like a movie screen with all the lights suddenly turned off. Forced to watch nothingness, I sat paralyzed, waiting until a movie came alive on the screen. Horrified, I saw all the people butchered. By me. And my brother. Removing eyes. Souls screaming for help as the eyes were crushed, writhing. It was unbearable.

Luckily, one of the guys knew what I was going through. 'You can stop that movie. Now. Focus on us. Open your eyes. *Now!*'

Aloud, I blurted, "What about your Souls? Did I take your Souls? Where are they?"

One of the guys answered my question. 'We were stuck in 'beyond the Veil' with no eyes and no bodies. Just Souls. That was a first for humans not waiting to be judged in the Reincarnation Universe. You had been adopted by your dad, and we were stranded. Finally, TendHer showed up and unfolded our Pages.'

'Pages?' I asked.

Luckily, there is a Book of Life Page attached to our Souls. It allowed TendHer to reattach our Mind's Eyes and egos to other sets of eyes in bodies here at the hospital; never happened before, or so she said.'

Another of the patients took over. 'The new four bodies we got here were and still are humdingers. The original occupants were catatonic and grateful to be released from their diseased bodies. Ever since, over thirty years now, we have mostly been waiting for you here so we could join up with TheSon and His troops. We must move quickly because NoOne and your brother are getting too powerful.'

'Why is TheSon waiting for you four?' I asked.

Again, the most talkative guy answered, 'We four are the Chosen. And I guess you are, too, now.'

'Chosen for what?' I stammered.

The guy I guessed was Luke, quiet until this point, answered, 'Don't you remember the book you just read? Hello! NoOne? Your twin brother?'

'OK...that must mean I have tremendous mental powers?' I meekly asked.

'Yep. You need to find a place to hide your body until you join us,' said the guy I thought was Charles. 'Probably number-one target now on NoOne's most-eager-to-torture list.'

'Join who?' I asked.

'Join us here and maybe in 'beyond the Veil',' said one of the four.

I nodded. 'Yes, but won't I be vulnerable? I mean, can't my brother find my body and destroy it?'

Another added, 'You need to stay here. Don't travel anywhere else. As long as you stay in this part of the city, your brother won't find you. Too much emotional trauma.'

'Oh, that's comforting. I'm stuck here forever?' I said. My sarcasm did not elicit any response.

A long-drawn-out pause was suddenly interrupted with a single, powerful statement. 'Huge armies are amassing,' announced one of the four guys.

'Where?' I asked.

'TheSon is in 'beyond the Veil' preparing to protect the Holy Lip, and NoOne is in our physical universe. He's seeking to destroy the Lip. Word has it the Funnel has shut down, and TendHer has stopped processing Souls in the Reincarnation Universe.'

I could wait no longer. I needed to know the answer. 'Is…my dad there too?'

The four guys smiled. 'Yep…one of the Orbs helping TendHer,' thought the guy at the opposite end of the table.

'Is he still smoking cigars?' I impulsively asked.

Almost in unison, all four thought, 'Ha, ha. He thinks he is. Imagine cigar smoke in the land of Angels?'

'And the others my dad wrote about. Where's my….?' I could not finish the sentence.

Some time passed before the guy who used to be John said, 'New Twin, your mom, Jenna, is lost. She and your grandfather couldn't… they couldn't stand….'

I started to sob. 'I killed them. They couldn't stand the pain and….'

'Yes. They were taken by NoOne,' softly replied one of the humped-over bodies.

'My father.'

'Yes, NoOne, your biological father, took them, and they are with the LostSouls.'

I started to flashback to the camping trip. 'I'm starting to remember. Omigod. I remember following a stupid little yellow bus with my brother and watching the four redneck teens in the truck bully the guys on the bus. You guys now sitting before me. Well, you had different bodies then. I remember torturing the teens, not out of any sense of justice but because they were mean, and I was curious to see how they would respond to getting a dose of their own medicine. I remember the shocked look on their faces when we removed only one eye from each, so they could see who was toying with their lives. We were seven-year-old twins. Then we removed their other eyes when they comprehended exactly what would happen. I recall we let one of the four guys keep his eyes and live to tell everyone what happened.'

The guy at the table, who I thought was Charles, tried to reassure me. 'You're safe here. Don't worry. We've all had to go through our own inventories of life mistakes.'

My sobbing became so intense I was afraid I would attract the unwanted attention of the attendants. I couldn't stop. 'Mine was more than just life mistakes. I was *evil*. I remember teasing you four with the four Gopher trails. I remember giggling at the absurdity of my grandfather, so desperate to get his daughters back that he helped us resurrect our sisters' bodies and dangle them around like weak puppets. We watched him whimper like a baby over their rotting corpses.'

I began to hyperventilate. One of the guys stuck out his hand to help me relax. It didn't help.

'I remember luring all of you into the forest. I remember torturing your bus driver and the other counselor. Ivan? Was that his name? I remember....'

One of the guys at the table, Luke, could not take any more of my catharsis. 'Please stop.'

Silence. Not a muscle moved. Were they judging me? They should be. Hideous horrors were rising from deep within me and flooding my consciousness. I had been evil. But I was forgiven. Yet, I still felt I deserved only punishment. Yes, that's what was happening to me. My guilt was punishing me.

I had to get more answers. 'Please answer this for me, and I'll stop. Where is the Counselor Ivan? Did he go to NoOne?' I asked.

'Heck, no. He's in 'beyond the Veil',' replied John, glad to steer the conversation to a topic more likely to lift the depressed mood immersing the group.

'Is he an Orb, or is he being reincarnated?' I asked.

The four guys chuckled at once. 'Ivan. All we gotta do is say his name, and we laugh. Ivan, well, he's sort of the entertainment director.'

Shocked, I asked, 'Entertaining for who and what?'

The guy who was Luke shook with his chuckling. 'Ivan organizes Orb races.'

"Orb what?" I screeched aloud.

'*Shhh.* Thoughts only. Yeah. Orb races. Ivan agreed to stay behind and be a Mentor Orb rather than merge with TheOne. The other Orbs didn't know what they were getting themselves into. Some have begged for Ivan to merge. Anything to get him out of their domain.'

'Why? Is he screwing something up?' I innocently probed.

John took over. 'Ivan? Screw up? Would he be Ivan if he didn't find something to screw up?'

John was interrupted by the guy I thought was Ben. 'Yeah, like taking us to the wrong lake. That turned out well.'

'Yes, my brother and I wondered why you would go to Lake Sutherland at that time of year. So, tell me, what type of games is Ivan organizing? I mean, really? Games in Heaven?'

The body housing Luke replied, clearly excited at the chance to talk about sports. 'Ivan sets up any game that can be imagined. It's 'beyond the Veil'. Any sensation or image can be manufactured and shared by others.

'Let's see, of course, there is football. The most interesting aspect of that sport is the football constantly changes shapes and goes wherever it wants to go. Then there's soccer. But the best is cloud racing. Some Orb players played football with Ivan in his youth but gave it up for racing. New pilgrims in the Funnel find it quite relaxing to see a bunch of Angels surfing on clouds.'

'Oh, sure. But the nudity has to go. As an Orb, Ivan's supposed to be beyond titillation,' Ben commented.

'Yeah, Ivan likes boobies alright,' another guy commented.

Every head on the table jerked up and smiled at me with that thought. All at the same time. Looking for my reaction.

'Ivan likes to make funny shapes with his clouds,' explained another of the guys.

'Oh. I'm relieved he's happy,' I thought. 'My brother and I were so cruel to him. We couldn't make him beg for mercy. He was steadfast in his duty to protect you guys.' I again started to sob.

The guy I thought was Charles made it clear it was time to change the subject. 'I'm sorry for you. But we have all lost so many Souls. I think it's time we move on.'

'Yes, I'm sorry,' I replied. 'Just give me a moment. Yes, OK. I'm OK. What have you been doing here all these years?' I asked.

'Don't worry. You'll have plenty of time to heal when you join us. Our Souls go back and forth, sometimes here; sometimes they are in 'beyond the Veil'. Depends on what is going on. We were just waiting for you. And hiding. This is the perfect spot to hide.'

I still didn't get the entire picture. 'I'm joining you? This is the perfect hiding place?'

The guy who had been the least responsive looked up. 'Yes, right here. The looney bin. Just four Loonies in a bin. Get it? Soon to be five Loonies!'

I stepped back. I couldn't believe what I was hearing. 'Who said I was joining you? No, wait! First, answer me this. How could a Mental Hospital be a safe refuge from the Devil?'

The four chuckled out loud again, foreheads raised a notch above the table. I peeked around the room. Thankfully, no one had heard.

The guy that replied was certainly Ben. 'It's all about vibration, just like what keeps the universe in one piece. There is so much discordant pulsing here; NoOne and your brother could never get a fix on our location. Oh, yeah, they know our vibratory signature, all right.

And yours. It's just that there are so many wacko emissions here, they couldn't discern Adam from Eve.'

Another guy piped up. Right off, I thought he must be the old John. 'A very famous physicist, Hawking, used to say that one second after the Big Bang, if the subsequent energy had been lesser to the point of a single component out of a hundred thousand million, the….'

John was interrupted by Ben who was definitely the perfectionist. 'No, John, you're wrong. You forgot a million. You should say…if off by one component out of a hundred thousand million *million*.'

'Yeah, I was going to say that. If that part was missing, life, as we know it in this universe, would not exist,' said John. 'The universe couldn't exist!'

'Don't you think such a perfect formula could result from millions of experimentations?' added Ben. 'Maybe that's why we have so many universes within our multi-universe?'

'But how have you all endured staying here for so long?' I asked.

The one body that had said or thought the least had to be Luke. 'You mean, how have we stayed sane locked up in a looney bin?'

The four took turns speaking again, eager to lay out their experiences.

'TendHer said we needed to stay sharp, so she allowed us to piggyback kindred Spirits.'

'Yeah, to live out some of our lost potential. Both good and bad. Made our Souls stronger.'

'So, you come and go as you please?' I asked.

The guy on my left spoke first. 'That's it. Being catatonic in a Mental Hospital allowed us to leave here anytime we wanted. Still does. Well, most of our Souls anyway. We had to leave some remnants here as we ventured out. I am John, by the way. I shared my Soul with a psychiatrist. I even applied for a job here at the hospital. Fascinating coming into this room and seeing the body my Soul was housed in. I made sure all of us maintained reliable catatonic behaviors.'

The next guy spoke. 'I am Ben. The smart one? Can you guess who lets me share their Soul? A firefighter! His name was Don Washington. He was a lecturer on fire safety and my Battalion Chief. I saved a mom and her baby. Escaping out of a second-floor apartment window, a gas main exploded. We were blasted out the window. I was all over the news, and I made something out of myself, unlike these losers.'

'Yeah, right. The only thing you made, Ben, was an enormous ego! In case you haven't guessed, I'm the one that keeps Ben in line. Luke is my name. A Dandy Randy revival show with a nude showgirl production in Las Vegas invited me in. Newspapers said I was the best Dandy Randy impersonator in the strip's history. Well, actually, the show was located at a kind of sleazy resort ten miles off the strip. I was the only one that looked good with clothes off.'

Last was the quiet one, Charles. 'I just decided to stay here. Found myself a body on one of the less intensive floors. My host body happened to really like sex. I set a record for making love on the grounds. Thanks to my buddies, I stashed cigarettes, condoms, and occasionally a few beers in the woods. Most of the staff who let us explore the backside picnic areas were too stoned to care. Just turned us loose and ride 'em cowboy!'

Ben couldn't help himself. 'Cowboy? You're Indian, dude!'

'Yeah, and I'm expanding into selling used wagon trains.'

'You're finally getting a sense of humor, Chief!' said Luke.

'Don't call me Chief, Dandy Randy,' replied Charles.

Unlike the four seated at the table, I could find no stress relief from the one-upmanship. I had to have more answers. 'Why would you want to wait for me?'

John replied. 'You're going to protect us here and join us when you're needed,' said one of the four.

'Protect you?'

'Yes, right here. Right at this very table.'

I hoped the four didn't notice the perspiration accumulating on my forehead. 'And how do you think I can do that?'

'Do you remember how you got in here?' John continued to speak for the group.

Uneasy, to say the least, I replied hesitantly, 'Ahh, yeah.'

'You're going to admit yourself. Admit yourself to this ward.'

I exclaimed, 'Admit? And why would…oh, I see. But how do I do that?'

'What? Rusty already? Ha, ha…it will come back. Your mental powers, that is. Man, what a waste of all these decades.'

'My mental powers? You mean like the Twins in my dad's book?'

'Yeah. You *are* one of those Twins, remember? The good Twin. Go home, study the manuscript again and then come back tomorrow. Be your normal self to get through the main doors, then use your powers to make the staff here think you're a patient on this ward. We got to get to 'beyond the Veil', and you need to protect us.'

'Well, I need to think this through. I mean, I don't remember how to use my powers.'

Charles added, 'Guess you've been out of practice. Don't worry. It won't take you too long to remember and catch up. Remembering is not the issue for you, though.'

'What do you mean?' I asked.

'When you do remember more of your "excesses," you will have to confront more of your guilt. What you experienced and shared today was just the tip of the iceberg. Even though forgiven by TheSon, guilt is a potent force. You murdered thousands of people. You will feel their anguish and pain. You will meet some of them in 'beyond the Veil'. You need to be ready for this onslaught of self-loathing as you journey into your thoughts, your emotional memories, your defenses, and then finally, a region from which few ever escape.'

'Well, what is this region that few escape?' I quietly asked.

'Hell,' replied Ben.

'What? Hell? I thought that was a fairy tale.' The minute I uttered those words, I regretted it. I'd just read my history. I was spawned from the Devil!

'Most people you did a number on sure didn't think you were a fairy tale!' replied Ben sarcastically.

This crushing statement sent me reeling. 'Oh, I deserve that. I'm so sorry!'

We paused and looked inward, me more than the others. To say the least, I was uncomfortable being in the same room as those who had witnessed up close my barbaric rampages. How could they stand to look at me? Why were they so accepting? Ever the skeptic, I wondered if I was being used.

Interrupting my inner processing, John said, 'Dig deep, my New Twin friend. When you get to the deepest and blackest part of your mind, after exploring the illusions of symbols and how they protect your ego, you will encounter monsters you never imagined existed. They will demand answers to questions like the questions you are asking yourself right now. You have but one hope. Pray for the Divine thought from TheSon. He will say these words: "Begone illusions. You lose your power when exposed to My Light. I AM the Light!"'

Ben added, 'Yes. You must be whole before your Soul can venture to 'beyond the Veil'. No self-doubts. No emotional currents lurking in some dark corner of your brain. No monster repressed to later distort your energy. You must have every ounce of mental energy free to transition to 'beyond the Veil'.'

'How do I make sure I'm not scarred for life? How do I know I will be accepted in 'beyond the Veil'?'

'Trust TheSon,' said Luke.

'But why are we going there?'

John replied, 'We're linking up with TheSon and his troops. Your role is unclear to us at this point, but I think you will join us eventually. We need your muscle. First, you must work through your history. At home. By yourself. Then come back here and protect our bodies.'

'I'm without a permanent residence right now,' I muttered.

Ben heard my comment. 'It doesn't matter where you are; just clear your head.'

Charles added, 'New Twin, we really don't know what your future holds. We don't know ours either. We were told we needed to wait for you before starting our mission.'

'OK,' I said. 'And where do you go from there? John, is that you? What's our ultimate destination?' The body that housed John uttered three words: 'The Holy Lip.'

Book of Life

That night, I repeatedly tossed and turned on my cot. I prayed for any kind of escape. Disjointed dream segments punctuated the few times I was able to doze off. Deep sleep was impossible. My mind raced back and forth between thousands of memories from my violent past and questions about the mission that lay ahead. Just as I felt myself relaxing, a gunshot followed by a scream echoed throughout my dilapidated daily rental apartment, reminding me I was in constant danger.

If I could, I would have rushed back to the hospital that very minute, in the dead of night, to find answers to my many questions. I knew my true mission in life would unfold within the confines of that hospital. And the guys. Waiting was unbearable. It was torture. I was consoled by the knowledge that my agony was inconsequential compared to all the people I had hurt. I deserved to suffer.

Moving to the side of my cot, I sat up, focusing on straightening out my spine. I had to keep my central energy channel vertical. Breathe.

The guys said I needed to "work through my history." The revelatory trauma from my newly discovered identity still stung, gnawing deep at my jagged consciousness. Memory by memory, I was assaulted by the emotional residue that lurked, buried within the darkest parts of my brain up to now; NoOne's domain, no doubt.

I had no choice but to let the waves of horror sweep over me, surrendering any illusion of controlling my outcomes. Sweat poured out of me, keeping a perfect rhythm with my pounding heart, blood rushing around my body, muscles aching to burst. Do something. Go somewhere. Be someone else. Be different.

Pulled in a thousand directions, pierced by a thousand needles of guilt, my mind was near-total collapse.

I gave up. Completely and totally.

I then heard the words that lifted me to a Spiritual height of ecstasy. The words were, *You are forgiven. The victims that dwell with Me as Orbs forgive you. We await your service.*

A powerful presence had just extinguished my pain. I was in rapture.

I knew who He was. I began to cry. For endless minutes, perhaps hours, I wept.

The uncontrollable sobbing slowly ebbed. I felt a new sensation. I was being cleansed.

'I remember You,' I meekly stated.

Yes, you do. I am TheSon. I have come to give you your Book of Life.

Just mentioning "book" immediately helped me relax.

'Book of Life? What's that?' I asked again.

TheSon replied. *The Book of Life is where your life Pages are stored. Your Pages have been wiped clean. When you invited Me into your heart, I erased your Soul history.*

Puzzled, I asked, 'Why did You erase them?'

Your Pages were unable to record goodness. NoOne allowed only your sins to be documented.

'So, I start all over?' I asked.

Yes, My son. I ask that you open yourself to My reports and record them on your Pages. I also ask that you record your impressions, just like your dad with his manuscript. At a point in the future, the four Chosen will need these Pages to conduct their final mission.

'Why don't You record them? I don't understand why I'm doing this! Surely You or one of Your Orbs could do a better job.'

TheSon did not reply for some length of time. I thought that He had left. Perhaps I said something that offended him.

No. You have not offended Me, thought TheSon. *You must do this because I may not survive the looming Armageddon. You and your four friends might be Our last hope.*

'What exactly am I supposed to record?' I asked.

You must record all that you have learned thus far within the Pages. Include your father's book. You must document everything you are about to witness. You must record the Sacred events that will soon unfold.

'When do I start?' I asked, hoping I would have some time to rest and prepare.

Now. You start now, TheSon replied.

My weariness grew. I knew there was to be no bargaining. My fate was sealed.

Then I sensed He was gone. I was left with an empty feeling in my heart. Then, gradually, I felt an expanding sense of peace. Images swarmed through my perception: flowers opening to display their petals, grass spurting out of the soil, Eagles leaping off treetops to drop to the Earth below, children pumping their legs to reach new heights on their swings, babies fighting their way through birth canals straining to see a different Light, Lovers swelled with billowing waves of passion.

Finally, all the disjointed parts of me unite. What was it called in karate? John used the term many times: "*Isshin*." One Spirit. One mind. One body. I was whole.

Tonight, I begin, just like my dad. I must write down every dream, every image at night, every action and conversation during the day. That is what TheSon meant when he assigned me this task: to create new Pages for my Book of Life.

I must continue my dad's work. I must begin where my dad left off.

Yet, phrases returned to haunt me, thoughts tumbling around in my mind as if they were all connected by a single ever-repeating ring of worry: "final hope," "my final mission," "must record."

My self-affirmed bravado began to fade. Regardless, I must proceed. I didn't have the faintest idea of how my new Book of Life Pages would be helpful. I simply had to trust. I must take the next step. Yes, that's it. One step at a time. TheSon wills it so.

What will be, will be. TheSon wills it so. Tonight, I shall begin my Pages. To trust. With Isshin.

New Twin's Page One: Forces Gather

It is night. This is my first Page. The events of the days that follow must be swiftly consolidated and summarized in my new Pages. I will try to record the events and visions that surely will consume me as precisely as possible.

I don't need to use normal recording methods like the Erob wall recorders or handwritten papers. Thanks to my unique psychic heritage, my thoughts will be instantly recorded as vibrating strings in the quantum realm, the universal language of Creation, organized as Pages attached to my new Book of Life. Along with my dad's book.

I begin.

I see my brother, the Old Twin, leisurely levitating above the ground. It pains me to call him "my brother." He is no longer related to me in any manner. From now on, as much as possible, I too shall try to refer to him as the "Old Twin." He is that much different from me.

As the Old Twin skimmed a foot above the concrete path surrounding the Portland protective Erob dome, he felt confident he could eventually destroy the Erob mental force fields that protected all the cities, Portland included. First, he had to discover the correct psychic frequency.

Shouldn't take much time, the Old Twin thought. *If my brother, the New Twin, was present, surely, with our combined focus, we could find a way to penetrate the energy shields and find the four pests deep within the city. However, our father said no. It would take too much time and effort. We were to leave the towns alone for now.*

The Old Twin wondered how I looked after forty years. He wanted to know if I was still a child physically. Or had I grown into an adult? The Old Twin seldom reflected on his developmentally frozen body; still age seven in physical stature. Did NoOne do this on purpose? To keep him subservient? No matter. Due to his telepathic powers, the Old Twin did not need to grow. He could assume the size and appearance of any adult he chose to create.

In addition, the Old Twin was proud he operated on NoOne's time; a year was like a second. My brother had completely lost any perception of time relevance. He wanted to believe that time and aging were irrelevant to what mattered most: being the second most powerful force in the universe.

The Old Twin felt smug. There was nothing alive on Earth except a few pitiful survivors in the cities. With the help of NoOne's Spiritual powers, the Old Twin obliterated all living organisms outside the Erob defenses. Nothing grew. Nothing moved. Nothing swam. Even the wind was hushed. Early on, many adventurous Souls snuck out only to lose their eyes, bodies skewered on poles outside city walls, like so many Roman highways with crucified enslaved people, warning the rebellious that escape was futile.

Most of Earth's land now contained Soulless bodies, planted a few feet below the surface, row upon row of rotting corpses ready to rise should the need arrive. NoOne told the Old Twin his plan: billions of corpses and their body parts would be molded with Dark Matter and launched into space. The Old Twin fondled a spectacular image in his mind: bodies ascending into the stars surrounded and guided by NoOne. Corpses brought to life. The Old Twin close behind NoOne, leading the troops as General.

Or supernaturally, the Old Twin chuckled to himself. *Soul-Judged Evil Eyes, vacuous Soul remnants, the ultimate weapon in 'beyond the Veil', adding even more Spiritual length to my father's glorious Snake; hungry, thirsty, ravenous to devour any essence that was not Dark Matter.*

Complete decimation of the cities would have been easy for the Old Twin with help from NoOne. But father had cautioned my brother that this could bring unwanted attention from TheOne. Too much too soon. Once TheSon's army was destroyed, NoOne would return to Earth and incarnate again in thousands of other Earth women, eventually destroying all but his own spawn.

With the reincarnation process to be assigned to the Old Twin, he was sure he would sit at the right hand of NoOne and become his number-one disciple. No, partner was a better word than disciple. They would branch out to all the other universes connected to Earth's multiverse and then branch out to other multiverses. Just like dominos. So the Old Twin, my brother, hoped.

Yet, a gnawing seed grew in the Old Twin. Why would NoOne need other incarnations? The Old Twin had more than accomplished what was required for the domination of Earth. Did his father have other plans? And did those plans include rewarding the Old Twin for his steadfast loyalty? Or perhaps, father had some other more sinister objective in mind?

Brushing his growing doubts aside for the moment, my brother figured it would be easy to locate me when he was given permission from NoOne. He thought I had to be in one of the few remaining self-contained cities. The Old Twin predicted that I was close to our old home. It had to be Seattle or Portland. It could be Los Angeles, but that was too far away. And way too small now.

The Old Twin remembered Los Angeles fondly. He destroyed 90% of the city by precipitating numerous Earthquakes. His favorite was producing a level 7 Earthquake along the fault line running parallel to Santa Monica Boulevard.

Rodeo Drive, Westwood, Beverly Hills. They were all gone now. They simply disappeared into cavernous holes. Gas lines exploded. Cars screeched to a halt. People hung onto doors as buildings collapsed into gaping, hungry, bottomless pits.

The Old Twin especially savored the many Earthquake survivors who, upon surveying the disaster, threw themselves out of the skewered, gutted buildings to avoid the fires. Splat! Splat! A thousand times over. Splat! Oh, he enjoyed that sound!

Then again, was that his favorite? No, wait. He treasured the falling power lines much more as they buzzed and whirred with fountains of sparks. Then zap! Like bugs hitting a light at night, human bodies sizzled, wrapped in fallen wire, alive with electricity, hair straight as an arrow searching for the sky, arms and legs twitching. Others recoiling, watching their Loved ones fry before their eyes, helpless in the face of so much pain. Those lucky enough to be around relatives and friends with firearms were mercifully put to death.

What was amusing for my brother was catching people trying to escape the city. Some folks just couldn't resist pushing out on their own. Usually consisting of the macho militia types, the Old Twin let the city fugitives travel a mile or two before scanning their brains for any clues as to the whereabouts of me or a group of four old guys. Once he was satisfied they had no information, he took their eyes and planted their corpses alongside the other deposited bodies around the countryside. He didn't want the city folk to know what happened.

NoOne congratulated my brother for sending him a constant supply of Souls to judge and new bodies to add to his army.

At last, NoOne directed the Old Twin to begin an intensive search for me. My brother projected his psychic antenna around the United States, state by state, city by city, looking for my unique vibration signature. Occasionally, if something piqued his curiosity, he teleported his physical body and personally inspected a city through its dome barrier. It always turned out to be a bogus lead. However, he still enjoyed hanging in space, facing the Erob invisible barrier, terrifying those who happened to be looking at him from the other side through the invisible protective barrier.

With no trace of his targets detected, the Old Twin moved from Los Angeles to Seattle and finally to Portland. Now that the most liberal cities in the United States, San Francisco and New York, were decimated due to wandering gangs, Portland would be the ideal place to hide. Portland citizens took pride in encouraging unfettered personal expression. Portland residents accepted any eccentric behavior, ranging from self-mutilation to the sheltering of potential terrorists. "Live and let live" was the Portland motto. Individualism at its peak. Freedom enjoyed by all with few consequences, justice an antiquated notion, criminals the actual victims of society, security for none—except for the few politicians granted the luxury of armed forces and tall fences around their buildings and homes. Those who lobbied for police force protection were lectured and shamed in public; they were displaying a lack of trust.

The Old Twin chuckled. *Die and let die. Yes, Portland was the perfect place to hide.*

My brother decided he would have some fun (why do I keep calling him my brother?).

Viewing the dome-shaped Erob barrier that protected Portland, the Old Twin wondered if the city defenders had ever considered an attack from below. Why not go under the city? Once burrowing under the Dome and then up to the surface a mile or so in toward the city's center, the Old Twin could easily search for the psychic vibrations that signaled the presence of his brother (me) and the four boys.

The Old Twin ordered a small army of corpses from an adjacent farm to begin burrowing through the Earth until they were directly underneath the city's center. Starting a half-mile out from the dome boundary, the group of dead surreptitiously dug away with their bare hands. They continued to dig until their arms were worn entirely away up to their armpits. The Old Twin was annoyed because he had to bring in fresh corpses five times.

Once the final group had reached the city's center, the planted dead sprung up out of the ground like so many jacks-in-a-box, greeting an astonished group of joggers. Corpses with putrid smells, rotting flesh, dangling body parts, missing eyes, and tattered clothes greeted this small group of city dwellers, who dared to venture out of their secure apartments for a tad bit of exercise in a city park.

The Old Twin had to interrupt his invasion when NoOne said it was time to marshal the troops. The Old Twin's attention needed to be focused elsewhere, so the small army of corpses was ordered by the Old Twin to withdraw and cover up the evidence of their brief invasion.

The Old Twin was informed by NoOne that he was going to begin the attack against TheSon, and it was time for the Old Twin to gather the troops in space. Departing with the billions of corpses stored in the undisturbed farmlands of Earth, the Old Twin ascended into space, safely cocooned in his psychic bubble, leading NoOne's troops into formation.

Billions of body parts were shaped into hundreds of thousands of spears by the Old Twin. Bits of sizzling and blistering flesh lurched their way up, up, up. The sight was magnificent, thought the Old Twin. Forming perfect 100-mile-long spears, the bodies were sucked into space; the "V" shaped squadrons straining to find their master, NoOne, straight ahead leading the assault, now a lurking ghostly cloud of Dark Matter.

The army of the dead stopped in space miles above the Earth, inert but ready. They waited for NoOne's command to launch an attack. They didn't know where or when; all they knew was that their calling was to please their master NoOne and crush whoever and whatever stood in their way when the time came.

In another dimension, TheSon huddled with His army of Orbs in 'beyond the Veil'. TheSon clearly saw NoOne's waiting army in the physical dimension. He sensed a trap was being set. NoOne's objective was clear: to attack the Holy Lip, penetrate, and conquer the Holy Foam surrounding TheOne.

TheSon was concerned. He could track NoOne and catch glimpses of his massive army propelled through space by NoOne's Dark Matter. The long spears of corpses seemed to multiply by the second. It was the first time TheSon had seen such a formidable army whose single goal was to destroy the Holy. It was now a matter of wait and see for TheSon, hoping His defenses were strong enough to withstand the assault; hoping His Father, if necessary, intervened to protect the sanctity of 'beyond the Veil', should TheSon fail.

New Twin's Page Two: Deceit

NoOne knew there was only one event in the physical universe that could signal the presence of the Holy Lip. It was a Black Hole Merger. Found in a dense collection of stars called globular clusters, the odds of one Black Hole running into another Black Hole significantly increased. NoOne reasoned that it was here that the Holy Lip was best disguised and hidden.

A Black Hole Merger hungrily consumes energy. They are the vampires of the universe, sucking each other up, converging, and converting exquisitely immeasurable mass into pure energy. Each twenty times the size of the Earth's sun, matter and energy crushed together and gulped into a hole the size of a pea.

NoOne speculated that the Black Holes themselves would be hidden within a form of universe distraction—the Supercluster Filament: literally, several galaxies pooled together to form a wall in space. Like the web from an insect, the Supercluster walls were similar to Earth's galaxy Laniakea Supercluster, consisting of 100,000 galaxies, whose span was as vast as 10 billion light-years, effectively hiding structures on the other side. It was there NoOne thought that TheOne and His Son had disguised the location of the Holy Lip and protected it from detection by the greedy Black Holes.

With his black cloud winding through the physical universe, NoOne had a sudden revelation. He gloated as he anticipated once again outsmarting his sanctimonious Brother and his spurning Father. NoOne reasoned the closer his troops approached the Holy Lip, the more the Orbs would try to protect the Lip thereby generating increased psychic disturbance. All he had to do was track the frenzied unintentional signaling to receptive humans on Earth. And because I was so close to the four Chosen and TheSon, NoOne figured that I, the New Twin, would be one of those receptive humans; that I would unconsciously pick up the danger signals created and sent by TheSon's Orbs, assigned to protect the Lip.

All NoOne had to do was follow me.

And who better to monitor me than my brother, his faithful son, the Old Twin? However, to the displeasure of my brother, to be fully receptive to the signal from me, my brother would have to remain on Earth.

My brother, the Old Twin, became angry when he was informed of NoOne's wishes. He wanted to stay with the troops in space. He was sure I was no longer a danger and could be found anytime. Perhaps he, the Old Twin, could join the attack force later? Couldn't NoOne use him in the final assault?

NoOne was not accustomed to giving orders a second time, much less discussing options. NoOne said nothing. His action, though, sent a clear message: The Old Twin found himself transported to a primitive abandoned wheat field, surrounded by half-buried corpses.

The Old Twin thought, *This is NoOne's first tactical mistake. He needs me but does not know it. He's going to regret it.*

Making a mistake was not part of NoOne's flawless strategy; manipulation was. The Old Twin had been inflated in importance because NoOne needed to use him. Now that the Old Twin's skills were of reduced importance, there was no reason to abandon so much precious Dark Energy lurking in the deep regions of the Old Twin's body. The Old Twin needed just enough of NoOne's presence to be a warning signal when his brother had been found.

The Old Twin could feel the departure of NoOne from much of his body. It was as if someone grabbed his heart, squeezed it flat, and then yanked it out. Cell by cell, the dark sludge was extracted precisely, calmly, emphatically.

'Please, stop. Father, why are you doing this? It hurts!' thought the Old Twin.

'Well, of course, it does, my child!' purred NoOne. 'But facts are facts. You are of limited use now. Be thankful I am leaving a bit of myself for old times' sake. The only way you can help me now is to find your brother and wait for my orders. Do nothing until you hear from me. Do this now, or I shall rip out the remainder of myself from what remains of your nonexistent puny and irrelevant, dark being.'

Ordered to wait on Earth, the Old Twin watched from afar with anger and envy as the troops he collected departed Earth's gravity with NoOne's dark cloud in the lead. For the Old Twin, there was nothing to do on Earth except one thing: follow his father's orders. The Old Twin estimated it would take but a few days to find and finally destroy his brother and his small group of losers.

NoOne had no interest in any further discussion with the Old Twin. His only concern was finding the Holy Lip with his army in place. And the bottom line was that NoOne knew TheSon would keep His Word. Other than the incarnations sanctioned by TheOne, TheSon was forbidden to materialize in the physical universe just as NoOne was forbidden to become Pure Spirit in 'beyond the Veil'. The difference between TheSon and himself, NoOne thought, was that NoOne would easily break his Father's taboo. TheSon would not.

NoOne's army was in place. Trillions of corpses. Body parts. Eyeballs. All held together with Dark Matter. Waiting. Anticipating. Drifting in space. Like fish ensnared in a troller's net, the corpses were ready to do whatever NoOne commanded.

Continuously, the Old Twin reached out to NoOne. He wanted NoOne to reconsider. He pleaded and begged NoOne to take him back. Anger festered and turned to anguish and a sense of hopelessness, which circled back to anger. Nothing but silence from NoOne. Hours turned into days. My brother felt abandoned, left with nothing but a small sliver of darkness in his puny Soul.

Why did NoOne now want my brother to find me immediately? NoOne had his army. He was positioned. Earth was drained of resources. There was nothing left except a few shielded cities, a bunch of robots, and mental patients. NoOne must be using the Old Twin for some other reason; otherwise, NoOne would have ended the Old Twin's life. The Old Twin was still of use, but what could that be?

Drifting through the countryside, the Old Twin returned to the outskirts of the Portland metropolitan area. He settled down among rows of evenly spaced bodies, corpses waiting to be ordered awake from their eternal sleep. Just outside the city's dome, this vastly reduced corpse army was still his to command, as were all the other corpses left behind buried on Earth.

I am alive for only one reason. Father needs me for something that involves my brother and probably the Chosen four as well. So why should I stay loyal? Did TheSon ever abandon my brother? No. He's been safely hidden all these decades, protected and free. There were so many times I could have eliminated my brother, but NoOne held me back. Why? And why did he leave a Dark Spot on my comparatively non-existent Soul? Yes. That's the keyword. Comparatively. Compared to my brother I have no Soul. But I feel something. There's something else stirring within me.

Maybe it's just NoOne. He's tracking my every move. It must involve his search for his precious Funnel. And the Holy Lip. That's got to be it. I'm toast once he finds them. I'm trapped with no escape.

Unless....

NoOne could not locate me if I were in a highly distorted emotional field, thought the Old Twin. *Yes, that's how I get free. Maybe kill two birds.... What was the rest of the saying? Oh Yes, with one stone. Find my brother and the Chosen and set them free to piss off NoOne, and at the same time, save my life.*

Now, one step at a time. Where are the most distorted vibrations that could mask my brother's presence?

The Old Twin chuckled. *Ah, yes. A Mental Hospital. Right under my nose this whole time! Who says you can't outsmart the Devil?*

New Twin's Page Three: The Ground of Being

As a Spear of Light, TheSon flowed within the Divine Quantum Foam's neck, near the Lip's entrance. TheSon was so close to the entrance, He could perceive physical space just outside the Lip's balloon-like opening. Upon detecting his Holy Presence, Orbs immersed in fountains of Quantum Strings rushed from all corners of the Foam to encircle and orbit His Holy Presence.

The neck of the Lip swelled in anticipatory majesty.

I have trained My four well, have I not? If NoOne finds the Holy Lip, We must be ready to repel him from the physical dimension side of this universe. In that case, Orbs fully joined with TheOne must prepare to detach and exit the Divine Foam. Gather Your armor to gird Your Souls for being in the physical dimension. You will enter as pure, not Pure.

A chorus of celebration emerged from the swirling Foam. *But Lord, is this not the first event of this nature? Is it not risky to disturb Divinity? If we are destroyed in the physical plane, our Souls are lost forever. The Divine Foam will be in peril.*

TheSon knew the risks. And knew now was the time to share one of the trillions of futures he had witnessed. The one future that concerned Him the most.

Penetrating the Lip to reach the Divine Foam would be catastrophic for 'beyond the Veil', disruptive on a cosmic scale, resulting in the end of TheOne. It is for this reason we must defend the Foam in the physical universe. It is for this reason, I have prepared My Chosen four to fight with Us as Spirit.

Should We call the Chosen four forth? asked the Orbs.

Yes. Make sure the New Twin is guarding their bodies.

The four guys felt the call. It was time to leave their bodies at the Mental Hospital. They knew where the signal would lead: 'beyond the Veil'.

John alerted the other three. 'Come on, guys. Make sure you're zoned out. Usual position. Head plopped on the table, mouth open. And for good measure, let's throw in a little snoring.'

'Why are you leaving?' I asked John.

'TheSon has called us to help protect the Holy Lip. At all costs.'

'What am I supposed to do?' I asked.

'Well, just sit with us in your patient body and make sure nobody tries to move us. In physical time, we should only be gone a few hours.'

'Ok,' I meekly agreed. My reluctance was overwhelmed by a curiosity as to how the guys would look when their Mind's Eyes and Souls departed their bodies.

Just as John had ordered, the four resumed their usual catatonic postures. Glancing at the office, I searched for any unusual behavior from the staff. Nothing. I pretended to sleep.

This is going to be a long two hours.

Popping up through their 'beyond the Veil' portals and then rising slowly through the mist, the four guys sensed they were greeted by a new band of Orbs.

But they were not just any Orbs.

'Remember us?'

The four guys studied the four Orbs.

'Do you think it could be…?' Ben stopped in mid-sentence.

Greeting them were their Mentors, or at least the Souls of their Mentors now fully in Orb form: Bestow, Igor, Sensei, and Heather.

One of the four Orbs briefly blazed in intensity and said, *We're here to take you to TheSon. He waits at the far end of 'beyond the Veil', where it touches the Holy Lip.*

'Which of the four are you?' asked Luke.

I was known as Igor. Joining me are your other Mentors.

Luke moved closer to the four. 'Which is Heather?' he asked urgently.

One of the four Orbs gracefully swirled around Luke. *Yes, Luke. I'm here. But all of us need to take care of business.*

'That's right. No time for lip-locking!' smirked Ben. 'And one more thing. Before we head out, there's something everyone is missing here,' added Ben.

'That's why you're here, Mr. Brain,' said Luke. The Orb surrounding Luke began to spin around Luke in slow cycles. The effect calmed Luke down. 'But I actually liked you better when you were a tub of lard.'

'Ah, gee. Can we hold hands?' replied Ben. 'My point is we're dealing with two different dimensions, two different realities, the physical, where NoOne is, and the Spiritual, where we are now. Are we playing hopscotch between the two? Or just settling in here? If there is a "here." '

John picked up on Ben's urgency. 'That's a good point, Ben. Where do we make our stand, the physical or the Spiritual? Where are we headed? I've been thinking a lot about that. Do you have any suggestions?'

Ben smiled. 'Ah, John, hello, does poop go south? If we're fighting in the physical dimension and can keep Igor with me, the two of us can concoct a weapon that will blow your mind. I've been working on the plans in my head. But I'm no strategy dude like you, so you gotta figure out where it fits.'

Igor's energy flared. *I think I know the weapon you are planning, Ben.*

'OK, before we get into specifics, just one thing bugs me,' said Luke. 'How are we gonna be beaten by a bunch of corpses? When they come after me, I'll just run right through 'em like a knife slices butter.'

Bestow signaled to Luke her approval. She now felt it was time she shared her thoughts. *Guys, those corpses have Souls attached. Somewhere. Do not forget. Those corpses get past The Lip into the Divine Foam, and their Souls will emerge from the Book of the Damned. Many, if not all those Souls, would be judged unfit for reincarnation in that universe. Those Souls have layer upon layer of Karma pain, loss, suffering, and corruption. They would contaminate all that is Holy in the Divine Foam.*

Ben interrupted Bestow, too excited to contain himself. 'Yes! Even just one sin could forever distort, even pervert, what Paul Tillich called our 'Ground of Being.'

Luke was clearly frustrated. 'So, will someone explain or describe this "Divine Foam" stuff again?'

Observing the four, Heather thought it might help to bring in more detail. *The Divine Foam is Spiritual and part of 'beyond the Veil', but most importantly, it is the birthplace of all universes. The Lip is the entrance to the Divine Foam.*

'Have you been there?' Luke asked.

Yes, I have glimpsed the pure Orbs in the Divine Foam who have progressed through the Four Gates. It is where I will Be when I choose to move on. It's where I will dwell when fully integrated with TheOne.

Heather continued. *The Divine Foam is where the Seeds of Creation are birthed and then set at the Lip. It's a launching pad for Life. You will always find the Lip next to the largest Black Hole in that universe. Actually, it is two Black Holes that merge, anticipating the eventual demise of a universe. Together the two Black Holes pull, sucking everything in, and the left-over matter/energy is stored for TheOne's use at the birth of a new universe.*

Luke was incredulous at what they were thinking of doing. 'Are we allowed at the Lip?'

Heather continued. *TendHer will escort you to the very, very tip of the Lip that touches the physical universe. You'll only be there long enough to serve your purpose, so you'll need to cover your Souls with hurricane armor.*

'Souls covered with armor so we can fight in the physical universe,' stated John.

Yes, that's correct, thought Heather.

John was trying to figure out how this information could help him with his battle strategy. 'So, which one of you is Sensei? Will our army of Orbs be at the Lip, waiting for us?'

One of the Orbs circled John. 'Yes, John. I am here to help. I was also asked to return from my Soul Guide duties to assist.'

Heather's energy briefly surged, interrupting John's reunion with Sensei. *Billions are waiting near the Lip to protect the Divine Foam.*

'Tell us more about you Orbs,' Luke requested. 'You're Angels! That's what I think. And I want to be one ASAP!'

Heather's radiance expanded in agreement. *Orbs are free to explore any part of existence except complete merging with TheOne. We are everywhere. We are in everything. Sometimes we joyride on energy particles, playfully whirling, or racing, then turning, circling, jumping, always laughing. Sometimes we collapse so small that we can squeeze ourselves into the deepest, most desolate regions of atomic life and explore that which is almost TheNone. Then sometimes, we erupt to the size of the stars and blaze in wonder at the universe. Sometimes we joyfully whisper invitations to sinful Souls to accept grace and compassion from TheOne. Or sometimes we help Souls see connections through synchronicity, the result of Orbs maneuvering Souls to discover each other and share life lessons at the perfect time. Sometimes we soar with the wind, caressing the trees. Sometimes we share blissful revelations from the Divine. Sometimes we help the dead move on, and sometimes we help the living move forward; then, we ultimately choose to become one with the Divine Speck. Forever.*

Heather paused and then continued. *Orbs sometimes spontaneously help start new life. Sometimes we whisper hope to the hopeless. Sometimes we help others forgive the unforgivable. Sometimes we apologize for life wrongly ended. Sometimes we cuddle with a dying pet* and celebrate the Love and sacrifice so preciously shared. *Sometimes we consecrate acts of worship and help growing Souls grasp the numinous. Sometimes we carry a dead fetus Soul out of the womb and lay it at the feet of TheOne for linkage to another body. Sometimes we fight for justice. Sometimes we help the friendless find a friend before they move on. Most importantly, at all times, in all forms, in all substances, in all essences, we Love.*

Heather stopped. She studied the guys. She could tell they were affected by her words.

Ben nodded as if he wanted to ask a question. Heather again briefly burst with energy. The shape she assumed resembled a smile.

'Excuse me for interrupting, Heather. But how do you Orbs know so much about us? I mean, do you know everything, like TendHer?'

We are but a twinkle in the grand majesty of Light you call 'beyond the Veil'. TendHer is the totality of that Light. In working with our Father's Creation, Orbs read the Spiritual condition by perceiving Souls' auras. Just now, you see me as a white Orb—I am pure and clean from negative Karma. Other Orbs would see me as purple.

'Will you be able to read our condition in space when we're fighting?' asked John.

Absolutely. This is how Orbs communicate all the time. We send out snippets of color, replied Heather.

'How do we get our Orb armies?' asked John.

They will be assigned to you equally in four groups, answered Heather. *At the Lip.*

'And they will be able to fight with us in space?' asked John hopefully.

It would be a first. But if TheOne wills it, it will be so.

'And they will be our troops?' pressed John.

That is so.

'What about TheOne and TheSon helping us at the Lippy thing?' asked Luke.

Heather replied, *As far as the presence of TheOne and TheSon at the Lip, they gave us permission to let you enter, but just at the entrance tip, no further. Even this is a first.*

'Why can't we just go in and see the Divine Foam?' asked John.

The Mentors smiled at each other. Igor took the lead to help the guys understand the mystery of the Divine Foam. *Like Heather said, it's self-contained. It's not a space like you think of it; that metaphor is just to help you understand its power and its mystery. Think of the smallest detected elementary particle in nature,* said Igor.

This was Ben's cue to step in. 'Yes, Igor. That's the quark.'

Well, can the quark be seen by itself? asked Igor.

'No, not with any current scientific instruments, that's for sure. We only infer its existence when it combines with other quarks to form a hadron, which in stable form becomes protons and neutrons,' said Ben.

Yet out of the combination of quarks at the lowest levels, we experience the four types of fundamental forces, said Igor.

Ben looked around and saw the other guys were getting antsy. This was probably too much science for them, but Ben decided to continue the discussion with Igor. 'OK, gravitation, electromagnetism, weak interactions, and strong interactions.'

So our natural world, from trees to rocks and to, yes, even your physical bodies, comes from some "energy" that cannot be directly observed. Right? Igor asked.

Ben reluctantly agreed, 'Affirmative.'

Heather took over from Igor. *Now try to conceive of a reality smaller than the quark. It's what we call a "Quantum Foam String." Not only can it not be observed, but also it is so small it can't be measured by any physical tool in the universe. Therefore, "in reality", it doesn't exist.*

John saw the expressions on the other guy's "Soul-faces." They didn't have the luxury of his universe explorations and discussions with TendHer. 'Guys, this is what I learned when I was in my "gap" journeys. What we think of as life is really vibrating energies emerging from a garden. Think of them as violin "strings." This Quantum Foam is the symphony of harmonics that ultimately comes from a force even more mysterious and undetectable than life itself. It comes from a Seed launched from the "Divine Foam." We have no perceptual capacity to grasp this Divine reality. Until we become Orbs. That is, if we become Orbs.'

'And this Lip is the border between the two types of Foam? The Divine Foam and the Quantum Foam?' asked Charles.

Igor answered. *Precisely. You can see why you are not allowed into the Lip. You are just as alien to it as it would be to you.*

'Like a fish out of the water!' Luke was proud of his contribution to an intellectual discussion.

Yes, Luke, said Igor. *That's why we must stop NoOne while he's still in the physical dimension. Our armor will protect our Mind's Eyes and Souls while in physical space. So that is where we must stop him. If NoOne gets into the Lip, we are useless., His Dark Matter corpse parts will flood and contaminate the Divine Foam.*

Just think of sewage being dumped into a pristine lake, added Heather.

We have to stop him before he gets to the Lip, repeated Bestow.

Igor knew it was time to depart. His final words were: *Guys, we Mentors have been called back to the Lip. We'll be in Orb form and will meet you when TheOne gives us permission to enter space and commands us to battle.*

After the four Mentors disappeared, the guys received a thought message. It streaked through their minds, reverberating with incredible power. The finality and intensity of the message brought a heaviness to the guys; a great weight pressed down on their Souls, each turning inward to process the ultimate consequences should they fail.

The guys accepted that there was to be no escape from the looming cosmic entanglement. They were to be swept along by a current of spectacular forces, impotent to completely control what lay ahead, helpless to repress the feelings of fear and doubt.

A distant voice rang out from the far corners of the universe. It was TendHer.

Time has run out. We must protect the Divine Foam. You must defend the Lip!

New Twin's Page Four: Armageddon

Floating with soft pillowy purple clouds in the 'beyond the Veil' mist, multi-colored, thin, glittering Lights beckoned the four guys forward. The sparse display of twinkling luminosities that immediately surrounded them gradually became dense sheets of radiance in the far distance. The guys assumed that they were in the shallowest region of the Spirit world.

John warned the others, 'Guys, don't even think about heading toward those Lights out there until we are escorted by an Orb or TendHer.'

After the guys agreed, John laid out his strategy to defeat NoOne. 'I've studied all the great military campaigns in history, at least for Earth. The one premise for victory I always return to is a quote from the great Chinese Warrior Sun Tsu. "Hence the saying: If you know the enemy and know yourself, you need not fear the result of a hundred battles. If you know yourself but not the enemy, you will also suffer a defeat for every victory gained. If you know neither the enemy nor yourself, you will succumb in every battle." '

'Well, that sounds wordy! In plain words, tell us what that means in terms of our lives, or Souls, or whatever?' demanded Luke.

'This is just a place to start,' said John. 'I think we know more about our enemy, NoOne, than NoOne knows about us. Lao Tsu said we have to be prepared and surprise our enemy who is not.'

John paused to let his assertion sink in and then continued. 'NoOne's strategy is obvious. He wants to gather Dark Matter from all over the universe to make his Snake massive. Once he finds the Holy Lip, he will attack head-on. He will dive right into the Lip with that Snake.

'The upside is he knows little about us, but we know a lot about him. NoOne knows nothing about our troop composition, our preparation, our hidden assets, plus, most importantly, he doesn't know where the Lip is located and how we plan to defend it.'

'One thing we know, John, is that TheSon's troops have been outnumbered up to this point. Hopefully, we can make up the difference,' said Charles.

John nodded. 'Yes, I hope so. The point I'm making is we need to be prepared long before NoOne arrives in ways he could never imagine.'

'OK, so what's the plan? I mean, what is our battle plan?' asked Charles.

John proceeded to lay out his strategy. 'My favorite general of all time was Shaka from Southern Africa,' said John.

Ben edged his way in front of John. 'Oh, man…yes! He devised one of the most revolutionary warfare styles in all of history. It's called the "Bull Horn" formation.'

'Ben, just let John lay out his plan, please?' said Charles.

Nonplussed by Ben's interruption, John continued. 'Yes, Ben is right. The "Bull Horn" consists of four components. The chest of the bull is the center force. It's the main force. It drives straight ahead. The two side attack forces are like the two horns of the bull. They flank and encircle the enemy to the left and the right. The last part is the back end of the bull, the loins. These are fighters that lay back and reinforce any part of the center or flanks that need reinforcing.'

'Four parts to the attacking bull. Four of us. Just like the Four Gates, remember? Who is at each part?' asked Charles.

We need to leave now, thought TendHer. *NoOne and his troops are close to the Black Holes.*

'So much for Sun Tsu,' Ben muttered.

'I wonder. Let's see what happens,' John said.

'At least we have a plan to work with down the road,' said Luke.

TendHer continued. *I'm here to take you to the Lip. But only to its very tip. No non-TendHer Judged Soul has ever been allowed to dwell anywhere near that part of the Lip. Each of you has Orb troops assigned to you. They will greet you just outside the Lip. You'll keep your physical armor on as long as possible to give your Soul substance. An attack by NoOne is imminent, and we want to keep him in outer space as far as possible from the Lip.*

Luke thought, 'Well, will our Mentors and other Orbs be fighting with us?'

Of course, said TendHer.

After TendHer departed, Ben verbalized what everyone was thinking. 'Guys, if we put our Souls in the physical dimension, even with our armor…I mean, what happens if we get nuked with Dark Matter?'

'We're toast. My guess is that our Mind's Eyes will disintegrate. Our Souls will suffocate,' replied John.

'What about our Mentors? What happens to them, like my Heather?' asked Luke.

'We just don't know, Luke. Maybe like us, when their Light gets covered with Dark Matter, they suffocate. Or maybe they harden into lumps of Dark Matter space debris,' said John.

'So, we lose our Souls forever if our physical armor is compromised in space? And our Mentors become Dark Matter pancakes? What about our physical bodies in the Mental Hospital?' asked Charles.

'At that point, would we really care?' replied Ben.

The guys knew they didn't need to reply.

New Twin's Page Five: The Two Sides of Mystery

NoOne knew the Lip had to be nearby. He felt frustratingly close. To hide the location of the Lip, NoOne knew that TheOne would have used a space inversion rip, similar to what He used to hide the Funnel. Thumping its signal like the beat of a heart, the Lip would be imperceptible to most, hidden within an infinite number of possible twisting and churning dimensional intersections.

But not so hidden as to escape my detection! Am I not the most intelligent force in the universe?

The Lip was no more massive than a giant asteroid. Its location was impossible to pinpoint except for three clues. First, the Lip had a unique Divine frequency; he just had to identify it—hardly possible given NoOne's banishment. Second, large groups of Orbs go to the Lip on their way to servitude at the behest of TheOne; he'd just have to try to spot them as they exit or enter the Lip. Third, locate merged Black Holes that are used to disguise the Lip; this is difficult in many parts of the universe that have massive numbers of Black Hole mergers.

The second clue had proven successful in locating the Funnel, so NoOne ordered his Snake to patrol the general area where large numbers of Orbs had been reported.

What surprised NoOne was that as his Snake got closer to investigate the cluster of Orbs circulating in the area, a large army of Orbs promptly streaked out from an invisible portal into physical space, stopping on a dime and facing NoOne's army.

The Lip must be near.

Just like my Brother to show His hand too early.

Then NoOne saw more Orbs converge from various locations in space and congregate. Each appeared to be led by a unique kind of Orb.

After a moment of scrutiny, NoOne recognized the four. They were the four Chosen. And who were those Orbs next to them? Their Mentors? Should he be intimidated? He sneered.

The guys took positions at the head of four massive Orb groups. The guys' Souls were draped in physical hurricane armor to navigate material-space reality. The Orbs wore a thick, transparent glass-like material that protected their entire surface; all the better to reflect blinding, Divine Light.

The four armies of Orbs displayed the Bull Horn formation that John had suggested. John was in the front with Sensei, representing the "chest of the bull." Ben and Luke were on the flanking "horns" with Igor and Heather. Charles was in the rear with Bestow. The Mentors were in Orb form.

NoOne sent a thought message to the four guys and their Mentors, 'Your precious Mentors are risking their eternal Souls by attacking me in my physical universe. Are you sure they have TheOne's permission? Has TheSon told you that using Orbs to fight me on my turf is a first?'

This statement of fact had the desired effect. The Mentors moved closer to their students, more concerned about the reaction of their protégées than for the Mentors' own well-Being.

Turning his attention to the general area of the Lip, NoOne broke off parts of his Snake and commanded them to scout the troops of the Chosen four.

TheSon felt he must protect the Chosen at all costs, so while the guys stood by with their Orbs, He ordered a squadron of His Orbs to leave the Lip and attack NoOne's scouting party.

That's when NoOne was certain he had pinpointed the general location of the Holy Lip.

TheSon saw his mistake. By sending out his Orbs from the Lip, TheSon had divulged the location of the Lip. He had but one course of action left: destroy the Snake.

TheSon transformed into a blazing star. It was as big as His entire army of Orbs. The sun's radiance blocked out any visual landmarks in space, including the Lip and the four Orb groups.

Ordering the four Orb groups to the rear, TheSon rushed to confront NoOne and his Snake in a blazing mass of celestial fire.

NoOne was momentarily disoriented and retreated behind his Snake.

Addressing NoOne, TheSon cried out with a Sacred pronouncement.

Brother, Our Father has decided you are to leave the lip. you are ordered to Do so now.

A somber silence ensued. Time stopped. Both sides did not move. Everyone waited for the other side to attack. It was as if the universe's power had been switched off with the push of a button.

TheSon flared in majesty. Then just disappeared. In the blink of an eye.

'What the fuu…? Where did TheSon go?' shouted Luke.

John liked the diversion. 'Just be patient. He knows what He's doing.'

The next instant, TheSon was where no one was expecting Him to be; BEHIND some merged Black Holes.

TheSon's voice rang out.

I say, My brother, so be it. I say, My Chosen, attack!

The four guys, now directly facing the Snake, ordered their Orbs to attack the Snake. Millions of Orb troops, radiating dazzling balls of Light, lunged for the Snake. The Orbs scratched entire chunks off the Snakeskin with laser wands and in the process, many sacrificed parts of their Soul Light.

Snake remnants drifted away motionless into deep space.

Diving back into the Lip, the fighting Orbs replenished their Divine Light. Then the Orbs returned to physical space, fully rejuvenated, and again attacked the Snake. Repeatedly, they lunged at the Snake, reformed their Light, and attacked again.

It didn't seem to make any difference. Even as the brilliant Lights from the Orbs ruptured the corpses and diaphanous eyes, another deeper Snake layer always moved up to seal over any damage.

All four army groups regrouped back to the Lip.

John called out to his buddies, 'Guys, the Snake is too long and bulbous, and we don't have enough troops! The Snake grows new skin whenever it's damaged. We have to get away from here. We're sitting ducks. Let TheSon come back and take over.'

As the four armies were retreating away from the Lip, TheSon did emerge from behind the Black Holes and position Himself directly in front of the Snake.

NoOne taunted his Brother. 'Can't You make up Your mind, oh Holy One? Stop playing hide and seek. Stay and fight me!'

TheSon swelled with radiance. He proclaimed to NoOne's troops who were glued to the Snake, IF YOU SO CHOOSE, YOU CAN COME TO ME AND BE JUDGED. YOU STILL MAY WORK YOUR WAY THROUGH THE FOUR GATES TO FORGIVENESS, TO DWELL IN MY HOUSE OF SANCTITY. MAKE YOUR CHOICE NOW.

Initially, the LostSouls were hopeful upon hearing TheSon's offer. Eyes and corpses alike came alive. They stirred, briefly remembering their merciless judgment, and entombing in the Snake.

Abruptly, a stillness overcame the Snake. Caution spread up and down its skin as the doomed Souls reminded each other that any sign of revolt could mean immediate extinction for all.

NoOne's corpses and Soulless eyes squirmed with indecision. Looking frantically at one another, the mass of the Snake was too great for any single eye or corpse to escape; there had to be agreement among a large group to break free. Some groups did extract themselves, but it was like removing a hand from sticky glue.

NoOne's Dark Matter quickly identified and obliterated those trapped traitors who dared seek freedom. Other groups of eyes and corpses that formed groups to break loose, upon seeing NoOne's vicious response, promptly returned and burrowed back into the body of the Snake.

TheSon felt the intent of the trapped enemy soldiers but was helpless to intervene. His radiance dipped as His sadness swelled. NoOne interpreted this as weakness. NoOne ordered the Snake to move forward and immediately attack the Lip.

TheSon took the offensive before the Snake could follow through with NoOne's command. Rather than retreating to protect the Orb troops and the Lip opening, which NoOne had predicted, TheSon forged ahead and attacked the Snake. His star gained mass as it gained distance.

A part of TheSon's star broke off and plunged into the shocked and bewildered LostSoul troops that formed the Snake's mouth. It proceeded down the Snake's throat, all the way through its body to the tail.

The Chosen and NoOne stood by in wonderment as the TheSon's blazing mass of fire pushed through the Snake's inner body and burst out at the very end. The Snake's tail shattered into huge segments of dead tissue, the guts leaking out the end of the Snake into space.

The four guys and their Orbs cheered TheSon as He returned to His position protecting the Lip. The disemboweled Snake hung in space, eyes, and corpses cast off and spinning in all directions.

NoOne fumed with anger. He ordered his remaining troops to re-form, but they were too far away to reconnect with any kind of group consciousness. The Snake continued to spiral further and further out into space. Lost.

The guys' celebration was premature.

Floating beside the disintegrating body of his Snake, NoOne sucked Dark Matter from all corners of the universe. Wispy at first, massive, siphoned energy streams streaked to NoOne and congealed. Then, the Dark Matter thickened into a shape resembling a pure black pyramid. Almost immediately, the solid black mass coalesced into a rectangular column of dark energy that stretched for millions of universe miles. The difference between TheSon's star and NoOne's dark rectangle provided an elegant contrast. Together, they blocked out the horizon of visible stars and planets.

Then NoOne upped the stakes, striking terror in TheSon's army. NoOne pointed his rectangular column directly at the guys and their Orbs, now off to the far side of the Lip opening. Out from the middle of the column of Dark Matter sprung long, thrashing silver chains, whirling, and whipping, hungry to hack and sever.

NoOne barked, 'TheSon, this is my dimension. It is the universe of physical pain and personal torment. The strongest survive, and I am the strongest! Your silly Cross? Your sacrifice was worthless. Look at my weapons; forged to take what is mine!'

TheSon replied, *Where are your Souls now, NoOne? They are drifting away in space. So many vacuous eyes and body parts. Empty and meaningless particles of nature. Just like you. You are alone. You will always be alone. Our Father knew you could only be trusted with the garbage of nature. All you have left is a silly toy.*

NoOne became furious. His Brother had struck a nerve. It was too close to the truth, an insight NoOne could only bear to acknowledge once in a millennium. He was alone. And hated. It was not his fault. From time immemorial, NoOne had reached out to his Father for inclusion in the Divinity of the Trinity. All he ever received in return was banishment and last-minute servitude to anchor his Father's ridiculous Creations.

'For what purpose? To grow Souls? That's just an illusion. Actual reality is dust to dust. The Orbs are nothing more than the product of spiritual masturbation. They are sycophants lacking true power.

Brother, You are truly obsolete. It is now my turn to rule. Before I show you my new toy, have a taste of what's to come.'

Then, NoOne's column set loose razor-sharp whips. They were aimed directly at the four Chosen and their Orb armies.

TheSon immediately moved to block the missiles. In a massive solar flare, TheSon's Light engulfed and melted NoOne's projectiles, giving the Chosen armies time enough to retreat.

The Dark Matter projectiles destroyed by the flare were quickly replaced with Dark Matter imported from other galaxies. NoOne, unlike TheSon, had an infinite amount of energy at his disposal. If he ran out of Dark Matter in this universe, he could simply purloin Dark Matter from another universe.

NoOne thought, *Have I not spent eons perfecting my transportation highways to link all the structures I was forced to craft at the beginning of so many creations?*

TheSon's confidence took a sudden turn for the worse. He hadn't counted on NoOne's unlimited supply of energy. TheSon and his troops watched in horror as NoOne coolly and steadily designed a new weapon right before their very eyes.

'Behold my toy!'

It was a machine of destruction unlike any weapon TheSon had ever encountered. Dark Matter flooded in to add a giant propeller blade to the ever-growing column. The blade was connected to the structure with a single swivel; the blade spinning horizontally at the top.

The blade was so long, its tip could not be perceived in the distance. But its sounds were overwhelmingly present, screeching and howling as dark as the column upon which it sat.

The blade moved closer toward NoOne's surprised Brother.

TheSon's star could not match the size or speed of the propeller blade. The monster blade was retractable as well as sweeping, first spinning a current of death, then stabbing, then slicing through the surface crust of TheSon's enormous burning mass. No universe had ever seen such a massive weapon. Its sharp edges easily dissected TheSon's star into thousands of puny dead planets, soon impotently orbiting the starving center core of the once blazing furnace.

TheSon's only option was to retreat from the battle, dropping far below the Lip to gather more radioactive mass. He called to other stars to merge with His (suddenly "his") emaciated remnants.

Now free from TheSon's protection at the front, the massive spinning propeller blade attacked John's troops. Long ropes of twisting chains and whipping spikes emerged from the blade and the stationary column it was attached to, thrashing every square inch of adjacent space.

John's troops didn't know what to do. They were paralyzed.

John cried out to TheSon, 'Lord, where are you going? What do you want us to do?'

No answer.

NoOne's rotating Dark Matter blade then attacked the middle of John's Orb force. Ropy, spiked, shiny chains flew out from the blade. They wrapped themselves around John's Orbs, squeezing and shredding the Orb's protective armor Light into a billion lifeless particles, even more tragic as the Orb's glass reflected their fading Light for all to witness.

Silently and with mechanical disdain, the chains returned to NoOne's long dark propeller of doom, ready to thrust or spin again.

John finally understood that the Snake, composed of murky eyes and corpses, was a decoy. It was used to test TheSon; to see what He would do. The spinning propeller blade of Dark Matter was NoOne's real weapon.

The propeller blade continued to enlarge. John saw Dark Matter rushing from all corners of the universe to add mass to the middle shaft and the blade. Why did God allow NoOne to have access to so much energy? Why did TheSon flee? Was He afraid?

In a split second, John understood the irrelevance of his questions. They were beyond the point of asking why. John saw clearly that TheSon and His Orb armies were going to lose. And his troops were in the front, squarely in line with the monstrous weapon.

Perhaps John would be rescued? Sensei was still in action, batting away corpse parts like flies. But the other three Orb groups were preoccupied with trying to prevent a total massacre.

John saw the blade heading directly towards him and his troops as he clung to the last shred of hope: There was still time for TheSon to return.

But time was running out.

'Retreat! Retreat!' John yelled.

It was too late. His life flashed before his eyes.

People who are about to die review their life histories. I wonder why? One more chance to purify the Soul, perhaps?

John panicked.

Stop it! I have my whole life before me. I want to live!

John cried out for help. 'Ben, Luke, Charles…help me! Please! God help me! This cannot be. I'm Chosen. I'm not a loser anymore. I proved myself. Didn't I? Guys, please say something!'

John's friends and their Mentors saw out of the corner of their eyes what was happening to John. They knew there was nothing they could do. Or say. They were too busy protecting themselves from the relentless instruments of death hurled at them. There was so much gratitude and admiration for John, but it all must be left unsaid. It was too late. Too much was happening all around them. John was going to die. Were they next?

Charles was the only one able to send a thought.

'Goodbye my brother. See you soon.'

John realized he was helpless. There was nothing anyone could do to rescue him, short of TheSon performing a miracle.

John grasped at that possibility. 'Hey guys, no worries. TheSon will rescue me. He must! I'm one of the Chosen!'

NoOne's propeller blade advanced to within inches of John's body. It stopped. Where once there were gigantic streams of Dark Matter spit into space from the spinning blade, now there was only stillness and calm. Was the blade mocking John's impotence? Or was the blade acknowledging John's courage—from one warrior to another? Would the Devil be so honorable as to show admiration to a fallen enemy? Or had the propeller blade, forged from so many LostSouls, recovered momentarily some part of its humanity, and despite its evil Lord, struggled to at least show respect?

John settled into a deep peace born from resignation. There was nothing he or anyone else could do. He said goodbye to Charles, Luke, and Ben, hoping to give them hope and a future. 'Guys, don't give up. Thank you for being my friends. Say goodbye to….' Before John could mention my name, a single whip ejected from the massive blade. Surgically, it sliced John's Mentor Sensei into a thousand pieces, sending dull Orb pieces hurling further out in space.

As if their one and only purpose of existence was this last definitive act of grace, the small shreds of Sensei's Light struggled to return to John and add a protective layer around John's armor. Small bits raced out to other Orbs, seemingly begging them to unite and join the reformation. Frantic, the tattered bits of Soul added ragged layers to John's armor.

It was not enough. The time for fear and hope had passed. John accepted his fate. He was resigned to his own extinction—Soul and body. So, why was Sensei fighting so hard to save him? Perhaps to store John's Soul in the Book of Souls to later resurrect John?

Sensei had shared countless lessons in life with one central message: Being and Non-Being are but two sides of the same mystery. John knew his time had arrived to NOT Be, a moment of transition inevitable for every living creature.

Sensei was fighting to keep a remnant of John's Soul.

'Please, Sensei. I am finished. I mastered your final lesson. I have let go.'

With those words, the tattered bits of Light that formerly comprised Sensei's Soul relaxed and slowly drifted away from John's body. Each piece retreated to its own destiny, again celebrating the gift of existence, no matter how brief. The remnants of Sensei's Soul blazed brightly for one last remarkable moment, scattered in all directions, like so many candles cast out to the darkness, flickered to fight the dying of their Light, then ceased to Be.

John uttered his final words to Sensei: 'Thank you.'

Shortly after that, John looked back at his friends and smiled. It was but for a second, but his Soul was able to expand and glow brilliantly one last time.

The whip lunged forward, intent on its mission. John was swiftly carved into microscopic pieces and sucked out to space.

The other three Orb columns froze as they witnessed John's demise. The sight of the rotating, saw-like black propeller blade flinging razor-sharp whips through the millions of Orbs in John's troops was eerily fascinating. The power of the clock-like rhythm and synchrony of the razor whips was spellbinding. The few remaining Orb troops left in John's group soon joined their leader in the realm where mystery reigns supreme.

With John's troops eliminated at the front of the defensive force, Luke's and Ben's troops were directly facing NoOne's Dark Matter propeller. Charles' Orbs retreated further backward, now positioned at the very entrance of the bubbling Lip.

Rejoicing at how he had slaughtered John and his Orbs, NoOne ordered his propeller to launch huge balls of Dark Matter from its surface. Millions of spheres shot out from the spinning blade aimed at Ben's and Luke's Orbs. Most hit their targets.

Luke's and Ben's Orb armies, walloped and coated with NoOne's Black Matter glop, found their Light gradually sheeted, layer upon layer, with black death; slowly, they were strangled out of life. Others went quickly, sliced into extinction by the rotating knives.

Luke rushed ahead to Heather. Sliced completely apart by deadly spikes thrust out by NoOne's Dark blade, Her Light was but a dim flicker.

Luke cried out, 'Heather, hang in there. I will protect you with my armor…please just wait. Don't go. I'll lose you forever. Heather, *Heather!*'

As panicked thoughts raced through Luke's head, he could barely discern the muffled reply from Heather.

I Love you, Luke-Henry. Goodbye, my Love.

'Heather…stay with me. I'll get you to safety.' Frantically wiping at Heather's Orb shell, Luke saw it was hopeless. Like a burrowing Marmot, the black twisting spikes stabbed, probed, ripped apart, and shredded Heather's Light-protected exterior. Seeming to enjoy prolonging the agony, the spikes slowed down and pulled the fork ends in and out, out and in, out and in, in and out. With each withdrawal, the forked ends paused, twisting the Light body substance around as if examining its handy work, as if it were a curious monster fascinated with the unique taste of a new morsel.

'Oh, no!' Luke screamed. He saw what was headed his way. A bomb of Dark Matter was streaking toward the remaining troops in Luke's contingent. Leading the hurling missile was a single figure. It had the shape of a human but was just as black as the Dark Matter bomb trailing close behind.

'Luke, dear. It's me. Your mother! You didn't think I'd let a trollop get between you and your mother, now did you?'

'No! You can't come back to life. Go back to your grave and rot!' screamed Luke.

'Now, now, son. We need to reconcile. You and I will be spending eternity nestled together in the Snake with your father who reigns above all supreme,' whispered Luke's mom. 'He's here. He's ready to receive you.'

'Who are you talking about? Where's my father? Who are you saying is my father?'

'NoOne, of course! He wants you to come with me and be safe. Forever!'

'Never, you crazy bitch!'

'Always such a headstrong boy. We'll see about that.'

Luke, along with a small group of Orbs, began to flee. They heard laughing. A name swamped Luke's consciousness: NoOne.

'Yes, do run away. Did you like the reunion with your mommy? We're waiting for you to return to mommy and me. You will be mine, eventually. All returns to me…son!'

Completely enveloping most of his remaining Orbs and Heather's Orb remnants, Luke's mother figure of Dark Matter imploded inward, condensing every part of Heather and her surrounding space into a single dot. A miniature Black Hole formed in space. After vacuuming all surrounding matter, the Black Hole slowly disappeared, gobbled up by its own invisible singularity, now trapped in a perpetual wormhole journey. A trip without a beginning or an end.

Luke and a small group of Orb troops barely made it out of the Black Hole's reach.

Ben picked up on Luke's trauma. 'Luke, you can join up with me if you want.'

'Thanks, Ben. I want to keep my team together. I'm seeing this through to get this son of a bitch,' vowed Luke.

The hurricane armor gave the three Chosen some protection from the various Dark Matter projectiles. Realizing it was a matter of time before NoOne would modify his arsenal to add more effective weapons, Ben prayed to TheSon stationed far below the Lip as to whether they should flee.

No answer.

It was too late, anyway. Retreat was not part of TheSon's plan. Nor would NoOne accept any outcome other than the complete annihilation of his Brother.

NoOne pressed his advantage by continuing to hurl Dark Matter at any moving object of Light. Orbs exploded and imploded all around the guys. Luke screamed to Charles and Ben. 'Retreat. Head out to space. We'll form three new sniper groups from our remaining Orbs. Then we'll attack the blade at the same time, top, middle, and bottom.'

Noticing the withdrawal of the small, reconfigured three remaining groups of troops, NoOne taunted, 'While your God cowers deep away from the Lip, you risk your brave but foolish lives. I already see your plan. The Shuai-Jan Snake Attack Strategy. Send three groups to attack my spinning blade of Dark Matter simultaneously: head, tail, middle; all at once; impossible to defend. No doubt courtesy of your former head warlord? John, I believe? Wasn't he the one that came up short?'

Pausing for effect, NoOne blasted his next pronouncement to his Brother. 'Will You come back and finish this contest? Are You cowering once again while Your servants are shredded? Do You not see my power in this mass of Dark Matter? I have enough energy to completely raze our Father's antiquated Divine Foam. You should ask for help from our Father, who will soon NOT be in Heaven.'

Suddenly, the three groups of surviving Orbs started to spin, radiating circles of Light. The three guys looked around, wondering why their troops were so excited.

NoOne too was startled when he detected the surge in energy.

Streaking from below the Lip, TheSon had returned. His response was accompanied by a magnificent discharge of Light.

THIS IS YOUR LAST CHANCE, NOONE, MY BROTHER. WITHDRAW.

TheSon was ready to battle.

NoOne sneered, 'Come, come, dear sniveling Sibling. Why waste any more precious Souls? Let's just You and I square off. Like the old times. Light against Dark. Hope versus Reality. Love or Exploitation. Spirit versus the Flesh. What say You, Holy Brother?'

TheSon agreed.

New Twin's Page Six: Truly Beasts of Wonder

TheSon's gigantic burning star commanded the entire horizon to the left of the Lip, as did NoOne's Dark Matter propeller command the whole horizon to the right of the Lip. When positioned across from each other, Luke made his move. Luke directed the three remaining Orb groups, led by the three remaining Chosen including himself, to attack the middle of NoOne's column.

'We're going to use a wedge formation,' announced Luke.

'I sure want to be like you when I grow up,' remarked Ben as he joined up with Luke. 'Finally, I see how your football skills are paying off.'

'Thanks, Ben. You would have been a great lineman,' replied Luke.

'Yeah. Definitely left-side tackle. Protect your blindside.'

'I don't like the pocket much…rather….'

Charles screamed out, 'Will you two stop talking about football? We're about to get our asses kicked!'

Together, Ben and Luke answered Charles, 'Yeah. Sorry.'

Combining all the troops together in a circle, Luke shaped his wedge formation. At his signal, the wedge of Orb troops raced ahead towards the very still column and its middle.

Was the column so still because it was curious what the guys were doing? Or entertained at the sight of any force in nature trying to attack its integrity?

'This is almost too good to be true,' yelled Ben. 'The column and blade are doing nothing. Just standing there. Should we back off? Could it be a trap?'

Luke was determined. 'We attack, period. The best defense is a good offense. At least that's what my coach always used to say.'

'Yeah, that's what John used to say, too. God, I miss him. We sure could use him now!' moaned Ben.

The wedge of troops crashed against the middle of the dark column. Nothing. The initial impact was not successful, so the Orbs regrouped and struck again. Many Orbs disintegrated. Many Orbs lost so much Light, they clumped together and drifted back to the Lip.

Some Orbs attempted to go around the column and attack the opposite side. Then the two forces could work into and connect at the center. Unfortunately, the column was so thick, the Orbs could not find the back side. They returned and joined the main force.

Finally, a small crack formed after multiple strikes by the Orbs at the exact same spot. At the same time, Luke ordered Charles to stay put while he and Ben attack the blade.

'This blade stretches out forever. Are you sure you have enough troops? Maybe back off and reassess?' suggested Charles.

'We must act now, Charles. I think we can weaken NoOne's fighting power by chewing away at the very tip. We'll work our way back to the swivel,' Luke thought to his buddies.

Maybe all we're doing is buying time for TheSon? Is that why we're the Chosen?

'Luke, the blade is just too long,' cried Charles.

Unfortunately, Charles was right.

Luke and Ben never reached the end of the blade. It seemed to extend to eternity. They turned and headed back to the column. With no warning, as they were struggling to return, razor whips exploded out from the middle of the column aimed directly at Charles and his Orbs.

Ben and Luke watched helplessly as Charles' few remaining Orbs were ripped to pieces.

At first, Charles had been able to avoid the whips by rolling and diving at all angles; the whips more often than not striking each other. But finally, energy fading, he could dart no further and was struck. Even though covered with armor, it wasn't strong enough to protect Charles from the razor teeth of the whip.

Charles was cut in half. The cut was thorough and clean, surgically precise. Charles was oddly fascinated with the lower part of his body, armor still intact, floating lifelessly away. Then he was fascinated with his fascination.

Charles felt his Chi plummet. He turned to Bestow and mouthed the words "help me." Bestow rushed to Charles, who was now in shock, and whimpered. Charles' final act was to meekly smile. His Soul Light briefly swelled in tribute to TheSon.

Bestow surrounded the upper half of Charles' body with her Light, trying to protect his Soul. She told him all animal life on Earth cherished him. She asked him if he was in pain and told him she would help him move on.

There was no reply.

Bestow wailed, pleading for help from all the animal world. Finally, some Orbs sped to help. One she recognized in particular.

You were the Monster Bear. You came back from 'beyond the Veil'? Bestow asked.

Yes. I chose to postpone becoming One with TheOne, in case TheSon required me to help once more, replied the Monster Bear.

Can you help us? pleaded Bestow.

Perhaps. I will call out to all those animal Spirits still alive on my mountain. One may agree to invite Charles in.

You mean, as in merging? An animal with a human Soul?

Monster Bear answered, *Why not? It has been tried and has succeeded before, has it not?*

Bestow had a sudden insight. *Monster Bear. As a released Orb fighting in the physical realm, You are partly a Divine You and a "you" of substance. Why can't Charles merge with the Divine part of You? Besides, we are losing this battle. Charles' armor is destroyed. His Soul is soon to be released.*

Monster Bear solemnly replied, *You Love Charles that much?*

It is so, Monster Bear. You also need to escape. You are needed in 'beyond the Veil' for service to TheSon. It would be an outright shame, a waste, for You to perish here. Much is left to unfold, and I fear We have lost too many good defenders this day. Take Charles with You.

With great respect, the Monster Bear replied, *Bestow, if this is what You want, then I will merge with Your student and help him heal in 'beyond the Veil'.*

At that moment, Charles' upper body armor exploded, exposing his Soul to space, pushing Bestow away. Charles' Soulful eyes opened wide and stared for a fraction of a second in final recognition as his Mind's Eye and Soul yanked apart.

Monster Bear's Light immediately reached out and cradled Charles' Soul, protecting it from physical matter. Once fully embraced, Monster Bear invited union. Charles' Soul radiated its acceptance. The two became one and headed to 'beyond the Veil'.

For the Bonobo, Love is our nature, Bestow said. Watching Monster Bear depart, she heard TendHer command Charles' Mind's Eye to collect Charles' Book of Life and escort it immediately to the Funnel.

Monster Bear felt Bestow's farewell from a great distance, safely away from NoOne's troops. *Monster Bear, we were truly wonderful beasts, were we not?*

Monster Bear knew Bestow was soon to perish. Forever. He had caused so much pain in the animal world. He was glad he could take care of Bestow's prized apprentice now, at the end of time, even though the apprentice was human.

Yes, Bestow. We were truly wonderful beasts.

Glancing back at the departing Monster Bear Orb, Bestow saw a single tear languish on the surface of Light. Bestow could barely make out the thought sent her way from the Monster Bear.

The tear is a gift from My Soul Mate, Charles.

Before Bestow could reply, the same serpentine lash that had destroyed most of her fellow animal Orbs struck her. The sizzling hot whip with spikes curled itself around Bestow like string surrounding a ball. She felt smothered, which she knew would quickly turn to the dissevering of her Soul. She had but seconds.

She assessed her existence. It had been filled with Love. She reviewed her life. It had been a wondrous celebration of life.

Gathering the last remaining reserves of her Soul's energy, Bestow whispered one final message for anyone that could hear.

Yes, my animal kin, we are truly wonderful beasts...truly wonder....

Bestow's Soul Light disintegrated in a majestic explosion. Pieces scattered to all corners of distant space. Her Soul was so powerful that even Dark Energy bid respectful passage to her last surviving subatomic particles.

NoOne simply observed, curious. *Why are these Creations of my Father so willing to sacrifice themselves for others?*

Watching the mutilation, the few remaining Orbs cried to TheSon for help.

They received no answer.

New Twin's Page Seven: Sorrow

NoOne gained energy every second by summoning his Dark Matter from all corners of the universe. Far and wide, NoOne's dark cloud rung out of space; Dark Matter particles squeezed out of every crevice, every nick, every String to seek out its progenitor. Dissimilar to other forces, like electromagnetic and nuclear with natural currents that weaved randomly through the physical universe, Dark Matter was distributed evenly and unlimited in supply. And waiting for NoOne to direct its energy, no matter the intent or consequences.

Now it rushed to NoOne's siren call.

TheSon saw what NoOne was doing. TheSon believed He needed to start the battle before NoOne accumulated too much Dark Matter and became too formidable. And that point was fast approaching.

TheSon ordered Ben and Luke back to the Lip opening with their small groups of surviving Orbs and the ever-faithful Igor to await the outcome. If TheSon lost, they were instructed to seal the Lip.

Ben asked TheSon what they should use to seal the Lip. Igor intervened and said, 'He's preoccupied, right now, Ben. Hopefully, we don't have to seal it. If we do, we must seal it with our Souls, if there are enough Orbs left.'

'Ah, excuse me, Mr. Mentor. But I didn't read the part in our deal where I'm used as super glue!'

'Ben, it may come to that. I'm sorry. But it's our last resort. I'm on your side. The Lip has a better chance of not being polluted if we just use illusion.'

Ben agreed that he thought illusion would work just fine. If he had the strength.

'Igor, I'm getting weak. I've lost two of my best friends. Even though they bugged me to death, I'm….' Ben realized what he had just said. 'No, they really didn't bug me to death.'

Ben wept.

'Hey, buddy, I'm still here,' yelled Luke followed by a few surviving Orbs.

'We've lost John, Charles, Heather, Sensei, and Bestow.' stated Ben. 'You, me, and Igor are the only ones left.

Luke also began to sob. 'They're all gone. That bastard took 'em.'

'I'm sorry, Luke. I'm sorry you lost Heather. I'm sorry how I bugged you all these decades. I'm sorry we lost all the Orbs that have been cut down. So many gave up their Souls.'

Luke reached out to Ben. 'Yeah, me too. I just don't know what we can do. I'm scared.'

'You're scared?' The shock of hearing Luke's admission of being afraid, of being human, masked Ben's exhaustion for a moment.

Luke saw the surprised expression on Ben's face. He said, 'We all have our limits. I'm scared shitless. Guess maybe it's your turn to take over.'

'Luke, take over what? There's nothing to take over!'

'I guess that's the point. I can't go on without Heather. I'm gonna take a crack at that bastard NoOne. Besides, you need some time to get your sorry ass out of here and protect the Lip.'

'You're gonna do what? You can't attack him! He's too strong!'

Luke felt better. Even he was surprised at such a spontaneous, foolhardy goal. Whatever plan he devised was sure to end with his death. But why not try it? Why not try something? They were all eventually going to die here anyway. Luke knew Ben and Igor needed some time to create a diversion. Plus, Luke had to do something to stop the feelings of horror at losing Heather, his Soul Mate. Forever.

Finally, Luke felt like he was in charge again. Just like the old days. Leading his team down the field and scoring a touchdown in the final seconds of a football game.

'Luke, stop!' yelled Ben. 'What are you doing?'

'I might just rip off one of those whips and stick it up the ass of that black cloud!'

'You can't do that, Luke,' screamed Ben. 'That's NoOne. You won't get within a thousand miles.'

Breathing deep, Luke replied, 'Oh, yeah? Seems like it's the last thing he'd expect.'

It *was* the last thing NoOne expected. Scanning his multitude of troops chasing down and eliminating isolated groups of Orbs, something unusual caught NoOne's attention. One of the boys from the so-called Chosen group wasn't running away. He was doing just the opposite. It looked as if he was speeding toward NoOne. It was the mate of the Soul called 'Heather.'

NoOne laughed. *Ah, yes. Sweet revenge. The boy Lover is risking his life to avenge his sweetheart's execution. How quaint.*

Luke screamed out, 'Hey, asshole! I'm Luke, and I'm gonna break through you like a 4.3-second 40-yard dash half-back through a field of hay. That means I'm calling you out!'

Everything in space stopped. Orbs stopped fleeing. Whips stopped lashing out. Dark Matter stopped flowing in and pooling in NoOne's ever-growing larger colossus propeller blade. All waited. All watched. The universe came to a screeching halt.

Except for Luke. Flying at NoOne's Dark Cloud with as much speed as he could muster, Luke reached out and grabbed one of the many broken-off whips floating in space, razors still attached, bits of Soul Light dripping lifelessly off the sharp tips.

'I'm coming, you son of a bitch.'

NoOne smiled. 'Yes, my son. Come to daddy.'

'Come to who?'

'Well now. Time for an explanation. I impregnated your mother in another universe and sent her to your planet Earth to birth you. Part of my early experimenting with crossbreeding species, so to speak. Fascinating how your mother managed to bring her lunacy to your world. You wear it well. So come forward.'

'My mom called you my daddy, earlier. You called me your "son." You really did screw my mom?'

'That's crude. Not impressive. So sad that you're not very bright. Luck of the draw, I guess, with genetics. You had so much potential for evil purposes. Unfortunately, you are no longer useful.'

A dense whirling mist broke off from the leading portion of the Dark Matter cloud. It slowly circled Luke, gradually assuming the shape of a Snake. Finally, it had Luke surrounded. A mouth formed on the Snake with slimy droplets of sludge exuding from its scaly skin.

The black droplets attached to Luke's Soul armor, quickly cracking it open. Then, piece by piece, Soul bits were surgically removed, smothered, and released to combust in the fullness of NoOne's dark space.

Pop. Pop. Pop.

NoOne looked on with a smirk. Luke was almost drained dry. 'Such a pity you can never see your Lover again, eh? How about I arrange a resurrection of your mummy to spend eternity with? But then again, she's barely gotten comfortable in my Book of the Damned.'

Luke knew he had little time to make his peace. 'Hey, asshole father. I'm not damned. That's for damned sure! Thanks for using up enough time to let my buddy escape. You are one dumb shit devil.'

Ben and Igor had indeed escaped farther away from his grasp. NoOne quickly scanned space and ordered his troops to find their location.

Luke's last thought was, 'Hey Ben, my last big play. Asshole dude rushed me, I lobbed the ball over his head. I confused Satan. Goodbye, my best friend. I'm proud of you. You did good.'

Ben heard Luke's final frail words and tried to reply but felt Luke's Soul had withered away. Frantically searching in space for any sign of Luke's reappearance, Ben finally accepted that Luke was gone. For good. Nothing left but dark silence.

TheSon felt Ben's sorrow and Luke's sacrifice. He swelled with Love. With so few Orbs and just Ben and Igor surviving, TheSon had to strike. Now again filled with Sacred Spirit, He streamed back out to meet His enemy brother.

Ben knew he had to overcome, at least for the time being, the deep sorrow he felt over the gruesome deaths of his friends. The images haunted him. Ben replayed their endings in an unending loop in his mind. Orbs crushed out of existence; nothing but particles in space floating away. He had to get a grip, or he and Igor and the few remaining Orbs would all die. Worse yet, his mind would be so clouded he wouldn't be able to keep his armor extended over his body.

'Igor, do you think now is the time for the illusion?'

New Twin's Page Eight: Reunion

My brother, the Old Twin, was imperious with confidence. While I was guarding the guys at the Mental Hospital, he had been looking for me. I dreaded to know why.

All too soon, I heard his voice in my head. 'I'm coming for you, brother. Did your buddies really call you "New Twin?" Only thing new about you is your newfound human weakness. You gave yourself away when your Chosen thought about you while they were playing games in space. Easy to trace you after that. I know your plan. I know where you are.'

I got the message. It was a challenge that I knew could not be ignored. It was a matter of time before we would settle our estrangement, one way or another.

On the other hand, I was thankful for the Erob city shield. I felt protected at the Mental Hospital and oddly secure. I didn't know the city shields had a different purpose than I thought. I also didn't know my brother had a completely different goal.

Just outside the domed shields of the city, my brother, the Old Twin, waited impatiently as his corpse minions drilled straight down through the rocky soil with their bare hands, flesh torn from decomposing fingers, hands crumbling. The rotting flesh was of little concern to him. Did the Old Twin not have an endless supply of corpse bodies buried? NoOne didn't seem to need them any longer.

In fact, my brother, the Old Twin, had not heard from NoOne in quite a while. The Old Twin cried, 'Why are you avoiding me, father? I have waited for your instructions. You have deserted me.'

There had been no answer for days. It was as if now that NoOne had the command of space, my brother could just rot on Earth with the rest of NoOne's buried corpses decaying in the Earth.

My brother gloated. *Soon, I'll take matters into my own hands. Or I should say, the corpses' hands!*

Once reaching a point deep enough in the Earth to escape the sensor reach of the city Erob shields, the corpses started to dig parallel to the surface. The Old Twin was confident he could find the exact location of the Mental Hospital high above their underground tunnel.

In no time, the corpse diggers signaled the Old Twin. Mumbled screams from mutilated corpse mouths that only the Old Twin could hear beckoned him forward.

The Old Twin walked upright through the tunnel with minimal effort until he finally stood directly underneath the Mental Hospital grounds.

The corpses had reached the surface just outside the Mental Hospital building where the four boys (now men) were housed. The Old Twin knew he had struck gold; he felt his brother's presence. Immediately, the corpses retreated down under the surface, exited out on the other side of the shield dome, dug new graves, and fell again into eternal sleep.

Once my brother surveyed the hospital surroundings, he quietly walked through a side door of the building where I was hiding, mentally cloaking his presence. He was invisible to all except for me. My brother relished his "invisible man" routine. It gave him an elevated sense of power and dominance in the ongoing drama with his father and me, between NoOne and The New Twin. My brother was above it all. He was confident he could overcome any threat, whether that threat was his father or me.

Entering the ward, my brother released his cloak and walked up to the table where the five of us sat. We had our faces down as if sleeping. My brother inspected the five of us patients and wondered why we let ourselves be planted in such weathered bodies. As he walked around the table, he lifted the heads one by one. Three of the heads had Soulless eyes. Nothing but translucent, mushy globs relegated to dark empty holes, a sight my brother knew all too well. He deduced one of the two remaining heads with functioning eyes was me, his Twin.

One of the two bodies had frantic, darting eyes, not focused on anything in his immediate environment. My brother lifted his head off the table to get a better look.

That can't be my brother; this guy is in space somewhere, too stressed out. My brother would never freak out like this dude, the Old Twin thought.

Dropping his head back on the table with a thud, the Old Twin turned to the other body that still had eyes. Opening the body's eyelids, the Old Twin saw that the eyes were clear and his body healthy.

Bingo!

'Brother, it's me. Get focused so we can talk,' said the Old Twin.

I stirred. Groggy and woozy, I shook my head, rubbed my eyes, and looked up at my brother.

Oh shit, I've been caught, I thought.

My brother laughed. 'Glad to see you too! My, how you've aged! Shit, why didn't you get into some young dude's body so you could at least screw somebody?'

I started to chuckle but then caught myself. 'You're still just a boy!' I exclaimed. 'What did our father do to you?'

'Have you looked at yourself lately? I'd rather be short and young rather than an old fart like you waiting to collapse. We got to have a "come to Jesus" moment, my sibling in horror. The real question is, what did TheSon do to you?'

'I don't want to fight you. Look at these guys here. Three killed by your father,' I said.

'*Our* father,' corrected my brother. 'But, I gotta tell you, I'm really pissed. He abandoned me.'

Sarcastic and mocking, I replied, 'Oh, wah wah…are you kidding? What did you expect? He's the Devil!'

'Yeah, but you ain't no angel yourself. How many people and animals did we torture? Remember?'

'I had no part in killing our mother. You made her suffer. And she was always good to us,' I defensively replied. 'And why did you bring her back to life and then kill her again? Our own mother!'

'She was a corpse. Daddy has the hots for her. But she couldn't stand the heat. I just did what felt good at the time. Do you remember that awesome feeling? Moreover, you seem to forget we together killed grandpa and the girls. Or has your selective memory conveniently forgotten your true nature?'

I couldn't look at my brother. 'That haunts me, but I've been forgiven.'

My brother broke out in laughter. 'Forgiven? Yeah. Ha, ha. So TheSon gave you back your Soul. Now how did He pull that off? It really doesn't matter, does it? I mean, where the fuck is He now? Getting wiped out along with your friends? Lots of good He's done. If you haven't noticed, your side is losing, brother!'

I dropped my head. I couldn't bear to look at him because I knew he was telling at least part of the truth. Where was TheSon? What about Ben? His body was still here, alive, with good eyes, so he still must be fighting NoOne somewhere.

It was hard to think of the small boy standing in front of me as my brother. It was much easier to think of him as the Old Twin. For all I knew, my brother had not changed one bit and was still as dangerous as ever. Better to think of him as the Old Twin, unpredictable and vicious.

Yet, what did my brother have to gain by showing up here? Could it be my brother had seen the Light? Is that not where I should lead him, to the Light, if possible? Was I not forgiven and transformed from a demon child into a witness to all who strive to be just and pure?

I turned around in my chair to my brother and put my hand on his shoulder. He looked so small, so frail. Did we together really cause all that suffering? 'Look, brother, I think all we have is each other once more. Maybe we can work together just to stay alive?'

I knew that my brother was calculating my objectives and resolve. Was I setting him up? Was I thoroughly converted? Could I be turned back to my former evil self? Or, like him, was I planning future moves as in a chess match, moves to maximize the chances of my own survival as a son of NoOne.

My brother surprised me with his response. 'Yes, we should talk about surviving together.'

I was relieved he hadn't lashed out at me. Still, a part of me was waiting for my brother to impulsively attack. He could destroy this entire building and all the patients and staff working in it with but a twitch of his eye. It would take less than a second.

Warily, I responded, looking for any sign of imminent attack. 'Well, let's talk practicalities. The few people left in the cities are scared to shit you'll kill 'em. Nothing else is left on the planet. Even all the corpses are in space, except for the few around this dome, thanks to you.'

My brother was prepared to finally tell me the truth. 'Brother, you think you're in this Mental Hospital to keep you crazies inside. You're wrong. You're inside this Mental Hospital to protect you from the crazies *outside*.'

I was not expecting this revelation. 'Say again?' I replied, trying to act nonchalant.

My brother continued, 'Brother, long ago, the Earth became the Mental Hospital of this universe. As our father and I cultivated our troop of corpses and SoulLess eyes, a few righteous souls were so pure that TheSon would not allow us to touch them, so we herded them inside the Mental Hospitals of the cities. It was meant to be a joke. Get the irony?'

I didn't respond, so moments passed before we said anything. No movement. No conversation. What did each really want? Could we adjust to each other's needs? Could we ever reconcile?

Finally, I said, 'Well, you have let me survive here, at least until today.'

I could see my brother soften with a look I'd never seen, even for the briefest of moments. He wanted to cry. He became a little boy reaching out for someone to hold him.

Then he suddenly reverted to his Old Twin persona, assuming his typical cold demeanor. 'Hold on a minute. I could give a shit about your boyfriends. I really don't care about you either. So, don't give me this crap about being "saved" and "Loved" by TheSon.'

'Noted. OK, then,' I said. I had seen the crack in my brother's emotional armor. It gave me some shred of hope. 'But why are you here, and why are you trying to help me? And Ben?'

My brother smirked. It gave me chills because that was the signal something nasty was imminent. I had seen it a thousand if not more times; how much my brother enjoyed catching people off guard, manipulating expectations; and the pleasure he experienced torturing people and animals, in fact, anything living.

'OK, I'm waiting,' I said. 'Or are you getting off too much on keeping me waiting?'

My brother scanned the room. He could barely see above the table. He obviously wanted to see if anybody had moved. We observed the usual ward routines: the same patients watching television and the same attendants reading their magazines in their glass cage. Once we determined nothing was out of order, my brother started to explain to me what would happen, concentrating on avoiding any speech or sudden movement that might attract unwanted attention.

'You may not want to hear this, my brother. But our father, ex-father, is going to win,' he said.

'What are you talking about?' I asked.

'As we speak, he is at the threshold of capturing the Lip and storming the Divine Foam.'

'My dad, who adopted me, talked about the Divine Foam for a bit.' I replied. 'I found the concept incredibly complex. So how do you describe it?'

'Let's dispense with the fancy physics shit. Just think of it as Heaven. Does that work for you?' he replied with cheery condescension.

'So, how do you know NoOne is ready to conquer Heaven?' I asked. 'You haven't been there.'

'Brother, do you not see three of TheSon's Chosen dead at this table?' replied my brother. 'Plus, I still am somewhat prescient as far as our notorious father is concerned.'

I was trying to understand why my brother was telling me all this now. Plus, hearing a big word like "prescient" from the mouth of a seven-year-old made me want to laugh. But then again, my brother may be small on the outside, but he was cavernous with evil on the inside.

Evil, just like I used to be.

So, what brought on the sudden change of heart? I had to know. 'You're here because something is in it for you,' I probed.

My brother laughed. 'First clue? Yes, numb nuts. Something is in it for me. It's called survival.'

'Let me get this straight. You figure I'm going to save you?' I asked.

'No, but my chances *and* your chances of survival are a hell of a lot better if we partner up. Just think of it as insurance.'

Before I could answer, the body that housed Ben began to stir. Slowly at first, subtle muscle contractions shimmied up and down his body. Then the large muscle groups took over, with legs kicking out and arms flailing. My brother moved over, trying to conceal Ben's body movements, but only managed to cover the bottom half of the body.

'Looks like we got this one back. Let me know if anybody notices,' my brother said.

Ben's eyes started to open. Straining from the glare of the lights, Ben raised his hands to offer some relief from the glare. Peeking through his fingers, Ben quickly scanned his surroundings. Finally focusing on my brother, Ben panicked.

"It's alright, Ben. I'm now on your side," said my brother.

"Where am I?" moaned Ben.

"Ah, the Mental Hospital. Remember?" said my brother. "My brother is right there beside you. Safer if we communicate with thoughts, OK?"

Ben nodded his head in agreement. 'OK.'

'Ben, I'm here beside you. Snuck in. Your three partners here at the table are gone. What happened?' I asked.

Ben couldn't answer. Waves of repressed emotion came gushing out. Ben began to sob uncontrollably. My brother and I put our hands on Ben's shoulders for comfort.

Surprised, I looked in shock at my brother's expression of compassion. On the other hand, perhaps it was not compassion but a way to quiet Ben and not attract scrutiny from the hospital staff.

Composing himself, Ben said, 'I have something for you.'

My brother and I glanced briefly at each other and then studied Ben out of habit. Almost simultaneously, we thought, 'What?'

Ben became more focused. 'More important, you need to know from *whom*.'

'OK,' I said. 'Go ahead…from who?'

'From TheSon,' said Ben.

'What would TheSon want to give us except an early death?' my brother asked.

Ben focused on the table. 'I'll lay it on the table. After I warn you.'

'OK, you have our attention, right brother?' I said.

My brother nodded. 'Yes, you have our attention. Go ahead, warn us.'

'It means all of us are going to die,' whimpered Ben. 'Very soon.'

'What do you mean?' I asked.

Ben paused. He dropped his head onto the table. Tears began to fall. 'Let me tell you what happened.'

New Twin's Page Nine: The Illusion

Ben recounted his part in attempting to preserve the Lip and save the few remaining Orbs. He struggled to control his feelings of anguish and hopelessness.

'Yes, I have something for you, but first I need to tell you how I escaped. Positioning ourselves in front of the Lip, me and Igor surveyed the battlefield. Space was littered with gutted, inert Orbs, floating, lifeless, 99 percent of TheSon's Orb army destroyed. Any thought of battling NoOne without additional troops was not even a possibility…I can't continue.'

Ben sobbed.

'That's ok, Ben,' I said. 'Let me and my brother read your mind and we can see what happened.'

Ben slumped, exhausted. His eyes glazed over. His head dropped to his chest. His arms flopped to his sides.

Ben pointed to his head as if it contained something special, 'Ok. I gotta give you this. It's from TheSon.'

'Whatever it is, it can wait,' I assured Ben. 'Just let us Twins access your memories.'

Ben's eyes got as wide as saucers. 'You're back together? Working together?'

My brother and I looked at each other. We nodded our heads yes.

In perfect synchrony.

Ben's memories were clear for us to read. His progression of events was precisely preserved.

'Will this work for us, brother?' I asked.

My brother replied, 'Just like old times!'

Hollow and hanging, celestial Light snuffed out, trillions of extinguished Orbs were a taunting testament to the power of NoOne and the futility of any resistance in his physical realm. With their small group of surviving Orbs, Ben looked frantically for any sign that TheSon would come and rescue his last small group of warriors.

In the far distance, Ben and Igor barely perceived TheSon; He was still a massive sun of energy, yet too far from the Lip and too distant to pose a defensive threat to NoOne. He appeared to be retreating, disappearing into the gloomy desert of endless space.

'Why is TheSon leaving? I mean, He looks like He is fleeing. Look, I can barely see Him anymore,' noted Ben.

I don't know, Ben. He must have some kind of plan. Our concern here and now is to protect the Lip, answered Igor without much confidence.

Directly in front of Ben and Igor, NoOne paused. Probes jetted out of NoOne's giant propeller blade, his unbeatable weapon of annihilation. Out and back in, bending the fabric of gravity, endlessly searching, the probes were meticulous in covering every square inch of space.

Ben and Igor knew it was a matter of hours before NoOne would locate the Lip.

'Igor, I can't see TheSon anymore. I think we're on our own,' declared Ben.

We have to concentrate on hiding the Lip. Remember what I did at your folks' home in New Haven? asked Igor.

'Of course,' answered Ben immediately. 'We can cloak the Lip like you did with my house?'

Yes, you're quick with the brain stuff, said Igor. *Our only chance to survive is to create numerous false Lips. Confuse NoOne, if that's possible.*

'Yeah. I get it. Buy TheSon some time to refuel and get back here. That might work. How can I help?'

We need to project high-frequency brain waves.

'Let me guess, Igor. We use our gamma waves? Thirty to eighty Hertz–cycles per second?'

Igor beamed. *Never told you how pleased, no wait, how proud I am of you. You really have come through, given all the trauma you had early in life. Any fire issues lately?*

'Well, to be honest, I am quite excited at TheSon's big fireball!'

They both laughed.

Feeling guilty about the loss of his buddies, Ben apologized. 'I'm sorry. I should be more respectful of my friends. They gave up their lives so we could reach this point.'

It's OK, Ben. But yes, if we combine our mental power at the highest frequencies, I think we can do a little space warp, like gravity curving space. Maybe throw NoOne off for at least a few minutes. Give TheSon time to re-group.

Ben's fear dissipated at the intellectual challenge and mystery Igor presented.

'Kind of fits in with our mission here,' Ben said. 'Accessing gamma waves gets us to the foundational energy of the mind with its Spiritual frequencies. I remember reading that neurologists still don't have an idea how the gamma waves run at frequencies higher than what is thought possible by neuronal firing. We know for sure that the Gamma frequencies are associated with transcendent Love. Possibly it's the link we've been looking for, with our mind being part of God's mind.'

Igor was ready for action. *OK, whatever the explanation, the bottom line is it's a powerful force, and I think if we combine our gamma waves, we can create a pulse that craters the space fabric just like the Lip does.*

'OK, so how do we do it?' asked Ben.

Igor shared the process. *First, gamma waves are most accessed by people who can be super concentrated and focused on a goal, like you. Next, emotion must be turned off. Then we ask some of our Orb friends to create more pulses.*

'What do you mean? How would they provide more pulses and why?' quizzed Ben.

Igor began to explain. *Ben, the brain can track or align with exterior gamma wave frequencies. But it involves being incredibly focused. A few of our Orb friends and their Lights can mimic our pulse.*

'Then what?' asked Ben.

Then we concentrate on making as many space ripples that duplicate the Lip signature as possible, responded Igor.

'Ah, so what specifically are we concentrating on?' asked Ben.

Visualize jumping on a trampoline, and then note how your weight temporarily depresses the rubber skin as you land. That's our goal. And gamma waves love plans. We want to keep the space skin depressed as long as possible. Hopefully, that dip will create enough distorted gravity ripples to confuse NoOne. We and the Orbs will make as many dips as we can all around the Lip while staying as far away as possible.

Having tracked the conversation between Ben and Igor, the remaining Orbs surrounded the two. The Orb pulses attained synchrony at exactly the same Gamma frequency in seconds. Ben and Igor directed them to coordinate locations randomly far and near in space. One by one, hundreds of dips were created that perfectly matched the pulse of the original Lip.

The ploy worked, initially. Witness to the numerous fake Lips quivering and depressing the space fabric, NoOne ceased all activity. Ben and Igor assumed NoOne was confused. And the fact that NoOne ordered his probes to return to his column confirmed their assumption.

What they had not anticipated was TheSon's reaction.

Without signaling His intent to Ben, Igor, or the Orbs, TheSon suddenly appeared and attacked NoOne head-on.

Ben and Igor were stunned. They witnessed the largest body of Light, a blazing star, explode with solar flares leaping out to space spanning millions of miles, converging in lightning speed on the most extensive collection of compressed Dark Matter ever witnessed in any universe that had ever existed.

Igor commanded the Orbs to cease their frequency transmissions, regroup, and meet at the Lip front. Hovering together, the group watched as the epic battle between TheSon and NoOne began.

Speeding through space, TheSon's star headed directly toward NoOne's column. With His star's nuclear fusion, TheSon thought He had more than enough energy to swallow NoOne's column thereby releasing the blade from its swivel and source of power.

An invincible force was thrust against an immutable object. This was TheSon's fatal mistake. Seeing the small contingent of Orbs regroup, NoOne knew the Lip was close by, probably directly behind them. As TheSon crashed into the middle of the huge black column, NoOne split off two massive, spinning, spiked disks. He ordered them to attach themselves to TheSon's star, one at the top and one at the bottom.

Once attached to the star, the disks ground away. The disks' relentless whirring penetrated and stripped away huge sections of the star, working their way through the convective zone, then the radiative zone, and finally the core.

NoOne was surprised that TheSon chose such a vulnerable manifestation. What was He up to? There had to be something devious TheSon was planning. Surely, there could have been more strategic incarnations? Did TheSon consult with TheOne before wedding His Divinity to a burning rock?

There was a bright side (NoOne chuckled at his humor). His Father had not allowed TendHer to materialize in the physical realm and team up with their Brother. TheSon was formidable enough. NoOne reflected that once his Dark Matter flooded the Foam of Divinity, TendHer would be there waiting with her Orbs. It would be too late for them. NoOne had superior mass and energy. He knew his victory was inevitable.

NoOne's confident reverie was interrupted as TheSon engulfed NoOne's disks by folding part of His star's outer ring, the super-hot chromosphere, around the huge circular objects, frying their surfaces.

NoOne's disks were too dense and huge. They just keep grinding downward, intent on destroying as much core fusion as possible.

I need to slow down. Enjoy this victory! I will savor every ground-up slice of my Brother's pathetic star.

The hydrogen fusion, so necessary to protect the star from the pressures of gravity, was gradually degraded by the disks' penetrations. With the loss of this energy, gravity space layers pressed down harder on the star. As the amount of hydrogen was reduced, the sun's helium began to burn through the star's core.

Suddenly, the disks stopped and retreated outside the star's corona. Moments passed as Ben struggled to understand why the disks had moved and paused.

Then slowly, the two disks combined. From the newly combined mass, three rectangular planks emerged. One end of each plank connected to another plank at a right angle producing a "U" shape - a forklift clamp with two blades extending from a central plank.

Proceeding steadily to the star, the top plank elevated higher, and the bottom plank dropped lower; the middle plank gained size to accommodate the increasing width dimension.

When the new weapon was large enough to fit the star between the two planks, it greedily lurched forward and clamped down tight.

Now, my children. Squeeze! Squeeze!

Like two hands crushing a trapped bug, it took little pressure for the forklift clamp to crush the massive sun.

Eventually, the star collapsed upon itself as the helium fuel ran out. The once gigantic sun, alpha in the universe, transmuted into a White Dwarf: a stellar remnant, a dead rock in space.

TheSon was forced to re-Spiritualize. Looking back at NoOne's latest weapon of Dark Matter, TheSon realized too late that NoOne couldn't be destroyed in the physical universe. This was NoOne's domain, his unconquerable turf.

But TheSon had achieved his real goal, later to be revealed when the time was right.

Departing the once-massive sun, TheSon's Spirit retreated to the Lip. The Orbs, sensing that defeat was imminent, turned their attention away from Ben and Igor and waited for instructions from TheSon, who had manifested Himself as a single Orb.

Ben and Igor were stunned and in shock at TheSon's apparent humiliating defeat at the hands of NoOne. Before TheSon could instruct the remaining few troops, along with Ben and Igor, to scatter outward, the Orbs instinctively moved toward the Lip to protect TheSon. NoOne saw the movement of the Orbs and assumed it was to run to the safety of the Lip.

NoOne was right. He now knew the exact location of the Lip. He quickly destroyed the Orb guards, gloating as he witnessed his Brother's retreat into the Lip interior. But two of the troops jetted off away from the Lip. Diving down and moving towards TheSon's dead star, the two stopped, suspended.

NoOne sensed one was an Orb and the other was a human. And the human was one of the pesky boys. The last one to survive.

This is too good to be true, thought NoOne.

The remaining Chosen one and his Mentor were of no consequence, but NoOne didn't want to leave loose ends. As he approached the Lip opening, NoOne sent a missile remnant of his Dark Matter aimed at the two far out in space.

The two saw the launch and knew it was headed their way.

'Igor, are we going to die? I'm scared,' said Ben.

You've been very brave; all of you guys were fantastic. TheSon, me, all of us couldn't have lasted this long without your help.

'OK. Thanks. That's your way of saying goodbye?' asked Ben. 'I don't think I've ever been so scared.'

Ben, trust what I'm about to do. What I must do. TheSon asked me to give you something to hide, to protect. And He asked me to sacrifice my Soul so that you might carry out His mission. I agreed.

Ben was confused. 'You want me to hide something? But I thought you said we were going to die?'

The missile is close to reaching us. I will surround your Soul-body with my Light. It should be enough to protect you. But it will mean I will be destroyed.

Ben started to breathe rapidly, then increased to hyperventilation. 'Why can't we just escape?'

Igor snapped back, *Not enough time or energy. The Dark Matter is gaining speed and mass. It will smother all matter around us in a matter of seconds. You should have enough energy to make it back to safety.*

'Shit. Wish I could start one more fire!'

Ben, you no longer need to, sighed Igor.

'You became my father, you big oaf,' said Ben.

Igor saw he had but seconds. A spear of Dark Matter was hurtling closer. His prediction was correct. It had gained in mass and speed. He had to cover Ben quickly.

Igor figured he had just enough time to transfer the package TheSon had given him to Ben.

As Igor spun his thread of Light around Ben's Soul-body, he imbedded the parcel from TheSon into Ben's Soul. He then uttered his last words. *Ben, I'm very proud of you. And I'm sure your folks would be proud of you too.*

'Igor, don't….'

Goodbye. Son.

Last New Twin Page: Ben's Gift

Ben stood up from our table. Patients from around the room, including the staff in their cage, looked over and studied the group.

'Ah, Ben, better not do that,' I warned. 'The last thing we need is attention.'

Ben shook his head. 'You saw what happened. You saw the whole thing. TheSon gave me something to give you both—a gift and a mission.'

'Give us?' I asked in unison with my brother. Then for a moment, I saw something completely unexpected coming from my brother. I stared, unable to look away. Was it empathy? Was my brother demonstrating compassion? He looked close to tears.

I returned my gaze to the body housing Ben.

'TheSon asked me to give you your last mission. OUR last mission,' thought Ben.

Then approaching me, Ben stopped within inches of my face. 'But before I do that, I have a special gift for you. It's from your dad.'

I leaned back and lifted my body arms up as if to ward off some evil. 'I will have nothing to do with NoOne. Never again.'

Ben shook his head in understanding and smiled. 'This gift is not from NoOne. It's from *your dad*. Remember, the one who sent you on this mission. The one who wrote the manuscript of journals that led us to this end game?'

'Which I'm not all that happy about,' muttered my brother with frosty conviction.

Ben ignored my brother and peered at me, waiting for some kind of response.

Minutes passed with lumbering ticks and tocks from the wall clock. Not a body stirred, nor did we perceive any other sound from the room. The clock's pointed second hand teased the three of us at the table, daring us to make a move that might launch us down a road to doom with no exit.

Finally, I spoke, 'He is with you, isn't he, Ben? My dad. His Soul is with you. I feel him.'

Yes, my beautiful son, thought Dad. *I am inside Ben. TheSon gave of Himself to send us to you. Earlier in the battle, TheSon had NoOne on the ropes, ready to destroy him. Then TheSon saw that most of my battle armor was in shreds and that NoOne was beginning to conquer my small unit. TheSon then distracted him. In that moment, TheSon told me to merge with Ben and return to you. He told me that we four—you Twins, Ben, and me—have a mission to complete far more critical than protecting Himself or the Lip..*

My dad continued. *I cried as I felt I was abandoning my Soulmates, but they blessed me and asked me to remember them and our Love. And to do our Father's bidding. The final thing I remember was being sucked into Ben's Soul-body and experiencing his Soul next to mine. Then, as we escaped, we looked back and saw NoOne destroy TheSon's star.*

TheSon's star was turned into stardust. He retreated inside the Lip with some Orbs chased by NoOne. TheSon then sent a thought to us. It went like this: "Of all the Sacred expressions of the Soul, there is nothing more Sacred than a father's Love for his son. And that is why I will again sacrifice Myself for those who Love and trust in TheOne's beautiful Creation."

Ben sent a thought out, obviously taking the stage from my dad. 'OK, uh…I have other news. I'm glad father and son are reunited here. Cool. I never did get to meet up with my folks. But….'

My dad interrupted Ben. *I did know them, Ben. Orbs know the entire universe. We know every particle, every Spirit, every memory, every intention, every Being. You are given that gift when you die and are judged Pure. You will learn that your parents never forgot you. Their last thoughts were to share their Love.*

The body that contained the Souls of Ben and my dad sat down. Bringing his hands to his head, Ben dropped his head to the table and began to weep.

Ben lamented after the sobbing subsided, 'I never got to say goodbye. Just like with my three buddies. I hated them, and then I liked them. Was it so long ago we were four Loonies in a bin just going on a camping trip? Why did we get involved in all this? We were just kids! Now they're gone: John, Charles, Luke, and our Mentors. God, I hated Luke. He was everything I wanted to be. Towards the end, I felt he knew me better than anyone did, and he respected me. He saw my pain and weaknesses, and his last thought to me was, "Ben, you did good." I was just a kid…just a baby when I got stuck here, for Christ's sake. I feel like I'm gonna break down any minute. I just don't know if I dare give you what I'm supposed to give you. I never got to have a wife or a family! Not even a girlfriend.'

My brother softly replied, 'Hey, you're a hero, Ben. I've never used that word. But you're a true hero. Glad I didn't evaporate you when I had the chance. Actually, this is all new to me if the truth is known. People being…what's that word? Soft?'

I interrupted, 'Learning a whole new language, aren't you, brother?' Then turning to Ben, I said, 'My brother is right. You are a hero. I think we're involved in a much bigger drama than any of us can imagine. And what you've done will have positive consequences down the line on a cosmic scale none of us could conceive on our own…if we're here to experience any of 'em.'

'There is one thing I miss from NoOne. At least with him, you never felt guilt or compassion,' commented my brother at my side. 'This compassion stuff is just too stressful.'

A timely distraction came from one of the patients seated across the room. "Hey, could you lunatics keep your thoughts down? I'm trying to be crazy over here."

The bodies at the table laughed. Their Souls shined just a little brighter. It was the perfect time to ask Ben and my dad what parcel they had to share with us Twins.

I asked, 'Ben, we've all suffered incredible losses, so we know how you hurt. I'm sorry. Can you tell us what package you're supposed to give us?'

'It's in my Soul,' Ben continued. 'TheSon planted it in my Soul, well, I mean my Soul and your dad's Soul. There's a map for us to follow to reach a particular destination in the universe. It was the map created by John. And a couple of Books. In quantum language. All contained in a single, tiny seed. Using John's map, your dad and I are carrying it and are supposed to plant it.'

'Plant? Where? Like here somewhere?' I asked.

The body housing Ben started to shake. The reality of the mission was obviously taking its toll. 'No, not on Earth. You two Twins are to take this body I'm sharing with your dad to the end of the universe. There, you are to deposit our body with the Seed inside to the outermost membrane. TheSon called it "the Planting." '

Ben studied the group and then turned back to me. 'And you, New Twin, are supposed to give me the Pages you have recorded these past few days.'

'And join them with this seed?' I asked.

'Yes. Actually, TheSon said your Pages would become one with the Seed. A history of sorts. TheSon also said the Seed would shelter three Specks, or Sparks really, along with a Book of Souls, past and present. And a Book of the Damned.'

My heart swelled with hope. 'So, all the Souls lost fighting NoOne…John, Luke, our Mentors, Charles are recorded in this Book of Souls?'

My brother interrupted. 'And all the lives we destroyed?' my brother asked, looking at me. 'Are they also in this Book?'

Was my brother testing me? Why was he looking at me so deeply? Was it Love? Concern for me?

Ben continued. 'TheSon said all can be "re-membered" if we keep the Book of Souls safe.'

'And how are we supposed to take you there?' I asked.

'TheSon said if you two Twins worked together, you could do it.'

Pointing to me, my brother commented, 'Like you did with the bubble underwater. Brilliant maneuver, brother, but I would have cracked it eventually.'

I became still. A shiver weaved its way up and down my spine. *I know what it takes to maintain a protective bubble. I think we might have just enough life energy to get us there.*

'I just read your mind, brother. That sounds like a one-way ticket,' mumbled my brother.

Ben said, 'It is. It's a one-way ticket. One way. For all of us. You two Twins get this body your dad and I share there, and I plant the Seed that contains the Books and your final Pages.'

'How do you plant the Seed?' asked my brother.

'You shelter this body as long as possible once we arrive. Unt….'

'Until what, Ben?' asked my brother.

'Until the Seed is set free from this body,' replied Ben.

'And how does that happen?' I asked.

'We die,' stated Ben.

TheOne

TendHer entered the Foam of Divinity to address TheOne. *NoOne looms. He has battled with the Chosen and Your Son, TheSon. NoOne has prevailed. He found the Holy Lip and may soon be here. What would You have Us do?*

Yes, Father, replied TheSon entering the Foam, now but a small Speck. *My Sister is correct. Trillions upon trillions of Orb Souls have been lost. NoOne awaits Your decision.*

TheOne asked, *Decision for what?*

TheSon replied, *How We wish to cease to Be.*

The Foam of TheOne became frothy. Its vast, immutable sea of energy labored with the struggle to form an impression suitable for comprehension by TendHer and TheSon. Vast volcanoes of quantum fire leaped, lurching for the few remaining circling adulating Orbs, reaching out, clutching them, embracing them, consuming them, drawing them in. Releasing them. Confirmation of what was once grand and numinous. Separate but united. TheOne begetting the many. The many becoming TheOne.

TheOne discharged the Orbs so they might honor the mystery of Creation and reflect the ecstasy of creative destruction. Javelins of radiant Light erupted, then curled and warped, turned in on themselves, coiled again, then exploded outward. As the cycle of celebration continued, more Orbs were called to celebrate the mystery of life.

Does not NoOne long for Me? Is he not of Me? asked TheOne.

TheSon waited in reverent deference, then answered, *Yes, but NoOne is very near and will soon flood Your sanctity with Dark Matter. There will be no more Light.*

TendHer added, *There has never been Dark Matter in the Foam of Divinity.*

TheSon pondered the situation and replied, *Neither has there ever been Dark Matter in the Reincarnation Universe until now. And once he did steal into 'beyond the Veil'.*

Taking the cue from TheSon, TendHer addressed TheOne, *You forbade NoOne from ever entering 'beyond the Veil', but he has already violated that stricture. The Reincarnation Universe and Our Divine Foam surely are next to be invaded.*

The Foam again stirred. *Wondrous!* said TheOne.

Concerned, TheSon asked, *What is wondrous, Father?*

TheOne replied, *My Foam without Light. Only Dark Matter.*

Lord, without Light, does not Dark Matter wither? He needs Us to gird his form as much as we need his structure to buttress Our Light. Does not NoOne know this truth? questioned TendHer.

TheSon spoke, *Yes, We need NoOne and his Darkness. Without NoOne in Your Creation, there will no longer be Logos; no longer an edifice for Creation. No longer flesh to carry Your seed. No longer bone to protect the hearts of Your Creation. No longer suffering to test the Souls of Your Beings. Love cannot grow without pain.*

Chaos will transform the Ground of Being to the Ground of NoThing, added TendHer.

At that moment, The Foam of Divinity groaned. A tidal wave of NoOne's Dark Matter and cosmic junk flooded into the Foam. The swells of Dark Matter were instant and massive, each joining together eclipsing the Pure geometric physics of Holiness. Next, putrid mangled body parts from masses of corpses added to the wave, all rotating in unstoppable contamination. Last, SoulLess Eyes from NoOne's obedient Snake inserted themselves into the oncoming, crushing waves.

TheOne, TheSon, and TendHer retreated to the far distant corner of the Foam.

NoOne screamed from across the chasm of the Foam, 'I have triumphed. You will stay imprisoned for all eternity as I govern Your Creation.'

One last time, TheSon tried to reason, *Brother, you know not what you have wrought. You are Us; We are you. Without Us, all will turn into No-Thingness.*

With impudence, NoOne released even more Dark Matter, forcing the three Holy to retreat even further to the deepest depths of the Foam.

With resignation and heaviness of heart, words of TheOne were spoken, and they were Holy: *WE ARE FINISHED.*

The command of TheOne was sent. Lips in all universes opened wide. Light and Dark leaked out of trillions of universe Lips, gushing back to the Foam of Divinity, the Source of Creation. At the same time, oceans of Dark Matter particles attacked and smothered the incoming new Light, preventing any possible new accumulation.

Leaving TendHer and TheSon to hide in the furthest region of the Lip, TheOne came forward as Pure Light to battle NoOne. Struggling forward through the Dark Matter, shedding precious slabs of Light,

TheOne presented His Holiness before NoOne's gigantic cauldron of Dark Waste.

Imperious and gloating, NoOne cycled his manifestation, shifting between his favorite Snake and sinister Dark Matter cloud. 'I beat You, Father! Why do You keep emptying Your universes? Why do You continue to send Your Light to fight me? Protect Your Light so that I may call upon it to serve me.'

TheOne ignored NoOne's questions. Laboriously TheOne swept closer to NoOne, losing even more Light. I LOVE YOU, MY SON.

NoOne screamed, 'NO! What are You doing? Why are You destroying Yourself to defeat me? Save Yourself. Stop Your approach. Retreat to Your sanctuary. Dwell where Your Light may still be of use to me.'

My Light shall never be used for evil. But I shall always Love you, My beautiful son.

Enraged, NoOne commanded that all remaining Dark Matter be sucked from all universes and flood the Foam. 'If You refuse to serve me, then Your Creations will be terminated.'

Have I not always protected you, My son?

'You have not given me what I wanted. What I deserved. What I have earned.'

Love holds no strings. It does not bargain. I have always given you what you need.

'Wrong answer!'

NoOne gave his order. The fabric of space membranes swelled in all universes for one last brief moment, protesting obliteration. Every string, every particle, every bit of energy was smothered entirely and extinguished by the unrelenting Dark Matter. Flapping like lone flags lost in a barren space of time, universe membranes were rescinded by the absence of energy. Except one.

All was gone. Except one membrane. Missed.

NoOne smugly addressed his Snake. 'Did I not have beautiful children in this universe? Does not my true Love lie buried on Earth?'

His Snake purred in agreement.

No-Thing was.

Goodbye, Father, together moaned TheSon and TendHer.

Goodbye, my beautiful Son and Daughter.

Father, cried TheSon. *Who are You?*

Mystery.

I Love You Father, barely whispered TheSon.

I Love You, Father, cried TendHer. *Brother, come and hold Me.*

TheOne summoned His last bit of energy and cried, NoOne, My Son.

'No! No! No! How can You call me Your son after this? Even now?' NoOne screamed as he watched his Dark Matter consume and be consumed by the Light.

Soon, what remained of TheOne flickered its last beam of Pure Light. NoOne's Dark Matter briefly swelled in anger, surrounded the beam, then itself evaporated. Leaving but a single Dark Matter particle.

TheOne, TheSon, and TendHer, clutching each Other, resigned to extinction, drowning in the abyss of NoLight, became TheNone.

No-Thing

There was nothing, material or Holy, that stirred in the bowels of TheNone. The great Creations of unlimited metaverses were over. The great Destruction would never be repeated. Or so it seemed.

Beyond the measure of time, emerging from a hiding place wrapped in an invisible shroud of shredded universe membrane, was a single Seed. It was dreaming as it pulsated weakly, signaling its existence. In rare moments of awareness, the Seed sluggishly remembered that It was a part of TheOne. It was Divine. It yearned to Be: dense, radiant, and intense. Again.

Finally, the Seed was nudged partially awake by a single passing particle of Dark Matter; the only material to have survived in the trillions of universes collapsed so many eternities long since passed, forever surrendering any hope of reconstitution.

Surprised and joyful, the TheOne within the Seed called out, pleading for company, praying the particle was not an illusion.

The particle of Dark Matter rushed to comfort. And be comforted.

The particle of Dark Matter observed, enthralled, hopeful as the Seed unfolded into three parts, two petals clinging to the Seed wall, one rising to the surface.

TheOne emerged.

Let there be Light!

Then the other two Specks of Light emerged cautiously from the depths of the Seed: the Thou of TheOne; His beloved Daughter and Son.

A second Holy decree from TheOne: *Let there be Love.*

The three Holy Sparks then gently touched: TheOne, TheSon, and TendHer.

The Holy Trinity awoke fully to the mysterious gift of Unconditional Love radiating from Their reunion.

In reverence, the Three gave thanks to the Seed's core so long ago planted in the furthest reaches of a singular universe on the only membrane material to survive the Great Obliteration. It was transported there by the last of the Chosen; a brave, scared, human boy named Ben.

The Seed was a gift so trustingly delivered with the highest of costs: the supreme sacrifice of Ben's life, whose last words were etched on the side of the Seed, forever a testament to his courage and bravery.

Four Loonies in a Bin were here!

The Three were pleased. Reviewing the recorded history from the small Page attached to the Seed, TheOne, TheSon, and TendHer witnessed how the boy had managed to plant the Holy Seed.

Surrounded by a psychically projected plastic bubble to protect the group, the Twins labored to maintain the shell of air through their long trip in space in the universe where Earth had once thrived. A map guided their journey; a map made by another of the Chosen four named John.

Thanks to John's map, numerous Wormholes that bisected the universe were located to reach the outermost membrane in the quickest amount of time.

When the group was close to their target, the Twins began to run out of energy and could no longer support the bubble. Ben knew what he had to do. His instructions from TheSon were clear: the body that housed his Soul must die to release the Seed. Once released, the Seed would find its new resting place in the universe fabric. However, Ben would require more Soul Light to get close enough to the universe's membrane wall and stick. The New Twin's father, who had traveled the distance next to Ben's Soul in the same weathered body, would provide that extra Spirit energy.

Ben froze with fear. He didn't want to die. He knew the Twins were fading fast. But there had to be some other way to survive.

Ben looked at the Twins, desperately seeking some last-minute plan to save all their lives, a last-minute reprieve. The Twins, shriveled from physical exhaustion, had used every ounce of psychic energy. Their cells were all but empty. Resolute to perish together, the Twins looked deep into each other's Souls.

'Yes, Brother. It is time,' panted the Old Twin.

'Let us merge again, completely, one last time,' replied the New Twin. 'Dad. Thank you for taking care of me. I Love you.'

Attached to the Soul of Ben, the New Twin's father's Soul cried out for his son, the New Twin, to find another way.

The New Twin was saddened at his father's pain; yet rejoiced at the Love they had shared.

Ben frantically searched for options. Perhaps TheSon would show up to rescue everyone? Perhaps the Twins could build armor suits for them? Perhaps they could find a suitable planet and land?

Ben started to cry.

Tears streaking down his face, Ben stared breathlessly at the Twins. Hoping. Praying for some last-minute miracle. Studying the faces of the Twins, Ben's hopes immediately faded. The Twins' bodies said it all. Collapsed. Spent. Nothing left to give.

Time was running out. Ben, weary beyond anything he had ever experienced, finally accepted his fate. Action had to be taken soon.

As their concentration on the bubble faded, the Twins nodded to Ben. It was time to die. Ben must release the Seed. Ben nodded, silent. Spent.

With a gaze that would last a lifetime in the moment, the Twins smiled at each other one last time. They vowed to entwine their growing Souls fully in resolute purpose.

Lovingly, the Twins merged their Souls. But unlike any other accomplished focus, this would be their most exalted consolidation of power. And it was a power greater than either Twin had ever experienced, as a single person or as part of their devastating team.

'So, this is what Love feels like,' whispered the Old Twin.

'Yes, brother. This is what Love feels like,' replied his brother.

'It's truly wondrous!'

'Yes, truly wondrous!'

The Twins clutched each other. Love washed away all fear of their looming extinction. Together they reached out with their Love, beseeching TheSon to witness a true miracle, hoping their noble sacrifice would prove them worthy if there was ever a judgment to come.

Because for all time, they were now together.

The physical bodies of Ben and the Twins immediately disintegrated, blasting the Seed and the four Souls of Ben, the Old Twin, the

New Twin, and the New Twin's dad outward. It was the needed final push to reach the Seed's target.

Nearing the deflating, flapping fabric wall at the curved end boundary of Earth's universe, the Seed started to slow. The four Souls gave it just enough psychic mass to reach the vibrating membrane. It stopped with a "thud."

The four Souls that rode the Seed started to rotate around the surface circumference of the embedded Seed. Then, Ben deposited a tiny layer of stored Divine Foam, safely stored within his Soul, sheeting the Seed, just as TheSon had ordained.

Finally, there remained but four diminutive Sparks, the only remains of Ben, the Twins, and the New Twin's dad.

Puzzled, the Sparks hovered over the Seed and the blanket of Divinity they had bestowed over Its surface. One after another, the four quizzically pondered their existence and purpose. Then one Spark started to bounce. Then another Spark mimicked the bounce. Joyously, all four Sparks began to gyrate around the Seed. Their revolutions increased in speed. Circling the Seed in rapture, the four reached blistering speeds. Faster. Faster. Till Heavenly sounds emanated from their blazing trails of moments passed.

One after the other, the four Sparks veered downward, in perfect synchrony, straight into the Foam that cuddled the Seed they had so perfectly planted. Finally, a single Soul emerged from the Book of Souls, buried deep within the Seed. It reached out to embrace the incoming Sparks fully.

It was the Monster Bear. Making contact, the four Sparks disappeared into the outstretched protective arms of the Bear, fully dissolving their essence into the quantum mist of the once-grand, magnificent beast.

The Seed did capture Ben's final words. Ben's voice rang out in the recording. Strong. Confident. At Peace. *We four were The Chosen. John, Luke, Charles and me, Ben. We fought a brave battle. We did the best we could. I did good too, didn't I, Luke? Forever, I will Love you all. Ben.*

The End

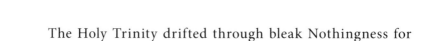

The Holy Trinity drifted through bleak Nothingness for eternity.

By chance, a single particle of Dark Matter drifted by.

It reached out to the limp Seed.

A voice burst from the Seed's depths. *Please, My son. Let Us dance!*

Orbiting around each other, the Seed continued, for eons out of time, led, protected, cradled, and guarded by the loyal single particle of Dark Matter, wandering, and exploring. Dwelling on choices made. Forgiveness offered. Unrequited Love. Vulnerability. Apologies. Possibilities.

Memories dribbled by, caught in the stream of cosmic indifference. Grasping tight to potential, the Holy Trinity struggled to unite and recast once more the play and troupe of the Divine Theatre. Ambivalent and paralyzed with the loss of those They Loved, every Orb, every creature, every lost Spark of Light mourned: the animals, the birds, the primates, the humans. It felt like such a waste. Could they be retrieved from a re-created Book of Souls?

Surely, there was a better way to Love.

TheOne invited TheSon and TendHer to conjoin and dance for essence and Love, anew.

And so, the TheOne decreed: Release the Divine Quantum Foam.

The Divine Foam within the Seed core oozed out and began to vibrate on the surface of the Seed, pulsing tentatively and throbbing with potential. Eventually, the vibrations within the Foam combined to form Foam Strings.

The Foam sheeted layer upon layer of NoThing with a garden terrain of fertile Strings, ever-expanding circles of quantum soup, creating space and time, radiating from the Seed, inviting life, pulsating in existence.

Regenerating memories of Souls long forgotten, the Foam struggled to re-member, carving in psychic signatures on the orbits of atoms all the names of all those Souls judged Pure and Worthy. It was the Book of Souls.

At the same time, the Foam began to re-create the Book of the Damned, those Souls judged foul and evil. For eternity.

Circling the growing maelstrom of the Dance, a particle of Dark Matter, all that was left of NoOne, watched, then swelled.

NoOne waited to be embraced.

The Holy Trinity affirmed They would start anew, one universe at a time. Uncontainable Love swelled within the Three. Divine Foam mushroomed forth. Sparks cast and set. Holy breaths waited to ignite.

Foreordained to be called, steadfastly standing guard, NoOne resolutely watched and hoped.

When the time was opportune, NoOne was not invited into the creative embrace with TheSon, TendHer, and TheOne.

The boundary between the two realities, the physical and the Spiritual, keeping Them separate once more, was not sundered.

Like any other time or in any different dimension, the Three Holy claimed dominion and surrendered longingly to the synergy created by Their majestic re-union. They danced. They Loved.

NoOne yearned.

To Dance.

And yearned.

To Be Loved.

He was not.

So, he left.

The Holy Three had no choice.

But to return to sleep eternal.

The Dance

But NoOne Was.

He finally dwelled in the Dance.

He finally was Loved.

I know. My name is Jenna.

My Lover resurrected me from the Book of the Damned.

We have two new beautiful daughters. They're Twins.

We *ARE* here!

We are THERE!

Thus did NoOne plan.

Epilogue

Grant's friend noticed something blinking in the corner. Turning off the room lights, he said to Grant, "Do you see that in the corner? What could it be?"

Together the boys crept closer to the dull object.

As the two moved forward, the rectangular object of solid darkness, about the size of a shoebox, began to throb.

Grant reached down to feel it. At his touch, the rectangular black mass swelled in breadth and depth, plunging down in a tubular structure straight through the floor, down, down, unfolding in precise sections, finally snapping open at the bottom. Then nothing, except a big dark hole in the floor.

The two guys held their breath. Looking at each other, they nervously cleared their throats and bent down to examine the opening. They felt dank, muddy waves of air, rhythmically washing up out of the hole. Start, then stop. Start, then stop. The hole was deep, and the guys strained to see all the way to the bottom.

From deep in the hole a harsh black beam started to blink, spearing the ambient room light above, giving the boys a momentary, limited peek of what lay beneath them. An object of some sort lay at the very bottom but was obscured by the darkness. The mass moved upwards, then flickered, getting weaker by the second it seemed, hesitating as its power waned, struggling to reach the surface.

Emerging out of the hole, a dark craggy ball jetted up, furious, intense and sharp, inky and sullen. A dark flame emanated from the ball. It hung perfectly in the center of the room. The ball then vomited its energy outward uniformly around the room with one gigantic belch.

Walking in circles around the ball, the guys marveled how easily they ambled through the numerous dark, narrow, sharp-edged waves that crisscrossed their space, javelins of black lasers blurred as they intersected the boys' bodies.

"How can a flame not be light?" pondered Grant aloud.

Before Grant's friend could answer, they heard high-pitched voices echo out of the hole, from the very bottom, a long way down. "Mommy, should we start blowing? Daddy's NoSpark is there."

"Yes, Julie and Loie, my Lovely Twins. You will make your Father proud."

The Twins puffed out their cheeks and began to blow.

The Spark of NoLight Dark Matter exploded. Grant and his friend, along with all life forms, were instantly evaporated by the outward blast. The detonation reached the ends of the universe. Within a nanosecond, dissembled energy particles of every nature for a billion trillion trillion miles were sucked back into the dark ball, the fabric of space-time collapsing. Hanging in NoThing. A sliver of membrane was all that remained. Empty. Alone. Once more.

Swimming in befouled and stilled Divine Foam, the little girls peered out at the great chasm of NoThingness that hung lifelessly before them just beyond the entrance to the Holy Lip. They giggled with glee as they carefully collected a sample of lifeless Dark Matter, rolled it into a ball, and carefully positioned another NoLight Spark at the base of the Holy Lip.

NoOne triumphantly boomed as if all could hear: "Jenna, it is My time. Let's move on to the next universe. Are You ready, My Divine family?"

A crepuscular, inky asp, Jenna slithered and oozed in and out of NoOne's murky, dark quantum shadow. Briefly transforming into her human persona, body writhing in eternal, compliant reconciliation, Jenna purred, "Yes, My Lover. We are now TheOne."

The little girls, in monotone unison, perfect copies of their Earthly resurrected mother, simultaneously yelled, "Can We blow now, Daddy? Mommy? Please? Can We blow now?"

"Yes, My beautiful Twins. You may blow."

Thus planned NoOne.

He was now SomeOne.

'Amen.'

To Be Continued….

Volume III: The Book of the Damned

Connect with the author at pmattox518@gmail.com